The
GIRL
with a
SECRET

BOOKS BY KATE HEWITT

KATE HEWITT

The
GIRL
with a
SECRET

Bookouture

Published by Bookouture in 2024

An imprint of Storyfire Ltd.
Carmelite House
50 Victoria Embankment
London EC4Y 0DZ

www.bookouture.com

ISBN: 978-1-83790-293-4
eBook ISBN: 978-1-83790-292-7

PROLOGUE

JUNE 1946—PARIS

The little café in the shadow of the Eiffel Tower was a nondescript place, faded writing on its wooden sign, a few rickety tables out front. Inside, a handful of customers sipped coffee or liqueur as the sunlight slanted across the square, its long rays glossing the River Seine with a golden sheen. Inside, a deathly silence fell as three women stared at each other, transfixed, horrified by what they'd just heard.

"*Dead?*" The woman standing by the bar clutched her scarf to her throat as she whispered what had just been spoken. She could not believe it—not now, not after all this time, when they were so close to all being together...

"Yes. Dead." The woman in the doorway nodded, her mouth downturned as pain darkened her eyes. She wore a shabby coat, and a scarf covered her hair. "I saw it happen."

How? Seven years ago, four friends had agreed to meet in this café after the war was over. Back then, the war hadn't even begun, yet they'd all known it was coming—a dark thundercloud on the horizon, looming ever closer as they'd fled Germany on the SS *St Louis*, destined for Havana, doomed never to gain entry. They'd all been forced to go their separate ways—to America, to England, to the Netherlands, to France. Before they'd separated, they'd split an emerald into four, each taking a precious piece, and made a vow to meet again... and three of them had kept it.

But where was the fourth? *Dead?* No, surely not...

The woman pulled the scarf more closely about her throat, as if it could guard her against the truth. "No..." The word slipped from between her lips, half-hearted yet pleading.

"How did you see it?" the third woman asked, her tone almost harsh, accusatory. "Where were you together? It doesn't make any sense—"

The woman drew a deep breath, let it out in a shudder. "I know it doesn't," she said quietly. "I never expected to see her again." Her voice caught. "I never expected her to give her life for me... but she did."

CHAPTER 1

MAY 1939—HAMBURG, GERMANY

"Fritz! Fritz, they want to take our photograph!"

Rosa Herzelfeld bit her lip to keep from saying something sharp as her mother preened for the photographer in her floor-length evening gown of emerald satin. She looked dressed for the opera or a ball, a fur stole thrown over her shoulders and a diamond bracelet sliding down one wrist, instead of what they were actually doing—standing in a long line of weary passengers waiting to embark on a refugee ship to Cuba. Her mother, Rosa reflected, had no sense of occasion, or perhaps too much of one.

Rosa watched, her dark eyes narrowed and her mouth pursed, as her mother angled her head for the camera, one hand planted on her thrust-out hip. Her father's chest predictably puffed out, his eyes gleaming with the opportunity to be noticed and admired, which he invariably was. Fighting a sense of humiliation at her parents' theatrics, Rosa lifted her gaze to find a young woman behind her in the line looking straight at her, clearly bemused by their behavior. Out of habit, as much a form of self-protection as anything else, Rosa rolled her eyes, and the woman suddenly smiled.

Rosa's weary heart improbably lifted. In the world her parents inhabited, she hadn't encountered many kindred spirits. *Save one...* And in the end, he hadn't been truly kindred at all— a cruel reality she still struggled to come to terms with. But she had no intention of thinking about him now, on the cusp of her brand-new life.

Rosa smiled back, and the woman's own smile widened in return. She was a pretty little thing, so different from Rosa's own tall, dark, almost mannish looks—straight hair, a long, sallow face, strong nose and mouth and a straight, tall body. This young woman was all blond hair and big eyes, and Rosa doubted she could be more than eighteen or nineteen. Not that she was much older herself—only twenty-one, yet she *felt* so much older. Although, considering everyone in the stifling shed on the Hamburg harborside was a Jew fleeing Germany for their very life, perhaps they all felt old, even the towheaded little boy tugging the young woman's hand.

Rosa glanced back at her parents, who were still preening, although the photographer wasn't actually taking any pictures. He'd lowered his camera, a look of surly impatience on his face.

"You are not the kind of subjects the Reich wishes to photograph," he stated stiffly, and Rosa watched as her mother's mouth dropped open in outrage.

"*What?*"

"What on earth do you mean?" her father demanded, adopting the stentorian tone that suited him so well as a leading physician back in Berlin—confident, commanding, a little bit officious.

The photographer was looking positively mutinous now. "Move along," he said angrily, and Rosa saw her father's face redden as his chest swelled once more, this time with indignation.

Instinctively, she glanced back at the woman she'd spotted before, and saw she was watching the whole scene, more confused than censorious. Rosa smiled again, wryly, and rolled her eyes once more. The woman smiled back, and she felt as if they'd shared something. A joke, or perhaps a sigh. Maybe both.

"Mother, Father, please, let's not make a scene," Rosa said in a low voice as she stepped forward. "We're just trying to board the ship, after all, not go to a party."

Her mother threw her a furious glare, which Rosa was used to. Her mother had never had all that much time for her, but for the last several years, she had acted as if she positively loathed her, and the truth was, Rosa couldn't entirely blame her. That didn't mean she had to like it, though.

She ignored her mother's look as she moved ahead, her head held high, paying no attention to the surly photographer, only to stop and turn when she heard a furious voice behind her.

"How *dare* you take photographs of my passengers!" a short, officious-looking man declared as he strode toward the photographer. "How dare you insinuate yourself in here, with your vicious and inappropriate propaganda!" Rosa watched, bemused, as he pushed the photographer's shoulder, so the man almost dropped his camera. "*Out!*" he exclaimed, spittle flying from his mouth. "Out of this shed—out, *out!*"

"I am here on orders of the Reich," the photographer protested, staggering back as the man continued to rain slaps down upon him. "You cannot keep me from following my—"

"This embarkation shed is the property of the Hamburg-American Line," the other man replied. "And here, I, as captain of the SS *St Louis*, am in charge. If you do not leave at once, you will find yourself forcibly removed, and your equipment confiscated. *Out!*"

Rosa's mother drew back, looking annoyed by the whole embarrassing altercation, while her father eyed the captain thoughtfully. Tension banded Rosa's temples and tightened her stomach as she felt the curious—and judgmental—stares of the other passengers, no doubt wondering who this jumped-up couple was, thinking themselves so important.

Instinctively, Rosa took a step away from her parents, and then glanced back at the petite blond woman further back in the line. She saw her taking in the whole scene with a look of bafflement and Rosa raised her eyebrows sardonically, determined to set herself apart from her parents' behavior. The woman grinned back, and the tension in her stomach eased a little.

"Please, Mother, Father," she murmured in a low, urgent voice. "Let's just board the ship..."

"Oh, very well, then," her mother replied testily, and she flounced past Rosa, pulling her long, satin skirts away from the dirty floor.

"After you, darling," her father said, giving her a teasing smile, which Rosa forced herself to return, if only a little. Her father had always been so sure of his ability to charm her, and too often he'd been right.

Not any longer, she told herself as she marched toward the first-class boarding gate. She didn't look back once.

A few minutes later, after they'd walked past various sumptuously elegant lounges and halls, a steward led them to their first-class suite—one of the best on the entire ship. Nothing, Rosa knew, was too good for the Herzelfelds. They had two bedrooms as well as a private sitting room, all of it expensively and tastefully furnished with sofas and armoires, bureaus and desks, a porthole in each chamber overlooking the harbor.

Her mother shrugged off her fur stole as she ran her fingertips along the top of a cherrywood dressing table, as if checking for dust. "We've been on better ships," she remarked, and Rosa almost rolled her eyes, except this time she had no smiling audience.

"Well, this one will do the job," her father answered rather shortly. "It's not a pleasure cruise, Elsa, after all."

"Darling, I know." As always when her father became the

tiniest bit terse, her mother turned instantly placating. It was a pattern Rosa was familiar with, and made her want to grit her teeth, as well as cringe in shame, for it was one she all too often participated in, as well. Her father had the sort of domineering and charismatic personality that made her and her mother want to both please and appease him, even when Rosa wished she didn't. "I was only remarking upon it," her mother continued, resting a hand on her father's sleeve, her lacquered nails digging in. "You know I believe you deserve only the best."

Rosa turned away from them to find her own room, sepa-rated from her parents by the sitting room. It was slightly smaller, with a single bed, desk, and dresser, its porthole over-looking the harborside. She glanced outside at the dock in the distance, still bustling with activity. Her last view of Germany, the only country she'd ever known as home. What would Ernst be doing right now, she wondered, and then cursed herself for thinking of him at all. How he could still occupy a place in her brain, never mind her heart, remained an intensely frustrating mystery, and one she chose not to unravel.

"Fritz, let's celebrate!" she heard her mother cry, her voice rising anxiously, as if she sensed he was slipping away from her already. "Why don't you send for champagne—"

"Not just now," her father replied, his voice managing to sound both charming and irritable, a tone he'd perfected over the years, whether he'd meant to or not. "Perhaps after we've sailed, Elsa, when we're truly safely away. Don't you think that would be better? We'll raise a glass then, almost certainly. Now, you look tired. Why don't you sit down..." Her father's voice dropped to a coaxing murmur and Rosa closed the door of her cabin, grateful to have some privacy, as well as some space from her parents' theatrics. Already it felt as if it would be a long voyage, cooped up in these few rooms—a far cry from the pala-tial villa they'd once lived in on the banks of the Wannsee, before the Nazi government had requisitioned it. Her father had seen the writing on the wall then, she thought sourly. It had been about time.

And now they were on the *St Louis* at long last, looking ahead to their new lives and all their possibilities, either in Havana or America, if they were lucky enough to get visas for the latter. Her father certainly seemed confident that they would, but privately Rosa had her doubts. The shaky prestige her father had enjoyed in Berlin might not, she feared, stretch to Cuba or the United States. It might not even stretch on board this ship.

A light tap on her cabin door startled her out of her thoughts. She rose from the bed and went to open it.

"Rosa, *Hase*." Bunny. It had always been her father's pet nickname for her, an endearment only he used. "Shall we explore the ship?"

"What about Mother?"

Her father shrugged, the movement, as so much about him was, expansive. "She was overwrought from our journey. I gave her a spoonful of Luminal to calm her nerves."

A barbiturate and strong sleeping aid that her father prescribed her mother with rather reckless abandon, considering it was lethal in larger doses.

"All right," Rosa said after a second's pause, because she wanted to explore the ship as much as he did, even while she felt guiltily glad that her mother wouldn't be accompanying them. Alone with her father, Rosa could often forget how much his behavior disgusted her—and simply enjoy his company. "Let me just get my hat," she told him, and hurried to fetch it.

Her father was waiting by the door of his cabin, her mother already sprawled on the bed, still in her evening gown and deeply asleep.

"You didn't have her change?" Rosa asked, unable to mask her disapproval. Her father's expansive bonhomie could so easily tilt into cavalier callousness, maybe even cruelty.

He shrugged, smiling. "What does it matter? She looks comfortable enough."

Only because she was drugged to the gills, Rosa thought, but did not say. Her mother would have taken the Luminal willingly enough; in fact, she might have even asked for it.

Still, Rosa couldn't keep from going over and slipping off the high-heeled sandals and drawing the coverlet across her slender, supine form. Her mother might act as if she loathed the sight of her, but the feeling was not mutual. At least, not always.

Rosa straightened as she turned away from her mother. "All right," she said, and could not keep from feeling a flicker of excitement at the prospect of exploring the ship, despite her mother snoring softly on the bed. "Let's go."

CHAPTER 2

They headed down the corridor to the center of the ship, where the main first-class areas were—an elegant dining hall, a wood-paneled reading room and library, a two-story social hall with a wrought-iron balcony above, and then the sports deck and swimming pool. Plenty of other people were wandering about, their expressions often of cautious hope, the brightness in their eyes dimmed by a certain wariness. After all, the ship had not left Germany yet. As Rosa and her father strolled through the social hall, she couldn't help but wonder, like so many others, if it was all too good to be true.

"Well, whatever your mother says, it seems a good, solid ship," her father remarked in his booming, jocular tone that was clearly meant to carry to the other passengers, let them know his opinion mattered.

A few people gave them speculative or even suspicious sideways glances as they walked along; Rosa couldn't tell what they thought of her father from their faces. She suspected it was a sort of baffled bemusement—he was impressive to look at, with his dark, brillantined hair swept back from a high, aristocratic forehead, his wide, white smile that he beamed on just about everyone. He stood several inches over six feet, with broad shoulders and chest, and he didn't so much inhabit a space as overwhelm it. He didn't walk quite so much as strut, one hand tucked into the front pocket of his waistcoat in a style that Rosa thought was uncomfortably reminiscent of the Führer. Next to him, she felt like a drab sparrow—her plain, belted dress did no favors to her straight, boyish figure, and her dark hair had been scraped back in a bun. Once she'd enjoyed dressing up, playing a certain part, but not anymore. Maybe never again.

"With plenty of entertainments to be had," her father continued as he slid her a smiling glance. "Should we visit the nightclub?"

"I doubt there's anything happening there now," Rosa replied, cringing at how prim she sounded. Her father often brought this out in her; his expansiveness, for whatever reason, made her shrink.

As a child, she'd adored being in the radiant beam of his gaze, but now, older and wiser, she tried to avoid it. Yet she'd still gone out to stroll with him, she reflected with a flicker of bitterness, and left her mother alone and asleep. Maybe she hadn't changed as much as she wished she had.

"Well, why don't we see," her father replied easily, rolling right over any objections as Rosa knew he would. "I was hoping to meet some of the crew, maybe even the captain. He was impressive back there in the shed, with that weaselly photographer, wasn't he? I heard he was a man of some reputation, although he didn't fight in the war."

Her father was very proud of his four years of war service, in North Africa rather than Europe. From the photographs she'd seen, he seemed to have spent a good deal of time in souks and cafés, smiling broadly and sipping mint tea. Although she supposed that wasn't really fair; he'd come out of the conflict with an Iron Cross, first class.

"Very well," she replied, and they headed away from the

social hall towards the nightclub Tanzplatz, on C deck. Rosa took in the wood-paneled walls, the chandeliers and crystal and gold lighting fixtures, the thick carpet under her feet. Yes, it was a nice ship, nicer than any she'd been on, at any rate, since she'd never been on a cruise liner before. Her parents had cruised both the Mediterranean and the Black Sea, but they'd left her behind both times with a nanny.

Still, while Rosa was impressed by the ship's amenities, she hadn't actually been expecting this voyage to be *entertaining*, as her father had remarked, but rather simply a way to get from point A to point B—Germany to Cuba. Treachery and shame to freedom and hope.

She didn't particularly want it to be anything else. She'd had enough of parties and dances, of glittering social occasions that teetered on the edge of danger, disaster, even death itself. How many times, while entertaining her father's guests, had her heart lurched, her breathing become staccato with fear, even as she'd laughed and chatted and drank? Then the moment would, invariably, pass, like a thundercloud moving over the Wannsee, ruffling and darkening its waters, smoothing them out again... until the next storm.

No, she wanted to leave that all behind in Germany—and start a new life. A simpler, quieter one, in Cuba or America. She glanced at her father, his head thrown back, whistling as he walked, or, rather, strutted, and she wondered if that would ever even be possible.

As they approached the nightclub, the sound of piano music, accompanied by raucous voices, could be heard. It only took Rosa a few seconds to realize what they were singing—the odious *Horst Wessel* song, the Nazis' angry, unofficial anthem.

"Comrades shot by the red and reaction, March in spirit with us and our ranks!"

It had to be members of the crew singing, and surely on

purpose, as all the first-class passengers had to pass the night-club to get to their berths.

"Let's go back," Rosa said quickly, grabbing her father's arm and already starting to turn, desperate to get away from those awful voices. It brought back too many painful memories—the crash and bang of the piano keys, the men singing lustily, a jeering note to their voices. It was just like before, only this time she didn't have to stay there and listen to it.

"No." Her father shook off her hand, threw back his shoulders. "I'm not going to meekly creep away. We paid for our fare on this ship, and we damned well won't be serenaded with these Nazi songs!"

And yet he'd listened to that very song in his own sitting room, Rosa recalled sickly. He'd smiled faintly all the while, as if it was all a wonderful joke, and one that he was in on, rather than the painful butt of. How could he be hypocritical enough to protest now? And yet she knew he could, because it was surely safer to do so here than it had been in his own home, with SS Obersturmführer Eichmann at the piano, a smirk on his face, eyebrows slightly raised, as if he were daring Fritz Herzelfeld, eminent physician, a friend to Nazis and yet a Jew, to say so much as a word.

Her father hadn't, but it seemed he would now.

Rosa watched, apprehensive, as he threw open the door, filling the space with his presence, his shoulders brushing the doorframe, his chest puffed out. "What is the meaning of this?" he boomed, as the singing suddenly stopped, and with a last bang of the keys, the piano fell silent.

"And who the hell are *you*, you jumped-up Jew?" a man sneered. He had the rough, gravelly voice of the working class, with a Berliner's accent, far below her own family's station.

"Who are *you*," her father replied stiffly, "playing such a song, in such a place as this?"

Rosa winced as she heard the scrape of a chair, the sound of a heavyset man lumbering to his feet. She saw her father stiffen, his hands clenching into fists at his sides before he deliberately unclenched them.

"You're going to protest against your Führer's favorite song, hey?" the man jeered. "Maybe you should sing it with us, you dirty Jew. Do you know the words? I bet you do. And if you don't, I'll teach them to you..."

Footsteps, coming closer. Rosa stood, poised on the balls of her feet, tension thrumming through her, ready to run. Her father, standing completely still, didn't so much as blink. Was he frightened, or just angry? She knew what she was—terrified. She didn't want a dangerous and painful scene, right at the beginning of their new start, their second chance. She didn't want her father to force one.

The moment seemed to spin on forever, until an irate voice suddenly crashed over them.

"*What* is the meaning of this?"

Rosa whirled around to see the ship's captain marching down the corridor, looking even more furious than he had back at the shed, when he'd chased the photographer away. His blue eyes snapped with icy fire, his short form bristling with fury.

"I had quite the same thought," her father replied with dignified asperity, throwing his shoulders back as he stepped back to let the captain into the nightclub. "It is an outrage, to hear such music at a time like this."

The captain barely glanced at him as he stormed into the room; Rosa doubted he'd heard a word her father had said.

"Stop this at once!" the captain demanded of the men who had been singing. "At once! I will not have this music playing while these people board my ship. Back to your posts, immediately."

"That will sort them out," Rosa's father remarked in approval, straightening the cuffs of his jacket.

The captain continued to berate the crewmen, and Rosa had a prickling, urgent desire to escape.

"Father, let's go somewhere else," she implored in a low voice. "It will be dinner soon. Maybe we should go back to the cabin, check on Mother before we change for dinner."

"In a moment, Rosa," her father replied with a flinty smile. "I wish to have a word with the captain first."

Of course he did. Suppressing a sigh of frustration, Rosa stepped back toward the wall as several men slouched out of the nightclub. They were all crew of the ship, a rough sort of men whose expression of sulky discontent morphed to true malevolence when they caught sight of Rosa and her father.

"*Juden raus*," a man with a pockmarked, pouchy face hissed, and Rosa felt a fleck of spittle on her cheek as he glared at her.

Jews, out. Well, they were *going*, weren't they? They were leaving not just Germany, but all of Europe. What more did these stupid oafs want? She almost laughed at the thought, imagining if she had the courage to say it. She knew she didn't, however. As the rest of the men filed past, she averted her eyes.

"Ah, Captain Schroeder." Her father's voice was rich and plummy as he stepped into the nightclub once the crewmen had gone. Rosa lingered in the hall outside, torn between joining her father and not wanting to be part of the conversation.

"Yes?" Captain Schroeder's voice was polite but guarded.

"My name is Friedrich Herzelfeld," her father continued. "I am a doctor from Berlin. Perhaps you've heard of me?"

A slight, startled pause and Rosa closed her eyes, silently shaking her head.

"No," the captain answered, "I'm afraid I have not, but, admittedly, I do not travel in medical circles, Herr Doktor."

"No matter," her father remarked jovially, "you look like a man in excellent health at any rate! I applaud your handling of those men just now. Clearly that sort of behavior cannot be allowed on this ship—in any circumstances." He paused, as if waiting for the captain's agreement, or perhaps even his admiration.

"Indeed not," the captain replied. "I apologize for any distress it may have caused you, Herr Doktor."

"Thank you," Rosa's father answered. "I trust such a thing will not happen again." Although his tone was gracious, Rosa still winced. Lecturing the captain about the behavior of his own crew, on his own ship! It was unforgivable; could her father not see that? *Feel* it, even?

"Indeed, it will not," the captain replied after another pause, this one seeming a shade cooler than the one before.

"Excellent." Rosa heard the sound of her father rocking back on his heels, and imagined his satisfied expression, his hand tucked into the pocket of his waistcoat. "I trust we will see each other again. I hope to have the pleasure of dining at your table one evening." Before the captain could reply to this, her father continued swiftly, "But I am sure you are a busy man, with much to attend to. *Guten Abend*, Captain."

"*Guten Abend*," the captain answered. He walked swiftly out of the room, throwing Rosa a startled glance, before he gave a brief nod and then strode down the corridor.

"A good man, I think," her father remarked as he rejoined her. "Took a firm hand with those crew members. It's important, you know, Rosa, to be a strong leader."

As if her father knew anything about strength, Rosa thought, looking away. She felt too weary to be truly scornful of him; he seemed so completely oblivious of his own arrogance.

"We should go back to the cabin," she said instead as she started back. "Mother might wake up soon, and we need to dress for dinner."

"Ah, Rosa, ever so practical." Her father fell into step beside her, dropping a jocular arm around her shoulders for a quick, fatherly squeeze. "I think it's going to be a pleasant voyage, don't you?"

Rosa could only shake her head. She didn't particularly care if it was a pleasant voyage or not. She just wanted to escape Germany... even if she knew her memories would follow her all the way across the Atlantic.

CHAPTER 3

MAY 13, 1939

Dinner had been, for Rosa, predictably interminable. They'd been seated at a table of eight, with two middle-aged couples and an elderly gentleman whose chin had drooped toward his chest, his eyelids fluttering, for most of the meal. Her father had dominated the entire table's conversation with his many booming pronouncements and sweeping statements, and her mother had been in a dazed stupor from the effect of the Luminal, gazing around blearily as she'd sipped her champagne.

Rosa had practically bolted all five courses of her meal, wanting only to get away from them both. She'd looked around for the young blond woman she'd seen earlier in the shed in the line for first-class passengers, thinking perhaps she could make a friend, but the woman was nowhere to be seen in the first-class dining room. Perhaps she and her family had eaten privately.

Up on deck after the meal, Rosa stood by herself at the railing as the *St Louis* finally freed itself from its ropes, its gangplanks removed. The deck was crowded with passengers, yet they were all curiously silent, as if they were witnessing a ceremony, too sacred for words. Or perhaps they were all just afraid to trust in this moment, in the reality that nearly a thousand Jews had actually been allowed to leave Germany.

Even Rosa found herself holding her breath, wondering if somehow it was all going to go wrong. She could picture it perfectly—the enormous ship suddenly stilling right there in the water, the slack ropes becoming taut once more as the ship slowly turned back to harbor. She could picture the sneering faces of the crew members who had crowded around the piano, exulting in the refugees' misfortune.

Did you really think we were going to let you go? How stupid can you be?

"The space between the ship and land," someone called, as if in amazement. "It's growing!"

Someone else tittered at the obvious statement, yet Rosa understood the incredulous wonder behind it. They were actually *leaving*. Leaving *Germany*. Even as she watched, the harborside was receding. Germany, and all it represented, was inexorably becoming part of the past.

Rosa turned abruptly from the sight; she found suddenly she didn't want to watch the Hamburg harborside slowly becoming a speck. She wanted to leave it all behind, immediately and abruptly, forever. If only she could banish the memories that still lingered and taunted her, in the disquiet of her own mind, when she allowed them to...

Rosa walked quickly away from the railing, down the deck, away from the passengers who now, after their silence, were beginning to murmur in hope and joy. She didn't feel either— not now, not yet. She *wanted* to—heaven knew, she wanted to desperately—and yet there was something inside her that was hard and cold and empty, and she found she couldn't shift it.

She rounded the deck, stopping in surprise as she saw a woman leaning halfway over the railing, her face downturned so she was gazing at the sea below. With a jolt, Rosa realized it was the young woman from the shed. She'd found her, after all.

Rosa started walking toward her, but the woman didn't notice her approach. Rosa stopped, folding her arms, and then called out wryly, "You're not going to jump, are you?"

Startled, the young woman straightened and turned toward her, her eyes widening as she recognized Rosa, just as Rosa had recognized her. The knowledge gave her a little dart of satisfaction.

"Jump?" the young woman repeated with a little laugh. "No, certainly not."

Rosa nodded towards the woman's hands, still curled around the railing. "Well, you looked as if you might have," she remarked, smiling, "but I'm glad to hear it's not a possibility. It would be a shame, having finally got *on* this ship, to get off it again so soon."

"It certainly would." The woman took a step back from the railing as she eyed Rosa up and down, making Rosa straighten a little under her obvious inspection.

She knew she wasn't pretty, not the way this young woman was, with her blond hair and blue eyes, her neat little figure. Rosa was too tall, too mannish, her body going straight from shoulder to hip without much change. Her face wasn't any better—large eyes, straight nose, full lips, all of it a bit too *much*, as if she didn't have enough room for every feature. She'd been called *striking*, which, she felt, was a far cry from beautiful, although she'd been gratified by the compliment at the time, more fool her.

"Finished your inspection?" Rosa asked, doing her best to sound amused, for she suspected she came up wanting, compared to this woman's looks, the ideal of Nazi beauty, never mind that she was Jewish.

The woman blushed and ducked her head. "Sorry. I was just... curious. I recognize you, from before."

"Yes, I know." Rosa nodded. "I recognized you, as well. You

came with your parents?" She'd seen them standing next to her —a father who had looked elderly and anxious, a woman who clearly bore the strain, and a little boy, as well, she recalled, holding this woman's hand, tugging at it in his childish excitement.

"My father and stepmother," the woman replied. "And my half-brother. He's only five."

"Ah." Rosa nodded; judging from what she'd seen before, she thought she understood the dynamic. This woman, all of maybe twenty years old, had been enlisted as her brother's nanny.

"And you?" the woman asked. "Are you traveling alone?"

Rosa let out a short laugh, now genuinely amused. "No," she replied, "didn't you notice my parents making the usual display of themselves for that Nazi photographer?" She shook her head, smiling faintly at the idea that this woman had assumed they couldn't be related to her. It both amused and stung, just a little. Were they so outlandish—or was she so plain? Both, perhaps, and Rosa knew she shouldn't fault it; she'd chosen to be this way, after all. She'd chosen to be neither striking nor beautiful, to be as invisible as it was possible to be, because, in the end, she'd decided that was better than being seen... and rejected. "I'm with them," she explained.

"They're your *parents*?" the woman exclaimed in surprise. "But—"

"I know, I know," Rosa cut her off with what she suspected was a slightly hard laugh, "they're nothing like me. Or, really, I'm nothing like them, thank goodness. But yes, they are my parents." She tried for another, lighter laugh. "Not that you'd know it. I suppose you thought I was their personal secretary or something?" The woman stared at her helplessly, clearly embarrassed by what she'd assumed. "Sometimes I do feel like that," Rosa confessed. Or like a useless appendage, no more than a nuisance to the people who, in theory, were meant to love her most. She let out a little sigh, feeling the weight of depression start to settle on her, before she gave a shake of her head, determined to cast it off. Here, after all, was a potential friend, something she hadn't had in a long while. "Anyway," she said. "I'm Rosa Herzelfeld." She stuck out a hand for the woman to shake.

"Sophie Weiss." She took her hand, and Rosa shook hers firmly. "Pleased to meet you."

"Likewise. I was hoping I'd see you on board." Rosa paused and then confessed with more bravado than true confidence, "I haven't always been very good at making friends, but you seemed something of a kindred spirit."

Rosa suspected she had been too academic and serious for the girls at school, and too Jewish for others. It had left her feeling lonely, craving the attention and affection her parents so rarely gave her, and finding it in exactly the wrong place.

"Do you really think so?" Sophie asked, sounding pleased, which made Rosa smile. Maybe she'd found another person who didn't feel like she fit in.

"Well, you laughed at my parents' ridiculousness, after all," Rosa replied dryly. "So that's something. Will you be staying in Havana, or will your family try to obtain visas for America?"

"America," Sophie replied. "New York. At least, I hope so. My father is—well, was, really—a lawyer, and he has some connections in New York and Washington."

"Always good to have connections," Rosa replied. Her father certainly thought so, at any rate.

"I imagine your father must have some, as well?" Sophie ventured.

So, Sophie had noticed her father's expansive charm and accompanying arrogance. Who else on this ship had? Her father walked the very thin line between impressive and pathetically ridiculous. She wondered which one Sophie thought he was.

"He collects connections the way other men collect

stamps," she joked. "So, yes. But whether they are the right ones..." She shrugged, looking away, not wanting to go into what kind of connections her father had made in the past. The passengers aboard this ship certainly wouldn't be impressed by those. "Who knows?"

"Will you stay in Havana, then?" Sophie asked.

"We'll stay where my father can be most successful," Rosa replied. "He's a doctor." She wasn't about to go into what sort of doctor he'd become, treating the most unmentionable of diseases for philandering Nazis.

There was a slightly tense pause, and Rosa realized that even without mentioning the specifics of her father's profession, she'd sounded too condemning. She was going to have to hide her emotions a little bit better than she was currently managing to do, she thought, especially if she wanted to make a success not just of this voyage, but the possibility of a new life. Deriding her father for the choices he'd made—*and hadn't she made some as well?*—served no purpose now. She had to look toward the future.

"Well, I'm looking forward to ten days on this ship," Sophie finally remarked in a bright voice. "Food and dancing and entertainment—I heard there is a cinema on board, and there is even going to be a costume ball on the second to last night."

All the entertainments her father was looking forward to, as well. "Yes, I heard the same," Rosa replied after a moment. She didn't want to dim her new friend's enthusiasm; why shouldn't she look forward to such things, even if Rosa couldn't care less about them? "It sounds like good fun," she continued, injecting some much-needed cheer into her voice. "What are you going to dress up as? My mother's brought a Cleopatra costume, of all things, a wig included! She'll probably look a complete fright."

"I haven't thought that far ahead," Sophie admitted. "But it's nice just to think of being able to do such things again," she said, "not that I ever really did them before."

"Yes, I know what you mean." *She'd* done them before, Rosa thought with a touch of bitterness. She'd laughed and danced and flirted and teased, but all those enticing things had only entrapped and humiliated her, in the end. She longed to be away from all that, every last smug smile, every knowing look, every subtle dig. And the *guilt*, oh, the guilt... Suddenly, Rosa flung her arms wide as she tilted her face to the night sky, breathed in the cool, sea-scented air. "We finally get a chance to *live!*" she exclaimed, desperate to believe it. "*Really* live. I can't wait."

"What do you want to do in Havana?" Sophie asked, sounding uncertain. Rosa's theatrics, worthy of her parents, had probably alarmed her. "Or America, if it comes to that?"

Rosa lowered her face as she dropped her arms, the memories of those parties in Berlin still chasing through her, souring every thought, every hope. "*Anything*," she said in a low, throbbing voice. Anything, that was, other than what she'd been doing before... to her own shame.

Suddenly, she heard heavy footsteps coming from behind them. Rosa tensed and Sophie turned as a man sneered.

"Ah, two little *Jewesses* enjoying the night air. Better be careful you don't fall over—or get a push."

As he came closer, Rosa saw it was one of the crew members who had been singing at the nightclub earlier. She recognized his voice, too—he was the one who had called her father a jumped-up Jew. She'd been too timid to say anything then, but she told herself she wouldn't be now. Feeling reckless and defiant, she remarked coolly, thankful her voice didn't shake, "I'd say the same of you. Your little piano concert wasn't very popular this afternoon, as I recall, with the captain."

The man's face twisted with malevolence and inwardly Rosa trembled. It took all her willpower not to cringe and cower back. "Shut up, you dirty little Jew," he told her in a growl. "Or you really will need to be careful."

The man loomed over her, close enough she could feel his hot breath on her face. Rosa stayed completely still, her fists clenched at her sides, her heart beating like a hummingbird in her chest, fast and hard. Somehow, she summoned the strength to straighten, gazing at him haughtily as she replied, "Shall I tell Captain Schroeder about this little conversation? I'm sure he'd be interested to hear how his crew are treating the passengers, especially as First Officer Ostermeyer was so keen to make a good impression on us. The reputation of the Hapag Line is at stake, after all." She kept the man's gaze, biting her lip as the man raised one heavy fist as if he was about to strike her. It took all her willpower not to flinch under his scornful gaze.

An endless moment passed as they stared at each other, and then, slowly, the man lowered his fist. Rosa's stomach churned and her head felt light, but she'd done it, hadn't she? She'd faced someone down. *Finally.*

"I'll be watching you," he growled, and then he pushed past her, hitting her hard in the shoulder, so she staggered and had to clutch it; she suspected she'd have a bruise by tomorrow.

As his footsteps faded into the darkness, Sophie hurried to her side. "Are you all right?" she asked anxiously, as Rosa massaged her shoulder. "I can't believe your courage!"

Her *courage*? She had never felt more frightened in her life. Rosa started to smile, but then she felt her churning stomach rise up, and she darted over to the ship's railing, where she humiliatingly emptied the contents of her stomach into the sea.

She hung there for a moment, half over the railing, her eyes closed as she recalled the look of naked hatred on the crewman's face. Had she been brave, she wondered, or just incredibly foolish? What if that man did as he'd promised, and looked out for her? It would be easy enough for such a man to make her life a misery on this ship. She might not have been interested in the cruise liner's entertainments, but Rosa knew she did not want this voyage to be *dangerous.* And really, she'd only stood up to that stupid man because she'd said nothing before—all the *many* times before. Pity her father hadn't been watching.

Rosa straightened, taking out her handkerchief to wipe her mouth. Poor Sophie was looking anxious, indeed. "I refuse to be cowed by some toady little stool pigeon like that," Rosa declared with more conviction than she actually felt. She'd certainly *felt* cowed. She managed a wry smile. "Even if the prospect of standing up to him was enough to make me lose my supper," she added as she grimaced, glancing down at her dirty handkerchief. "I do apologize for such a display. I didn't think I'd actually be *sick!*"

"Never mind that," Sophie told her. "I thought you were amazingly brave. I never could have spoken out the way you did."

Rosa was still amazed that she'd actually done it. "If courage is feeling terrified and doing it anyway, then maybe," she stated a bit shakily, as she folded her dirty handkerchief and slipped it into her pocket. "Although it might just have been sheer foolishness." She was afraid it had been. "I'm just so *tired* of people like that—thinking they're better than I am, and for what?" Her voice wobbled a little as she continued, "An accident of birth? A J stamped in my passport?" She hadn't realized just how many people she'd cared about had thought that way. Even Ernst. *Especially* Ernst. And the fact that she'd convinced herself he didn't, he couldn't, was so ludicrous as to be offensive, absurd. She shook her head, determined to forget Ernst as well as that odious member of the crew. "Anyway, never mind that lout. Captain Schroeder is on our side, at least, as far as I can tell."

"Is he?" Sophie asked.

Rosa shrugged, not wanting to explain what she and her father had overheard. "Didn't you see him shout down that photographer, back in the shed?"

"Yes, but..." Sophie's forehead furrowed. "Why was he there in the first place, do you know?" she asked.

"To take photographs of Jews cringing and scraping and looking dirty and poor," Rosa stated. She'd realized it as soon as the man had lowered his camera, refusing to take any snaps of her parents and their posing and preening. "That's why he didn't want to photograph my parents," she explained, an edge entering her voice as she recalled how her father had puffed out his chest, her mother had angled her perfectly coiffed head. "They were far too glamorous for the Reich's newsreels that show good Germans how Jews are little better than rats—a nasty, germ-ridden infestation they'd best get rid of."

Her lips twisted in memory. *Really, Herzelfeld, those of your unfortunate race are like a bunch of rats, scrabbling about—don't you agree?* Her father had managed a rather strangled laugh in reply, color surging into his face as the officer had tossed back his best schnapps.

"No, he didn't want a photo of my parents, that much is certain," Rosa stated flatly. "My father has made a career out of looking like the right sort of person."

"And yet he couldn't escape being Jewish, I suppose," Sophie pointed out with a small smile.

"Well, he gave it a good try," Rosa replied shortly. "But never mind that. I should get back, not that my parents will miss me. But why don't we meet up in the morning, have a wander around the ship? I want to have a good explore of everything." And she'd like to get to know Sophie better. She seemed a friendly, uncomplicated sort of person; she certainly didn't seem as if she were hiding the kinds of secrets Rosa was.

Sophie beamed in reply before giving a slight grimace of apology. "I'm afraid I'll most likely have my little brother with me—"

So, she really was as good as an unpaid nanny.

Rosa shrugged. "I don't mind if you don't."

"He'll probably be very excitable," Sophie warned. "But, yes, if you don't mind, then I certainly don't! And I'm desperate

to explore the ship. What I've seen so far has looked amazing."
She smiled, and Rosa smiled back, glad that their friendship
seemed firmly forged.

"Then it's a date," she said, before giving her new friend a
little wave and heading back down the deck, to the main
corridor that led to the first-class cabins.

Back in their cabin, her mother was seated at her dressing
table, looking bleary-eyed and disconsolate. Her father was
nowhere to be seen.

"Where have you been?" her mother asked accusingly as
Rosa closed the door and then took off her coat.

"I went to see the ship set sail. We've left Germany at last."
Rosa kept her tone pitched light, although she was aware of her
mother's surly glance. "Where's Father?"

"Who knows." Her mother let out a weary sigh as she stared
at her reflection; her face powder had collected in the creases
between her mouth and nose, and she looked every one of her
forty-eight years. "Meeting new people, I suppose, as he loves
to do."

Rosa regarded her quietly for a moment. "You could go out
with him?" she ventured. "Stay by his side?"

Her mother's eyes narrowed to slits as she glared at Rosa. "I
don't recall asking for your advice," she stated coolly, before
deliberately turning away from her daughter.

Rosa watched silently as her mother began to smooth cold
cream over the tired lines of her face. She felt as if she should
apologize, but she knew it was far too late for that. Besides, what
was she meant to apologize for? Knowing the truth, or simply
existing in the first place? Her mother had resented her presence in their lives for as long as Rosa could remember. It was
only when she had realized what Rosa knew—and had kept
from her—that that resentment had turned into something
resembling hatred.

Without a word, Rosa walked past her mother and then

through the shared parlor to her own cabin, closing the door quietly but firmly behind her. A breath escaped her in a shaky rush as she leaned against the door. Now more than ever, she was looking forward to spending some time with Sophie tomorrow. Now more than ever, she needed a friend.

CHAPTER 4

SATURDAY, MAY 27, 1939—HAVANA, CUBA

A dawn mist moved in ghostly shreds across the still harbor as Rosa stood at the ship's railing. She'd watched a few moments ago as a small launch had chugged across the expanse of water, bearing several Cuban immigration officials to the ship. They'd spoken cheerfully in Spanish, gesticulating broadly, seeming as if they were off for a holiday jaunt rather than inspecting a thousand desperate passengers for entry into their country. For some reason, their easy bonhomie had made Rosa feel uneasy, but it was far from the first thing on this journey that had given her pause. After two weeks traveling across the Atlantic, the *St Louis* had finally arrived at its destination... almost.

Last night, the ship had docked outside of the harbor, but when the passengers had awoken early this morning, ready to disembark, there had been a flurry of confusion and alarm, as everyone saw that the ship had not been allowed into the bustling port. Even at just past dawn, rumors were already flying—the ship's papers were not in order; the *passengers'* papers were not in order. It was a mere formality; it was a cause for concern. With everyone up at the crack of dawn in the hope of disembarking, tempers were already starting to fray; the men were tight-lipped, the women pale-faced, the children tearful or fractious. Everyone wanted information, and no one seemed to have it.

As Rosa watched the last of the mist clear, a now-familiar dread settled in her stomach. While many aspects of the voyage had been pleasant—including the entertainments her father had spoken about—others had left Rosa feeling uneasy and uncertain, even fearful. Early on, it had become clear that the voyage of the St Louis was not without its perplexities and dangers— the presence of the Gestapo firemen aboard the ship; the visas everyone had received with what Rosa's father had remarked was far too much ease; the news that traveled in whispers that Cuba might not be as welcoming as they had been led to believe when they'd booked their passage.

The first warning had come only a day into their journey. Rosa had spent a very pleasant day exploring the ship with Sophie and her brother Heinrich. Away from her own family, and with a kindred spirit, she'd felt that deep-seated cynicism she so often cloaked herself with soften a bit, at its edges. They'd even made another friend—Hannah, only eighteen years old and from Dusseldorf, traveling with her shy little sister, Lotte.

Rosa had felt a deep sympathy for the young woman, who was on her own and yet clearly very protective of her. Their father had been working in Havana for the last few years, and their mother, a gentile, had abandoned them to marry an SS officer, a fact Hannah had offered up with great bitterness, and which had made Rosa wince.

Hannah had taken some of the other children traveling on the St Louis on their own under her wing, and Rosa and Sophie had also pitched in, while Heinrich and Lotte played together.

Everyone seemed to get on very well, but on that very first night, when they'd gone to the cinema, they'd been shocked by a virulent newsreel of Hitler ranting about the Jews that had been shown before the film. Sophie's poor father had run out of the theater in terrible distress; Rosa's father, on the hand, had paraded down the aisle like an angry peacock, and then demanded to speak to the purser about the lamentable state of affairs that had a hundred Jews subjected to a Nazi newsreel, as if they'd never seen such a thing before, back when they'd been allowed in the cinemas.

Rosa had been embarrassed by his posturing, as well as annoyed by his hypocrisy. She'd also felt ashamed, that her father had protested—and she hadn't. It had created a welter of unhappy emotions inside her, but, in any case, the captain himself had apologized to her father, and, shortly after, asked him to be part of a select "passenger committee"—a group of the more prominent men on the ship, to liaise with the captain about the concerns of the other passengers.

It was through that committee that Rosa had come to hear of things she'd rather not have—the death of a passenger that was deliberately kept quiet, his body slipping into the water with a gentle splash late at night; the suicide of a Russian Jewish crew member; and worst of all, the growing disquiet on Captain Schroeder's part that Cuba would not welcome the St Louis and the nearly thousand Jewish souls on it, which Rosa now feared might be coming true, as she looked out at the distant harbor and wondered why they had not anchored closer.

Amidst all this, there had been many pleasures—not least making such good friends as Sophie, Hannah and then Rachel, a young woman in tourist class who had joined their little group after she'd helped Sophie and her father when he'd bolted from the cinema. Rachel was married to Franz, a man still suffering from his months of incarceration at Dachau, and Rosa greatly admired Rachel's seeming serenity in the midst of such obvious hardship. She was always ready with a soft word, a quiet smile, and she'd provided a steadying presence in their little group, especially when Hannah, protective of her sister and anxious about her father, could sometimes be volatile.

The four of them had spent many happy afternoons learning Spanish, with Sophie as their instructor, or having coffee and cake in the social hall, or simply strolling the deck, chatting and laughing, while Heinrich and Lotte played, and Franz walked quietly beside them. They'd even gone swimming in the pool, and there had been a wonderful costume ball the night before last, where they'd all toasted their bright futures with champagne, vowing to be firm friends forever, no matter where their fortunes took them.

As she'd hoisted her own glass, Rosa had managed to suppress the cramp of fear that so often assailed her, tightening her stomach, straining her nerves, that those bright, shining futures might not happen at all. She'd spoken of some of her concerns to her friends, especially to Sophie, but she already could tell that neither Hannah nor Rachel wanted to hear of her doubts. Hannah in particular was focused on her future in Havana; her father was already there, waiting for her, just across the harbor, and she did not want to hear anyone say otherwise.

No, Rosa decided as she straightened up from the railing. She would not bore or distress her friends with the nebulous fears that still plagued her. She wanted to be cheerful, hopeful, focused on the future the way they were. After all, worrying would accomplish nothing.

With a determined spring in her step, she turned from the railing to go in search of her friends. They'd all agreed to meet in the morning, in the hope that by the afternoon they would be disembarking. Rosa thought that unlikely.

As she walked down the corridor toward the social hall, she saw a member of the crew moving swiftly toward her, his head down, his manner furtive. With a lurch of alarm, she realized it was the same man who had threatened her on the first night of the voyage, calling her a dirty Jew and shoving her hard in the shoulder; she *had* developed a bruise.

There was no one else in the corridor but the two of them, and Rosa feared an ugly scene, or worse, if she came across him alone. She'd managed to avoid him for the entire journey; she certainly didn't want to run into him now, when they were— hopefully—on the cusp of disembarking.

She glanced around for some place to go or hide, but the corridor was straight and narrow and there was nowhere to go but backward. The man, she realized, hadn't even seen her yet; he was too occupied with what he was doing, holding something in his hand. She should turn around and run, Rosa knew, and yet somehow, she couldn't make herself do such a cowardly thing. Why not brazen it out the way she had before, even if she'd been, quite literally, sick with nerves?

Frozen with indecision, her heart starting to hammer, Rosa watched as the man came toward her and then stopped, a mere dozen feet away, still oblivious to her presence. He was, she realized, unscrewing the top of a fountain pen. Several endless seconds passed, each one more torturous than the last, as Rosa stood there, still frozen, while the man peered into the pen. What on earth was he doing? Nothing, Rosa suspected, that he wanted her to see. As quietly as she could, she took a step backward, realizing that there was cowardly and then there was simply foolish—and letting this man see her now seemed likely to be the latter.

Another step, and then another, and then her heel caught on the carpet, and she let out a rush of surprised breath.

The man looked up, and Rosa saw the naked fear on his face before his mouth twisted into an ugly snarl.

"So, you're a sneaky little spy as well as a dirty Jew," he sneered, slipping the pen quickly into his pocket.

"I don't think *I'm* the spy," Rosa retorted before she could think better of it.

The man closed the space between them in three long strides and then, his meaty hands on her shoulders, pushed her up against the wall hard enough to knock the wind out of her, her head slamming back. Dazed, Rosa could only stare at him, shock giving way to terror as he brought his face near to hers, his breath hot and smelling of onions.

"You'd better be careful, my little Jewess," he said, stepping even closer to her so his body was pressed up against hers. Rosa could feel the length of his thighs and the jut of his hips against her own, and her stomach swirled in rebellion. "Not that being careful is going to help you now," he added thoughtfully. His hands moved from her shoulders to her throat, his thumb pressing gently on her windpipe, yet hard enough for her to feel it and let out a choking sound.

Please… She almost begged him, but she bit the word back before it escaped. This odious man would relish her begging and then being able to reject her pleas. Rosa forced herself to stay silent, even though her whole body was icy with terror, and with the man's thumb on her windpipe, she struggled to breathe.

"You know Cuba doesn't want you, don't you?" he continued, pressing his thumb a bit harder, so Rosa let out an inelegant, gurgling gasp. "Oh, they might pretend they do, and we'll go through all the rigmarole of acting like you're getting off this ship, but trust me, my little Jewess, you *aren't*."

With a mocking grin, he thrust his hips, grinding into her own, and a pathetic, mewling sound escaped Rosa before she clamped her lips together.

The man chuckled softly. "Too bad I don't like Jewesses," he told her. "You could have seen what a *real* man can do."

He stepped back, eyeing her consideringly, while Rosa, unable to stop herself, pressed one hand to her throat. Her heart was thundering, and her vision swam. She felt as if she could slide right down to the floor in a trembling heap.

"Schiendick!" someone called out, walking briskly down the corridor. "What are you doing? You are wanted on deck."

"Remember, I'm watching you," the man—Schiendick—told her, and then he walked off with the other member of crew.

Rosa's legs trembled and, for a second, she did almost slide to the floor before, on shaky legs, she forced herself to straighten.

Her mind was whirling with what Schiendick had said—*you aren't getting off this ship*—and also what she'd seen. Had he been going to hide something in that pen? It had certainly seemed like it, which made her wonder, with a thrill of incredulous terror, that he was part of the Abwehr, Germany's spy network. Could the Abwehr be here, right here on the ship...?

Or maybe, Rosa told herself rather desperately, she was being ridiculous. He was just a petty little thug of a man; maybe he'd simply been fixing his pen.

Rosa scrunched her eyes shut, wishing she hadn't witnessed a thing, because already she knew there was absolutely nothing she could do about it—if there were Abwehr on the ship along with Gestapo, it did not bode well for the fortunes of the passengers... at all.

Rosa didn't want to believe it, not when they'd finally arrived. And yet...

No. She wouldn't believe it. She wouldn't let herself. Schiendick couldn't possibly know what he was talking about. Straightening, smoothing down her skirt with hands that trembled slightly, Rosa walked back down the corridor, her head held high.

Even so, Schiendick's ominous words echoed through her. *We'll go through all the rigmarole of acting like you're getting off this ship, but trust me, you aren't...*

CHAPTER 5

The rest of the day passed in a flurry of activity, a haze of exhaustion. They all had to line up in the social hall for a medical inspection; the health inspector's gaze barely flicked over each passenger as they walked past. There were no forms to fill, no boxes to tick. It was, Rosa feared, simply a charade, the rigmarole that Schiendick had suggested, to make it seem as if they had some chance of getting off this ship.

Still, so many hoped. Fishing boats bobbed in the sea alongside the *St Louis*, some of them selling fruit to the passengers, others carrying passengers' relatives eager for a glimpse of their loved ones. The excitement grew, and then fell again, as the hours passed with no news.

In the late afternoon, a German woman and her two children were allowed to disembark, sending people into a frenzy of expectation, only to subside again when no one else's name was called.

"Why them and not us?" Hannah demanded, her voice rising to a near-wail as she clutched Lotte to her.

"It will be our turn soon, Hannah," Rachel said quietly, laying a hand on her arm. "Why shouldn't it be? We've come

this far, and heaven knows we can't stay on this ship forever."
She smiled, as if inviting them all to share the joke, but only
Sophie smile weakly.

Can't we, Rosa wondered, but chose not to say. If the
Cubans didn't want them, just as the Germans hadn't... who
would take them? Where would they go?

She kept these questions to herself, but she saw Sophie
shoot her an uncertain glance, and knew her friend was
wondering about the nature of her unhappy thoughts.

"I'm sure you're right," she forced herself to say, injecting a
bright note into her voice. "Today was bound to be a bit of a
muddle. We'll have news tomorrow." Rosa saw how her friends
seemed relieved at her words; somehow she'd become the unofficial leader of their little group, perhaps because her father was
on the captain's passenger committee, and so she had more
information than most. In any case, she felt the unwanted
responsibility keenly; she needed to keep everyone's spirits up,
her own included.

As dusk fell, Rosa left her friends and went back to her
cabin to change for dinner. They would not be disembarking
today. She felt too tired to be anxious now; if anything, she felt
no more than a weary resignation. Slipping inside, she saw her
mother was in bed, asleep, her mouth agape, her dark hair
spread across the pillow and her limbs akimbo. Her father sat at
the desk, staring out of the porthole with narrowed eyes as he
smoked furiously, the filter of his cigarette glowing an angry
orange every time he sucked in a breath.

"You gave her more Luminal?" Rosa asked, unable to keep
the note of accusation from her voice. Her father was a little too
free with that bottle.

"She was agitated, Rosa, and I am a doctor. She needed a
sedative." His tone was tense rather than its usual expansively
implacable.

Slowly, a sense of dread creeping over her like the mist over the harbor, Rosa closed the door behind her.

"Do you know something?" she asked quietly. "Why have we not been able to leave the ship?"

Her father shook his head, a twitchy sort of movement, as he blew out a stream of smoke.

"Father, *please*," Rosa insisted, keeping her voice low for the sake of her mother, although she looked as if she wouldn't wake even if the ship sounded its klaxon. "I know you talk to the captain," she continued. "What's going on? Why can't we leave?"

"Nothing is going on," her father burst out. He stubbed out his cigarette in the ashtray in one vicious movement. "*Nothing.*"

"What does that mean exactly?" Rosa asked, folding her arms.

She didn't like the wild look in her father's eyes, the way his hands shook. He was a man who relished being in control, who delighted in seeming confident and at ease, in command of everything he saw. Yet right now he looked as if he'd been pushed to the brink, as if he were teetering on its razor-thin edge. It unnerved Rosa more than she cared to acknowledge. She might disdain her father's cozying up to the Nazis, but in that moment, she realized she'd always liked feeling that he was in control.

"It means, Rosa," he told her, and now his voice held an acid edge, "that we are most likely not going to be able to get off this ship today, tomorrow, or *ever*. Cuba doesn't want us. The Abwehr have been stirring up hatred against Jews in Havana for weeks now, in preparation for our arrival, and it looks as if all their fat, smug pigeons have come home to roost."

The Abwehr again. That man Schiendick must be involved somehow, Rosa thought. Did it even matter, though? She knew there was nothing she could do about it.

"How do you know this?" she asked. "Did the captain say so?"

Her father shrugged impatiently. "More or less, yes. He was visited by an agent in Havana who came on board, not that he wants to say as much, but it was obvious by the agent's oily manner. I saw him, and he wasn't even hiding it." He let out a heavy sigh. "He made it clear what the point of this voyage was, and it *wasn't*, Rosa, to allow a thousand Jews to leave—and live—freely, as the captain or any of us might hope."

Rosa swallowed hard. So, it had all been an exercise in propaganda? "But..." She licked her lips, started again. "What does it mean for all of us?"

"It means that the Nazis are doing whatever they can to keep us from getting off this ship. Not that the Abwehr even cares about that," her father amended bitterly. "I'm sure the agent just wanted to pass on some information or some such. But it will certainly be a delight for the Reich if it can be shown that *no one* wants the Jews, Cuba included." He shook his head slowly. "Should we be surprised? Why do you think the Nazis let us go in the first place? It wasn't out of the kindness of their hearts, that much is for certain."

It was a question Rosa had asked Sophie earlier in the voyage, but in the face of her friend's hopefulness, she realized now that she'd been content to let it remain unanswered. Of *course* the Nazis didn't want the Jews to go merrily on their way and settle happily in Havana, to show the whole world how they could be successful somewhere else. It would be the very last thing they'd seek! What they wanted was just what her father had said—for the world to see how *no one* welcomed the Jews... not Germany, not Cuba. Not anyone, anywhere.

"What will happen?" she asked, her voice little more than a whisper.

"I have no idea." Her father stood up, straightening the cuffs of his jacket. "But I can assure you, I will not take this lying down. We paid for our passage, as well as our visas, and we deserve to be treated appropriately. If the captain cannot manage to get off this wretched ship, then maybe someone else can." He'd adopted the pompous tone he usually reserved for people he wanted to impress. "I intend to speak to him about it immediately." He nodded toward her mother, still asleep on the bed. "You can keep an eye on your mother, since you always seem so concerned about her."

And with that cutting remark, he left the cabin, while Rosa sank onto a chair, burying her face in her hands.

What, she wondered despondently, was going to happen to them all now?

That evening, Rosa heard from a cheerful Rachel that nothing could happen until after Sunday, the Christian holiday of Pentecost.

"That's what the immigration officials were saying—*después de Pentecost!*" She shook her head in smiling wonder. "I'd never heard of it before."

"Nor I." Rosa wanted to believe that was the only reason for the delay, wanted to believe it desperately... and yet she didn't.

An hour before, her father had returned from his brief meeting with the captain fuming at the lack of information, the false promises.

"Something is clearly amiss," he'd stated, caught between fury and fear. "The Gestapo firemen have been knocking on cabin doors, roughing people up. They broke a man's *rib* in tourist class."

Rosa had thought of the crew member she'd seen earlier, his sneering, fleshy face, the furtive way he'd peered into the pen. No, she thought as she tried to smile at Rachel, she certainly didn't believe that they would all be allowed to disembark *después de Pentecost*.

The question that remained, and one she didn't dare voice aloud, was—would they ever?

The days passed in sweltering, stultifying slowness. Some of the younger people seemed to view the delay as some sort of extended holiday, especially after First Officer Ostermeyer announced there would be no class distinctions, and tourist and first-class passengers could use all the same lounges and social areas, which they did with merry abandon—the first-class lounges now heaving with people, the swimming pool a seething mass of bare-skinned humanity.

The heat, the crowds, and the growing sense of tension left Rosa feeling tetchy and restless. She argued with Hannah about their future; Hannah insisted they would be let off the ship soon, and she absolutely did not want to hear anything to the contrary. Her father had waved at her and Lotte from a boat, and she'd been overjoyed. Rosa couldn't bear to dampen her determined enthusiasm, and yet it was becoming harder and harder to stay silent. She felt the need to warn her friends, to prepare them, but it was abundantly clear that they did not appreciate such sentiments.

When Pentecost passed and nothing changed, the mood on the ship began to darken into deep despair. At one point, women rushed to a ladder, desperate to get off, and were pushed back by Gestapo, some of them badly injured, which only added to the sense of frightened futility. Rosa's father was frantically sending cables, trying to trade on the connections it seemed he no longer had. Rosa had stopped asking him for news; it only made him furious that he didn't have any. Her mother remained in a sedative-laced stupor, barely leaving the cabin. When, on Wednesday afternoon, Rosa beseeched her to take some air, she batted her away.

"Don't mollycoddle me, Rosa, I'm not your child," she

snapped. "You might feel guilty for the way you've treated me over the years, but you can't make up for that now."

Rosa had to bite her tongue. *The way she'd treated her?* She could have bandied that accusation right back at her! The only thing Rosa had ever done to her mother was hide a horrible truth from her, for her *own* sake. It was something she'd discovered her mother would never forgive.

"Leave me," her mother commanded, rolling over on her bed so her back was to her daughter. "I don't want your company anymore."

You never did, Rosa thought with a mixture of sorrow and anger, but she didn't say the accusatory words. Instead, she slipped out of the cabin, taking a deep breath to steady herself. It annoyed her that her mother's barbed comments could still hurt her so deeply. After years of them, she surely should be immune, but, to her shame, she wasn't. Her only defense was to act as if she didn't care, but right now she couldn't summon the strength.

She started toward the social hall, thinking she'd find her friends, only to realize she felt too dispirited to jolly them along as she'd so often tried to do, promising they'd be toasting each other with cocktails at the Inglaterra Hotel in Havana in just a few days' time. Well, they wouldn't, she didn't believe it for a minute, and she couldn't pretend any longer. She didn't even want to.

They weren't *ever* going to get off this ship, Rosa thought despondently as she slipped out onto A deck and gazed out at the placid harbor, fishing boats bobbing alongside several cruise liners—three ships had come and gone since the *St Louis'* arrival, their passengers disembarking without any trouble. How could anyone believe that it was all going to turn out all right for them?

Just then, the ship's horn gave a single, long blast—the traditional signal for "man overboard." Rosa's heart lurched. What had happened now? Had someone else fallen—or jumped? She shuddered to think.

She saw a commotion happening much farther down the ship's deck; people were shouting and gesticulating, and a police launch was cutting through the water far below, churning up white-flecked foam on either side of the little boat. Rosa started hurrying down the deck, only to nearly smack into Hannah halfway along. She stumbled backward, one hand pressed to her chest.

"Rosa, there you are!" Hannah's blond hair, usually pulled back into a neat bun, was half-falling down about her face, which was flushed from exertion, her voice breathless as she pulled Lotte behind her, the young girl pale-faced and wide-eyed. "The most dreadful thing has happened," she exclaimed, drawing Lotte closer to her side, her arm around the girl's thin shoulders. "Too terrible for words!"

"Did someone fall overboard?" Rosa's stomach dropped at the thought. There had already been a death and a suicide on board. Another casualty would surely plunge everyone into even deeper despair.

"It's Sophie's father!" Hannah told her, her voice dropping to a hushed whisper. "He's gone and thrown himself off the ship. Cut his wrists first as well, the poor man. He was absolutely distraught. I saw it all happen myself—they're just fishing him out of the water now."

"*What...*" The word escaped Rosa in a breath. She'd known Sophie's father was emotionally fragile, but she hadn't realized just how on the brink he must have been, to do something so drastic, especially with his own children on board. "Is he... is he...?" She couldn't make herself say it.

"He's alive," Hannah replied, "and a member of the crew said they're going to take him to hospital in Havana." Her face creased with worry as she hugged Lotte to her. "Poor Sophie is beside herself. And little Heinrich! How has it come to this, that

a man thinks he's better off dead than on this wretched ship?"
Hannah clutched Lotte more tightly, and Rosa saw the
anguished question in her friend's eyes that she didn't want to
voice aloud.

What if they *were* better off dead than on the doomed St
Louis?

CHAPTER 6

FRIDAY, JUNE 2, 1939

Rosa had thought that the bleak mood on the ship couldn't get any worse, but after Sophie's father's attempted suicide, it darkened even more dramatically, as the fleeting holiday mood vanished, replaced by thinly concealed terror. Members of the crew were put on suicide watch, patrolling the corridors each night to make sure no one else flung themselves off the ship. Police launches cruised through the water, surrounding the ship, and leaving the passengers feeling all the more as if they were in a floating prison, with no escape—and no news. Sophie's father, at least, was in stable condition in a hospital in Havana, and would be returned to the ship as soon as possible.

"Although what for, I don't know," Sophie remarked bleakly to Rosa, when she'd told her the news. "If we aren't allowed in Cuba, where will we go?"

On Friday morning, news came at last, and it was even more unwelcome. The Cuban President, Federico Brú, had ordered the *St Louis* to depart from Cuban waters. They might not know where they were going, Rosa thought, but it seemed they still had to leave.

When she asked her father about it while they had coffee in

the social hall, he was both encouraging and dismissive. "Captain Schroeder says he cannot possibly heave anchor until tomorrow night. We still have some time before Brú's command must come to pass."

"Time?" Rosa eyed her father uneasily. His normally immaculately brillantined hair was disheveled, a stray lock flopping greasily onto his forehead. His shirt was wrinkled, and there was a stain on the cuff of his smoking jacket. For a man who prided himself on his appearance, he looked unsettlingly unkempt. He reached for the coffee pot and sloshed some into his cup, not meeting her gaze. "Time for what, Father?" she pressed. He didn't reply, and she stated flatly, "You haven't been able to reach anyone of note, have you?"

"It is not for lack of trying," her father replied with an edge. "The passenger committee has cabled many dignitaries and politicians in the United States, as well as various American and European newspapers, to get the media's attention, but they don't seem very interested in a thousand homeless Jews, as it turns out. The Joint Distribution Committee has become involved, as well—they've been attempting to broker a deal with the Dominican Republic, but they want half a million dollars just to take us!" His voice quivered in indignation. "It's an outrage! As if we are beggars, caps in hand, when every person on this ship has paid for passage as well as a visa..." He trailed off, for he'd already told Rosa himself that the visas were worthless, handed out by a Cuban government worker on the take, with no real authority. "There has been talk of the ship going to Miami or Washington, but..." He let out an aggrieved sigh. "Considering how much money the Dominican Republic wants, I'm afraid it seems like so much wishful thinking at the moment."

Rosa knew the Joint Distribution Committee was a Jewish charity in the States that had been trying, quite successfully, to get refugees out of Europe. But if even they couldn't manage to save the *St Louis*, then who could?

And what would happen if no one did? They couldn't cruise the Caribbean seas forever, with no port in view. They would run out of food and fresh water, as well as fuel. Logically, the ship had to go somewhere, but *where*?

Rosa knew the answer before she'd even made herself ask the question. The place—the *only* place—they could go to was Germany. Sent back to the country where they'd been reviled and excluded and even worse... the thought was utterly horrifying. Just imagining it made her stomach hollow out and her heart start to race. Their house by the Wannsee had already been taken from them, given to an SS officer her father had once treated, a turn of events which had precipitated his decision to emigrate. They'd sold all their possessions—the antiques and the Art Deco furniture and art the Reich found degenerate—and her father had moved as much of his money as he could out of the country, which in the end had not been nearly enough. But they had nothing back in Germany. *Nothing*.

And that was assuming they wouldn't first be arrested, or worse...

"Your little friend's mother has been sending her fair share of cables," her father remarked acidly as he took a sip of coffee. "She's in the telegram office every day, sending something or other to someone important, or so it seems."

"Sophie's father has some connections in the States," Rosa replied, keeping her tone deliberately mild. "Through the legal profession. I'm sure they want to make good use of them."

"I suppose so," her father replied with an ill-disguised harrumph, his handsome face screwed up in a momentary scowl. He obviously didn't like the idea that someone might be better connected than he was, and yet that was, Rosa knew, the unfortunate truth of the matter.

"It's too bad all your connections are back in Germany," she couldn't keep from saying, her voice possessing its own touch of acid. "Not very useful now, are they?"

Her father's eyes narrowed briefly to ice-blue slits before his fleshy lips turned upward in a steely smile. "Is that a hornets' nest you wish to prod, my dear?" he asked pleasantly. "For you had some rather intimate *connections* yourself."

Rosa flushed and looked away. She'd been stupid to say anything; it was just that her father's arrogance got to her after a while, even though she knew she shouldn't let it. *Are you really any better?* she silently mocked herself, which made her flush all the more in shame. She had to take a few steadying breaths before she could manage a reply.

"There's no need to bring any of that up," she stated quietly, looking down at her lap so her father wouldn't see the miserable expression on her face. "You know it's over."

"You were the one who forced the issue," he pointed out in that same, dangerously pleasant voice. "If we're sent back to Germany, Rosa, I imagine you could have quite a *touching* reunion with dear Ernst."

At that awful prospect, Rosa's stomach heaved, and she had to press her hand to her middle to keep the few sips of coffee she'd had down. She could not bear even to think about such a thing.

"Rosa!" Rachel walked up to their table, smiling, and Rosa had to force a smile onto her own stiff lips. She didn't think Rachel had overheard their conversation, but she shuddered to think what conclusions she might draw if she had. She liked the other woman, with her dark blue eyes and her tranquil expression, and was glad that she'd joined their little friendship circle.

Married to a man who had been imprisoned at Dachau until just a few weeks ago, Rachel had a surprising and enviable placidity about her demeanor. Her husband, Franz, had, like Sophie's father, become anxious about the lamentable state of affairs on the ship and was often wandering away, lost in his own dazed world, barely uttering a word when he was found and led back, trotting next to his wife with a vacant look on his face. Rachel never seemed particularly distressed by such episodes, always speaking tenderly to him, with the patience of a mother with her child. It both saddened and heartened Rosa, to see them together, and she half-wished she possessed the same kind of calm equanimity about the people in her own life.

"I was wondering where you were," Rachel continued, a slight furrow between her eyebrows as she glanced between Rosa and her father, no doubt sensing the tense undercurrents that still pulsated between them. "Herr Doktor," she greeted him with a nod. "I hope you are keeping well?"

"As well as can be expected, considering these trying circumstances." Her father flashed Rachel a quick, gleaming smile, reverting to his charming form with disquieting ease. "How is your husband, Herr Blau, keeping?"

"Like you, as well as can be expected. We all just want to hear some news."

"I wish I had some to give you on this occasion, but I'm afraid at the moment the passenger committee knows little more than you do."

Rosa watched, a sardonic twist to her lips, as her father's chest swelled slightly; he loved any opportunity to remind everyone he was one of the select members of the passenger committee, who had the captain's ear on so many matters, little good it seemed to have done anyone. She had to suppress a smile as she saw a flicker of amusement flash through Rachel's blue eyes before she nodded soberly.

"It must be quite a daunting responsibility, to represent all the passengers and their views," she remarked, and with a jolt, Rosa wondered if Rachel, always so kind and calm, was actually being gently sarcastic. But no, surely not...!

"Indeed, it is," her father replied with a sagacious nod. "Indeed, it is."

Rosa didn't think she could stomach any more of his unrelenting pontificating. Abruptly, she rose from the table. "Were you on your way to see Sophie and Hannah?" she asked Rachel. She'd still been half-avoiding her friends, not wanting to darken their moods with her own worries, but now she felt she needed a respite from her father—and his mocking threats. *If we're sent back to Germany, Rosa, I imagine you could have quite a touching reunion...*

"Yes..." Rachel glanced uncertainly between Rosa and her father, who had remained seated, his charming smile starting to wilt a little at its edges.

"I'll come with you," Rosa said quickly. She tossed her father a careless glance. "You can keep an eye on Mother, since you always seem so concerned about her," she added, parroting his earlier words to her back at him. She didn't miss the flash of anger in his eyes as she strode quickly away.

"I won't ask," Rachel murmured as they made their way to the reading room, where Sophie and Hannah were, attempting to entertain Heinrich and Lotte. "Everyone's tempers are fraying these days, aren't they?"

"Yours isn't," Rosa replied, trying to sound lightly wry and failing. "In any case, I'm afraid it's more than that," she continued, as she looked away. "I've never got on with my parents, and I don't suppose I ever will."

To her surprise, Rachel stopped right there in the corridor, and laid a hand on Rosa's arm. "They are your *family*, Rosa," she admonished gently, her deep blue eyes crinkling at the corners, "and they are all you have now. My own parents are dead, and I regret every cross word I ever spoke to them. Now more than ever, you need your family about you. Don't jettison your closest relationships out of mere perversity." Her lips curved in a small, understanding smile. "You know what they say. *Das Kind mit dem Bade ausschütten.*"

"Don't throw out the baby with the bathwater?" Rosa let out

a hard little laugh as she gently but deliberately shook off Rachel's arm. "There's small chance of that. They chucked the baby out with the bath a long time ago. It's not been my doing, Rachel, it's theirs." *Or it was mostly*, she told herself.

Rachel let out a quiet sigh, and Rosa suddenly felt childish, as if she'd had a temper tantrum, pouting and stamping her foot. She didn't like to think she'd disappointed her friend. "Even so," Rachel stated quietly. "Even so."

Sophie was sitting in a quiet corner of the reading room as they arrived, looking tense and anxious, while Franz, Rachel's husband, sat nearby, a book abandoned in his lap as he stared dreamily off into the distance.

"Where's Hannah?" Rosa asked, bending to kiss her friend's cheek. She'd been trying to keep vigil with Sophie as much as she could, although it was difficult, with the demands of her family. "And Heinrich and Lotte?"

"Hannah took them both swimming. Heinrich has been fussing terribly about going in the pool, but it's so crowded now, and he's not the strongest swimmer. I haven't wanted to take him." She sighed, tucking a stray blond tendril behind her ear. "That's the least of my worries now, though."

"Has there been any news of your father?" Rachel asked as she joined them, having ordered coffee and cake.

"No, not since yesterday." Sophie shook her head. "He's still in hospital. They won't tell us more than that."

Rachel sighed as she glanced around the reading room with its various clusters of morose-looking passengers, her gaze resting briefly on her husband, her expression becoming momentarily tender before she turned back to her friends. "Does the captain have a plan, do you think?" she asked.

Sophie shrugged, and Rosa followed suit. No one knew anything.

"What happens," Sophie wondered aloud after a moment, "if my father is still in hospital when we leave?" Her lips trembled and she pressed them together. "I'd like to think he'd be safe," she'd continued quietly, "but I just don't know..."

At least on this matter, she could offer some encouragement, Rosa thought. "Captain Schroeder has said they can't possibly leave tonight," she told Sophie bracingly. "He has to take on fresh food and water first. My father says we won't move off at least until tomorrow afternoon."

"That's something, then," Rachel offered with a small smile.

"But where will we go?" Sophie asked.

"Some are saying Miami," Rosa offered, although her father had said it was wishful thinking, and she thought he was probably right. "Maybe Washington." She wished she could believe it. "Not too far."

The sudden click of heels on the parquet floor of the reading room had all three women turning. Sophie's stepmother walked toward them, her face alight with fierce purpose. She wore a smart, belted dress of black taffeta, and her face was powdered, her lips slicked with crimson, her eyes burning darkly in her pale face. What, Rosa wondered, had happened now?

"Margarete—" Sophie half-rose from her chair as she looked at her stepmother in alarmed query. "Has something happened? Have you had any news?"

"Of your father? No." Margarete's tone was tense. Her gaze flicked to Rachel and Rosa, and then back to Sophie again. "We must talk in private, Sophie."

"Of course." Rachel rose from her seat with quiet dignity while Rosa could only bristle at the abrupt dismissal. "We will leave you in peace."

"There's no need," Margarete replied briefly, without meeting the other woman's eye. "We'll go back to our cabin."

Sophie turned back to her friends. "Can you look after Heinrich for me, if I'm not here when Hannah brings him back—?"

"Of course," Rachel said again, quickly, while Rosa watched Margarete; the older woman looked as if she was going to burst out of her skin. What could be going on? "We are always here to help."

As Sophie left with her stepmother, a steward came with a tray of coffee and several delicious, apple-filled slices of *Apfelkuchen*.

"Ladies," he stated genteelly as he set the tray down, and Rachel murmured her thanks. Rosa watched Sophie hurry after her stepmother.

"What do you think that was all about?" she asked after the steward had left.

Rachel shook her head as she poured the coffee. "I have no idea."

Rosa thought she did. Her father had said Sophie's step-mother had been sending cables to America; the likelihood was she'd finally had a reply. A shaming sensation of envy twisted Rosa's gut. If Sophie was saved and she was not... Well, she'd be glad for her friend. She would not begrudge Sophie a chance at happiness, at *life*, and yet... *oh!* How she wished for it for herself. How she wished her father hadn't set himself up as a Nazi stooge and that she was the one with a prospect, a possibil-ity, and yet she didn't even know if that was why Sophie's step-mother had summoned her.

They found out just half an hour later. Rosa and Rachel had gone out to the deck and were lolling in chairs, wilting in the heat, trying to keep their anxiety at bay when Rachel caught sight of Sophie, hurrying toward them.

"Sophie!" Rachel straightened in her chair. "What did your stepmother want?"

"Where is Hannah?" Sophie asked, her voice tight with tension. "And Heinrich?"

Rachel frowned. "They're still at the pool."

"I need to speak to you all," Sophie said. Her voice hitched and now Rosa was the one frowning. Why did Sophie look so upset?

"Sophie," she began, "what—"

"Please, wait. Let's get Heinrich and Lotte settled, and then..." She bit her lip, almost as if she were holding back tears.

She'd been right, Rosa realized with a lurch of understanding. Sophie was going to be rescued, and she clearly felt guilty about abandoning them all, as she would, being so tender-hearted. Rosa felt a stab of shame; she didn't think *she* would feel that guilty. She'd sprint straight off this ship if she could, without looking back. What kind of person did that make her? "What's happened?" she asked, her voice turning sharp. "Something has happened." It was painfully obvious.

"Yes, but... please. I'll tell you. Just..." Sophie shook her head. "Let me settle Heinrich first."

Rachel and Rosa waited in a tense silence as Sophie went to find her brother. A quarter of an hour later, she was back, with Hannah as well, the four of them gathered around the table in the corner of the reading room.

"Sophie, what on earth is going on?" Rosa asked, and she heard the impatience in her voice, needling through the concern like holes being picked in a cloth. She tried for a laugh and didn't manage it. "All this mystery and drama!" Her voice sounded high and brittle, and her fists had clenched of their own accord.

"No mystery, no drama." Sophie's voice trembled. "I just wanted to tell you what... what is happening."

"What *is* happening?" Hannah demanded, frowning.

Rosa thought she looked caught between anger and alarm, as she so often was. Rachel simply shook her head slightly, looking both concerned and confused. Rosa tried to school her expression into something pleasant and interested, when inside she felt like shrieking. *Don't leave us*, she wanted to cry. *Don't leave* me.

Since she'd met Sophie on the first evening, or even since she'd seen her as they'd boarded in the embarkation shed, she'd felt as if she'd found a true kindred spirit. A real one, not the kind of sham one she'd put her trust in before, with Ernst. Not that she wanted to think about Ernst now, she thought with a shudder. But to lose Sophie, the closest friend she'd ever had...

And yet, Rosa thought, of course Sophie should go if she had the opportunity. There was no question about that, none at all, in her own mind. She knew that full well.

Sophie gazed between them all, her eyes filled with tears. "My stepmother..." she began, and then had to stop again.

Rosa tutted, and wished she hadn't, but she felt as if something inside her was about to break.

"My father has connections in America," Sophie explained in a rush. "A family in Washington. My stepmother sent a cable... she has arranged for me to leave the ship... to go to America..." She trailed off at the look of shock Rosa knew was on all three of their faces.

So, it was just as she had suspected, although she hadn't considered that Sophie might go alone, leaving her entire family behind. "You're... *leaving?*" she managed.

Sophie nodded.

"When?" Rachel asked, still looking stunned.

"Tonight. Very soon, in fact. I came to... to say goodbye." Her voice caught as she glanced at Hannah, who Rosa realized still hadn't spoken. She'd folded her arms, and her lips were pursed, her eyes narrowed nearly to slits. She was angry, Rosa realized, and she probably felt betrayed, just as she did, even if there was no reason to. Sophie *had* to take this chance. "I'm so sorry..." Sophie choked.

"How can you be *leaving,*" Hannah spat suddenly, "when Lotte and I are not able to? My father is in Havana! He's *right there!*" She flung one hand out, a shudder going through her whole body as she struggled not to cry.

"I'm so sorry," Sophie said again, wringing her hands. "I didn't want to go, but my stepmother—Margarete—she insisted." She touched her cheek, and Rosa saw the faint, pink imprint of a hand. Had Margarete *slapped* her? "She said it would be wrong for me *not* to go, after the sacrifices my family has made. It's what my father would have wanted—"

"It's what we *all* want," Hannah burst out bitterly. "Lucky you, though."

"Hannah." Rachel sounded quietly reproving. "Sophie must take this chance. You would take it, if you'd been offered it. You know you would."

They all would, Rosa thought, yet she didn't have the strength to say anything to Sophie, to reassure her that she understood. She felt bitterly disappointed, and yes, betrayed, and also guilty for being so selfish as to resent Sophie for finding her freedom. If she'd been given this same chance, Rosa knew, she would have taken it with both hands, without a single second's hesitation.

"I don't want this to be farewell forever," Sophie insisted, her voice breaking. "You three have been my best friends. I haven't..." She paused, struggling to keep her voice even. "My best friend back in Berlin, Ilse, was a gentile. After the race laws, she turned her back on me completely. I... I never had another friend like her, not until I met you three. *Please...*"

Rosa couldn't take anymore. Her resentment evaporated like the mist over the harbor, in the face of her friend's obvious distress. "Oh, Sophie," she said quietly. "I hope and pray we'll see each other again, as well." She could not truly imagine such a thing happening, but she hoped it might, one day.

"Listen," Sophie said. "I have a jewel, an emerald, from my mother." She held up a little bag, made of blue velvet. "I split it into four shards, so we can each have a piece to remember one another by. And one day—*one day*—we'll meet again." She gazed at them all defiantly. "We will."

Rosa frowned. "You should keep any jewels," she said, nodding to the bag. "You might need them." Even if Sophie was getting off this wretched ship, the future would still be terribly uncertain.

"No." Sophie shook her head, seeming vehement. "I want us each to have a piece. A talisman of sorts. And when we're together again—and we will be—we'll fit the pieces back together. We'll be whole again."

"Oh, very well," Hannah replied, sounding restive; Rosa suspected she was trying to hide her anxiety. "It's a bit dramatic, but if you insist."

Carefully, Sophie withdrew the jewel's shards, jagged and green, and handed them solemnly to each woman. Rosa studied the piece of emerald resting in the palm of her hand, glinting under the light of the lamp, and wondered if she would ever see Sophie again. She would be in America, and Rosa—she would be... where? In Germany? Somewhere else? Still on this ship? She had no idea, and that felt terrifying. The future loomed in front of her like a gloomy, endless fog, entirely unknown.

She closed her fingers over the emerald, letting the jagged edge of the jewel bite into her skin. They would see each other again, she vowed. She'd make sure of it. She wouldn't let this ship, these circumstances, defeat her. *Them.* Somehow, some way, she would triumph. They all would... and they would find each other again, because, Rosa knew, these were the dearest friends she'd ever had.

"How on earth did you manage to split it?" Rachel asked as she glanced down at her own shard. "Emeralds are almost as hard as diamonds."

"It wasn't easy," Sophie replied. "But my father had brought jeweler's tools."

"Still," Rachel remarked, her eyebrows raised, "you must have had to give it a good whack."

It didn't matter how it was split, Rosa thought, only that it was, and that they would each have their own precious piece to remind them of each other. "And now what?" she asked, gazing down once more at the splinter of emerald in the palm of her hand. She wanted to be practical, to make a plan. "How on earth will we ever find each other again? We don't even know where we're going."

"I'll send a cable when I arrive, so you know my address," Sophie replied quickly. "And you can write to me, with your own addresses, when you know them. Please write," she implored. "Let me know when you're settled, so I can write you back. We must keep in touch. We *must*."

"And one day," Rachel finished softly, "we'll meet again. Where?"

"In New York?" Rosa suggested, managing to make her tone wry when, in truth, she simply felt frightened, and worse, despairing. "Somewhere in America, where we'll all be living."

A brief silence rested on the little group, and Rosa knew her light words hadn't fooled anyone. No one knew where they would be... or if they would even still be alive.

"In America," Sophie agreed after a pause, "or maybe somewhere in Europe—Paris? Somewhere wonderful. We can decide later, because we're all going to stay in touch." She gazed at each of them, a look of desperation in her wide blue eyes. "Aren't we?"

"Yes, we are," Hannah said quietly, before Rosa could reply. Her heart felt heavy, her stomach like lead. She wasn't sure she believed any of it. If they were forced back to Germany... well, the chances were, they would never see Sophie again.

And yet... right now, they needed to believe. To hope.

Hannah raised her shard of emerald. "We're the Emerald Sisters," she quipped, smiling faintly, yet her eyes as hard as the jewel she held. "And the next time we see each other, it will be somewhere elegant in Paris or New York or who knows where, drinking champagne!"

"Or piña coladas," Rachel added, with a small smile.

"I think Paris," Rosa said decisively. She could enter into the spirit of the thing, she decided; she *needed* to... for her own sake, as well as for Sophie's and her other friends'. She needed to hope, to *believe*. "There's a little café by the Eiffel Tower that I've been to," she continued, recalling the place, its shabby comfort. "Henri's. We'll meet there on the same day as today, the second of June, at..." She glanced at her watch. "Four o'clock!" As if it were a date they could all pencil into their diaries. If only it could be.

"What year?" Hannah asked, sounding skeptical, and Rosa shrugged, determined to be defiant, even insouciant, much as it cost her.

"As soon as it's safe."

They all fell silent, not needing to acknowledge that none of them had any idea when that would be.

But it *would* happen, Rosa thought. She would make sure of it. Slowly, deliberately, she raised her shard of emerald as Hannah had done, and after a second's pause, Sophie and Rachel followed, lifting their hands high in the air, their expressions solemn, almost devout. They all stood there, their hands raised, the light catching the shattered jewels, and making them glint, the moment becoming something sacred.

"To the Emerald Sisters," Rosa reiterated, and the others followed, turning the words into a solemn vow, and one that despite her own best intentions, Rosa already feared they could not possibly keep... especially if the *St Louis* was bound for Germany.

CHAPTER 7

TUESDAY, JUNE 6, 1939—SOMEWHERE OFF THE COAST OF THE UNITED STATES

Rosa startled awake, gasping for breath as if she'd been running a race—or been trapped in the claws of a nightmare, its talons sunk deep inside her. A shuddering breath escaped her as she blinked the sleep from her eyes and glanced around the cabin wildly, although she did not even know what she was looking for. *Who* she was looking for, she realized with a sickening lurch. In her dream—the nightmare—she'd been back in Germany, at their house on the Wannsee. She'd been in the garden...

Another shudder went through her. The room was completely dark, save for a sliver of moonlight from the porthole that slanted across the floor, but in her mind's eyes, she was in their sunlit garden, with the lawn tumbling down to the lake, the birch trees in verdant leaf, the air full of birdsong. She'd seen Ernst standing by the shore, and her heart had leapt at the sight of his deep blue eyes shot through with gold, like sunlight dancing on the sea. She'd felt her spirits lift, her hands reach out, and then he'd caught sight of her, and his mouth had twisted...

Rosa fell back against her pillows, squeezing her eyes shut, but a tear trickled out anyway. A tear of shame, but also of grief.

She *missed* him. How could she possibly miss him?

Against her own will, she found herself recalling Ernst as she'd first seen him, in the drawing room of their house, one elbow propped on top of the grand piano, a glass of schnapps in his long-fingered hand. His hair, the color of ripe wheat, had been brushed off his forehead; he wore it longer than most good Aryan Germans did, and certainly those in the army.

She'd been arrested by the sheer, careless beauty of him, even though she hadn't wanted to be, because she knew what he was. At least, she'd *thought* she knew what he was, simply by the uniform he wore.

But then he'd convinced her to think otherwise.

Oh, how he had convinced her...

Another groan escaped her, and she wiped her eyes, only to still feel as if the bed was shifting beneath her. No, not the bed, not even the floor, but the whole *ship*.

Rosa froze, her hands still covering her eyes, as she felt the ship move, like some great behemoth of a beast, slowly and inexorably turning its vast, lumbering body.

Yesterday, Captain Schroeder had set course to return to Cuban waters, with the hope that they would be able to disembark on the Isle of Pines, Cuba's second largest island. The passenger committee had been told they might be able to stay there at least temporarily, until a final destination was arranged. Everyone had gone to bed with a sense of cautious optimism and relief, that there was a solution at hand, but through her father, Rosa knew the truth—approaches had already been made to Venezuela, Ecuador, Chile, Colombia, and Paraguay... and they had all refused to take the refugees.

President Brú had no intention, her father had told her, of allowing now just over nine hundred Jews onto the Isle of Pines if they didn't have somewhere else to go. She hadn't said as much to her friends, however, knowing they wouldn't welcome the news, and not wanting to be the bearer of it.

Now, however, as she felt the ship shift, Rosa had a leaden sense of what the truth was. Another country had not been found. Surely they were heading east... back toward Europe.

She hurried out of bed, pressing her face to the beveled glass of the porthole, but there was nothing to see but dark, endless ocean, under a sky scattered faintly with stars. She threw on her dressing gown and stormed into her parents' bedroom, heedless of her mother still lying in bed, asleep.

"What's happening?" she demanded of her father, who was already out of bed, a shirt pulled on over his pajamas. Fear made her sound angry.

"You could knock, Rosa, really," her mother harrumphed sleepily as she sat up in bed, looking rumpled and dazed, her dark hair loose about her shoulders; she'd been taking far too much of the sedative her father doled out to her whenever she asked, as well as often when she didn't.

"We're turning," Rosa stated, her eyes on her father, who was buttoning his shirt. "We're heading east."

He glowered at her before he reached for his trousers. "I know."

"Why?" The word was torn from her lips, like the plaintive cry of a child.

Her father's mouth firmed, his blue eyes flashing with anger.

"I imagine you can guess as easily as I can, Rosa," he replied tersely. "I'm going to see the captain now."

He finished dressing and slammed out of the cabin, while, with a sigh, Rosa's mother snuggled back under the covers. Rosa stared at her, caught between despondency and frustration.

"Mother," she burst out, "aren't you worried? We're heading *east*. To Europe! Back to *Germany*."

"Your father will sort it out," her mother replied in a half-mumble as she pulled the cover over her shoulders. Thanks, no doubt, to the sedative, she was already falling back asleep.

"He will, will he?" Rosa muttered under her breath. The only person who had more faith in her father than he did himself was her mother. She worshipped the man, even when she knew his failings just as Rosa did. It made no sense to her, just as her mother's anger at her, simply for knowing this truth, did not.

With a groan of frustration, she went back to her cabin. It was just after midnight, with hours of darkness stretching ahead of them, and yet Rosa felt the need to get dressed, to go out and *do* something. She didn't, though, too afraid to wander the ship alone at this time of night, especially when she thought of the odious crew member, Schiendick. She certainly didn't want to run into him late at night, she thought with a shudder, but she still longed to know what was happening. Had Hannah or Rachel felt the ship turning? Did they know what it meant? At least Sophie was safe.

Rosa paced the small confines of her cabin, her shard of emerald clutched in one hand, before, after an endless hour, her father finally returned.

"The captain refused to see anyone," he fumed as he came into the cabin; Rosa's mother was snoring quietly in the bed. "How *dare* he! He formed the passenger committee, after all—"

"If he didn't want to see you," Rosa cut him off, her tone wooden, "then it must be because he doesn't want to tell you what's happening—that we're going back to Germany." She felt as if she was hollowing out as she said the words, everything in her becoming terrifyingly empty, a void no longer of ignorance, but of knowledge, which felt far worse.

Back to Germany... it was too horrifying to think about. What would happen to them, if they were forced back to the country that despised and reviled them?

"If he told the passenger committee," she continued,

working it out as she spoke, "you'd be obligated to tell all the passengers... and then there could be a riot. Or a mutiny." Or more suicides. There were many people on board, Rosa suspected, who would, quite literally, rather die than go back to Germany... just as Sophie's father had said he would.

Was she one of them?

Her father whirled away from her, driving his hands through his hair. "There has to be another way..." he muttered.

Rosa stared at him helplessly. It scared her, to see her father at such a loss. It was easy enough to deride his arrogance as so much folly, and yet... like her mother, she'd *trusted* him. No matter what his own personal foibles—and Rosa knew there were many—he'd guided their little family through the treacherous riptides of Nazi Germany. He'd kept them safe, even if the methods he'd used were more than questionable.

But perhaps this was truly out of his control.

"*Schatzi!*" her mother called sleepily, lifting one pale arm to beckon her father. "Come back to bed."

Slowly, he turned around to face Rosa, his face gray with fatigue, with despair. He was fifty-one years old, but in that moment, he looked far older. His broad face sagged, his once-strong jawline was now jowly and wrinkled, and his eyes were bloodshot.

"Go back to your berth, Rosa," he said wearily. "There's nothing we can do until morning."

And, Rosa thought as she turned toward her cabin, there would most likely be nothing they could do then, either.

The next morning, Rosa stood on the deck, narrowing her eyes against the dull glare of the sun filtering through the thick cloud. The sea stretched flat and gray in every direction, underneath an equally flat, gray sky. They were hundreds of miles or more from the coast of the United States... and, as had been announced to the panicked passengers in the social hall, heading back to Europe... which surely meant Germany.

The member of the passenger committee, Josef, who had made that grim announcement, had not said it as bluntly or bleakly as that, of course. He'd tried to reassure the murmuring, milling crowd that although the *St Louis* was heading back to Europe, it did not necessarily have to mean to Germany. Another country might take them still, he'd insisted... the Joint Distribution Committee, back in America, as well as the captain, were both working hard to find a solution before the ship was scheduled to arrive in Hamburg in a week's time.

These petty assurances did little to assuage the dreadful fear that now gripped the passengers, like a terrible malaise, twisting their guts. Some stayed hidden in their cabins or drifted down corridors or through the social rooms, pale-faced and wide-eyed, dazed and silent, while others rebelled. There had been, to Rosa's shock, a potential coup, with several passengers attempting to take over the bridge. Rosa's father had told her that it had been a close-run thing, but the captain had managed to convince them to step down before any violence occurred.

It didn't help that now, into the fifth week of their journey, food and water had to be rationed. Gone were the elaborate menus of five-course meals with three choices for each course. Rosa hardly cared about such things, but it still shook her, to come to the first-class dining hall and simply be given one plain course to eat, and not much of it, at that. It made her feel even more like the prisoner she knew she was.

Still, she acknowledged, there had been small kindnesses amidst the hardship and uncertainty—a crew member had smuggled precious fresh fruit to Lotte, and a steward had given her father pipe tobacco when he'd run out. Yet even among these thoughtful gestures, a deeper, darker menace lurked. Rosa had managed to avoid Schiendick since that awful encounter in the corridor, but she'd heard stories of the Gestapo firemen continuing to rough people up. Rachel had told her that in tourist class, they'd broken a man's nose and thrown all his belongings over the side of the ship.

Rosa slipped her hand into her pocket and withdrew the shard of emerald that she'd taken to carrying with her everywhere, like the talisman Sophie had wanted it to be. Under the gray sky, it looked dark and dull, with no sunlight to catch its glinting depths. Its edge was jagged, its tip a rough point. Sophie hadn't done a very good job of splitting the stone neatly, Rosa thought wryly. She ran her finger along the edge to the point as a pang of grief assailed her, for the loss of her friend. She hoped Sophie was safe and happy. She *did*... and yet she still feared and lamented her own situation.

Rosa heard footsteps down the deck, and, quickly slipping the emerald back into her pocket, she turned to see Hannah coming toward her.

"Have you heard anything?" Hannah asked, and Rosa shook her head.

Hannah joined her at the deck, resting her slender hands on the railing, her blond hair blowing in wisps about her face. "You would tell me if you had, wouldn't you?" she asked quietly. "Even if it was bad news? I'd still want to know."

"Yes, I would," Rosa replied, although she wasn't sure she was telling the truth. Looking at Hannah, her pale face, her slender body that was already starting to seem gaunt and strained with anxiety, she didn't think her friend could withstand any further blows to her fragile hopes. "Where is Lotte?"

"With Rachel and Franz, in the gymnasium. Rachel insisted they all take some exercise. Heinrich went with them, as well, although only because I think his mother has been driven to distraction by him, now that she must care for Herr Weiss, since he is back on board." Hannah blew out a breath. "He is lost without Sophie, poor little boy. How do you think she is?" Sophie had sent a telegram a few days ago, giving her address in

Washington. Rosa wondered when she would be able to tell Sophie *her* address—and what country it would be in.

"She's doing better than we are, at any rate," she told Hannah. She'd meant to sound wry, but it came out bitter.

Hannah slid her a curious glance. "Do you resent her going?"

"No," Rosa answered after a pause, her gaze on the sea. "I can't make myself, although I want to, for some reason. But if I were in her position, I would have done the same thing. I know I would have." She returned Hannah's inquisitive glance with a questioning look of her own. "What about you?"

"I don't, not anymore. I was angry, at the start, because..." Her lips trembled and she pressed them together. "Because it felt so *unfair*. My father..." Her voice trembled then too, and she had to draw a quick, steadying breath. "He was right there, Rosa. You saw him, in the boat, calling up to us. He had a room all ready for us in his apartment in Havana. He told me about the things he'd bought, the bed covers and the curtains..." Now Hannah's voice cracked, and her shoulders shook as she pressed her hand to her mouth.

Rosa turned to put her arms around her. "Hush, *Hase*," she murmured as she stroked her hair. The endearment, bunny, had fallen naturally from her lips. She felt oddly protective towards Hannah, even though she was only a few years younger than her. Perhaps it was because Hannah had to take care of Lotte; it was a great and terrible responsibility for such a young woman.

"What will happen to Lotte, if we are forced back to Germany?" Hannah wept. "I don't mean just being Jewish... you know she has a stammer. And she walks with a limp. It's a silly thing, just that one leg is a bit longer than the other, hardly noticeable, but someone came to our door before we left and noted it. A nurse of some kind, from one of the Reich's committees... they marked it down on some paper... *why?*"

"I don't know why," Rosa replied, although she suspected it could not be for any reason Hannah would welcome.

"It's because she's not a perfect little *Aryan*," Hannah spat, pulling away from Rosa as she wiped her damp cheeks. "With golden hair and blue eyes and perfect, rounded limbs, everything just so. They can't stand anyone who is remotely different, a little Jew with a shortened leg and a bit of a lisp!"

"But you're only half-Jewish," Rosa reminded her gently. "Surely that counts for something, especially when it is your mother who isn't Jewish." According to tradition, Rosa knew, Jewishness was considered to pass through the maternal line; Rabbinic law decreed that a person with a gentile mother was not actually Jewish.

"The Nazis don't care so much about that," Hannah replied. "We were Jewish enough to be kicked out of school, to be forbidden entry to shops and all the rest of it. You know how it was."

Rosa kept silent, because the truth was, she *didn't* know how it had been, not the way her friends had. Her father, and the Faustian bargain he had made with the Nazis who needed his medical help, had made sure of that.

"I'm sorry," Rosa murmured, knowing the words were inadequate.

Hannah turned away, her face set into hard lines as she stared out at the endless ocean. "I'm scared," she whispered. "And I don't know what to do. I'd protect Lotte with my life, *gladly*, but what if I can't?"

"Would you ever appeal to your mother for help?" Rosa asked, and Hannah let out a hard huff of scornful laughter.

"My *mother*? Never." Her voice rang out with firm, condemning conviction. "I'd rather die first than go crawling to someone who climbed into bed with a Nazi."

Rosa willed her expression to stay bland as she kept her

gaze on the ocean. She had, she knew, absolutely no reply to make to that.

On Friday, the mood on the ship plunged even deeper into despair when a member of crew was found hanging by a rope in his locker. Apparently, he'd been Jewish, although no one had known. The Gestapo firemen had become even bolder, as well; the day before, they'd gathered in the social hall and sung rousing Nazi songs for over an hour, their voices ringing through the room, while passengers had eyed them uneasily before making themselves scarce. This time, Captain Schroeder did not come thundering down to tell them to leave; he was nowhere to be seen.

They were four days off the coast of England, and there had been no news, no solution set forward, as the ship steamed steadily toward Hamburg. Rosa's father had become like a man possessed. He was constantly trying to talk to the captain, or the other members of the passenger committee. He'd sent cables, although to whom Rosa had no idea, because the only connections her father had had—and he certainly didn't have them anymore—were in Germany.

"There's no point talking to the captain," he told her in a flat voice as they walked along the deck on Saturday morning, the freezing wind off the ocean buffeting them. After the tropical climes of Cuba, the chilly, gray weather in the mid-Atlantic felt unforgivingly cold, even in June. "He doesn't have any real power on this ship anymore."

"*What!*" Rosa stared at him in alarm as she pulled her cardigan more closely about her. "What do you mean?" She'd been able to draw some small comfort from knowing Captain Schroeder was sympathetic to the plight of the Jewish passengers, when it seemed so many of the crew were not.

"He has to follow orders," her father told her, "and the

orders from his Hapag superiors are to return to Germany." He paused to draw a shaky breath. "He's been trying to arrange for other countries to take us—England or France. One of the French officials said that if the *St Louis* returns to Hamburg, we will all be taken to concentration camps, straight from the dock."

Rosa stared at him in horror, one hand pressed to her middle. That terrible fear had been lurking in her mind like a dark shadow, yet she hadn't truly believed it could happen. Now it seemed as if it could... it *would*. "They wouldn't..." she began feebly.

"Why wouldn't they do such a thing, Rosa?" her father demanded, speaking to her as if she were a particularly slow-witted child. "They'd think they had every right. The world has rejected us... they've proved that *no one* wants us, not just the Nazis. They'll tell all the powers that be that they've taken care of us, gone out of their way to support us... by putting us in a camp. The Gestapo firemen have been telling that to passengers already—saying we'll never be heard from again, the moment we set foot off this ship, in Germany. One of the wretches saw me and drew his finger across his throat, smirking all the while."

Tears blurred her vision and she blinked rapidly to clear them, too angry to cry. "It's not fair..." she whispered.

Her father let out a weary laugh. "No," he agreed, and to her surprise, he put his arm around her shoulders, drawing her close to him, so her cheek rested against the lapel of his jacket, and she breathed in his familiar scent of tobacco and cologne. She closed her eyes, and for a second, she felt like a small child once more, safe in her father's arms. "It's not fair," he repeated quietly, his arm still around her. "But I intend to do something about it."

Rosa peered up at him, feeling both hopeful and apprehensive. "What can you do?" she asked.

"I'm going right to the source," her father replied. "Captain

Schroeder has no good plan—the best he has come up with is to run the ship aground, somewhere in England, and have us wade to shore as refugees!" He shook his head, entirely disparaging of the idea.

"Surely that's better than going back to Germany?" Rosa ventured, even though she had to agree that it didn't seem like much of a plan.

Rosa's father's mouth firmed, his eyes flashing. "There's a member of the Abwehr on board," he told Rosa. "He'll be calling the shots here soon, if he isn't already. I intend to speak directly with him."

"With the *Abwehr*!" Rosa drew back so her father's arm fell to his side. As appalled as she was by what he'd just said, she found she missed its comfort. "Father, you can't."

Her father narrowed his eyes, his mouth curling in displeasure; he was not a man who liked to be challenged. "And why can't I?"

"Because... because it's foolish!" Rosa burst out. Realization trickled icily through her. "I think I know the man you mean. Schiendick? He accosted me the first night on board, and..." She didn't want to mention the second time she'd run into the horrible man, the threats he'd made, his thumb on her windpipe, his body pressed to hers... "He's a thug, and probably a stupid one, as well."

"All the better," her father replied coolly. "He'll be easily impressed, then."

Rosa shook her head despairingly. Even now, her father clung to his old delusions of importance and grandeur. He'd been forbidden to practice medicine and kicked out of his own home by these people, he'd been mocked and derided endlessly, amusement dancing in their cold blue eyes as they'd forced him to laugh at their cruel jokes, and yet he still seemed to think he wielded some sort of influence over men who were carelessly determined to destroy him.

"*How?*"

Her father stared at her for a long moment, and then he let out a short, abrupt laugh. "Rosa, you're so naïve," he told her with a weary shake of his head. "You see things in black and white—like you did with your precious Ernst."

Rosa reeled back, shocked by the name they were usually both so careful not to mention. "He was never *my* Ernst," she said in a low voice. "And he certainly wasn't *precious*." She was lying, and they both knew it.

"He was angelically good," her father continued relentlessly, "and then he was demonically bad, with nothing in between." He shook his head. "You think like a child, Rosa."

Stung, she recoiled a little. "And how do you think?"

"Like a *pragmatist*. Do you think I like these people?" he demanded in a low voice that throbbed not just with anger, but with pain. He threw one arm out to encompass not just the ship, but the world they'd left behind. The people he'd courted so assiduously, his smile never faltering for a second as he'd offered his hospitality, his schnapps, his laughter when they'd mocked and ridiculed him. "Do you think I *enjoyed* having them in my house?" he continued, his tone turning raw. "Playing my piano, mocking me in my own home, to my own face, time and time again?"

Rosa blinked, speechless with surprise. She'd never thought her father had been able to see it that way, even though she certainly had. "I..." she began, and she found she could not continue.

She *had* thought he'd enjoyed it. She still thought he must have, at least a little, to have endured it so seemingly cheerfully for so long. To have courted it, to have ostensibly reveled in it. Her father could view the past in a more flattering light *now*, when they were far away from Berlin, but back then, he'd made the choices he had, and had stood by them. And for that Rosa didn't think she could ever trust or forgive him.

"They have too much power, Rosa," her father told her flatly. "You can't cross them. But you can *play* them, which is what I did—or at least I tried to do. I'm not ashamed of it. Why should I be? Do you know Hitler himself arranged for his childhood doctor, Bloch, to leave the country? And the doctor who treated him during the war, as well. They both escaped scot-free and with all their money and possessions, even though they were Jews." He raised his eyebrows, a small, cold smile playing about his mouth. "How do you think I got as much money out of the country as I did?" There was no mistaking the note of pride in his voice.

"How?" Rosa asked, meeting his mocking gaze with defiance.

"Eichmann. He owed me a favor."

She shook her head, wanting to deny it. "But Nazis don't owe Jews favors."

His smile flickered and then died. "*Sometimes* they do. They have their own peculiar code of honor, I suppose, or perhaps it's just a keen sense of self-preservation. In any case, I'm going to talk to this Schiendick. If he knows I have the ear of Eichmann, he might be willing to put in a good word for me when we get back to Germany."

A good word? When they'd just learned they would all be sent to a concentration camp as soon as they arrived? Her father might think he was being pragmatic, but Rosa feared he was still delusional... and incredibly foolish. He certainly didn't have the ear of Eichmann now, if he ever truly did. Any Nazi who had graced their house, thrown them a scrappy bone, had done so out of nothing more than indifferent amusement. The Nazis her father had rubbed shoulders with could have clapped him in jail as easily as they'd favored them with their presence, and, in truth, Rosa didn't think they'd see all that much difference between the two. And as for that little toad, Schiendick? Rosa was quite sure she'd got the measure of such a man.

"Father, don't, please..." she implored, catching his arm. "I told you, I've already run into Schiendick, and he's a petty little thug. He won't listen to you. He won't *want* to listen to you, and the fact that you are trying to impress him will just infuriate him and make him want to humiliate you all the more."

"Well, I don't have any other ideas," her father snapped. "Do *you*?"

Rosa turned back to the railing, gripping it hard with both hands. She thought of Sophie's father, flinging himself into the sea, and for a second, she was terribly tempted to do the same. The water was cold and deep; how long would she last in it? A few minutes of choking terror, and then oblivion. Peace, at last. She wouldn't have to face the terrible, yawning uncertainty of the future... going back to Germany, being arrested, imprisoned in a camp, maybe even tortured.

She thought of Rachel's husband Franz, who had endured such treatment, who even now looked and acted like a man haunted by demons. A few months in Dachau had stolen not just his sense of peace, but his sense of *self*. Rachel herself had admitted he wasn't the man he'd once been, although she wouldn't say any more than that.

Rosa couldn't stand the thought of something similar happening to her. As much as she dreaded the possibility of discomfort, pain, or even torture, the thought of losing herself— of becoming less than what she was, someone unrecognizable, pitiful—seemed even worse. She'd be living in a hellish world controlled by men like Schiendick, men who wanted to see her grovel, who would glory in her shame, pain, and abuse. She couldn't survive it. She wasn't brave enough. She liked to act like she was strong, just as her father did, but she wasn't. Not strong enough for that.

She gripped the railing even harder, her fingers aching with the effort. It would be so easy to fling herself over, to forget all her mistakes, never to have to face the future, whatever it contained. This was a different kind of courage, a cowardly one, but courage all the same...

"Rosa..." Her father put a heavy hand on her shoulder, almost as if he could guess what she was thinking.

"Rosa!"

Rosa turned her head to see Hannah hurrying down the deck, holding Lotte's hand, her eyes bright with excitement, her face wreathed in smiles. "The captain has just made an announcement! We aren't going to have to return to Germany!"

Rosa's fingers eased on the railing, her mind spinning.

Next to her, her father stared at Hannah, slack-jawed. "Where are we going, then?" he demanded hoarsely.

"England will take some of the passengers," Hannah explained breathlessly. "And France, I think, and maybe Belgium. They'll divide us between them—none of us will have to go back to Germany."

"We won't?" Rosa glanced down at the ocean churning far below and a shudder went through her. She didn't think she would have actually jumped, but the realization that she'd been tempted, even for a few seconds, scared her. She might be weak, but she'd still thought herself stronger than *that*. She stepped back from the railing on shaky legs.

"England..." Her father murmured in dazed relief. "Belgium and France..." He let out a shaky breath as he passed a hand over his forehead. "Thank God."

"Yes," Rosa echoed numbly as she stared down once more at the water far below. "Thank God."

CHAPTER 8

FRIDAY, JUNE 16, 1939—OFF THE COAST OF
BELGIUM

Passengers filled the social hall, their suitcases and trunks piled around them, as they waited to be told where—and when—they would go.

The mood was now one more of weariness than hope; they had been on the *St Louis* for so long, following too many false trails and finding too many dead ends, to summon much excitement. Although, just a few days ago, when the news had first been announced that the *St Louis* would not return to Germany, everyone had been ebullient. They had even thrown a party in the social hall they now waited in, and good-natured jests about cruises to Cuba had abounded, as if the last four weeks could be consigned to the punchline of a joke. Rosa had laughed along, but her heart had been strangely heavy. As relieved as she was not to be returning to Germany, the future still felt fearfully unknown.

Over the last few days, news had trickled out about the fate of the passengers—England would take a quarter of the refugees, Holland another quarter, France another and Belgium the last. Representatives from the four countries were meeting today to discuss which country took who; passengers with numbers high up on the immigration quota list for the United States, who could therefore be expected to move on fairly soon, were the most in demand, since they would not be too much trouble.

But even when they were to be taken in, Rosa had thought bitterly, they still wouldn't actually be wanted. The knowledge was both humbling and humiliating. She wasn't even sure where she wanted to go, not that she would have a choice. Her mother thought France, as she'd always been fond of Paris, her father Belgium or the Netherlands, since he knew some people there. England felt too strange, somehow; Rosa spoke some English, but she was far from fluent, and her parents were the same.

"Besides, the English will be at war with Germany soon," her father had stated, as if he had Hitler's ear on that matter, just as he had Captain Schroeder's.

"Wouldn't you rather be in England then, fighting the Nazis?" Rosa had asked, and her father had raised his eyebrows, his expression turning reproving.

"Rosa, we're still German."

But were they? They'd been as good as stripped of their citizenship, their home, their rights. Yet they were still German, in her father's eyes. "But surely you want Hitler to be defeated," she'd pressed, for she could not imagine him saying—or believing—the opposite.

"Yes," her father had answered after a pause. "Naturally. But do I want *Germany* defeated—the country of my birth, my homeland and hope? No."

"I think they're one and the same at the moment," Rosa had replied, and her father had slowly shaken his head, looking more sorrowful than she'd seen him in a long time.

"No," he'd told her. "They're not."

Now Rosa perched on the edge of her steamer trunk, her

chin propped in her hand as she waited for the purser to make the announcement of where everyone was meant to go.

"Any news?" Hannah asked as she joined her in the hall, her own cases piled nearby. Lotte, her fair hair in neat braids and wearing her best dress, stood slightly behind her.

"No, not yet," Rosa replied. "It feels as if we are forever waiting."

"I just want to know where we're going." Hannah rubbed her arms as if she were cold, even though the hall, filled with passengers as well as suitcase, was stifling. "It would be nice to be together."

"Yes, it would," Rosa agreed, although she did not know how likely that would be. Requests, her father had told her, would be neither allowed nor granted.

A sudden commotion at the doors to the social hall had everyone straightening, murmuring, and looking around. A group of officious-looking people filed in—representatives from all four governments of the countries that would take them in, as well as executives from America's Joint Distribution Committee. They'd arrived by tugboat from the Dutch port of Flushing that morning. The moment had finally come; the passengers' fates were about to be decided.

Hannah reached over to grasp Rosa's hand tightly. "Rosa, I'm scared," she whispered, her face pale and drawn.

"You don't need to be," Rosa assured her, summoning a strength she didn't feel for herself. "We're all going somewhere safe, Hannah, whether it's England or France, Belgium or the Netherlands. You don't need to be afraid."

"I... know," Hannah said, but she sounded doubtful. She hugged Lotte more closely to her.

The representatives settled themselves at several tables at the front of the hall, under the requisite but inauspicious portrait of Hitler that had frowned down at them the whole journey. Rosa's throat tightened with anxiety as she gazed at their serious faces. Had they already decided?

She soon discovered that they hadn't. After the necessary and formal welcomes, the men at the front began to discuss the passengers' fates among themselves, leaving the nearly thousand people to wait and wilt. Rachel and Franz joined their little group, both of them looking excited but anxious. Rosa glanced around the room for her parents; her father would be hobnobbing with the other elevated members of the passenger committee, not that they'd exercised any real power in the end. She couldn't see them anywhere.

Finally, after at least an hour, Morris Troper, the American in charge of the proceedings, began to say something. Almost as one, every passenger in the hall straightened, taut and alert, as each waited to hear their fate. He started by making only one assurance—that this makeshift committee would do its best to keep families together. Rosa saw Hannah grip Lotte's hand tightly as a shaky breath escaped her. Rosa doubted Hannah had ever considered the awful possibility that she might be separated from her beloved sister.

Rosa's breath caught as it suddenly occurred to her, rather ridiculously, that this was really happening. Until Mr. Morris Troper started speaking, she realized she hadn't truly believed they would *ever* get off the ship. It had felt like a prison, a *hell*, eternal damnation for the unwanted. Yet here was this American Jew, with his thin moustache and dark hair neatly brushed —reminding Rosa, oddly, a little of Hitler—and his calm voice telling them so matter-of-factly what was going to happen—and soon.

Instinctively, she turned to Hannah, who gave her a wondering, incredulous look, as if she too could hardly believe it. They smiled at each other, a bit abashedly, yet Rosa thought she still saw fear in Hannah's eyes. She felt it in herself.

Morris Troper cleared his throat before speaking in a loud,

clear voice. "I will now read the names of those who will disembark in Great Britain."

Almost as one, every passenger in the hall seemed to hold their breath. The air, once so sleepy and stifling, suddenly became electric as bodies leaned forward, fists clenched. Who had been chosen?

Troper began to read out the names. "Ackermann, Bertha. Adler, Berthold. Adler, Chaskel. Adler, Paul. Adler, Regina…"

The names droned on, and Rosa did her best to stay attentive, waiting for a name she recognized. Troper went through the Bs without mentioning Rachel or her husband Franz, their last name Blau.

Rachel put her arm around Franz as Rosa and Hannah shared an unhappy glance; it was fast becoming apparent from the other passengers' reactions, either delight or despair, that being allowed to disembark in England, far from Germany's military aspirations, was the best result any of them could hope for. "Never mind," Rachel said with a bracing smile. "One country is as good as another, I suppose."

The names went on—C, D, E. Rosa caught her breath as her heart started to race. Soon, he would be at the H's, and she would know her own fate. Would she and her parents get to go to England? She'd thought before that she wasn't sure where she wanted to end up, but now she realized she would rather be in England than anywhere else. Like Hannah had said, England was most likely the safest place for a Jew to be.

"Hausdorff, Arthur. Hausdorff, Gertrud. Heldenmuth, Alfred. Heldenmuth, Lilo. Heldenmuth, Selma."

Rosa's fists were now clenched in her lap, her whole body tense, as Troper continued: "Herzelfeld, Friedrich. Herzelfeld, Elsa. Herzelfeld, Rosa…"

Her breath came out in a rush, and she sagged forward, suddenly almost near tears. England. They were going to England.

"Oh, Rosa," Rachel exclaimed, sounding genuinely pleased. "How fortunate for you, although I'm sorry we won't be together."

"Yes, how lucky," Hannah breathed. "England! I wish..."

"Maybe you will, too," Rosa told her, her tone turning urgent as she straightened. "You and Lotte. Let's listen, they're almost at the Ls. They're sure to call out Levin."

They both waited in apprehensive silence as Morris Troper continued to call names. "Langnas, Leon. Lauchheimer, Ida. Leinkram, Aron. Leinkrem, Mina."

But the rest of the Ls went by without a mention of *Levin, Hannah* or her sister. Hannah's face crumpled for a second before she smoothed out her expression, almost as if she'd taken an iron to it.

"Never mind," she said before turning to her sister with a bright, determined smile. "The other countries are just as agreeable, aren't they, Lotte? Maybe we'll go to France and see the Eiffel Tower." Wordlessly, the girl nodded, and Hannah glanced back at Rosa and Rachel. "I'll be the first at Henri's," she said, half-teasing, half-serious, "when we all meet again."

"Oh, Hannah." A lump formed in Rosa's throat as she stared at her friend helplessly, wishing there was something she could do or say to make it better. Her heart ached for her friend but also, just a little bit, for herself. She wouldn't be with either Hannah or Rachel. She'd be facing this strange new world all alone, for she surely couldn't count on the help or support of her parents, who, as ever, would be absorbed with their own affairs.

"And that concludes those who will disembark in Great Britain," Mr. Troper finished, once he'd come to the end of the list. "The other lists will be announced this evening."

"We're not even going to find out now?" Hannah sounded aggrieved. "We're practically in Belgium as it is, and I heard those passengers would be disembarking tomorrow morning. Surely, they need to decide soon?"

"You'll know by this evening, they said earlier. It's all good news, Hannah," Rachel reminded her soothingly.

"Yes," Hannah replied after a moment, but she did not sound entirely convinced.

Later that afternoon, Rosa, Hannah, and Rachel, with Lotte and Franz, stood on the deck and watched as the St Louis was guided up the Scheldt estuary, to Antwerp. Wide, marshy fields stretched toward the horizon on either side of the channel, flat and green. They all watched in silence, the moment strangely solemn, almost like a ceremony of sorts, as the ship glided past.

It would be the first time the St Louis would actually dock at a port since they'd picked up passengers in France over a month ago. In just a few days, Rosa thought in both wonder and fear, she would be starting an entirely new life in an entirely new country. It seemed impossible, still, and she knew there were many passengers on board who still lived in fear of a cable being received and the St Louis turning for Germany. She'd heard one man mutter darkly that he would not believe they'd be delivered somewhere else until he was off the ship, his visa issued, and the St Louis had sailed far away, out of sight.

"They're announcing who is going!" someone called excitedly from down the deck, and Rosa, Hannah, and Rachel all turned.

They hurried down the deck, each of them caught between trepidation and hope, before shouldering their way into the hall that was now heaving with passengers, most of them looking as anxious as Rosa knew her friends felt.

"I will now read the names of those who will disembark for Belgium," Morris Troper announced, and once more he began, in an almost stern monotone.

Rachel and Franz were not named, and neither was Hannah; they both exhaled quietly, although whether in relief or disappointment, Rosa couldn't tell. Where did her friends want to go, now that they knew they would not be heading to England?

"Weiss, Heinrich," Troper announced, as he came to nearly the end of the list. "Weiss, Josef. Weiss, Margarete."

Rosa glanced over at Sophie's parents, who were across the hall, Josef looking pale and haggard, Margarete gripping little Heinrich's hand tightly. So, Sophie's family would be going to Belgium, she thought. She wondered if she would ever see them again, and thought she probably wouldn't. After Sophie's departure, the family had kept to themselves, save for when Hannah had been willing to help out with Heinrich.

After Troper had finished the Belgium list, he started on the Netherlands. "Blau, Franz. Blau, Rachel..."

Rachel let out a little cry of what Rosa hoped was happiness as she put her arms around her husband. "You see?" she told him, her face suffused with tenderness. "We shall be safe. Safe in the Netherlands."

Hannah and Lotte were not on the Netherlands list. "I suppose it must be France, then," she said, when it seemed Troper was not going to read out any other names. "By the process of elimination."

"You did say you wanted to see the Eiffel Tower," Rosa reminded her. "You will save us a table at Henri's!"

"Yes, you must, Hannah." Rachel came to slip an arm around her friend. "How strange, we're all going to different places. Even if Sophie hadn't left when she had, she'd be going to Belgium now. Each of us flung to the far corners of the world, or at least of Europe."

"But we will see each other again," Rosa reminded them, her tone turning strident. She felt a sudden, wild desperation that they keep in touch, as they'd promised. She'd been skeptical and slightly disparaging when Sophie had suggested such a thing, but now she felt it keenly. These were her friends, her dear friends... and the only ones she had.

"Of course we will," Rachel replied, smiling.

"But how?" The realization of what was happening thudded through Rosa. "None of us has an address yet, and we can't send a cable the way Sophie could." She stared at the other two women, distraught. "How on earth will we write to each other?"

Rachel's cheerful demeanor faltered, replaced by a dawning uncertainty. She clearly hadn't considered this, just as Rosa hadn't. "We'll find a way..." she insisted, a waver to her voice.

"I know," Hannah said suddenly. "You can write to me at Henri's! I'll ask for them to hold my letters."

"*Henri's*..." Rosa let out a trembling laugh. "Will you even be in Paris?"

Hannah shrugged. "If I'm not, I'll find a way to get there. And if you can't write to Henri's, then write to Sophie. She can write us back, with all our addresses."

"But that will take ages," Rosa protested. For a letter to be sent to America and back again might take months.

"Well, Henri's, then," Hannah replied. "We'll find a way. This isn't goodbye. We won't let it be."

"At least, not forever," Rosa replied, trying to smile. She slipped her hand into her pocket and took out her shard of emerald, holding it up.

With a grin, Rachel took hers out of her pocket, as did Hannah. They'd all been walking around with them, Rosa thought, and the knowledge heartened her.

"To the Emerald Sisters," she said, repeating the toast Hannah had made just a few weeks ago, when they'd been all four together—her, Hannah, Rachel, and Sophie. Now, poignantly, it was only three.

"And to when we meet again," Rachel added.

They held their shards up, giving each other tremulous

smiles. Rosa heard ringing assurance in her friends' voices, but she saw fear and uncertainty lurking in their eyes. As they remained there with their hands upraised, smiles in place, the sun slipped from between the clouds, and its light touched the emeralds, making them, for a brief moment, brightly gleam, before the clouds came over it again, and the sky darkened.

CHAPTER 9

JULY 1939—LONDON

"This is unacceptable."

Rosa avoided the eye of the woman from the Central British Fund for German Jewry who stood in the doorway, on the top floor of a dilapidated rowhouse in Belsize Park, northwest London that had been turned into flats. Even when she wasn't looking at the woman in her sensible blouse, skirt, and lace-up shoes, Rosa could sense her irritation. Her father's response to their new home was neither expected nor wanted. In the two weeks since they'd landed in England, Rosa had learned just how grateful they were expected to be, for being there at all.

And they *were*, she reminded herself now, firmly.

"The Fund has worked hard to procure suitable accommodation," the woman told her father, her tone rather stern. They were speaking in German, although the woman had greeted them off the train at Waterloo Station in English. But none of Rosa's family's English was good enough yet to have an actual, prolonged conversation, something they'd all quickly realized.

They'd been in Southampton since they'd disembarked from the *Rhakotis*, which had taken them from Antwerp, staying at a cramped boarding house, waiting to find out where they would be sent. Rosa, having already said goodbye to both Rachel and Hannah, had felt very alone as she'd gazed out at the strange city, her sliver of emerald clutched in her hand. Everything had looked so gray—the buildings, the sea, the sky. Admittedly, it was a cloudy day, and chilly for late June, but Rosa hadn't been terribly impressed by her first view of her new country. Neither had her mother, who had muttered something about preferring Paris, or her father, who had spent the restless weeks holed up in a shabby boarding house that smelled of boiled cabbage and drains trying to find someone important to impress. There hadn't been anyone, not anyone at all.

"Do you know where I lived in Berlin?" her father demanded of the woman, and Rosa made a choking sound. *As if that mattered now...*

"The rooms are a lovely size," she interjected, her tone firm. "And the view of the park is lovely." She could just see a scrap of green, beyond the farthest rooftops, if she stood on her tiptoes. She turned to the woman with an expectant smile. "What is it called?"

The woman thawed only slightly. "That is Hampstead Heath."

"Ah, yes."

A silence fell on them all, tense and unhappy. Her mother was standing by the pile of their suitcases and trunks, a fur draped over her shoulders, shivering in the damp cold. The weather wasn't *that* much worse than Berlin, although it had, apparently, been a cool, damp summer, but her mother seemed determined to act as if it was. Her father had paced the room as if measuring it for a carpet, and now stood, facing the window, his hands on his hips, his handsome face settled into a discontented frown.

Rosa felt like grabbing them both by the shoulders and shaking them until their teeth rattled. Since they'd arrived on these shores, her parents had been acting as if they were deserving of special treatment, as if a red carpet should be rolled out for them, their hosts counting it a privilege for them to walk on it. She knew her parents had always thought they were important; at least, her father had, and her mother had happily basked in his light. If a month on board the *St Louis*, and then an interminable two days in the cargo hold of the crowded *Rhakotis*, hadn't shown them that they weren't, then arriving in England, where Jewish refugees, even doctors, bankers, and lawyers, were unwelcomely plentiful, surely should have.

"So." The woman from the Fund cleared her throat. "You'll be sharing this flat with another family."

"What!" Rosa's father whirled around, his mouth agape. He looked genuinely astonished by this information. "But it's barely big enough for us."

"It has four rooms," the woman replied stiffly. "There are many British citizens here in London who do not have as much space."

"Of course, that is... acceptable," Rosa said quickly, stumbling slightly over the words.

Even she was taken aback by the woman's news, although she supposed she shouldn't be. In the two weeks they'd been in England, the poor and precarious nature of their situation had been more than apparent. They'd been sponsored by the Central British Fund for Germany Jewry, as well as the Quaker Relief Association, and so they depended on charity in a way they never had to before.

Her father had yet to procure the funds he'd sent abroad from Germany; he had had them sent to Havana, and getting the money transferred to England had so far been a tangled mess of bureaucratic red tape and intransigence—so many forms to fill in, so many cables to send, so many petty officials to impress, or at least convince. He was hopeful now that he was in London, rather than Southampton, he might make some headway.

"So." The woman drew herself up. "You have everything you need? The other family should be here in the next few days. And, as I believe you have been told before, you must look for work immediately. The Fund can only pay the rent on this flat until the end of the month."

"Yes, we understand," Rosa said quickly, before her father could make some further complaint. They had been issued visas that allowed them to work, although she had no idea what they would be able to do. "We look forward to working."

"Good." The woman nodded once, briskly. "Well, then. Welcome to Great Britain."

As she left the flat, closing the door behind her, her mother's breath came out in a great rush, and she turned toward her husband. "Fritz, this is impossible. We can't live here..."

"Well I know it," her father replied through gritted teeth. "As soon as I've managed to get our funds transferred to London, we'll find somewhere suitable to our station. I've been told Mayfair is a good area."

"Most of the Jewish refugees are in this area," Rosa pointed out. "Surely we want to stay with our own community?"

Her father made a little moue of distaste before turning away. Rosa didn't think her father or mother possessed any real faith, and she doubted either of them wanted to associate with the Jews they'd seen so far in this neighborhood—somber, dark-coated Hasidim, with their unfamiliar side curls and bushy beards, so different from their own very lightly worn faith. If it was jolting to Rosa, she imagined it was even more so for her parents.

"Mayfair sounds nice," her mother said firmly, drawing her fur more closely about her shoulders. She gave her husband a pointed yet pleading look. "You know I can't abide living like this for very long." She gave a theatrical shudder. "That dreadful ship was bad enough."

Their two and a half days on the *Rhakotis* hadn't been *that* bad, Rosa thought, and certainly better than most who had been on board. The eleven-year-old freighter had had first- and tourist-class berths for fifty passengers, but the ship had had to hold ten times that number, and its cargo holds had been converted into communal berths.

Fortunately, as a member of the passenger committee once again, her father had been granted a first-class cabin. It hadn't possessed quite the luxury of their adjoining berths on the *St Louis*, but it had been comfortable enough, especially when Rosa had seen what Hannah and Lotte had had to endure on their voyage to Boulogne. The cargo holds had been cramped and airless, with steel bunks along the sides and long tables running down the center. The lavatories, already inadequate, had been up on deck. Many passengers had chosen to sleep on deck, for the stale smell of sweat and unwashed humanity down in the cargo holds had soon become unbearable.

"I know, darling," her father said, giving his wife a quick, conciliatory smile. "It's an outrage for someone of your tender sensibilities. Perhaps you need to rest...?"

"Where?" her mother demanded. "The beds are filthy."

They were hardly *filthy*, although, Rosa acknowledged, in truth, the flat's furnishings did leave something to be desired. A rickety table, a couple of chairs, a few lumpy mattresses on severe iron bedsteads, and not much more than that. It was far from homely.

"At least we brought our own sheets," Rosa said, trying to sound cheerful. "Shall we unpack? I could make up the bed for you, Mother."

After a second's pause, her mother nodded stiffly, and Rosa went to open one of their trunks. In addition to their clothes and personal effects, they'd brought all their linens and her mother's full set of Meissen china, packed carefully between layers of paper. The delicate dishes, hand-painted in Meissen's tradi-tional onion pattern, would look rather incongruous on the rough wooden shelves that comprised their pantry, Rosa thought with a small smile.

"And we could be *truly* English," she continued as she lifted the blue and white painted teapot out of its paper wrappings, "and have a cup of tea."

Her mother sniffed and said nothing. Her father let out a gusty, discontented sigh.

Rosa suspected she knew what was really bothering them— it wasn't the flat, or the fact that they would have to share it. It was, in essence, the reality that they really were refugees, and were seen as such in this place. They didn't *want* to be refugees —needy, desperate, looked down upon by the general population. Her father had been a man of stature and importance back in Berlin, her mother standing proudly by his side. Neither of them was ready or willing for that to change... and yet it already had.

"I'll boil the kettle," Rosa said as she rose from the trunk to fetch the dented, tin kettle from its place on the shelf.

Despite her determined good humor, she was, in truth, feeling more than a little shaken by the abrupt change in their circumstances. While the flat's rooms possessed gracious proportions and good light, the cooker and water tap were out on the landing, to be shared with other residents, and the toilet and bath were down the hall. After the airy spaciousness of their villa on the Wannsee, it was a step down indeed. Perhaps, she reflected, as she went out to the landing to light the stove and boil the kettle, a house in Mayfair would be better.

As she was waiting for the kettle to boil, a woman emerged from the flat below, carrying her own pot. She looked to be in her thirties, with fair hair drawn back in a bun and her slender body swathed in a shapeless dress of worn gray cotton. She started at the sight of Rosa, and then nodded once.

"You are new here?" she asked in careful, accented English.

"Yes," Rosa replied in her own hesitant English. "We arrived today. Do you speak German?"

The woman's expression, which had been guarded, cleared, and she smiled. "*Ja*. My name is Anna Gruber," she replied in German. "I am here with my husband."

"Rosa Herzelfeld," Rosa replied in introduction. "I'm here with my mother and father."

"I am from Vienna originally," she explained. "You recently arrived?"

"From Berlin, yes. We came on the *St Louis*, but we have been in Southampton for the last two weeks."

Anna nodded her understanding. "We have been here a year, since right after the Anschluss."

A year?

Rosa tried to keep her expression interested and friendly, although inwardly she was appalled. In a whole year, Anna Gruber had not been able to improve her circumstances? She was still living in the rented flat provided by the Quaker Relief Association, lugging her cooking pot out to the landing, sharing a toilet with four other flats. Rosa hoped their situation would be markedly different.

"How have you found it?" she asked, and Anna raised her eyebrows, shrugging a little. "Better than under Hitler, yes?"

"Yes, it certainly is." Of that there could be no doubt, and Rosa told herself, rather sternly, not to be ungrateful. She could hardly lambast her parents for their sniffy attitudes if she was quietly feeling the same. "Do you work?" she asked. "We have been told we must look for jobs."

Anna nodded. "I came here on a domestic worker's visa. I am a maid for a grand house in St John's Wood. In Vienna, I was a psychologist." She smiled and shrugged again, while once more Rosa had to hide her horror.

A psychologist, now working as a maid? Admittedly, she'd known that sort of thing happened—plenty of people at the boarding house in Southampton had explained how Jews were unable to find professional jobs in Great Britain and had to make do scrubbing and sweeping. An acclaimed lawyer, Rosa had been told, now drove a bus. Still, she'd assumed, without even realizing she was doing it, that her father would be different. That *she* would.

And even now, she found herself refusing to believe that they wouldn't be. Anna Gruber might have had to work as a maid, but that didn't mean Rosa would. She wasn't on a domestic worker's visa, after all; according to the Quaker Relief Association, they could get any job they liked. Rosa was hoping, at the very least, to be a secretary or typist. She'd done well in school, especially in the sciences. She hadn't been able to go to university, thanks to the race laws, but she was smart and ambitious, and she wanted to do well for herself in this new country. More than being a maid, anyway. If that made her a snob, well then, so be it.

"If you are interested," Anna continued, "the Jewish Day Center here in Belsize Park offers classes in English. They are free, and have certainly been worthwhile."

"Thank you," Rosa replied. Already she knew she needed to improve her English—and quickly.

The kettle began to boil, and Rosa took it by its handle as she pulled it off the stove.

"It was a great pleasure to meet you," she told Anna, her voice politely formal, as if they were in a drawing room back in Berlin, making chitchat over champagne.

Anna smiled faintly, and Rosa had the uncomfortable feeling that the other woman had guessed at least some of her thoughts. "And you," she said, as she slapped her pot down on top of the cooker. "I'm sure we'll see more of each other."

They certainly would, sharing this cooker, along with the toilet, Rosa thought. She smiled in return before heading back to the flat. As she came inside, she saw her mother was sitting on one of the rickety chairs by the table, looking forlorn, while her father was adjusting his hat, ready to go out.

"I'm going to visit the bank," he announced. "And see what has happened to our funds. We surely won't have to endure these dreadful conditions for much longer."

"Thank you, Fritz, darling," her mother murmured, with a grateful, adoring look for her husband, the kind that made Rosa grit her teeth, because her mother knew what her husband was like. Just as Rosa did.

It wasn't until her father had left, closing the door smartly behind him, that Rosa realized they had no tea; they hadn't yet bought any food at all. She put the kettle on the rough worktop, suddenly feeling exhausted by that simple effort.

Although it wasn't just that, she knew. It was everything— the strangeness of their new lives, the list of chores she would have to do to make this place habitable, because she was already quite certain her mother wouldn't lift a finger. It was the knowledge that they would be sharing this space with strangers, that she would have to venture out into this foreign world, trying to speak a foreign language, and get a job of some sort, if she even could. Considering the state of her English, it was likely she'd be a maid, as well, Rosa thought despondently —and that was if she was lucky enough to be hired in the first place.

"Rosa," her mother said, a touch of impatience to her voice. "I thought you were making tea?"

"I'll have to go out to buy some," Rosa replied. Even that simple task felt daunting. She thought back to how she'd been on the ship, full of determined bravado, believing this brave new world had met its match in her. Now, with a painful lump in her throat, she realized how foolish and false that façade of courage really was. She almost—*almost*—wished she was back on the St Louis, sailing across the Atlantic and standing on the deck, a balmy breeze blowing over her as she chatted and laughed with her friends, dreaming of a future in Havana that had looked only bright.

Was Hannah feeling this same unsettling sense of lostness? Rosa wondered. Was Rachel? And what about Sophie? Rosa had assumed she was enjoying the high life in the United States, but maybe Washington DC was as strange and scary as London. The possibility gave her a sense of solidarity with her friends, now so far away, and she slipped her hand into her pocket, her fingers curling around the sliver of emerald she took with her everywhere. Then she straightened, determined not to be defeated at the first, admittedly small, hurdle.

"I'll go get some tea now," she told her mother, and with a firm, bright smile, she turned toward the door.

CHAPTER 10

Their money, it seemed, was nowhere to be found. Or at least, it was not in London. It wasn't in England, or even in Europe. The life savings Fritz Herzelfeld had boasted about being able to keep, thanks to his eminent Nazi connections, had disappeared into the ether, somewhere over the Atlantic, or maybe into the dark bowels of Havana's banks. Perhaps a crucial slip of paper had slid from some tottering stack, become wedged behind a filing cabinet or under a desk, forever forgotten. Or maybe, Rosa thought, the Nazis whose ears her father had so smugly thought he had, had simply taken it for themselves, laughing quietly into their sleeves. They might have breezily promised to help the Jewish doctor who cured their unmentionable diseases, but that didn't mean they actually *had*.

In any case, it was gone. Rosa's father came back from the bank that first day, pale and tight-lipped rather than florid and fuming, which scared her because it was so unlike him. There was no bombastic tirade, no insistence that he would complain to the management, demand better service, sort everything to his satisfaction, as he always did. He simply told them, his tone terse, that the money wasn't available and that was that.

"What do you mean, Fritz?" Rosa's mother had asked, appalled and trembling. She'd barely moved from her chair the whole time he was gone, even though Rosa had been to the shops and back again. "It can't just be *gone!*"

His lips had thinned as he'd reached for his pipe, only to toss it irritably aside when he realized he'd run out of tobacco. "It appears it can."

"But... but all our savings..." Her mother's voice had quavered with both indignation and fear. "They can be found, surely? They must be. They can't just *take* it all."

They could, Rosa had thought somberly, and did. Back in Germany, Jews had been having their assets unjustly seized for well over a year now. Did her mother not remember how they'd had to vacate their villa, with all its furnishings, while a crowd of gentile neighbors had watched and smirked? The grand piano, the modernist paintings... they'd had to leave it all behind, for someone else to enjoy. They'd been lucky to take what they had, their linens and the set of Meissen china off which they now ate, at the rough deal table, the sight of the delicate porcelain on the splintered wood seeming both incongruous and pathetically sad.

"I'll go again tomorrow and speak to someone higher up," her father had said, his tone repressive, the conversation clearly finished.

But when he'd gone the next day, the result had been exactly the same. No one had any record of the money. "No transfer was possible, as it appeared, Herr Doktor, to all intents and purposes, that the funds did not exist."

They were, *to all intents and purposes*, penniless, save for what small amount of savings they'd brought over with them on the ship, a fact that neither of her parents seemed to be able to come to grips with, and what it meant for their lives.

They'd been at the flat in Belsize Park for four days, and Rosa's mother had barely moved from the threadbare armchair by the window. She dressed every day in her silks and satins, doing her hair and makeup, putting on her pearls... and all just to sit in that wretched chair. Rosa had attempted to cajole her to take a stroll around the park, but her mother had refused.

"Your father will find our money," she'd said, "and then we'll get a flat in a more suitable location. You'll see." And until that day, Rosa supposed, her mother would simply sit in her chair and wait, while her father went out on his "business"— what that was, Rosa wasn't sure, but it occupied him from after breakfast until supper.

Meanwhile, Rosa was doing her best to acclimatize to this strange new world. On their first day, she'd ventured to the little market on the corner for tea and other supplies and had promptly forgotten all her English when she'd been at the till. The woman behind the counter had, thankfully, been kind.

"You're new here, love?" she'd said in sympathy. "Fresh off the boat, are you? You can point if you like. Show me what it is you're after."

But while Rosa had at least understood her, pointing had been almost as difficult, for she didn't recognize the packaging or labels of any of the items stacked on the shelves behind the till. She'd stared helplessly at the strange words and designs while the shopkeeper had looked on patiently, and had ended up descending to miming a charade of drinking tea, putting sugar in.

"Ah, I know what it is you're after," the woman had exclaimed, and proudly placed a tin of soup on the counter. Rosa had managed a smile and shaken her head, and then tried miming again, while the shopkeeper had watched in perplexity.

When she'd finally cottoned on that Rosa was asking for tea, she'd measured it out in a little brown paper bag, on an impressive set of brass scales.

"You're not for a career on the stage, that's for certain," she'd remarked, and then erupted into great gales of laughter, which had made Rosa burst into giggles, as well. They'd shared a long laugh while several customers had looked on, nonplussed, and then the woman had wiped the tears from her eyes. "Well, you've got the right attitude, love," she'd said as she'd handed Rosa her items. After some effort, she'd managed to procure sugar, tea, and coffee, which was sold in a bottle, the brown liquid looking something like gravy. Rosa had never seen anything like it before. "You'll go far in life if you can laugh at yourself, I say," the woman had finished with a smile, and then she'd kindly helped Rosa decipher the different notes and coins, so she was able to pay the right amount.

It had felt good and somehow healing, to laugh like that, Rosa had reflected as she'd left the grocer's, a new spring in her step. Maybe she didn't need to feel so nervous and uncertain, after all. With this newfound confidence, she'd entered a bakery on the corner of their road and had managed to say, in careful, cautious English, that she'd like a loaf of bread. She'd even been understood! At the butcher's, she'd bought a beef bone to flavor broth; she hadn't had enough money for anything more substantial, but she decided she would make it stretch with some onions, potatoes, and carrots from the greengrocer. In a spirit of determined optimism, she took it all home, the paper-wrapped parcels bulky in her arms because she had not thought to bring a string bag, as she saw so many other industrious housewives doing.

All of this was new for her, and not just because of the English. Back in Berlin, there had been a maid and cook to manage meals; Rosa had hardly ever shopped for food, and as for *making* it... Well, she refused to be daunted by these hurdles. This was her new life, her new chance, and she was determined to embrace it.

Back in the flat, she'd made her mother tea and then gamely peeled and chopped and boiled. The resulting pottage for their supper was edible, if only just. Unfortunately, she'd forgotten to buy any salt.

"I'll remember that for next time," Rosa had said cheerfully, while her mother had pushed her bowl away in disgust.

Then, yesterday, her father had returned to the flat, looking grimmer than ever. Rosa had thought it was about the money again, but in some ways, it was worse. He'd flung his medical certificate on the table, his face twisting in derision.

"*Worthless*," he spat. "Absolutely worthless in this country, it seems, and I've been a practicing physician—an eminent practicing physician—for *twenty years*."

Rosa had stared at the ornate script of the certificate, conferring his degree in medicine from Heidelberg University, back in Germany. "What do you mean, worthless?" she'd asked while her mother had looked on fearfully, fingering the pearls that lay cold and white against her throat.

"They won't even consider it," her father had explained, his voice taut with both frustration and fury. "One of the oldest and most distinguished universities in Europe, and it's as if I'd fished my degree out of a bin!" He shook his head, his face crumpling a bit, revealing the fear underneath the fury. "If I am to practice medicine in this country, they have told me I will have to retrain."

"Retrain?" Rosa's mother had straightened in her chair. "But that will take years..."

"And it is beneath my dignity," her father had replied stiffly. "To retrain, when I have over twenty years of experience! It is utterly outrageous."

"But then what will you do?" Rosa had asked. She hadn't been entirely surprised by the news; she had thought of their neighbor, Anna Gruber, on a domestic worker's visa despite her credentials. In Southampton, they had encountered too many refugee doctors and lawyers and businessmen who were now pushing mops or waiting tables to believe her father could waltz into a physician's role as simply as that, as much as she'd wanted to, because, well... because he was her father, and he'd always seemed to succeed at everything he did. This, it seemed, would defeat him.

"Could you take the medical exams here, at least?" she'd pressed. "Without retraining, since you have so much experience?" It seemed an obvious potential solution.

Her father had pressed his lips together. "I suppose I could, but it would have to be in English."

"Well, then," her mother had said, leaning back in her chair, confident that as in all things, her husband could manage this. "You must learn English."

He'd raked a hand through his hair, the gesture one of anger and impatience. "I don't want to take the exams again," he'd snapped, swinging away from them both. "And certainly not in English. Why should I have to?"

Rosa had stared at her father's taut back and had realized, in an instant, that if her father would not lower himself to take the medical exams, then he certainly wouldn't apply for a job driving a bus or sweeping floors. Which meant the only person in the family capable of earning a wage, she acknowledged heavily, was her.

And so, the next morning, Rosa resolutely left the flat, wearing a plain navy dress and sensible shoes, in the hope that she could be hired for work. She wasn't sure what she was suitable for, considering the state of her English and the unfortunate and decided lack of any recognizable skills, but she still had hopes that someone, somewhere, would recognize her intelligence and innate ability and give her a chance. Maybe a clerical job in an office, typing or filing? She wouldn't be much good at dictation, not until her English improved, but she knew she couldn't wait that long to start earning money.

Still, despite those worries, Rosa felt surprisingly cheerful. Although the weather of the last few weeks had been chilly and dull, today was balmy and breezy, the air full of warmth and birdsong, and underneath a pale blue sky, London looked freshly washed and appealing, with its rows of gracious, white stucco-fronted homes, far from the drab grayness she'd been so dispirited by when they'd first arrived.

It was a day for opportunity, Rosa decided, as well as optimism. Never mind that they had no money, that her English was poor, that her mother still sat in that awful chair and her father disappeared to his own devices. She was *free* here, freer than she'd ever been back in Berlin, hosting her father's parties and trying to seem so insouciant, all the while fighting a deep feeling of dread, of guilt.

Here she had none of that, only a determined sort of hope. That morning, she'd managed to make porridge and finally learned how to mix the bottled coffee—camp coffee, it was called—with hot water to make a drink that resembled what they were used to, somewhat, if not in its entirety. Her father had drunk it, at least, even if her mother had turned her nose up at it, as she did at so many things.

"I'd buy proper coffee," Rosa had told her in as conciliatory a manner as she could manage. She'd suspected her mother's attitude of disgust came not from mere snobbery, but from fear. "But we haven't got a coffee pot," she'd explained, "or the money to buy one."

"Does this country even know what proper coffee is?" her mother had demanded, her arms crossed over her body as she'd averted her head. Rosa had sipped hers in silence.

At least they were still enjoying the relative comfort of the flat by themselves, Rosa reflected as she walked down Haverstock Hill toward the high street and the underground station, her step brisk and her arms swinging by her sides. The family they were to share with had yet to arrive, and Rosa suspected her mother was hoping they never would. Well, she decided, she would take that development in her stride, when and if it happened.

This morning, she intended to buy a newspaper, scour the "help wanted" adverts, and then apply accordingly. It *sounded* simple, but she already recognized how challenging she would find it all, especially with her limited English. She'd taken to buying newspapers simply to practice reading English, but she had no English-German dictionary and it had started to feel like a somewhat hopeless endeavor, the articles crammed with words whose meanings she failed to grasp. Still, she certainly recognized the urgent need to improve her language skills if she were to get ahead in this country, which she fully intended to do. She thought of attending the classes Anna Gruber had mentioned, but first, importantly, a job.

In a newsagent on the high street, she bought a copy of *The Times*, as well as some stationery and envelopes. She intended to write to Sophie, and Hannah at Henri's; she would not be able to write to Rachel until she had an address, which Rosa unhappily acknowledged could take months. She'd meant to write sooner, but there been so little to say, at least so little that Rosa *wanted* to say. She didn't want to tell Sophie about the dreadful days of uncertainty aboard the *St Louis*, or the cramped and dispiriting conditions of the boarding house in Southampton, how the stale smell of cabbage had become, for Rosa, the very scent of hopelessness.

But she couldn't *not* say those things either, she reflected as she sat at a table in the window of a Lyons teashop, nibbling the end of her pen, the blank sheet on the table before her, along with a cup of coffee—proper coffee, not the regrettable bottled stuff. It had been a bit of an extravagance, considering the dire state of their finances, but Rosa had felt it was well worth it. She was going to find a job today, after all.

She gazed out the window at the summer sky fleeced with

puffy, white clouds, pedestrians walking along below, everyone seeming cheerful and full of purpose—a mother wheeling a big, silver pram; a businessman with the brim of his hat pulled low. A young woman in a smart dress, nipped in at the waist, her hair in fashionable brushed-out waves, heels clicking on the pavement.

It still amazed Rosa, that she could sit in this teashop and sip coffee, contemplate the world, and feel part of it, as well as completely at ease. True, she didn't know how they were going to get money; the Quaker Relief Association had promised to pay the rent on their flat only to the end of the month—a date that was coming up all too soon. And true, she was anxious about looking for a job, especially with her limited language ability, but she was still in a country that had no signs on the doors forbidding Jews from entering; she didn't have to worry about SS officers or Gestapo coming smartly down the street, looking for someone to harass or humiliate. More importantly, she didn't have to dread them sashaying their way into her house as if they owned the place, which they'd more or less done.

"Herr Doktor, we've got another patient for you. Give him some of your magic pills, won't you? If I didn't know better, I'd believe those rumors that you Jews practice some sort of witchcraft..."

Even now, Rosa could picture her father's ready smile, the easy laugh. The way he'd reach for the brandy decanter, pour a glass.

"Don't question the magic, Untersturmführer."

As if he was sharing the joke.

The memory made her stomach roil. That couldn't happen here, not any longer. Not ever again.

She pushed the thought away as she bent her head and put pen to paper.

Dear Sophie,

Well, I told you I'd write once I received your address, although I'm not sure how much there is to say. The voyage back to Europe was pretty dire—none of the jolly mood going over! We're staying in a flat in London, a rather shabby little place, it's true, but at least we're allowed in the shops, and no one asks for our papers.

She regaled Sophie with some of what had happened on board, keeping her tone breezy and light, even though the events themselves had been grim indeed, and finished with a brief description of her situation now.

"More coffee, miss?" The Lyons' waitress, known by Londoners as a nippy, and dressed in a starched cap, dark dress, and white apron, proffered the pot questioningly.

"Yes, please," Rosa replied, and signed off the letter before folding it carefully into its envelope. She then wrote a quicker missive to Hannah, letting her know her address, hoping her friend really would be able to collect letters from the café by the Eiffel Tower. Hannah hadn't known where she and Lotte would be sent after arriving in Boulogne.

With those tasks done, Rosa turned to *The Times*, flicking to the back pages, where the employment adverts were.

Rosa's coffee slowly went cold as she squinted down at the paper, scouring the tiny type of the adverts for various situations, only to realize that, just as she'd feared, very few seemed suitable for a young German woman with limited English. Many of the clerical jobs specifically requested that only men apply, and those that accepted women still wanted several years' experience with typing, dictation, and stenography— none of which Rosa possessed, in English *or* in German. As for the other jobs... well, maybe she'd be a maid, after all.

She rested her chin in her hand and took a sip of her now-lukewarm coffee as she gazed once more out the teashop's window at the busy street. Now, instead of viewing the scene with a burgeoning sense of belonging, she felt acutely conscious that everyone out there was walking as if they had some place to go, something important to do. The man with the bowler hat had a *job*, as did two young women clearly dressed for office work. And while just this morning, Rosa had been optimistic that she too would be like them, and find work, now she wondered—and doubted. She had no experience, just an education in another language that had ended at sixteen and a work ethic that was yet unproven. Why would anyone take a risk on her? Did she even want to try? She needed a job, a wage, *now*, or at least as soon as possible.

"May I take your cup, miss?" the nippy asked, and Rosa blinked up at her, startled out of her reverie.

"Yes..." she began, only to ask in English, in her careful, stilted way, "do you know... can you help me... do they... employ... here?"

The nippy's forehead creased in confusion. "Sorry...?"

Rosa gazed at her helplessly, wishing she had more words. "Work," she said bluntly. "I need work."

"Oh, I see." The woman's face cleared, to be replaced by a look of dubiousness. "Well, I dunno, miss, you could ask my manager, I suppose..."

Rosa knew the nippy sounded so uncertain because of her accent, her lack of English. Still, she was determined to try. She might not be able to get the kind of clerical job she'd first dreamed of, but she could still work here, perhaps.

"*Danke*," she told the woman, and then corrected herself hurriedly, "thank you."

The manager, a stout, hassled-looking woman in her forties, hands planted on her ample hips and with a plain, no-nonsense expression, listened to Rosa's fumbling attempt to explain herself tolerantly enough, although with a busy café to see to, she was also clearly impatient.

"If you're asking if you can work as a nippy, then the answer is certainly not," she replied with brisk asperity, after Rosa had trailed off, the extent of her English having reached its regrettable conclusion. "Not with that thick accent! You're Jewish, I suppose?"

There had been no censure in the woman's voice, but Rosa tensed anyway, before nodding. "Yes," she said simply. "I will work hard," she added. "At anything."

"Well, I'd like to help you," the woman told her, "because heaven knows it can't have been easy, to get this far." She blew out a breath as she tucked a strand of hair back into her graying bun. "Lorna's left the kitchen," she mused out loud. "I suppose I could find you a place there, doing the dishes." She glanced at Rosa skeptically. "It's hard work, though, and those nice, soft hands of yours will get red and rough. I don't appreciate quitters, either—if you're not up for it, it would be better for you not to start at all."

Rosa didn't understand everything the woman had said, but she thought she caught the no-nonsense gist. "Yes," she told her. "That is, I will not quit."

"It isn't paid particularly well," the woman continued, a warning. "Twenty-eight shillings a week, for sixty hours." She eyed Rosa appraisingly. "You look a strong girl, never mind those soft, lily-white hands! Do you want to do it?"

Rosa hesitated for no more than a split second; she had no idea how much twenty-eight shillings was, but the woman had as good as said it wasn't very much. And sixty hours! There wouldn't be much time to do anything else—learn English, or explore this city, or properly live. She hadn't come all the way to England to work as a skivvy day and night, and yet... what choice did she really have, if her parents wouldn't find work?

The rent would be due at the end of the month, and what savings they'd brought with them on the *St Louis* were already nearly gone. She didn't have the time to search for a job she most likely wouldn't get hired for. She turned back to the woman.

"Yes," she said firmly. "I will do it. Thank you."

CHAPTER 11

JULY 1939—LONDON

Rosa stood at the deep sink, elbow-deep in soapy, greasy water, as she tackled what felt like the twentieth cooking pot of the day. She'd been working in the kitchen at the Lyons teashop in Belsize Park for coming on three weeks, and they'd felt like the longest weeks of her life—up early every day to make breakfast and study English, and then a ten-hour shift before she tottered home for a quick meal and bed. It didn't feel like much of a life, but the twenty-eight shillings in her pocket at the end of each week made it all worth it.

She had one day off out of every seven, and she used it to do her laundry in the old mangle in their building's scrubby court-yard, or shop for food, or simply catch up on sleep. Once, she'd managed to make it to the British Museum, wandering its great rooms with a sense of wonder and awe, watching couples stroll by arm in arm, smartly dressed and smiling, and she'd felt, for a fleeting moment, as if there was a life for the taking, a happy, busy, and exciting one, only just out of her reach.

In the three weeks since she'd been working at Lyons, her parents, as far as Rosa could see, had not bestirred themselves to do very much at all. Her mother stayed in the flat, and her

father had started holding court in the Willow Café, a local
coffeehouse frequented by Jewish refugees. It was run by an
aging Austrian opera singer, Maria, who had first hosted
Russian aristocrats after the war, and now welcomed the latest
crop of homeless émigrés into her little sanctuary.

When Rosa had ventured into the ornate room, all gilt and
polished wood, a samovar in pride of place, it had reminded her
one of Berlin's elegant cafés on the Kurfürstendamm.
Gentlemen and a few women had sat at the tables, somehow
managing to look both regal and lost, as they sipped coffee or
nursed glasses of schnapps and talked about what the world
used to be like. Her father viewed himself, she thought, as something of a leader of this motley group of dissidents and ex-
professionals; none of the recent raft of refugees had yet been
able to find decent jobs, and so they spent their days waiting for
something to happen. But what would, if they didn't take any
action?

Rosa was trying to be patient with her parents; she knew
this step down in station was difficult for them, but her mother's
sniffy attitude, her father's imperious disdain, didn't make it
easy for her. Nor did their new housemates, with whom they
had to share the kitchen and living room, stepping over the
washing hung out on a line from window to door, or enduring
the stink of sauerkraut from the cooker in the hall, both of
which Rosa's mother found near unbearable.

A week into their new life, a young couple had shown up at
their door, with the same woman from the British Fund for
Germany Jewry standing behind them, looking resolute.

"Mr. and Mrs. Rosenbaum will be sharing this flat with
you," the woman had explained stiffly, eyeing Rosa's father with
a certain wary beadiness; she'd clearly remembered his objections from before and had no toleration for them now.

"Welcome," Rosa had responded quickly, stepping in front
of her father, who had just drawn a deep breath and seemed

ready to expound on something or other, nothing Rosa had suspected any of them wanted to hear. "My name is Rosa Herzelfeld, and these are my parents, Elsa and Friedrich Herzelfeld." She'd stuck out a hand for them to shake, which they'd merely looked at; Rosa thought they'd looked dazed, winded, and she'd wondered when they'd arrived. "We're very pleased to meet you," she finished, smiling, while her parents stood behind her, silent and a little sullen.

"My name is Moritz Rosenbaum," the man had replied in careful German. He'd then nodded at her hand, but did not take it, and after a second's pause, Rosa had awkwardly withdrawn it. Moritz Rosenbaum was dark-haired and bearded, pale and slight, with rounded shoulders underneath a long, shabby frock coat. "And this is my wife, Zlata." His wife was also pale and dark, small and slender. She'd worn a shapeless black dress with a black knit shawl draped over her shoulders, and a headscarf around her head.

Rosa had realized, far too belatedly perhaps, that they were Orthodox Jews, who followed far stricter laws about dress and behavior than the Herzelfelds, as secular, liberal Jews, did.

While the Rosenbaums had settled into one of the bedrooms, the woman from the Fund having left breathing, no doubt, a sigh of relief, Rosa's mother had drawn her aside.

"Rosa, they're *Orthodox*," she'd hissed, her fingernails digging into Rosa's arm. "And I don't think they're even German."

"They're *Jews*," Rosa had reminded her, removing her arm from her mother's claw-like grasp. "And they're *refugees*." She'd paused before adding pointedly, "Like us."

Still, even Rosa had been a bit taken aback by their new co-residents; they kept a Kosher kitchen and observed a strict Sabbath, neither of which the Herzelfelds did, or had ever done. Such things were utterly foreign to them, as foreign as their own secular habits were to the Rosenbaums.

"But who is your *Shabbat goy*?" Zlata had asked in bewilderment, when, on the first Sabbath, the Herzelfelds had been insultingly unbothered by the predicament of who would do such things as turn the lights on or off, an act forbidden to Orthodox Jews, and thus needing a gentile to perform them.

"We don't have one," Rosa's mother had replied stiffly.

A heavy and rather ominous silence had followed this pronouncement. Zlata and Moritz had looked at each other in confused alarm, before Rosa had intervened.

"We can act as your *Shabbat goy*, if you like. We'd be happy to."

Zlata had looked rather horrified by the idea that fellow Jews would take on the activities proscribed them. She'd shaken her head, disbelieving, and muttered, "Jews... acting as *goys*... I don't understand it."

With some difficulty, thanks to the Rosenbaums' reticence and her parents' standoffishness, Rosa had learned that the couple was from Breslau, a city in Silesia with a large Jewish, Polish-speaking population. The Rosenbaums spoke Yiddish first, Polish second, and German third. It was, Rosa had known, entirely the wrong order for her parents.

Moritz was a repairer of violins, and Zlata kept their home; although they were both in their thirties, they hadn't had any children and Rosa could tell it was a source of pain, and even shame, for Zlata in particular. She'd felt for them, trying to adapt to this new world, one that was surely even stranger than it was for Rosa and her parents.

Over the course of the next few weeks, they'd learned a way of living together that was both awkward and understanding in turns. Rosa, who did the family cooking, agreed to keep a Kosher kitchen, for she could see that anything else would be disastrous for Zlata. It meant two sets of dishes, cooking pots, and utensils, and never cooking dairy and meat together, which, with her limited repertoire and cooking skills, Rosa struggled to keep to.

They took turns using the tap and cooker on the landing, and Zlata was scrupulously neat with all her washing and tidying—far more than Rosa was, to her own embarrassment. When they weren't eating at the table, Moritz and Zlata mostly kept to their room, except for listening to the evening news on the radio in the living room, which they all did together, in silence, as if they were at synagogue, Rosa thought, although, in truth, she'd hardly been to synagogue enough to know.

When the Rosenbaums headed out, every Saturday evening, to the Sabbath services, Rosa felt a strange pang of something almost like envy. To have that community, that certainty that there was a greater hand at work in the world! To not just be Jewish because of how you'd been born, but because you *believed*. The lack of faith in her own family felt, for the first time, like something she missed. She thought it would give her great comfort, if she had it, but, in truth, she did not even know where to look.

Still, the two families managed to get along, although Rosa suspected that while she was at work, her parents did not do much to welcome the young couple; the Rosenbaums were simply too different.

Now, as she scrubbed a pot in the Lyons kitchen, her arms aching, her hair falling in damp tendrils about her flushed face, Rosa couldn't help but wonder about the future. She didn't know what it held, but she was certainly starting to grasp what she *didn't* want it to hold... which was endless, ten-hour shifts washing pots in the stifling kitchen in the back of the Belsize Park Lyons teashop. Although, she acknowledged as she blew a sweaty strand of hair away from her face, the teashop's manager, Winifred Hatley, had been kind to her.

She was strict but fair, and she'd given Rosa a chance, despite her limited English and decidedly German accent.

Admittedly, she insisted, quite sternly, that Rosa stay in the kitchen and not show her face—or, more to the point, reveal her voice—in the actual dining area, but Rosa didn't particularly mind that. The kitchen was managed by a round, affable cook named Hetty, who sang as she stirred and had accepted Rosa with a comfortable—and comforting—ease. Things could have, Rosa knew, been much worse.

But she still wanted something different—something *more*—for her future. The trouble was, what it would be—and how would she go about obtaining it?

"Shift's just about over," Hetty told her as she swiped at her own shiny forehead. "Goodness, but it's as hot as Hades in here! Go out and enjoy the cool of the day, love, while you can."

Rosa smiled gratefully as she finished scrubbing her pot and laid it upside down on the dish drainer to dry. She hadn't seen anything but this sink and its dirty pots for ten hours, save for the twenty minutes she'd taken to gobble down a meat paste sandwich, and she was desperate to get outside, to feel the cool evening air on her heated cheeks. Tomorrow was her day off and she had plenty of chores to do, but she also hoped to do something fun... go to a park or a museum, or maybe even try one of the English classes at the Jewish Day Center. She wasn't sure yet what she'd do, but something.

Rosa said goodbye to Hetty and then stepped out into Belsize Park's high street. It was eight o'clock in the evening, and the sun was just starting to sink below the buildings of white stucco, lighting the sky and turning the clouds vivid shades of orange and lavender. For a second, Rosa simply stood there, enjoying the moment and all it promised—freedom, possibility, *hope*.

Although, she acknowledged with a pang of anxiety, more and more there had been talk of war, both on the radio and in conversations she heard in the teashop. Still, she was *free* here, free in a way she'd never been before. Free from the Nazis' power, and also free from her own memories. She would not, she told herself as a young, laughing couple strolled past, enjoying the summer's evening, think of Ernst, or who she'd been with him, as carefree and light as that woman who ambled past her, with her curled hair and her bright smile.

She'd been so carelessly untroubled by all the pain and worry around her, even when it had been thrust right in her face, thinking only of herself, of the happiness she'd found, fleeting and false as it had been. She wouldn't, she resolved, let herself ever be like that again.

Slowly, her step sure and determined, Rosa headed for home, tilting her face to the last of the sun's dying rays as the sky separated into striated strands of vivid color, more stunning than any artist's canvas, a Monet or Renoir.

As Rosa let herself into the building, the persistent smell of sauerkraut and drains rose up to meet her in a stale, suffocating stench. The linoleum-tiled stairwell was dark and depressing, and she had to shrug off the sense of dread she felt at returning to the flat and, she suspected, her parents' simmering displeasure and restlessness with this new, unwelcome life of theirs.

Sure enough, as she let herself in, her mother was in her usual armchair by the window, looking as if she'd been sitting there for hours, quietly fuming. The Rosenbaums were shut up in their room, the light seeping from under the door, and her father was nowhere to be seen. The cloying, clay-like smell of overcooked lentils hung like a miasma in the air; Zlata must have already made supper.

"Where's Father?" Rosa asked as she closed the door and eased off her shoes; after ten hours of standing, her feet were aching. She glanced at the kitchen area, with its table and worktop, and thought she might make do with just some bread and cheese for their evening meal. She couldn't stomach the thought of cooking, not after ten hours in a hot kitchen.

"How should *I* know where he is?" her mother replied

tetchily, staring determinedly out the window at the falling darkness, the bright colors of just a few moments ago now replaced with a muted palette of lavender and gray. A certain heaviness settled inside Rosa as she recognized her mother's tone and what it meant. It hadn't taken her father long, she thought with an inward sigh. It never did.

"Is he at that coffeehouse he likes to visit?" she asked, keeping her voice mild.

"He's been gone all day." Her mother's voice rang with accusation, as if Rosa were to blame for this state of affairs, and in her mother's warped mind, Rosa thought with a suppressed sigh, she probably was, at least in part. Somehow, her mother had found a way to blame Rosa for her husband's indiscretions.

"He needs something to do," she told her mother in that same mild voice, kept now with effort. "And so do you, Mother."

"I am not the one *gallivanting* about," her mother snapped as she drew herself up, practically quivering in outrage.

"If you had something to do," Rosa replied, gentling her voice even more, "perhaps you wouldn't worry so much what Father is doing, wherever he goes. He's probably only at the coffeehouse, talking to the other refugees about the better days, as he usually does."

"*Émigrés*, Rosa, not refugees," her mother corrected. "We are not destitute."

They were entirely destitute, Rosa thought, but she decided not to argue the point. "Still," she said. "I wouldn't worry about him."

"I'm not worried." The reply was automatic, insistent, and entirely unbelievable. Her mother averted her head from Rosa's knowing gaze, craning her neck so far that Rosa thought she might strain a muscle. "I don't know why I talk to you about such things," she continued after a moment, her tone repressive. "You have no idea of what goes on between a husband and wife, Rosa, no idea at all."

She had *some* idea, but once again she had no desire to argue the point. "It's getting late," she said instead. "Why don't you get ready for bed, and I'll make us some hot cocoa? We can listen to something on the radio before we go to sleep. There's usually a concert on Radio Luxembourg at this hour." The alternative radio station was listened to more than the nationally licensed BBC, as people enjoyed its light music and variety programs.

Her mother remained upright, her body tense, and Rosa knew she was battling with herself. She wanted to give her usual snappish retort, but she couldn't quite make herself. She had to be terribly lonely, Rosa thought, sitting in this awful flat all day while her father went out to hold court and impress people; he was a man who would always find his captive audience. A rush of sympathy for her mother overcame her, and she took a step toward her, one hand outstretched.

"*Mutti*," she said, her voice quiet and gentle. "Shall I make some cocoa?"

Her mother gave a twitchy, restive shrug. "Oh, very well," she said at last, as if granting a concession, and she rose from her chair to stalk, her head held high, to the bedroom.

Rosa put a pan of milk on to boil on the cooker in the hall, and then went to change. It felt good to get out of her work clothes, to undo her hair from its scraped-back bun. She spooned cocoa and a precious bit of sugar into the pan of milk and then brought the cups back to the living room, giving one to her mother and taking one for herself.

"Shall we see what's on the wireless?" she asked, as she turned the dial of the big wooden set that someone from the Central Fund had kindly donated. Her parents might like to fashion themselves as émigrés, but they'd accepted such charity well enough, Rosa thought wryly as she searched for some light music.

Her mother pulled her dressing gown more tightly around

her as she gazed out at the darkening night. "It's getting so late," she murmured, and Rosa knew she was thinking of her father.

"*Mutti*," she said impulsively, "why don't you come out with me tomorrow? We could go to a museum, or to the park... there is a zoo, you know, at Regent's Park. They say it might have to close if there's a war, we should see it now, while we can."

"Oh, Rosa," her mother replied in a fretful tone, "don't talk about a war."

"But there *will* be one," Rosa said quietly. "You must know that, Mother. The newspapers are full of it." Every day there were alarming new articles about Germany's territorial aspirations, troops amassing on borders, Hitler's false accusations of Polish aggression.

There had also been distressing news about the treatment of Jews in Germany itself—just a few weeks ago, the last Jewish businesses had been forced to close. What would happen to them all, Rosa had wondered, without any work? What could the Nazis possibly be intending? She thought of what her father had said would have happened if the *St Louis* had been forced back to Hamburg—arrest and deportation. That might be the proposed fate of a thousand destitute refugees, but for every Jew in Germany? Surely not. Such a thing was mind-boggling, utterly impossible to conceive of.

"It's practically all anyone talks about," she continued. Even if people didn't want it; no one relished the prospect of war, not with the last war still fresh in many people's memories.

Her mother hunched her shoulders. "Well, I don't want to talk about it," she said, staring determinedly out the window.

Rosa sighed and took a sip of her hot chocolate. "We could go to a museum, then," she said. "Or even to the cinema..." She thought, briefly, of the last time they'd been to the cinema, back on the ship. "There would be no Nazi reels here," she remarked with a small smile.

Her mother, however, without even turning from her vantage point by the window, simply shook her head.

She'd tried, Rosa told herself, even as she wondered why she did. Her mother held her in such little regard, after all; why did she think she could convince her of anything? In any case, if her mother didn't want to make the most of this life, well, there wasn't very much she could do about it.

But she wasn't, Rosa knew, willing to share the same fate. *She* would do something tomorrow, whether her mother accompanied her or not. She would embrace this new life... whatever it looked like and however she could. She'd make sure of it.

CHAPTER 12

JULY 1939—LONDON

Rosa stood on the threshold of the meeting room of the Jewish Day Center, located in a slightly dilapidated-looking townhouse near Belsize Park's high street. She'd woken up that morning determined to make the most of her day, and so after completing her usual chores—cooking, washing, and shopping—she'd resolutely ignored her mother's baleful look and headed outside.

It was a balmy, blue-skied day, and already Rosa had been in London long enough to know how rare those were. She was wearing one of her usual somber-colored, belted frocks—she'd determinedly given up trying to look pretty after Ernst—but she'd done her hair a little less severely and pinched her cheeks for a bit of color. It was as far as she was willing to go in terms of vanity; she'd relentlessly squashed that natural feminine desire when she'd realized just how foolish, how utterly stupid, she'd been.

But she wasn't going to think about the past now, Rosa had told herself, on a day that felt so much about the future. But right then, standing on the edge of a room that was full of people, all of them Jewish refugees like herself and yet looking so much more confident and comfortable, she felt a flicker of insecurity. The class was in conversational English, and already she suspected everyone was miles above her in ability. They were talking in English to each other as they waited; Rosa always reverted to German with someone from home.

"Are you here for the English class?" the instructor, a young, serious-looking man with spectacles and a warm smile, asked her in English.

Wordlessly, every scrap of English flown from her head, Rosa nodded.

"Why don't you take a seat?" the man suggested kindly. "We're about to start."

Although she was fighting the impulse to turn tail and run, Rosa murmured her thanks—in English—and moved to a wooden chair on the edge of the room. She straightened her shoulders and lifted her chin, determined not to be defeated. Since when had she been so *scared* by such things? she asked herself.

Yes, but it was just bravado, came the remorseless—and honest—reply. Still, Rosa told herself, bravado was better than nothing.

The man who had addressed her moved to the front of the room, and the class began. He spoke in English, his tone precise and deliberately slow, but Rosa still missed every other word. She felt her cheeks warm as she glanced around the room; everyone else seemed attentive, understanding. No one, she thought, had the blank, gormless look she feared was on her own face.

She straightened, leaning forward slightly to try to hear better, but volume was not the issue. He spoke plenty loud enough. Still, at least she *looked* as if she were listening, which she realized belatedly was taking so much effort that she was now missing two words out of three. *Hopeless!*

So caught up was she in trying to understand what was going on that she hadn't realized they were meant to divide into pairs to practice speaking with one another until she looked around and saw everyone moving chairs and starting to chat. Perhaps this would be a good time to leave, after all...

"I see you're without a partner, and so am I," a male voice said from behind her, making her jump a little. It was a kind voice, with a hint of wry humor.

Rosa turned around to see a handsome young man, perhaps a few years older than her, smiling down at her. He was tall and slender, with dark hair that fell over his forehead and brown eyes that glinted with good humor. He was wearing a three-piece suit in tweed that looked as if it had seen better days; the patches on the elbows were shiny with use. He stood slightly angled down toward her, with one hand behind his back. "Shall we work together?" he asked in what seemed to Rosa to be flawless English.

She opened her mouth and again her language defeated her. "Yes," she finally said, incapable of forming a longer sentence.

"Good."

The man's smile deepened, revealing a dimple in one lean cheek, his eyes positively twinkling as he took a seat opposite her, pulling the chair to face hers, so their heads were quite close. Rosa breathed in the scent of his aftershave—bay rum, she thought—and her heart gave a funny little flutter.

"Very well. Would you like a cup of tea?"

Rosa blinked at him. "*Verzeihung...*?" she asked blankly. *Excuse me?* Why was he asking her if she wanted *tea*?

"We're meant to converse as if we are at a tea party," he explained in careful English she was able to follow. "But perhaps first I should introduce myself." He held out his left hand for her to shake, rather than his right, which he still kept tucked behind his back. "Peter Gelb, pleased to make your acquaintance."

Rosa took his hand and shook it. "Rosa Herzelfeld."

"Where are you from, Rosa?"

"Berlin." She wished she could say more, but she simply didn't have the language. "And you?" she managed.

"Frankfurt, originally. But I have been living in Swiss Cottage for two years now."

"You are... experienced, then," Rosa said carefully. "I am new."

His smile deepened. "I could tell."

She laughed then and shook her head. "I am... not surprised."

"You'll come on quickly, I'm sure. These classes are very helpful."

Rosa nodded, not quite believing it. Everything still felt like such a struggle, and right then she could not imagine it ever being much different, although she certainly wanted to.

"I mean it," Peter told her, leaning toward her so that his head was even closer to hers. "I know it can seem so overwhelming at first," he continued, "but it does get easier."

Rosa nodded again, managing a smile. She'd understood the gist of what he'd said, at least, but she knew she didn't have the English to make a sensible reply.

Peter, seeming to sense this, sat back as he raised his eyebrows. "Well, then. Shall we talk about tea?"

"Tea...?"

"Yes, shall we have tea or coffee? And shall I pour, or shall you?" He held out his hand and mimed pouring tea from a teapot.

"I will pour," Rosa said, smiling as she let herself get into the spirit of things. With exaggerated courtesy, she mimed taking the teapot from him, even going so far as to pretend it was heavy, and was rewarded with Peter's unabashed grin, which made a frisson of delight shoot through her, like a spark. "Do you take... cream?" she asked carefully, and he gave a nod of approval.

"And sugar, for my sins."

"One lump, or two?" This, at least, was language she knew, thanks to working in a teashop.

He raised his eyebrows. "Would it be very extravagant of me if I said two?"

She didn't know the word "extravagant," but again she guessed the gist. "Very," she told him, her tone solemn, and he laughed out loud, causing a few people nearby to turn and look at them curiously.

"I think your English is coming on very well," he told her, and this time Rosa was the one who laughed.

Shortly after, the teacher called them all back together, and Peter inclined his head, a wry smile touching his lips, as he moved his chair back. Rosa returned his smile before she looked away, shifting her attention to the front. She'd enjoyed their conversation, and it had very little to do with the English she'd practiced. She'd felt as if she'd made a friend, which was undoubtedly foolish, since they'd barely spoken, and then only about how they took their tea! Although, in point of fact, she hadn't even mentioned how she took hers, not that she actually liked tea very much. Not yet, anyway. She was determined to like the English drink eventually.

The rest of the class passed in something of a blur, as the teacher, Isaac, led them in repeating various phrases—*it's nice to meet you, how is the weather today, please, you go first.* The two dozen people in the classroom repeated each one obediently by rote, reminding Rosa of little schoolchildren reciting their letters.

By the end of the class, she felt tired, but also as if she'd achieved something, and surprisingly, strangely exhilarated. The last, she knew, had nothing to do with the English she'd spoken. She glanced around the room as she made to leave, smiling at a few people who met her eye, but mainly looking for Peter Gelb. Unfortunately, he seemed to have disappeared. Fighting a sense of disappointment, Rosa left the Day Center with no more than a few waves and nods at various people. Perhaps she'd see Peter at another English class. She had already resolved to go again on her next day off, and the possibility of seeing him again caused her a little frisson of excitement.

Outside, the day was still sunny and warm, and Rosa decided to make the most of it. She'd walk to the zoo, just as she'd suggested to her mother. She didn't think it was too far, maybe a little more than a mile. Besides, Rosa wanted to see the city, and *experience* it. The cost of entry to the zoo was only a shilling, and while it was still one she could not really afford, she would do so this once. With her arms swinging by her sides, a jauntiness to her step, she started down the street, only to be stopped halfway down by someone calling her.

"Miss... Miss Herzelfeld?"

Rosa turned to see Peter Gelb walking briskly toward her, his wry smile tinged with an endearing uncertainty. Her heart lifted, expanded, even as she schooled her features into an expression of nothing more than pleasant inquiry.

"Herr Gelb," she greeted him, afraid she might have sounded a bit too stiff.

"Did you enjoy the English class?" he asked as he stood in front of her. Rosa noticed that once again he had that curious way of standing, with his right hand tucked behind him. He was smiling in a manner she liked, open and friendly, his eyes warm. She felt that little flutter of excitement again, and strove not to reveal it.

"Yes," she replied with a small smile, "very much. But now perhaps we speak German?"

He laughed, and then switched language with fluent ease. "Yes, although I must warn you, we might get a few looks. The British aren't too keen on hearing German spoken just about now, as you might imagine."

Rosa raised her eyebrows. "Even though we're Jews?"

"I'm not sure they don't make too much of a distinction." He shrugged the sentiment aside as his smile returned. "But I came out here to find you, as you'd left before I could speak with you."

"I didn't see you in the classroom," Rosa replied, and then blushed, because she'd just made it obvious that she'd been looking for him.

"I was helping tidy up. Isaac, the teacher, is a friend of mine."

"So, you weren't there to learn English," Rosa replied on a laugh. "I wondered, for you are far too good."

He hung his head in mock abashment. "I thank you for the compliment."

They subsided into a slightly awkward yet smiling silence, as they both stood there on the sidewalk, the sun shining benevolently above. Why, Rosa wondered, had he come and found her? She longed to know, and yet she was not bold enough to ask.

"I was wondering," Peter said after a moment, his smile now a little crooked, "if you wished to get an *actual* cup of tea—or coffee—rather than a pretend one. With me," he clarified quickly, and then let out a soft laugh.

"Oh." A rush of pleasure filled her at the suggestion, surprising her. She hadn't looked at another man since Ernst. She hadn't wanted to. She'd done everything she could to avoid male attention, wearing drab clothes and dressing her hair plainly. She hadn't wanted to risk her heart again, and yet she couldn't deny the excitement that Peter Gelb's invitation caused her.

But then, he was just asking her for a cup of tea. It didn't necessarily mean anything besides friendship, and she still wasn't sure she wanted more than that—not now, and maybe not ever.

"Unless you had other plans?" he continued when Rosa had

made no reply for several seconds. "Were you going somewhere?"

She hesitated and then admitted, "I was going to the London Zoo. I've never been, you see."

"Oh—" He couldn't quite hide the disappointment on his face, which made Rosa blurt in a rush:

"Perhaps you'd like to go with me?" She knew it was very forward, to ask a strange man to accompany her as she'd just done. A trip to the zoo was a good deal more than a cup of tea! And yet she found she couldn't regret it. She missed her friends from the *St Louis*, and her days in London had felt long and lonely; she hadn't realized quite how much until that moment. "That is, if you..." She trailed away, flushing, unable to be quite so bold as to finish that sentence.

"Go to the zoo with you?" Peter looked surprised by the suggestion, but thankfully also pleased. "Why, yes, I'd be delighted to."

Rosa let out a short laugh of relief and he asked, "Were you planning to walk?"

She nodded. "I didn't think it was too far, and it is such a nice day."

"Indeed, a walk would be excellent." He fell into step beside her. "In fact, I can't imagine anything more pleasant."

Rosa let out another little laugh of both relief and pleasure as they started to walk. She thought of the couple she'd watched out the window of the Lyons teashop, strolling along just as they were now. They'd seemed so carefree and happy, those two strangers, and now Rosa felt as if she shared their joy and ease. *This* was what she'd been looking forward to, longing for—the simple pleasure of a day out, the company of a kindred spirit, and a handsome man at that...

And what about Ernst? That was what you'd wanted with him.

That ugly little voice whispering inside her head had her

faltering in her step, so Peter shot her a quick look of concern. Rosa didn't want to think about Ernst. She didn't want to remember how warm his blue eyes had seemed as he'd gazed down at her, shot through with gold, just like his hair. She didn't want to remember how she'd basked in his attention, how when he'd come into a room, she'd felt herself light up from the inside, and everything else had fallen away, utterly unimportant. She certainly didn't want to remember how she'd brushed aside all those treacherous fears, those little whispers of alarm, when he'd carelessly told her that "at least she didn't *look* Jewish," or when he'd refused to be seen with her in public, soothing the rejection with so many pretty words. *I adore you, Rosa, you know that, but we have to be sensible.* Most of all, she wasn't going to think about what he'd been doing on Kristallnacht, or how she'd seen him that very night with a cut on his lip and a wild glitter in his eyes and she'd chosen not to ask any questions. Not to know.

"Rosa?" Peter asked gently, and she realized she was simply standing there on the sidewalk, staring into space. "Are you all right?"

"Yes." Rosa shook her head as if she could dispel all those memories, the silly, stupid girl she'd been. If only she could! If only it were that wonderfully easy. Well, she was going to try her best, especially on a day like today, bright and warm and full of hope. She turned to Peter with a firm smile. "Yes," she said, her voice as sure as her smile. "I'm fine. I'm very fine, indeed."

CHAPTER 13

London Zoo was right in Regent's Park, with wrought gates and a handsome pergola at its entrance, below a sign announcing the "Zoological Gardens." Rosa had enjoyed chatting with Peter during their walk to the zoo; he'd told her a bit about himself—he was a student at King's College and lived with his sponsor, a friend of his father's, in Belsize Park, only a few streets from her. He also offered suggestions for days out, and how to get cheap theater tickets, and which restaurants served the best German and Jewish food.

It had been lovely to speak with another person in a way she hadn't in weeks, if not months... Not since she'd been with her friends on the *St Louis* had she been able to converse so freely or easily.

"Do you like London?" she asked as they queued for tickets at the zoo's north entrance.

"I like it better than Germany," he replied frankly. "As I imagine any Jew does."

"Yes." She fell silent, and he raised his eyebrows in query.

"You don't sound entirely sure?"

Rosa considered the question. "It's not that I'm unsure," she replied slowly. "It is better, very much so. It's just..." She thought of her hours washing dishes, the smell of drains and sauerkraut in the flat. She hadn't come to England for a life of scrubbing and cleaning, desperately trying to make ends meet. "I want to *be* someone here," she burst out. More than she currently was, anyway.

"Be someone?" Peter repeated, sounding nonplussed, and maybe even slightly disapproving. "Who, then, besides yourself? Or do you mean someone important?"

Belatedly, and with some horror, Rosa realized she'd sounded like her father, pontificating about his significance, wanting to be feted and admired. The thought that she was at all like him in that way was deeply unsettling. "No, not someone important," she amended hastily. "At least, not someone *very* important. I just want to learn English and get a decent job and feel as if... as if I *belong* here, I suppose."

Peter was silent for a moment, his head cocked thoughtfully to one side, his hand still tucked behind his back. "I don't know if any Jew will feel as if they truly belong in this country. Not properly," he said at last. "Please don't mistake me, the British have been very welcoming for the most part, but we're still strangers, and I suspect we always will be. It is the nature of being Jewish."

That was a rather dispiriting thought, and yet one Rosa had to acknowledge was very likely true.

"Perhaps," she allowed. "But surely we can make something of ourselves in this new country."

They'd reached the front of the queue, and Rose took out her change purse, only to have Peter wave her aside. "Please, let me."

"You don't have—"

"I want to." He gave her a quick smile before he reached for his billfold and counted out some coins; it was only then that Rosa finally saw his right hand, and she understood why he kept it tucked behind his back. His third, fourth, and fifth fingers were all twisted and bent, the knuckles swollen so the digits were barely usable, the fingernails missing, seemingly having never grown back after they'd been damaged. It was a terrible sight, although he presented the money to the man at the till with both confidence and alacrity. As he tucked his billfold away, he turned to Rosa with a wry grimace. "My hand."

"I'm sorry..." she began helplessly, not knowing what to say.

He nodded briskly and kept walking, pausing for a second so Rosa could fall in step beside him. "It's all right. I know it looks dreadful, which is why I tend to keep it hidden. I don't want to scare little children away." He gave her a humorous look before continuing, "But it doesn't pain me, at least not too much. Not anymore."

Rosa swallowed. "What... what happened?"

Peter gave a little shrug. "I was a politics student at the University of Münster. When the race laws were passed, a bunch of brownshirts stormed into our lecture hall, roughed up some of the Jewish students. One of them stomped on my hand with his jackboot—he made sure I felt it." There was only a slightly bitter twist to Peter's lips, but Rosa's heart ached for him.

She'd heard of such things; it was why so many Jews had been leaving Germany—not just because of the restrictions on opportunity, but also due to the persecution and outright abuse. It was just, Rosa acknowledged painfully, she hadn't actually *felt* it herself. Not like that, anyway. She may have been forbidden to attend university, and turned out of her home, and made to feel inferior in a thousand both subtle and not-so-subtle ways, but she'd never been abused. At least, not physically.

"I'm sorry," Rosa said again.

"The reason it didn't heal properly," Peter continued, his tone turning diffident, "was that a bunch of us were rounded up and sent to a camp for a few weeks after. Dachau. Not a pleasant place." He paused for a moment, his throat working, before he resumed, "Anyway, I didn't receive any medical attention for my hand. If the fingers had been straightened and set, well then, maybe they would have healed properly, but who knows?" He shrugged, his philosophical smile returning. "I make do, just as anyone would."

Rosa admired his positive attitude, even as she felt a strange, uncomfortable sense of guilt. His experience was so far from hers—what, really, had she suffered that wasn't from her own awful folly? But she wasn't about to explain any of that, and in any case, it didn't seem as if he wanted to dwell on the past.

This was proved true when he straightened, tucking his hand behind his back, his smile firmly in place and his eyebrows raised. "What shall we see first? The giraffes? The elephants? The pandas?"

For a second, Rosa was blinded by a flash of memory—visiting Berlin Zoo as a small child and begging her father to let her see the giraffes. He'd hoisted her on his broad shoulders, and she'd felt his deep laugh reverberating through his chest as she'd clutched the top of his head to keep her balance. It was a moment that had been one entirely of joy, and yet was now shot through with a sense of loss and regret. She'd adored him, back then, in the uncomplicated way of a child.

Rosa blinked Peter back into focus and saw he was looking at her quizzically. "All of them," she replied firmly as she smiled back. "Absolutely all of them."

They began to stroll through the zoo, stopping at various enclosures to view the animals—the penguins in their newly built, state-of-the-art pool, the elephants towering above them, with Peter offering knowledgeable facts about each one that he read from a brochure he'd picked up at the entrance.

"Do you know the word in English, 'jumbo,' comes from the first elephant housed here at the zoo?" he told her, his expression one of lively, humorous interest. "Its name was 'Jambo,' from Swahili for hello, and it became a byword for anything large."

"Jumbo," Rosa repeated, wrinkling her nose. "I'll have to add it to my vocabulary."

"Indeed." He glanced back down at the brochure. "And Winnipeg, a black bear rescued by a regiment of the Canadian army, was housed here, until fairly recently. She was the inspiration, apparently, for Winnie the Pooh." He glanced up from the brochure. "Do you know the children's story? Very popular here in Great Britain."

Rosa shook her head. She didn't think she knew any British children's stories.

"Ah well," Peter said, "it's your typical view of English arcadia. Perfect pastoral paradise in this green and pleasant land." He dropped his light tone as he looked at her seriously. "We are really very lucky to be here, you know."

He didn't sound censorious, but Rosa felt a sense of rebuke, and maybe even judgment, all the same. Did she not seem grateful enough, she wondered, for the opportunities she'd been given? Admittedly, their flat was shabby, the building smelled of drains, and her job at the Lyons teashop was far from what she wanted to be doing for the rest of her life, *and yet...* Peter was right. She was lucky to be here. She didn't ever want to lose sight of that, especially when she thought of her parents, fuming at their reduced circumstances, or more poignantly, of Hannah and Rachel. They both would have jumped at the chance of immigrating to England, Rosa knew. They'd been happy for her, but there had been a touch of wistfulness, even of envy, to their good wishes, and Rosa had understood it. It had been how she'd felt about Sophie going to America, after all.

"I know we are," she told him seriously. "Not everyone aboard the *St Louis* was so fortunate." She'd already told him, on their walk to the zoo, about the fraught and fearful voyage across the Atlantic. Peter had been both sympathetic and horrified. Now, thinking of Hannah and Rachel, she had to blink rapidly a few times to compose herself. She earnestly hoped her friends were safe and well. She longed to hear from them, to be reassured that they were all right, but she suspected it would be months before there was any word.

"Shall we see the pandas?" Peter asked, and there was a gentleness to his voice and eyes that made Rosa's smile, usually so firm, wobble at its edges.

"Yes," she agreed. "Let's see the pandas."

But when they made their way to the panda enclosure, they found it empty, the space no more than a stretch of dusty ground.

"What's happened to them?" Peter wondered aloud in English, and a woman holding the hands of two young, snotty-nosed boys paused to answer him.

"They've been taken to the zoo in Whipsnade," she told him. "More's the pity. The orangutans, too, and the giraffes. My boys were that disappointed. They say the elephants will be next. At this rate, there won't be so much as a dormouse left in the whole bloomin' place!" She shook her head, disgusted yet also resigned, while Rosa looked on in perplexity and Peter gave a slow, knowing nod.

"There might not be," he agreed soberly. "But I suppose the animals will be safer there."

"You've got that right," the woman replied, "but what about the likes of us?" She didn't bother waiting for his reply, just bobbed a farewell and hurried on, dragging the two boys along with her. One of them twisted around to give Peter and Rosa a cheeky grin, and then stick his tongue out at them. Rosa let out a surprised laugh, which subsided when she saw Peter's somber expression.

"What was she talking about?" she asked him in German. "I must confess, I only understood every other word, if that."

"They're moving some of the animals," Peter explained. "Out to the zoo near Dunstable."

"But why?"

He paused before answering quietly, "Well, I expect because they are worried the zoo here in London might be bombed, when the war comes."

Rosa gaped at him for a few seconds; he'd been speaking German, but it felt as if he might as well have been speaking English, or some other foreign language. *Bombed?* She'd read herself that the zoo might close if there was a war, but somehow, she had not connected it to actual bombs falling right where they stood. "You mean... by the Nazis?" she asked faintly, although she knew that was what he meant. Still, she found it almost impossible to believe, or at least to accept.

"Yes, by Germany," he replied, "if there's war. Or really, when there's a war. I don't think it will be long now, do you?"

Rosa shivered, despite the warmth of the day. Everyone had been speaking about war for ages now—months, if not years. Back in Germany, hardly a single day had passed without a military parade, a regiment of Wehrmacht marching by, a flyover by the Luftwaffe, or some similar display of Germany's military might. And yet, war had still seemed like a theoretical thing, a concept she could accept without letting herself imagine its consequences—bombs falling, right here in London.

"It is the only way Hitler will be defeated," Peter stated. "You must realize that." There was a hint of challenge to his usually mild voice that made Rosa flush, just a little.

"Yes," she agreed after a moment.

She'd been reading the newspapers, as well as listening to the wireless, and while her understanding of English limited her somewhat, she'd still understood that a potential pact between Great Britain, France, and the Soviet Union had collapsed over the course of the summer, and now it was feared the Soviets would align with the Nazis. Tensions had exploded over Hitler's insistence that the Polish city of Danzig be returned to Germany, and both England and France had made assurances that they would defend Poland's independence in this matter.

With every passing day, Europe felt more and more as if it were poised on the threshold of something terrible... and yet, as Peter had said, it was the only way Hitler would be defeated. That was certainly something Rosa wanted.

"Even so," Peter allowed, his tone still somber, "it is startling, to see the reality right there in front of you." He pointed to the empty panda enclosure. "To think they've already moved the animals... they must know it's coming, and soon."

Soon.

Rosa tilted her face to the hazy blue sky, barely a cloud in sight. She tried to imagine it darkened by German fighter planes —Messerschmitts and Heinkels. She'd seen them before, in flybys at one of the many military parades the Nazis loved, their ostentatious and awful displays of sheer might marching down Unter den Linden—Hitler had had the linden trees cut down to make room for tanks—and darkening the sky above.

But here, over England? Over France and Belgium, the Netherlands too, for surely all of Europe would be affected. Out of instinct, Rosa slipped her hand into the pocket of her dress, her fingers reaching for the sliver of emerald she carried everywhere, only to encounter an empty pocket. For a second, she froze, horrified to think she'd lost the precious jewel, only to remember she'd wrapped it in her slip in her underwear drawer this morning, because she'd been worried she might lose it as she walked around the city.

A small sigh of relief escaped her, and she took her hand out of her pocket. The emerald was safe... even if no one else was, with the world about to be at war.

"Yes, it is startling," she agreed quietly as they turned away from the empty panda enclosure. "I don't like to think of war, even though I know it might be necessary. But I'm worried for my friends in Europe."

"In Germany?"

Briefly she thought of Ernst, the way he'd been the last time they'd spoken, before she'd emigrated. His handsome face had been twisted with regret, his lovely blue eyes shadowed as he'd reached for her hands. *I wish things were different, Rosa, of course I do... don't you trust me? Love me?* Had it all been an act, or had he felt as conflicted as Rosa had been, her heart and mind both sundered apart? She feared she knew the answer.

"No," she told Peter after a second's pause. "No one in Germany, not really." Her parents' parents were all dead, and her father had been an only child, her mother estranged from her only sister, who had married beneath her. "But in France, yes. And the Netherlands. I made friends on the *St Louis*," she explained. "I know it was only for a few weeks, but it was such a strange time, and we became very close... as close as sisters. My friends had no choice about where they were sent, and I fear for them, if it comes to war. Some say Hitler won't stop at Czecho-slovakia, or even Poland. He might want all of Europe."

"I'm quite sure he wants all of Europe," Peter replied with a rather grim smile. "The question is whether he will be allowed to have it."

"He won't," Rosa answered, the knowledge heavy inside her. "And that's why it will come to war."

They were silent for a few moments, absorbing this dark truth, and then Peter shook himself, reminding Rosa of a dog shaking his wet coat, and said, "Enough of this depressing talk! I believe there is a restaurant in the Regent's Building—shall we be very British, and have tea and cake?"

"That would be lovely," Rosa replied, and they headed towards the café.

Just a few minutes later, they were settled at a table on the terrace, having ordered a pot of tea and a selection of buns.

"Do you have family still in Germany?" Rosa asked after the waitress had left with their order.

Peter's face darkened briefly, and he nodded. "My parents. They could have emigrated when I did, but my grandmother, my mother's mother, was too frail to travel. My mother couldn't leave her."

Rosa could not imagine how difficult such a situation must have been. She supposed her own family had been fortunate in that way, not having to leave anyone behind. "Will they join you later?" she asked.

Peter shrugged. "Not until my *Oma* dies, and I could hardly wish for such a thing. And soon I fear it may be too late. Once war is declared, it will surely not be so easy to emigrate—and, heaven knows, it isn't easy now."

"No." It had taken her father a lot of money and calling of favors to get them on board the *St Louis*... and they still hadn't recovered the savings he'd lost. Rosa didn't think they ever would.

"What about you?" Peter asked. "You are here with your parents?"

"Yes." She spoke cautiously, knowing she didn't particularly want to talk about them, their complicated past. Her father might still want to be someone important, but Rosa doubted he wanted his Nazi connections known in this new country. She certainly didn't want them known.

"How are they finding it?" Peter asked.

Rosa let out a quick, unhappy sigh. "Difficult. My father is —or really, *was*—a doctor, and he cannot practice here."

Peter frowned. "If he takes the medical exams, he could."

"Yes, but he refuses." Peter looked surprised by this, and Rosa could hardly blame him. It was a particularly petty decision on her father's part, and one that only hurt himself. "He says he can't take them in English," she explained, feeling she had to defend her father at least a little, even if he didn't entirely deserve it. The old childhood loyalty was still part of her, deep down; at heart, she was still that child perched on his shoulders, trusting him to lift her high, to keep her safe. The knowledge was both shaming and aggravating.

"Perhaps he should be the one attending the English classes at the day center," Peter remarked, and Rosa let out a slight laugh of acknowledgment.

"Yes, if he could bring himself to attend. But he's a proud man, and I don't think he wants to ask anyone for help."

Peter nodded his understanding. "It is that way for many," he agreed. "To come to this country with nothing, to be dependent on charity... it is very difficult." The waitress came with their tea and buns, and he raised his eyebrows, a playful smile curving his mouth. "Now we can practice our English from this morning," he told Rosa. "Shall you pour?"

It was late afternoon by the time Peter walked Rosa back to her flat in Belsize Park. He lived only a few streets away, so he'd insisted on walking her right to her door, and remarked that he hoped to see her again, perhaps at the next English class.

"Yes, I hope to attend," Rosa replied, trying to ignore the little sting of disappointment his words had caused her; he had not suggested they meet again on their own, apart from the class, and she realized she'd wanted him to. "I certainly need to improve my English," she added.

"It won't take long, I'm sure," he told her with a small smile, and then with a little wave, his right hand tucked behind his back, he headed back down the street.

A sigh escaped her as she watched his retreating back. She'd had such a nice time today; it had been the sort of outing she'd once hardly dared to imagine for herself, exploring the city, making a friend. She was sorry it was over, especially since it wasn't clear that she'd have another one. At least she'd see him at the English class.

Resolutely, Rosa turned back inside. As she opened the door to her flat, she steeled herself for the sight of her mother, sitting alone and dejected in her usual chair. She was surprised to see the chair was vacant, and there was the citrus scent of her mother's favorite perfume, Worth's *Je Reviens*, heavy on the air.

"Fritz? Is that you?" Her mother's heels clicked on the linoleum as she emerged from her bedroom. She was wearing a new dress in midnight-blue satin, with a diamanté-studded belt at her trim waist. She'd done her hair and makeup, and she was just pulling on a pair of white kid gloves.

"Mother!" Rosa exclaimed in surprise. "You're going out?"

"Your father is taking me to dinner." Her mother's voice held a faintly petulant tone that made Rosa tense.

"Is that dress new?" she asked, trying to sound interested rather than censorious. It looked couture, and they certainly didn't have the money for that.

"Yes, as it happens," her mother replied, turning away. "Now I must find my pearls."

She went back into her bedroom, while Rosa slowly followed, standing in the doorway as a sense of unease deepened inside her, spreading outward.

"Mother, where did you get the money for that dress?" she asked in a voice that sounded hollow. She *felt* hollow, with an emptiness inside that she knew would soon swirl with dread. "Did you sell something?" It was surely the only possibility.

"Oh, what does it matter?" her mother exclaimed, sounding impatient. "Really, Rosa, it is so unbecoming to argue over pennies. You are sounding more and more like a fishwife, and you look like one too." She nodded toward Rosa's hands, now clenched into fists at her sides. "You have positively ruined your skin, you know, at that little restaurant."

"That's because I spend *ten hours* a day scrubbing pots and pans to pay the rent!" Rosa retorted, her voice rising in her anger. "While you sit at home and fritter away those very precious pennies!"

Her mother's eyes narrowed, flashing with fury. "Those pennies belong to your father, every single one," she snapped, her tone turning dangerous. "And never forget it."

"I earn—"

"Pennies, yes. I am quite aware of how little you earn, Rosa."

Rosa bit her lip, hard enough to hurt, knowing there was no point having a reasonable discussion when her mother was in such a querulous mood. And she was in such a querulous mood, Rosa knew, because her father had not yet come home. Would he remember his promise to take her out for dinner? Rosa doubted it.

Still not trusting herself to speak, she left her mother's bedroom and went to her own, tossing her handbag onto the bed with a growl of frustration. Her mother's dress had to have cost more than a month of her wages. A sudden, unwelcome suspicion crept over her like a dark, dense fog. Surely not. *Surely her mother wouldn't have...*

With her heart starting to beat hard, Rosa ran to her dresser and yanked open the top drawer. She riffled through the few, well-worn garments there, but there was no reassuringly heavy sliver of stone nestled among the cotton and silk. Her precious shard of emerald was gone.

CHAPTER 14

An icy sense of disbelief stole through Rosa in a numbing wave. *Gone.* The emerald Sophie had given her, that she'd vowed to keep safe, was gone.

And Rosa knew what had happened to it.

She whirled away from her dresser and stalked out to the living room, where her mother was standing in front of a tarnished, age-spotted mirror, primping her hair. She stilled for a second, her hands to her hair, her narrowed gaze meeting Rosa's furious one in the mirror before she, quite deliberately, Rosa thought, continued to arrange her hair.

"Mother!" Rosa's voice shook. "What have you done with it?"

"Done with what?"

"My *emerald.*" Her voice split the air in a jagged cry. "Did you... *pawn* it? For that dress?" Rosa didn't even know why she was asking; it was already painfully obvious. How on earth else would her mother have been able to afford such a dress? Unless she'd sold her own jewels, but Rosa already knew she would never have done that.

"Oh, Rosa, really." Her mother expelled an exasperated

breath. "Such a childish fuss about what really amounted to little more than a trinket."

"A *trinket*? Some trinket that paid for *that*." Rosa pointed a shaking finger at her mother's glamorous ensemble. "How much did you get for it?"

Her mother pressed her lips together as she turned away from the mirror. "Not as much as I should have."

"*Why*?" The word burst out of her as she clenched her fists, her nails digging into her palms. "Why take my little bit of emerald, when you have a whole case of jewels?" She hadn't even realized her mother had known about it; she certainly hadn't told her. Sometimes, Rosa realized, she forgot how much her mother watched and understood.

Her mother drew herself up, her eyes flashing with genuine ire. "Rosa, my jewels are precious, given to me by your father. I would never sell them."

"But you'd sell *mine*."

"It was a little shard, given to you by a girl you barely knew," her mother snapped in dismissal. "And the reason I didn't get much for it was because it hadn't been cut properly."

Rosa stared at her mother, her palms positively itching to slap her. In that moment, she thought she genuinely hated her, this woman who had given birth to her, who was meant to love her absolutely. She *despised* her, for her utter selfishness, her arrogant refusal to see Rosa's perspective at all, ever. "You had no right," she said quietly. "No right at all."

"Rosa, I am your *mother*—"

"And when have you ever acted like it?" Rosa burst out; to her shame, she sounded more hurt than angry.

For a second, her mother stilled, and Rosa thought she saw something in her face—the twist of her lips, the shadow in her eyes—that made her wonder if her mother regretted their relationship, or lack of it. Then her mother looked away.

"You're overreacting, as usual."

"*I'm* overreacting?" Rosa repeated in disbelief. In all their years together, their family fractured from the first, her mother had been the one prone to theatrics. "You did this for Father," she stated quietly, her voice throbbing with emotion. "Bought a new dress and have done your hair, decked yourself out in jewels, and all in an attempt to keep the interest of your own husband, who will look anywhere else but at *you!*"

As soon as her words rang out into the taut stillness of the room, Rosa wished she could take them back. She'd never, *ever* stated the truth of her parents' marriage to her mother's face. They'd all tiptoed around it, everyone knowing the truth yet never admitting it out loud, not in its gruesome specifics. And now she just had... and she had no idea how her mother would react.

"*Mutti...*" she began, like the whimper of a child, and then she stopped.

Slowly, her mother turned around. Her face was drained of color, her lips bloodless and her eyes burning like dark coals in her face as she closed the space between them in a few sure steps. Then, without hesitating for a second, she drew back her hand and slapped Rosa hard across the face. Her diamond ring caught the corner of her lip, and as Rosa pressed her hand to her cheek, her eyes smarting with tears, she felt a warm trickle of blood seep from the edge of her mouth.

"Don't," her mother said in a low thrum of a voice, "speak about what you don't know and can't possibly understand. *Ever.*"

Rosa wiped the blood from her lip as she straightened. "Don't," she replied, her voice as deadly as her mother's, "steal from me ever again. Or you'll find it's *your* jewels that are the ones in the window of the pawn shop."

"How dare—"

"Where is it?" she cut across her mother, her voice now as sharp as a knife. "Where did you sell it?"

"It doesn't matter—"

"Tell me."

Her mother gave a restless shrug as she sighed. "Oh, very well, but you won't be able to get it back. Suttons, on Victoria Street, near the big cathedral."

Rosa shook her head slowly. "How did you hear of them?" She thought her mother hardly ever left the flat.

"The woman upstairs told me about them. She said they gave good value, but I'm not sure she was right."

As if Rosa wanted to discuss how much she'd pawned her emerald for! She started back to her room to get her coat and handbag.

"Rosa, what are you doing?" her mother demanded when she'd returned to the living room. "You haven't any money to redeem it."

"I don't suppose you'll give me one of your jewels to do it," Rosa flung at her.

Her mother eyed her coolly. "No, I won't."

For a second, Rosa was tempted to storm into her mother's bedroom, upend her precious jewelry box, and take what she could. But no, she wouldn't stoop to the level her mother had.

As Rosa headed out of the flat, she heard the creak of a door, and realized the Rosenbaums, so quiet in their room, had heard the entire altercation, with her railing at her mother like a fishwife.

Rosa found she was too upset to care what they thought of her.

Suttons, on Victoria Street, was an elegant shop, not the dingy, squalid place Rosa had been half-expecting. Diamonds nestled on black velvet in the window, along with an array of other expensive-looking items—necklaces and rings, watches and even a sparkling tiara.

As Rosa opened the door, a frock-coated gentleman stepped smartly from behind the glass-topped counter.

"May I help you, miss? I'm afraid we are just about to close."

For a second, Rosa could only stare at him, unable to find the words in English. It was ironic, she thought bitterly, that her mother had the best English of them all, and she so rarely went out. She'd managed to communicate what she wanted here, obviously.

"My mother was here today," she stated carefully; the man's bland expression didn't betray so much as a twitch at her German accent. "She sold a... jewel. A... bit of a jewel. I... wish... to buy it."

"You wish to buy it back, miss? Was this a piece of emerald, perhaps?" His voice was as bland as his expression, solicitous without giving away anything.

"Yes..." Her voice trembled and she lifted her chin.

The man nodded slowly. "Do you have the receipt for the item in question, miss?" Rosa stared at him blankly. "Your mother was given a ticket," he explained. "Suttons keeps any item for six months in case the seller wishes to buy it back, but, naturally, you must produce the item's receipt."

Rosa understood the gist of what he was saying, and it filled her with despair. Why on earth hadn't she asked her mother for the receipt? Such a thought had not even occurred to her.

"I don't have it..." she admitted, and she heard the catch of tears in her throat.

The man nodded, his expression kind but also firm. "As I said, we keep items for six months. You may bring the receipt back at any point in that time in order to redeem the item."

"*Bitte...* please... could you tell me how much it costs?"

The man hesitated, and then, seeming to take pity on her, he reached for a ledger kept under the counter and flipped it open, running his finger down the page. "The gemstone in question was just over a carat, and was of particular good quality and clarity, although the way it had been cut, unfortunately, diminished its value somewhat. Your mother received thirty pounds for it."

"Thirty pounds!" It was an unfathomable amount of money to her; she only made a little over a pound a week. She would never be able to buy it back, even if she saved every penny she earned for the next six months, which she couldn't possibly do, anyway.

For a second, tears misted her vision and she tried to wipe her eyes as discreetly as she could. The man, in a gesture of gentlemanly kindness, produced a crisp, folded handkerchief from his breast pocket. Rosa took it with murmured thanks.

"I'm sorry," she told him after she'd wiped her eyes. "I cannot..." She struggled to find the word before finally settling on, "pay."

"Perhaps in time..." he suggested.

"Perhaps," she agreed, not wanting to admit just how impossible it all was. Her sliver of emerald, the one thing that had connected her to friends and even herself, was gone. Forever. She felt as if she'd betrayed her friends, committed an act of treachery against them. Worse, it felt like an omen; if she could not keep her word, would she be able to meet them at Henri's? "*Danke*," she whispered, handing the handkerchief back. "Thank you."

Blindly, her vision still clouded by tears, she started toward the door. The incandescent anger she'd felt for her mother was gone now, replaced by only a deep, wearying despair. It was only a jewel, she told herself, trying to rally and utterly unable to. Only a tiny sliver of a jewel...

But it had been so much more than that. It had *meant* so much more to her. And she absolutely hated the thought that she'd lost something she'd promised to keep, only a few months into her journey. She'd broken a promise—the most precious one she'd ever made.

Rosa fumbled for the door handle, pulling it open, only to stop suddenly when someone stepped inside, toward her.

"Rosa."

Her father put his hands on her shoulder, heavy and sure, as he steered her back into the shop.

Rosa blinked and wiped her eyes. "*Vati*..." The childhood name slipped unthinkingly from her lips. "What are you doing here?"

"Your mother told me what happened."

"My emerald—" Her voice choked.

"Yes."

Rosa blinked up at him, the first tendrils of hope winding around her heart. "Why..." she asked hesitantly, wiping her eyes again. "Why are you here?"

"Wait outside the shop," he told her. "And leave it to me."

Dazed, hardly daring to hope, Rosa stepped outside the shop. It was getting late now, shops starting to close, many of them already shuttered, people hurrying by, heads tucked low as the balmy warmth of the summer's day seeped away. Rosa wrapped her arm around her middle as she tried to compose herself. Her emotions felt like fragile, breakable things, and far too close to the surface. She feared if her father left the shop without her emerald, she would burst into tears, or worse. If he left *with* the emerald, her reaction might be the same.

A few endless minutes passed before he emerged from the shop, closing the door carefully behind him. Silently he held out his palm; the sliver of emerald was glinting in the middle of it.

Rosa let out a tearful gasp of relief. "How did you..."

"It doesn't matter."

Had her mother had to part with her own jewels? Rosa could not imagine she would have done so with any willingness.

She took the jewel and slipped it carefully into her pocket, swallowing against the threat of tears in her throat.

"Thank you, *Vati*," she whispered, and he nodded brusquely. As he straightened his sleeve, she noticed, with a lurch of poignant understanding, that he was not wearing his Blancpain watch that he'd bought from the luxury workshop in Villeret, France, many years ago. It was one of his most prized possessions. "Father," she said shakily. "Your watch..."

"Why do I need to tell the time," he teased wryly, "when I have nowhere to go?"

"Oh, Father. *Vati*." Unthinkingly, Rosa rushed into his arms, and her father pulled her into a tight embrace. She pressed her cheek against the scratchy wool of his jacket as she closed her eyes. "I'm sorry," she whispered.

"You have nothing to be sorry for, *Hase*."

She pulled back, wiping her eyes. "Mother wouldn't have bought the dress in the first place if you didn't—" she blurted, only to stop abruptly at the forbidding look on her father's face.

"Rosa, don't." The two words were flat, final. They never talked about what he did—the evenings out, the smell of perfume on his jacket when he came home, the way her mother's face crumpled into agony. Long ago, Rosa had become complicit without even realizing she was—a chuck on the chin, a secret-sharing smile. *No need to tell your mother.* She'd felt *proud*, grownup enough to share a secret. To be trusted with one.

She'd long ago shed that childhood fancy, and yet she felt as good as complicit now, as her father put his arm around her, and they turned toward the underground station.

"Let's go home, eh?" he said, squeezing her shoulders. "I promised to take your mother out to supper, after all, and I can't go back on my promise."

He'd gone back on far more important and even sacred promises than that, Rosa thought as she slipped her hand in her pocket and closed her fingers tightly around the sliver of emerald. How many more promises would he break?

And how many secrets would she be forced to keep?

Her throat too tight to make a reply, she walked with her father to the underground station and home. As they headed down the street, she noticed piles of sandbags heaped against the sides of shops. For a second, she had no idea what they were for—surely this part of London wouldn't be flooded?

Her step faltered, and her father followed her gaze, his mouth tightening as he gave a nod. "They're for protecting the shops from bomb blasts," he told her. "When the war comes."

Rosa recalled the empty panda enclosure, and what Peter had said earlier in the day. "You think it will come?" she asked her father.

"Yes, and soon." His arm tightened around her. "And God knows how we'll be seen then."

"What do you mean?"

He gave her a somber look as he slid his arm from her shoulder. "We might be Jewish, Rosa, but we're still Germans."

"But we *left* Germany—"

"I fear there are many who won't see it that way. Haven't you ever noticed someone look at you askance, just for speaking German?"

Rosa thought of Peter saying the same thing. "Yes..." she admitted slowly. She'd had her fair share of suspicious looks whenever she opened her mouth.

"All the more reason to learn English, I suppose," her father replied with an attempt at cheerfulness. "Perhaps I should attend those classes with you, especially if I am going to retake my medical exams."

He didn't look at her as he kept walking, although surprise had made Rosa stop in the street. She hurried to keep up with him. "You are? Really?"

He shrugged. "Well, I can't have my daughter supporting me for all my days."

"Oh, *Vati*, I'm glad." Rosa reached for his hand and gave it a quick squeeze. She knew how proud her father was, and how hard and humbling a step this was for him. As difficult, arrogant and irritating as her father could be, Rosa still loved him, and always would. What he'd done for her today showed the true man beneath all the bluster. "Thank you," she said softly, and he merely nodded and kept walking.

Rosa slipped her hand into her pocket and took out the emerald. Tears stung her eyes, and she blinked them back fiercely. She would never part with it again, she vowed, no matter what happened. Clutching the jewel, she hurried after her father.

CHAPTER 15

SEPTEMBER 1939—LONDON

The room was tautly hushed as the Herzelfelds and Rosenbaums huddled around the wireless, their faces drawn in tense lines of fearful expectation. It was the morning of the third of September, and the Prime Minister, Neville Chamberlain, was due to give a report on yesterday's demand that Germany withdraw from Poland.

Over the last month, the news of war had become grimmer and grimmer, a shadow that seemed to hover over the entire country, darkening by the day. Those first telltale signs of it coming had become commonplace—sandbags in the street, newspapers advising what to do in a bombing raid, even well-meaning advice on how to dispose of your pets, which was an apparently merciful thing to do, so they wouldn't suffer when the country was bombed, and no one could take care of them.

Rosa had taken to searching the sky every time she went out, half-expecting fighter planes to veer menacingly across it. There were advertisements for gas masks and guidance on how to tape your windows. Blackouts had already been trialed in Nottingham and Leeds, and those in possession of a garden were instructed on how to erect an Anderson shelter, which were free to those who qualified. The Herzelfelds, in their fourth-floor flat, did not.

Despite all these preparations, the threat of war still somehow did not seem real, at least not to Rosa. Her days were the same, scrubbing pots in the kitchen of the Lyons teashop, such drudgery punctuated by weekly English lessons at the Jewish Day Center and occasional afternoons with Peter Gelb.

Rosa and Peter had become good friends over the course of August, although—to both Rosa's frustration and relief—not more than that. After the tempestuous passion that had been her experience with Ernst, friendship felt like a welcome and comforting thing. And yet... it was only friendship. And the more time Rosa spent with Peter, the more she liked him—his wry sense of humor, the teasing glint that so often lit up his eyes, his practical and cheerful way of looking at things. More than that, she liked the way his smile made her heart skip a beat, and when he'd once kissed her cheek in farewell, she'd felt dizzy. Nothing more had happened, but somehow that had made it all the sweeter.

Sometimes, when she thought about what Peter had endured in Germany, she was gripped with an uneasy sense of guilt, that he could be so accepting, so forgiving, while she still burned against the petty injustices she'd been dealt. What was losing a home—or your pride—compared to Peter's crippled hand? And yet he seemed to bear no resentment or bitterness for the way he'd been treated, choosing to look toward the future instead.

"What annoys me, if anything," he'd told her once when they'd been walking through Regent's Park in late August, "is that with this hand, I won't be able to fight when there is a war. I just hope Blighty finds another way for me to serve."

"Don't you think you've paid enough?" Rosa had blurted. "You've already lost so much, Peter. To risk your life—"

"To risk my life for a cause such as *this*?" he'd cut across her, his voice gentle. "To defeat Hitler and the great evil he is visiting upon the world? I want that opportunity, Rosa." He'd turned to look at her seriously. "If it comes to war, and it will, you'll have to do something, as well. Not fight, naturally, but serve in some way. A young, able-bodied woman? They might have you hoeing rows of potatoes, or welding planes together. Something, I'm sure."

"I haven't thought about it," Rosa had admitted. "But I want to do my duty." Especially if it got her out of the sweltering kitchen of the teashop.

Now, however, as they sat and waited for the Prime Minister to speak, the imminent reality of war felt all too terrifyingly possible. Germany had invaded Poland, without any warning or declaration, two days ago, less than a week after Great Britain had made a pact to defend that country, should it be invaded. Yesterday, Great Britain had presented a formal ultimatum to Germany, and at the same time, the National Conscription Act had been passed, to conscript for military servicemen between the ages of nineteen and forty-one. Now, it was past eleven o'clock in the morning, and Chamberlain was set to speak at any moment.

Did anyone think Germany actually would have withdrawn? Rosa wondered. She had heard on the wireless that martial law had already been declared in France as the country mobilized for war, and her heart ached for Hannah, as well as Rachel. Were her friends worried they might be next? Only Sophie seemed safe. The United States was clinging to its neutrality, with Roosevelt's only statement after Germany had invaded Poland that the Germans must desist in bombing civilians.

"Oh, those church bells," Rosa's mother exclaimed, for in addition to the sound of the Bow Bells on the wireless, the bells of St Peter's Church in Belsize Square had been ringing with mournful insistence for the last few minutes. She rose from her seat in one abrupt movement, agitatedly patting her neatly coiffed hair as she paced the room.

"They'll stop in a few moments, Elsa," Rosa's father told her quietly. "Come sit by me." He'd been gentler with her mother since the whole altercation with the emerald. But it hadn't stopped Elsa from refusing to speak to her daughter for two entire weeks. Some things, Rosa, had thought, never changed.

Another thing that hadn't changed was her father, at least not as much as she'd wanted him to. Despite what he'd told her that day by the pawn shop, he had yet to accompany her to any English lessons, so while Rosa's English was coming on in leaps and bounds, her father's remained worryingly limited. The prospect of taking the medical exams seemed as far away as ever.

The wireless suddenly crackled to life, and the sound of Bow Bells was replaced by the buzz of static, and then the voice of a BBC announcer. "This is London. You will now hear a statement by the Prime Minister."

Rosa's mother hurried to retake her seat, while Rosa and her father leaned forward, straining to listen. Zlata Rosenbaum looked fearfully at her husband, and he reached out to hold her hand.

"Shalom," he said softly. Peace. It seemed a strange thing to wish for when they were right on the cusp of war, yet perhaps the Rosenbaums' peace, Rosa thought, had a greater source. In any case, it seemed to calm Zlata; she nodded, swallowing back her tears, as she clung to his hand.

After several, interminable seconds, the grave, reedy voice of Neville Chamberlain came on the wireless.

"I am speaking to you from the Cabinet Room of 10 Downing Street. This morning the British ambassador in Berlin handed the German government a final note stating that unless we heard from them by eleven o'clock that they were prepared at once to withdraw their troops from Poland, a state of war would exist between us. I have to tell you now that no such undertaking has been received, and that consequently, this country is at war with Germany."

Several seconds of silence followed that somber statement, and the Herzelfelds and Rosenbaums exchanged wordless looks; there was a dazed look in everyone's eyes, an uncertain sort of blankness. Were they expecting bombs to come raining down the moment war had been declared? Rosa wondered. She glanced out the window; despite thunderstorms the day before, the morning was warm and bright. It did not feel like a day for war.

Chamberlain continued: "You can imagine what a bitter blow it is to me that all my long struggle to win peace has failed. Yet I cannot believe there is anything more, or anything different, that I could have done and that would have been more successful."

Rosa turned back to the window as the Prime Minister's mournful words droned on, expressing his regret. *War*... it had finally, truly come to war. There would be soldiers marching off, and fighting, and dying. There would be fighter planes overhead, and bombs being dropped, explosions and fire. There would be the high, piercing drone of the air-raid siren, which they'd already heard, several times, in practice. There would be fear and uncertainty, and suffering and pain.

Rosa closed her eyes as the Prime Minister finished his speech: "May God bless you all and may He defend the right, for it is evil things we will be fighting against—brute force, bad faith, injustice, oppression, and persecution, and against them I am certain the right will prevail."

Another few seconds passed, and no one spoke. Rosa wondered what on earth there could be to say. Then, the BBC Home Service's announcer came back on, his elegant voice so jarringly unruffled. "That is the end of the Prime Minister's announcement. Please stand by for important government announcements, which, as the Prime Minister has said, will follow almost immediately. That is the end of the announcement."

The wireless went to faint static before the sound of the Bow Bells came back on.

Rosa's mother turned to her father in alarm. "What announcements?" she asked in German. "Fritz, what do they mean?"

"How we must prepare for war, I imagine," her father replied steadily.

Once again, Rosa found herself glancing out the window, but there was nothing but blue sky.

"Oh, those *bells!*" her mother cried, as the sound of the bells continued on the wireless, tinnily ringing out.

"They will tell us soon," Moritz Rosenbaum stated with calm dignity. "We must wait."

Sure enough, after a full minute of ringing bells, another BBC Home Service announcer came on, his voice as smooth as ever.

"This is London. The government has given instructions for the following important announcements. Closing of places of entertainment. All cinemas, theaters, and other places of entertainment are to be closed immediately, until further notice. In the light of experience, it may be possible to allow the reopening of such places in some areas. They are being closed, because if they were hit by a bomb, large numbers would be killed or injured."

Zlata gave a little gasp at this, and Rosa's mother shook her head. Rosa could hardly take it in herself.

The announcer continued, "Sports gatherings, and all gatherings for the purposes of entertainment and amusement, whether outdoor or indoor, which involve large numbers congregating together, are prohibited until further notice. This refers especially to gatherings for purposes of entertainment."

So, there would be no fun anymore, Rosa thought sadly. She didn't mind too much, as she'd only been to the cinema once since she'd arrived, and she hadn't been to any other large gathering, but it still felt sobering, to think of how much would be banned... and why.

"But people are earnestly requested," the announcer continued, "not to crowd together, in any circumstance. Churches and other places of public worship will not be closed."

Moritz breathed a shaky sigh of relief as he clutched Zlata's hand. Rosa knew they went to the synagogue in Belsize Park every Saturday; her family had yet to darken its doors.

"Air-raid warnings," the announcer went on, and Rosa could hardly bear to listen, although she knew she needed to know what he said. No hooters or sirens to be sounded except on the instructions of the police. Short, intermittent blasts or a warbling note would alert anyone to a possible air raid, or else by police whistles. Swallowing a laugh of near hysteria, Rosa wondered how anyone would be able to tell—it didn't say which sound would be alerted where, and yet the tone of the BBC announcer suggested such air-raid sirens might be sounded any second. "When you hear any of these sounds, take shelter." Rosa swallowed hard. "If poison gas has been used, you will be warned by means of hand rattles."

Poison gas? Zlata let out a small sound of distress and grasped Moritz's hands. Rosa's mother simply shook her head, her face pale, her lips bloodless.

"If you hear hand rattles, do not leave your shelter until you hear signs that the poison gas has been cleared away."

Dear heaven. Rosa closed her eyes, then snapped them open as she kept listening.

"All schools in neutral and evacuation areas in England, Scotland, and Wales are to be closed to lessons for at least a week from today. General: keep off the street as much as possible. To expose yourself unnecessarily adds to your danger. Carry your gas mask with you always."

It all sounded so unrelentingly *awful*. Rosa suddenly lurched up from her seat, causing her parents and the Rosenbaums to look at her in surprise.

"Rosa—"

"I'm going out." She reached for her coat, shoving her arms into the sleeves. Her mother half-rose from her chair.

"Rosa, you *can't*. Didn't you hear what he said? It's not safe—"

"Even if the Germans sent fighter planes over this very moment, it would take some time for them to get here," Rosa pointed out, although, in truth, she had no idea how long it would take. "I'll just be gone for a few moments." She left quickly, before anyone could make a further protest, and hurried down the stairs to the street.

Outside, Rosa took a few deep breaths of fresh air and blinked up at the bright, clear sky. She saw no fighter planes racing across it, even though she'd been half bracing herself. The air was full of the sounds of the city—the rumble of a lorry, the chatter of children and the trill of birdsong. Rosa could hear no menacing drone of planes or the shrill notes of an air-raid siren. All was as it should be, as it had been, and yet...

War. It had come to these shores, to all of Europe. Everything had changed, even if Rosa couldn't see it. She could *feel* it.

She started walking, not realizing where she was going until she turned onto Peter's street, knowing she needed to see him, be reassured by his steadying presence. There were a few people about—couples taking a stroll, people late for church. Rosa had the urge to grab them all by the shoulders, shake them. *Don't you realize what this means?* she wanted to cry. *Don't you realize your whole life, the whole world, has changed?* And yet she was out here too, walking along as if she hadn't a care in the world. How could anyone know how their lives had changed, when the sky was still blue, and the sun was still shining?

She reached Peter's building and rang the bell. A few seconds later, he appeared, his dark hair mussed and in just his shirtsleeves.

"Rosa—"

"You heard?"

"Yes." His face was somber, but she thought she saw a flicker of something almost like excitement in his eyes, and she could not understand it. "Do you want to come in?" he asked. "Or go out?"

"I don't know what I want," she admitted. "Go out, I suppose. Are you free for a walk?"

"Yes, let me just get my coat."

A minute or so later, they were walking toward Belsize Park.

"I can't believe it's real," Rosa said numbly as they fell into step alongside each other. "Air-raid sirens and bomb shelters and gas masks..." She shook her head, almost wildly. "I don't want any of it!"

Peter was silent for a moment, his face drawn into thoughtful lines. "You knew it was coming," he said at last. "That it had to come to this."

"Yes." Rosa spoke heavily. "But I still don't *want* it, Peter. Do you?"

"I want Hitler to be defeated." His voice was steady, as was his gaze when she looked at him miserably. "Don't you?"

"Yes, but..." Was she so selfish, Rosa wondered, to not want such a great evil defeated, simply because it might impinge on her life?

No, she realized, she was simply scared—scared for herself, for her friends in Europe.

"I'm sorry," she said at last. "I do want Hitler defeated. I'm just... frightened."

"I know. I am, too." Peter's voice was gentle as he put his arm around her, the first time he'd ever done so. Rosa leaned gratefully into his shoulder, breathing in the scent of his bay rum cologne, drawing comfort from his solid presence.

"Your parents are still in Germany," she remarked after a moment, the realization trickling through her, making her feel even more selfish. "Peter, aren't you worried for them?"

"Yes." The single word was stark and heartfelt. "But I know they feel the same as I do. Hitler *must* be defeated."

"Yes." Rosa nodded jerkily. "Yes, he must be."

"Why don't we sit down, have a coffee?" Peter suggested as he nodded toward the steam-fogged doors of a café. "The world always seems more sensible when you've something warm to drink."

Rosa let out a shaky laugh. "That sounds like some sort of proverb."

"Isn't it one?" he teased with a warm smile, his arm still around her shoulders as he opened the door of the café. Rosa found she missed its comforting heaviness when he removed it as they sat down.

It wasn't until she looked around and saw several familiar faces that she realized where they were—the Willow Café, where her father liked to hold court. It was crowded with émigrés, many of them in a high state of emotion, thanks to the declaration of war, while others simply sat and sipped their coffee or tea, looking somber.

"Do you... do you think we'll be attacked... soon?" Rosa asked in a low voice. She looked outside at the pale blue sky, still reassuringly empty, before she turned back to Peter. "The way they were talking on the wireless... I thought we'd be hearing the air-raid siren immediately!"

"I suppose they want everyone prepared," Peter replied. "And, in truth, I don't know whether we will be or not. Hitler might want to strike while we're still in a daze, or he might wait until he can mount a more sophisticated attack." He smiled wryly. "I'm not a soldier, so I'm afraid I couldn't tell you."

Both possibilities sounded dreadful, Rosa thought, and yet she knew they needed to be prepared. "And will you volunteer?" she asked. "I know you can't fight, but there must be something you can do."

"I'll certainly offer my services. It might be my speaking German ends up being helpful—and for you, too, as much as your English has come along."

"My German?" Rosa repeated in surprise. "How?" She'd have to be careful not to speak German in public as much anymore, she thought. The last thing she wanted was some patriotic do-gooder thinking she was a spy.

Peter shrugged. "Who knows? But if Great Britain is at war with Germany, they'll need to know the language, certainly."

He must mean intelligence, Rosa realized. Spying, or at least interpreting what spies found. The thought sent a thrill of excitement as well as trepidation through her. To be involved with something like that...! Or was she being silly, acting as if she were in a film, even to be thinking about such skullduggery? She let out a little laugh as she shook her head, before remarking wryly, "If I'm assigned anything, it will probably be in a soldiers' mess somewhere, doing just what I am now—washing pots!"

Peter laughed. "Think big, Rosa, why not?" he exclaimed, throwing his arms wide for a moment. "This war might present opportunities you could only dream of before. All sorts of things might open up—it will be all hands on deck, after all. What would you *like* to do?" He leaned forward, his eyes alight with interest. "If you could choose something?"

It was an intoxicating and overwhelming question, and one Rosa had never really considered before. Back on the St Louis, she'd told Sophie she wanted to do anything. All she'd wanted was freedom, a life away from Nazi Germany and her memories. But more than that? She hadn't yet dared to dream.

"I don't know that I've let myself think that way before," she admitted slowly. "And I don't know that I can now. It feels wrong, somehow, to think of this war as an opportunity."

Peter nodded, his smile slipping from his face as his expression turned somber. "That's true, but maybe it's the only way we can get through it... whatever comes."

Whatever comes. Again, Rosa looked out at the hazy blue sky. "Yes, you might be right," she said quietly. "We'll need something to keep our spirits up, I suppose." Could she use her German somehow, for the good of this new country of hers? Could she do something important, maybe even exciting? The possibility felt ephemeral, yet also tantalizing.

"Well," Peter told her, "maybe you'll discover what you want one day." He rested his hand on hers and Rosa smiled back at him, a fluttery feeling starting in her stomach that made her think, fleetingly, of other sorts of dreams. Then Peter's hand tightened on hers, and his mouth turned down in an uncharacteristic scowl. "That pompous old windbag," he muttered, his face darkening, and Rosa twisted around to see who he was talking about.

When she saw who had just entered the café, his hair rumpled and a scarf draped theatrically over his shoulders, her heart sank and her hand tensed underneath Peter's.

It was her father.

CHAPTER 16

MAY 1940—LONDON

They began to call it "the Phoney War." Rosa hadn't known what the word phoney meant, and Peter had explained it to her.

"It means it doesn't feel real," he'd told her, "because nothing has really happened yet."

"Well, I for one am grateful not to be bombed," Rosa had replied with a small smile, and Peter had given her a smile in return, but Rosa had feared that it hadn't reached his eyes.

Ever since that afternoon at the coffeehouse, where he'd seen her father stride in with such careless arrogance, an uneasy awkwardness had sprung up between them that Rosa hated, yet knew she could do nothing about. Her father was who he was.

"Do you know him?" she'd asked Peter, when she'd registered his scowl aimed straight at her father.

"Not really. I've only seen him come in here and start pontificating about how much he knows and how important he was as a doctor back in Germany. I've heard some people say he even treated *Nazis*." His lips had twisted in derision.

Rosa's cheeks had burned as she had realized she could not stay silent. "He did," she'd told Peter quietly. "Although I don't know how much choice he really had in the matter." She'd felt ashamed for defending her father, when she'd *known* that the course of action he'd taken had been indefensible. "He was important," she'd finished, "although perhaps not as important as he thought."

Peter had turned to her in surprise. "*You* know him?"

Rosa had swallowed, forcing herself to meet Peter's gaze. "Yes, I do. He's my... father."

"Your *father!*" Peter had looked completely flummoxed. Rosa had gone to some trouble *not* to mention her parents, because of how complicated it all had been. Now, with her father just a few feet away, she'd had to. "But he..." Peter had begun, before he'd stopped. "I'm sorry," he'd said after a moment, his tone oddly formal as he'd glanced down at the table. "You must think me terribly rude."

"No," Rosa had replied with a trembling laugh. "Just honest."

A silence had fallen between them then unlike any other, tense and unhappy. Rosa had always felt comfortable in Peter's company, at ease with him and herself, but right then she'd felt awkward, apologetic, as if she were hiding secrets. And hadn't she been? She might have just been honest about her father, but not about herself.

Peter, she'd noticed wretchedly, hadn't even been able to look at her.

"Rosa—" he'd begun after a moment, but before he could continue, the loud, shrill shriek of an air-raid siren, rising insistently, pierced the air. Rosa had stared at him, her eyes widening with horrified realization, as the sound died away before relentlessly starting again.

"It's happening already..." she'd gasped. She could barely believe it.

"It might just be a practice," Peter had replied, but he looked worried. Already, people had scrambled up from their chairs as they looked around wildly. No one, including her father, had seemed to know where to go.

"To the cellar!" someone had called from the back of the café, and everyone had hurried after them, half-stumbling down the narrow stairs to crowd into the dank, dark space while the air-raid siren had continued, its note rising and then falling, over and over again.

No one had spoken as they'd stood in the cramped cellar, squinting in the darkness, the only sound the ragged draw and tear of panicked breathing, and the distant shriek of the siren. Rosa had stood with her arms wrapped around herself, her legs starting to cramp, her ears straining for the whine of fighter planes, the muffled thud of a bomb exploding—at least, that's what she'd *thought* it might sound like, but the truth was she had absolutely no idea. Peter stood next to her, tense and still, but she could not see her father in the dark, crowded space.

Finally, someone had ventured to speak. "I don't hear any bombs."

For some reason, this had been followed by a titter of nervous laughter that had rippled around the room and made everyone breathe a bit more easily. Eventually, after what had felt like an endless amount of time but, in reality, had most likely only been a few minutes, the all-clear sounded—a long, single note that stretched on and on, causing everyone to squint about uncertainly at each other, until someone had realized what it was, and again they'd laughed, a bit abashedly, as if they all should have been old hands at this, already.

When they'd emerged from the cellar, Rosa's father had seen her and strode over, wrapping her in his arms before Rosa could say a word. She'd returned the hug gratefully, yet with some reluctance, sensing Peter's gaze upon them. Peter had swiftly made some excuse about needing to return home, while Rosa's father had regarded him indifferently, and Rosa had let him go. She'd feared their friendship had been forever changed, and not for the better.

"I told you, you shouldn't have gone out," her father had said sternly.

"Actually, it was Mother who said that," she'd replied, "and you went out, as well, obviously."

Her father had harrumphed, and they hadn't spoken again as they'd returned home; the streets had been filled with milling crowds, everyone anxious and yet also strangely excited, wondering if any bombs had actually fallen. Later, they'd learned it had been, as Peter had thought, just a practice.

Rosa hadn't seen Peter for several weeks after that, an absence that had tried her sorely. They'd developed the habit of going out for coffee after English classes, but Peter had stopped going to the lessons at the Jewish Day Center now that his university lectures had begun again. As for their outings—to the cinema or for a walk—those were not even a possibility. The cinemas might have reopened after only a week of closure, but Rosa hadn't been brave enough to seek Peter out herself, and he didn't seek her out, either, which had made her days feel emptier than ever, nothing more than work and home and back again. She hadn't realized just how much his companionship had meant to her, how his presence had filled both her days and her thoughts, until he as good as disappeared—from the former, if not the latter.

Then, in early October, he had suddenly appeared in front of the Lyons teashop as she was leaving at the end of the day.

Rosa had stopped in surprise and hope, and Peter had given her a ruefully apologetic smile.

"Friends again?" he'd asked, and she'd felt a rush of both gratitude and joy that he was back in her life. She realized she was glad that he hadn't pretended he'd simply been busy with his university lectures. The knowledge of her father, who he was and what he'd done, would, Rosa had suspected, always be between them, but on that day, they'd made a silent pact not to discuss it, and it was one Rosa was willing to live with. Looking at Peter then, she had only felt relieved—and happy.

They'd gone out for a meal at a cheap café, and caught up on each other's news, although, in truth, Rosa hadn't had much. She'd finally heard from Sophie, who was now working at the Jewish Community Center in Washington DC, using her German in a way Rosa wasn't, at least not yet. She still hadn't heard from Hannah or Rachel, a fact which had worried her. What if they were never able to get in touch? She'd kept her emerald with her everywhere, after the experience with Suttons; she'd even slept with it, under her pillow or clutched in her hand. Her relationship with her mother had remained strained over the incident, although they were at least cordial to each other.

"Have you been interviewed by the Enemy Alien Board yet?" Peter had asked. As soon as war had been declared, a government board had been set up to interrogate every German refugee in Great Britain, to make sure they did not pose a danger to society, and more importantly, to the war effort. There were tribunals being formed all over the country, with several in London, to classify all Germans as either Category A, B, or C, with C being the least dangerous, and those classed as A to be interned elsewhere, possibly for the duration of the entire war. It made Rosa feel as if their acceptance into this country had been nothing more than a sham; she knew many Jews felt the same. Why, after months or even years of living in England, were they now being treated not just as aliens, but enemies?

"Not yet," she had told Peter. "Have you?"

He'd nodded. "Yes, just a few days ago. They didn't ask much, once they learned I was Jewish." He'd paused, and then said quite deliberately, "I'm sure it will be the same for you and your family."

Rosa had glanced down at her half-eaten meal, her appetite vanished. "You can't know that," she'd said quietly, like a confession. With just a little digging, a tribunal could discover that her father had treated Nazis, that he'd hosted Adolf Eichmann in his own house! It wouldn't be so hard, especially since some émigrés, including Peter himself, already knew, or at least suspected, something of what her father had done. Rosa's parents, however, had remained resolutely dismissive of such a possibility, and Rosa clung to their conviction with hope.

"No," Peter had agreed after a moment, "I don't know. But your father surely isn't a *danger* to the government, Rosa, no matter what Nazis he gave Salvarsan tablets to for their syphilis." His voice had held a slight edge that Rosa had done her best to ignore.

"I hope not," she'd replied quietly, and thankfully, they'd left it at that.

It had been a relief to make up with Peter, even if things, Rosa knew, hadn't been quite as they once were, and perhaps never would be.

As the months had gone by, the tension and anxiety caused by Great Britain's declaration of war subsided into a wary watchfulness, and then an almost bored indifference, as life had gone on, mostly as normal, much to everyone's surprise and relief.

Although Great Britain had a naval blockade against Germany in place, there had been no major military action, and no real disruption to daily life in London—every morning, Rosa showed at the teashop, and every evening she left with reddened, work-chafed hands and aching feet. She still cooked, cleaned, and spent her spare afternoons either exploring the city or practicing her English, meeting up with Peter every so often. They remained friends, but nothing more, and Rosa was achingly conscious of the slightly chilly distance that existed between them, even as they continued to spend time together.

As autumn had slipped into winter, it had felt almost easy to forget there was a war on at all, save for when someone gave Rosa a suspicious look when they heard her speaking German, or the Rosenbaums and Herzelfelds gathered together to listen to the evening news on the wireless, with its solemn summary of all Great Britain was doing to combat Hitler's evil.

One night, after the news briefing which had seemed particularly grim, Moritz, without any prompting, had brought out his violin. "May I play?" he'd asked hesitantly, and Rosa's parents had exchanged surprised looks.

"Yes, please," Rosa had said. "We'd be glad if you would."

He had tucked the violin under his chin and then, after a second's pause, drew the bow across the strings. The first note had been exquisitely mournful, a poignant and beautiful lament. As he'd continued to play, Rosa had felt tears sting her eyes. She didn't know the piece of music, and yet its sorrowful notes spoke to her soul—of grief and pain, of loss and fear, and yet also of hope, like an ember buried in the ashes, flickering to life.

Everyone had been silent, rapt, and when he'd finished the song, Rosa couldn't help but clap, softly, because it had felt too sacred for anything else. Her mother, she had seen, had been wiping a tear from her eye, as discreetly as she could.

"That was very good," her father had said gruffly. "Very good indeed."

"It is Klezmer music," Moritz had explained as he lowered his violin. "Yiddish. A song of lament, for surely that is what we should play in these times."

"And yet," Rosa remarked, leaning forward, "it felt hopeful too, at the end."

He had smiled at her, his dark eyes gleaming behind his glasses. "Ah, yes. Even in lament, there is always hope, for our

God is faithful." He had held her gaze for a moment. "Even in this."

Rosa had nodded slowly. And in that moment, the poignant notes of the music still reverberating through her, she had believed him.

As the months passed, Rosa did her best to use the time well; she practiced her English, and saved as much of her hard-earned wages as she could, and hoped for a day when she'd be able to serve her new country and maybe even dream a little bigger, just as Peter had once said.

She went for walks with Peter, or occasionally to the cinema, and listened to Moritz play the violin—other sad laments, but also some rousing folk music they danced to on her mother's birthday, everyone whirling about and laughing, even dour Zlata and her usually prune-mouthed mother.

Life had, somewhat to Rosa's surprise, taken on a shape she'd become used to, a form she could accept and even enjoy, in small and hesitant yet surer ways.

Then, in May, it all changed, and those fragile, barely-there dreams evaporated into an ephemeral mist as the grim reality of their situation came right to their door.

Rosa came back from work early one evening to find her mother in a state, pacing the living room and wringing her hands. Her father was nowhere to be seen. Over the last few months, her parents had done little to improve their circum-stances; her mother had met a few fellow Jewish refugees, elegant ladies like herself with whom she played cards and drank cocktails on occasion, although they could ill afford such frivolity. Her father still held court at the coffee shop, and talked about sitting his medical exams, although he'd done noth-ing, as far as Rosa could see, toward that end. They both seemed to be waiting for something to change, but what?

The Rosenbaums seemed far more industrious. Moritz had found a job in a music shop, repairing violins, and Zlata took in extra washing and sewing. Rosa suspected the couple viewed her parents with more mystification than disdain; they could not conceive of how people could be so very *useless*. Sometimes, neither could she.

"Where have you been?" her mother exclaimed, turning away from the window, a spray of pink cherry blossoms brushing the pane, as Rosa, tired and sweaty from ten hours spent in a hot kitchen, came through the door.

"Working, as always," Rosa replied, a slight edge to her voice. For over nine months, she'd been the only wage earner in their little household, and while she knew there was no point in giving vent to her frustration, the fact of it still rankled, especially when her mother acted so aggrieved that she wasn't always available.

"I think something terrible has happened," her mother pronounced, a tremble to her voice as she fluttered around Rosa like an agitated moth. "But my English isn't good enough to be sure." Rosa knew her English had surpassed her mother's some months ago. "Read this," her mother urged, "and tell me what it says." She thrust a single slip of paper in front of Rosa's face, so close its edge brushed her nose.

"Very well." Rosa took the paper and smoothed it out, fighting her own mounting anxiety at the prospect of bad news. For the last few weeks, ever since Germany had invaded Norway and Denmark, it had seemed to be on the cusp of attacking the Low Countries and France, and Rosa could hardly sleep for thinking about it.

While Rosa had had several letters from Sophie since she'd gone to America, it was only in the last few months that she'd finally heard from both Hannah and Rachel. Hannah was working as a secretary in Paris, and Rachel and Franz were living in an apartment in Haarlem. They'd both been managing to eke out an existence for themselves, but that would all change if Hitler invaded... But no, surely, he couldn't. Poland and Czechoslovakia had been bad enough, but *France*? The Maginot Line would hold. It would have to...

"*Rosa!*"

"I'm reading it, Mother."

Rosa would have liked to have sat down first, and taken her shoes off her aching feet, and maybe had something to eat or at least a cup of tea, a drink she had come to appreciate in her ten months on this isle, but she could see how upset her mother was, and it caused a corresponding tightening of anxiety in her stomach. What if something terrible *had* happened? She was thinking of Hannah and Rachel, and the threats they might face, when she saw the insignia on the top of the letter—the Aliens Department of the Home Office. This wasn't about her friends, or a potential invasion, Rosa realized. It had to be about her father.

The letter was succinct, a mere two sentences, requesting that Friedrich Herzelfeld report to the police station in Rochester Row, London, "forthwith upon receipt of this letter."

"But why?" her mother exclaimed once Rosa had explained the letter's contents. "*Why?* They finished with all the tribunals back in February. Your father was classed C, we all were—"

"Yes, I know," Rosa cut her off, her voice tense. During the tribunals, only a handful of Germans in Britain—five hundred or so out of seventy thousand—had been classified A, enough of a threat to intern. But now, with Germany having attacked Norway and Denmark and poised to invade France, maybe even Great Britain itself... Perhaps Germans—Germans like her father—were seen as more of a threat. "It might just be a formality," Rosa told her mother, although she wasn't sure she believed it. "Maybe he needs to fill out a form, or re-register, or something."

Her mother shook her head, a panicked back and forth. "What will we do without your father?"

It was not a question Rosa had ever asked herself. She would get along without her father just fine, she thought with a sudden spurt of bitterness. It wasn't as if he was providing for them, after all. In fact, they would save money with one less mouth to feed, and a rather substantial and demanding mouth at that. And yet... as much as he aggravated and exasperated her, she knew she did not want to lose him. She certainly didn't want him to suffer in some forsaken camp, who knew where, while she and her mother struggled on alone.

But she didn't say any of this to her mother. She merely folded up the letter and put it back in its envelope.

"Where is he?" she asked instead. "He should report to the police station as soon as possible, to show he has nothing to hide." Even if he *did* have something to hide... but maybe the police, the Aliens Department, already knew it? Was that why he had been summoned?

"I don't know where he is," her mother replied irritably. "At that wretched *coffeehouse*, no doubt." She pressed her lips together, clearly not wanting to say anything more. There had been no more late nights, since that episode back in August, when her mother had pawned her emerald and her father had taken her out to supper, smelling of another woman's perfume. "He's usually back in time for supper."

"Yes..." How long would the police be willing to wait? Rosa wondered. How urgent was this summons?

"Oh," her mother said, her tone dismissive as she turned away. "There was a letter for you, as well."

"A letter for me?" Rosa's heart lifted with hope. She longed to hear from Sophie or Hannah or Rachel. She'd had so very little news.

"Yes, on the table."

Rosa picked up the envelope; it had a London postmark and

looked very similar to the one for her father, from the Aliens Department, a fact which made her throat dry, and her heart do an unpleasant little flip. *Surely not...*

She slit the envelope and pulled out the letter. With a sickening lurch of realization, she saw that it was exactly the same. Just like her father, Rosa had been commanded to the Rochester Row Police Station "forthwith upon receipt of this letter."

CHAPTER 17

"Please follow me."

Rosa was entirely numb, her terror too deep to truly feel, as she followed the officer at Rochester Row to a police van, known to Londoners as a Black Maria, waiting outside the station of Victorian brick. Behind her, her father continued to swagger and bluster, as if he had some say over their fate, some power.

"What is the meaning of this?" he demanded. "We were both classed Category C months ago—"

"Please, silence," the police officer escorting them cut across him, his tone severe. "It will all be explained to you at the appropriate time."

Her father, still bristling, fell furiously silent.

It had only been an hour since Rosa had been back in their flat, reading the letter from the Aliens Department, but it had felt endless, as if days had passed and worlds had shifted in the space of sixty heart-rending minutes. She'd had to wait for her father to come home, her mind and heart both racing, while her mother had wrung her hands and moaned about what she would do, if both Rosa and her father were taken from her.

Rosa had been tempted to whirl around and snap at her mother what was *she* supposed to do, if she was interned heaven only knew where, but she hadn't wanted to put such a terrible prospect into words, make it more of a reality than it already was. Maybe it really was just a formality, she'd told herself, again and again.

Now, as she clambered into the back of the Black Maria, it felt far from a formality. The barred door clanged shut as her father scrambled in after her. They sat on rough wooden benches, opposite each other, as the van started.

"Are we being arrested?" Rosa asked after a moment, her voice sounding small. The back of the van smelled horribly stale, of urine and sweat, and she covered her nose with her hand.

"We are going to be questioned, I should think." Her father narrowed his eyes as he glanced out the window, through the bars. "I imagine, with the imminent invasion of France and the Low Countries, they want to be especially careful, although I fully intend to complain about our treatment. We are respectable, working people—"

She was a respectable, working person, Rosa thought rather sourly. Her father had not drawn a wage in the nearly a year since they'd arrived. But before she could put such a retort into words, the meaning of what he had said slammed into her. According to her father, an invasion of France wasn't a mere possibility, but *imminent*. Inevitable.

"France..." Rosa whispered. *Hannah*. And Rachel and Franz in the Netherlands, as well. "Will it really come to that?" she asked, as if he could possibly know for certain. Sometimes, Rosa thought, she acted the way everyone else seemed to—as if her father had special knowledge or power, as if his charisma would bridge chasms. Sitting in the back of a rattling Black Maria, the irony was bitter.

"Don't be a child, Rosa," her father tutted. "Of course, it will."

He sounded both certain and indifferent, and that stung more than his dismissive admonishment. She hated to think of her friends being under Nazi rule once again. What would they do? How would they survive?

How would she?

"There's no need," her father continued after a moment, his tone turning diffident, "if they ask, to go into what our life in Berlin was like. That has no relevance here. Obviously."

No need to talk about how they'd entertained Nazis in their home, he meant, Rosa thought scornfully. How they'd filed in, laughing, joking about the pills her father gave, how for a Jew he had the best schnapps. They'd been indulgent, with a razor-sharp edge of cruelty, and it had terrified Rosa, even as she'd done her best to keep her laughter light, the smile on her face, wondering when it would all start to go horribly wrong...

A sudden, overwhelming fury rose up in her in a howl. If her father hadn't sold his soul to the Nazis... If he hadn't cajoled her to help him host... *They're just men, Rosa, and they can help us, think of it that way...* If he'd just kept his head down, been willing to lose his medical license, like just about every other Jew in Germany... They wouldn't be here. They'd still be safely classed category C, under no suspicion, *surely.*

"The whole reason we're here," Rosa spat, "is because they must know all that already. They probably have a file on *you* an inch thick, Father."

Her father glared at her, his eyes narrowed. "Be quiet, Rosa," he snapped, and then glanced meaningfully at the driver, separated by a wooden partition. Rosa doubted he could hear them over the rumble of the van, and, in any case, they were speaking German. "I don't think we need to worry," her father continued. "I should think it unlikely that they know anything."

"And yet you were so *important*," Rosa couldn't keep from

reminding him. She knew she was behaving in a petty and petulant way, but right then she couldn't help it. She was *scared*...
and angry. They didn't have to be here. If her father had chosen
differently, back in Berlin, they wouldn't have been.

"Important enough to keep you in fine clothes and out of
harm's way, yes," her father replied coolly. "I suppose it's easy
for you to be so smugly self-righteous now, Rosa, but let me
remind you, *you're* in the back of this van with me."

His words caused a dam to break inside her, the emotions
rushing out. She doubled over, her arms wrapped around her
waist. "I never wanted any of this," she wept, the tears streaking
down her cheeks unchecked. "Not any of it, ever. You should
have kept me out of it—"

"With your mother out of her head half the time on seda-
tives?" Her father tutted again. "I needed a hostess, and don't
pretend, my dear, that you didn't enjoy it, at least a little. The
attention, the admiration. You lapped up every second. I saw
you myself."

"I didn't..." Rosa whispered. She scrunched her eyes shut, as
if she could block out her father's voice, the damning memories.
She hadn't *lapped it up*, but yes, she'd enjoyed Ernst's admiring
smile, the way his gaze had lingered...

Her father let out a huff of disbelieving laughter. Rosa
pressed her hot, tear-streaked face into her knees, desperately
wishing everything had been different. That she had.

"Everything I did," her father said after a moment, his tone
turning quiet and steely, "was to keep you and your mother
safe."

Rosa lifted her head. "And yourself," she felt compelled to
point out. "You've always thought of yourself." In her mind's
eye, she pictured her father back at their villa on the Wannsee—
dressed in black tie, holding a glass of champagne, smiling tolerantly at the Nazi officers who amused themselves by humoring
their pet Jew, until it had become impolitic and then even

dangerous to continue to do so. That was when her father had decided it was time to leave.

"Yes, and myself," her father agreed tautly. "Really, is that so wrong, Rosa?"

She clenched her hands into fists, bunching them in her lap. *Was* it wrong? She felt as if she didn't know anything anymore; all she could feel right then was fear, cold and creeping, drowning everything else out, an iciness in her soul, a scream in her head. "This was meant to be our new start," she whispered. "Away from Berlin. From... from everything there."

Her father was silent for a moment. When Rosa dared to look at him, she saw how old he looked, his gaze distant and reflective. Then he straightened, smiled with his usual jocularity. "Well, it's not as if they have anything on us," he resumed in the plummy tone she knew too well. "We've done nothing wrong, and we're certainly not spies. We have to be released. It's only a matter of time, Rosa, I'm quite sure of it." He pursed his lips. "And I'll have something to say about the way we've been treated!"

Half an hour later, Rosa found herself in a classroom at the Oratory School in Brompton, attached to the magnificent church, where an interrogation unit had been set up. Her father had been separated from her as soon as they had exited the Black Maria; wildly, Rosa had wondered when—and even if—she would ever see him again.

She'd briefly glimpsed the massive, ornate dome of the church before she'd been ushered into the school and brought to a hallway that had clearly been requisitioned for women who had been arrested. Classrooms had been turned into interrogation rooms, and various women—*suspects*—sat in chairs along the walls, waiting for their turn to be questioned. Rosa saw that some looked terrified, others resigned; some were dressed in their finest clothes, others shabbily, in garments that were well-worn and patched. There was a mother with two young children, one of them weeping quietly as she put her arms around her, and another woman who glared at everyone whose eye she chanced to meet. Some spoke German, in low, fearful voices; others spoke flawless English. Yet they were all here; they were all under suspicion... just as she was.

Rosa waited on a wooden chair outside one of the classrooms, her body twanging with tension, her eyes gritty with fatigue, her mind racing down dead-ends. What was happening to her father? What would her mother do, if both she and her father were, heaven forbid, taken somewhere? What about her job, her life? What about *Peter*? She shuddered to think how he might react, knowing she'd been called in for questioning. Having to tell him why...

Finally, after an endless hour, she was called into one of the classrooms.

Two stony-faced men in plain clothes sat at the front, a typed sheet that Rosa couldn't read lying on the desk before them. Managing to murmur a greeting, she perched on the edge of a chair set on the opposite of the desk, tucking her hands under her thighs. Already she felt queasy, lightheaded, her heart beginning to hammer.

Then the questions began—one after the other, relentless, merciless. *Did she support the German nation and its military and political aspirations? Had she been in contact with anyone of Nazi sympathies since she'd arrived in Great Britain? Had she given money to any organization that supported Nazi endeavors? Was she willing to engage in war work that would be to the detriment of her native country?*

"I am *Jewish*..." Rosa said, her tone turning more desperate with each answer, her German accent becoming more pronounced, in her agitation. "I have no allegiance to Germany... none at all... I left it because I didn't want to be

there... you *know* what the Nazis have been doing to Jews..."
Her voice trailed away as one of the officers folded his hands on
top of the table in a way that made her fear for what he would
say next.

"You see, Miss Herzelfeld," he remarked in a tone that was
decidedly cool, "we are in a bit of a quandary. For while it is
indeed true that you are Jewish, we have reason to believe that
during your time in Berlin, you fraternized with high-ranking
officers of the German government, and even the SS." He
glanced down at the paper before him. "I have it on good
authority that you were, in fact, a charming hostess for your
father's parties, at which many Nazi officials were present."

Rosa felt the blood drain from her face as she stared at the
steely-eyed man. She could think of nothing to say.

The man raised his eyebrows. "Would you say that is an
accurate statement?"

"I..." She licked her lips. Her English had improved greatly
over the last year, but right then, she struggled to form
sentences, to *think*. "My father had no choice but to treat Nazi
officers," she finally said in little more than a whisper. "Med-
ically. He could not refuse them, not as a Jew. You must know
this."

"Yes, he treated them for venereal diseases." The officer's
lips twisted as his iron gaze settled on her. "He was known for
his discretion, it seemed, which might have been why he was so
in demand. But that does not answer the question of why the
men he treated for such confidential conditions were subse-
quently entertained at *your home*."

Rosa steeled herself not to look away from his gaze, both
curious and condemning. *What kind of Jew did such a thing?*
He might as well have asked the question out loud.

"They... they liked him," she admitted in a low voice. She
didn't know what else to say. "At least, he amused them," she
made herself continue, after a moment. "For a little while, when

a Nazi could... could still associate with a Jew, without... without repercussions. He was like a... a pet to them. Nothing more." She looked down at her lap. "It was a way to survive," she finished in a low voice. "That was all."

An excruciating silence settled on the room, stretched between them like something about to snap. Then the other officer remarked acidly, "And yet many Jews, in fact just about *all* other Jews, did not use such means as a *way to survive*." The words rang through the room, falling into the stillness.

Once again, Rosa had no reply to make. How could she defend her father? *Herself*? She hadn't wanted to hear his excuses back in the Black Maria—why should this man, now? Misery swamped her, along with a terrible, endless guilt. "He was trying to protect us," she said at last, knowing how feeble she sounded. How feeble she *felt*.

"Protect you." The officer sounded derisive.

Rosa blinked hard and made herself stay silent. Her explanations, such as they were, seemed only likely to condemn her—and her father—all the more.

The second officer glanced down at the paper in front of him. "Did you ever meet Adolf Eichmann?" he asked abruptly.

Eichmann, coming back to haunt them! Her father had been so stupidly proud of that connection, of what it could do for them.

Rosa swallowed audibly. "Yes... once," she admitted. Or twice.

"He came to your home, I believe?" The man's expression was pitiless. "To one of these parties, where you acted as hostess?"

Only when her mother had been indisposed, yet Rosa could hardly explain about *that*—the sedative her mother took to block out the pain of her husband's infidelity, the evenings where she lay in bed and sobbed, refusing to come downstairs to grace her traitorous husband's arm, and so Rosa had taken her place. It hadn't been very often, she thought, and yet she knew it had been often enough.

And, in truth, her father had sometimes preferred her to be by his side on such occasions, young and charming, and most importantly, not jealous of any attention he gave elsewhere. Even more damningly, Rosa had *liked* being preferred, even if she'd dreaded the parties themselves—the knife-edge they all seemed to be balancing on. More than once, one of the Nazis' mocking laughter had taken a dangerously cruel edge, a wild glitter had entered their eyes. There had been the awful sense that the evening could end in arrest, or worse.

"Yes," she admitted, in little more than a breath of sound. "He did. But I did not always act as hostess—"

"Eichmann is currently the head of the department of Jewish Affairs in Berlin," the officer cut across her, forcing her to fall silent. "In particular with regards to emigration." He let a certain weight settle on the word, along with the implication that Eichmann had helped them, and for all Rosa knew, he might have.

"Eichmann was posted to Vienna before we left," she replied. She had no idea if her possession of this knowledge would harm or exonerate her, but she did know that the man had not been in Berlin by the time they'd emigrated, even if he was now. "I met him years ago, before all of this..."

"In 1938, I believe, right before he left for Vienna, to aid with emigration affairs there."

She bit her lip, hard enough to taste blood, its metallic tang flooding her mouth. How did they know so *much*? Had they been keeping track of them since they'd arrived? And how could they have possibly found out when the wretched Eichmann had come to their house? None of it boded well for her or her father, not at all. "I can't remember exactly when," she answered after a moment, struggling to hold onto her dignity. "But yes, around then, I suppose. What does it matter? Neither of us liked the man. At all. We would have preferred to have nothing to do with him."

Her protests were utterly ignored, and the officer continued as if she hadn't spoken, his tone both cordial and relentless, "Did Eichmann aid your own emigration? Perhaps he felt he owed your father a favor, or maybe he just wished to repay a certain kindness?" His eyebrows lifted while Rosa stared at him miserably. "According to our sources, your father was able to take a great deal of money with him, which, as I'm sure you know, is very unusual for Jewish refugees. The German government put strict regulations on what Jews could take out of the country." He paused while Rosa pressed her lips together, determined not to rise to his bait. It felt like anything she might say would incriminate her. "It suggests he was aided by an official..." he continued. "An important official."

"I... I don't know..." And if he was, she wondered, was that wrong? Surely, they weren't the only Jews who had tried to play the system. Who, really, could blame them?

The man cocked his head. "Come now, Miss Herzelfeld. You must know something about it. All that money? You seem a sensible girl." He smiled thinly. In the circumstances, it hardly felt like a compliment.

"I believe he did attempt to take money out," Rosa admitted after a moment, her voice scratchy, the words coming painfully. "I... I don't know if Eichmann aided him in that regard. But, in any case, my father never received the funds here in England. Surely you must know that?" She lifted her chin, despising herself for being so cringing and weak. She had nothing to hide, she told herself. She was not a Nazi sympathizer, and she certainly wasn't a spy.

Yes, she'd entertained Nazi officials in her home, along with her father—and her mother, who had somehow escaped this dreadful interrogation—but she hadn't enjoyed it, she hadn't curried favor, and she had no love of any Nazi—no, not *any*—

now. She'd simply done what she'd had to, in order to survive, just as she'd told the officers. Was that so wrong?

Belatedly, Rosa realized she was echoing what her father had asked her just hours ago, and she hated herself for it. She wasn't like him, she told herself, she *wasn't*.

She straightened, forcing herself to meet the officer's gaze. "I wouldn't be working sixty hours a week at a Lyons teashop," she told the man with some asperity, "if my father had received that money."

"I know the money didn't go into his account," the officer returned evenly. "Where it *did* go is another matter."

Rosa stared at him as realization trickled icily through her. "You think the money was used for some Nazi cause? That my father gave it away... to *Nazis*?" she surmised in a hollow voice. The idea was laughable, as well as utterly offensive. "But we're *Jewish*."

"Jews who fraternized with some of the highest-ranking Nazis in all of Germany." The man gave her a cold smile. "Strange, that."

Again, Rosa had no real reply to make. She knew they hadn't been the only Jews to make a deal with the devil, but it *was* strange. It was strange, and it was terrible, and when it came down to it, in a moment like this, she knew she had no real defense.

"I think we have enough information here," the man announced as he stood up, the interrogation clearly over.

Rosa looked at him fearfully, her hands gripping the side of her chair. "What..." She had to clear her throat and start again. "What have you decided?"

"You are being reclassed as Category B," the man replied, "which is enough to have you interned for the foreseeable future. You will be taken from here to Holloway Prison, and from there to a suitable location."

"*Prison...*" Rosa gaped at him before she lurched forward,

one hand outstretched, as if to grab his sleeve, although she did not possess the courage to actually touch him. "Please," she begged. "I'm Jewish, I hate the Nazis. I will do anything —*anything*—for this war. I'm not a spy. I don't know where the money is..." Her words became garbled, spoken half in German, which surely did not help her cause. Tears ran down her cheeks unchecked. "*Nein... bitte...*"

The officer looked down at her coolly; Rosa saw no pity in his eyes at all. "Good day, Miss Herzelfeld," he replied, and the two of them walked out of the room, leaving Rosa alone, sagging in her seat.

She'd barely had time to take a shaky breath and wipe her damp cheeks before a stony-faced woman entered.

"You're to come with me."

Rosa stood up on shaky legs; she felt as if she could collapse in a heap. "Where am I going?" she asked in a thready voice.

"Holloway."

"*Now?*" Her head felt as if it were spinning. "Please—may I go back to my flat first? I don't have any of my things. My clothes..."

The woman looked supremely unsympathetic. "You don't need any of your things," she replied, and she took Rosa's arm, none too gently.

Rosa tried to catch a glimpse of her father as she was marched through the corridors of the school to yet another Black Maria idling out front, but she couldn't see him anywhere. This van had half a dozen women inside it—some looked tearful, others surly. No one said a word as Rosa was half-flung inside, and then scrambled to sit on one of those benches, squeezed next to a small, prune-faced woman who averted her head.

This couldn't be happening, she thought numbly. It simply couldn't be! It made no sense. She was no *Nazi*, for heaven's sake...

For a second, she thought about shouting out, begging them to reconsider, but she knew it would do no good. She simply had to hope that the British government would come to their senses and release the Jews among the German internees before too long. Meanwhile, though, she would be taken to Holloway. To *prison*. She hadn't even had a chance to say goodbye to her mother... or Peter. What would either of them think? A strangled gasp escaped her, and she pressed her hand to her mouth as the Black Maria rumbled off.

No one spoke for the hour-long journey to the prison in North London; no one seemed even to want to look anyone else in the eye. Were her fellow prisoners Jews? Rosa wondered. Some of them, she realized, might well be Nazis, or at least Nazi sympathizers. And she'd be living cheek by jowl with them, for who knew how long! It was a horrendous thought, and one that was also perfectly ridiculous; for a second, a bubble of hysterical laughter rose in Rosa's throat, but she forced herself to swallow it down. She could not collapse into hysterics here, of all places. She needed her wits about her.

As the Black Maria drove into the prison courtyard, Rosa glimpsed its forbidding, crenelated towers looming up toward a darkening sky. Then the gate shut with a clang behind them, locking them in—for how long? How on earth would she get out of this desperate situation?

Closing her eyes, whispering a wordless prayer, Rosa slipped her hand into her pocket, her fingers closing over the sliver of emerald. It had not served as much of a talisman so far, but it felt like her only comfort now, her only friend.

CHAPTER 18

JUNE 1940—ISLE OF MAN

The little island perched on the surface of the flat, gray water like the last outpost of humanity, the Irish Sea stretching all the way to a blank horizon. As Rosa disembarked the ferry that had transported several hundred female internees across the sea, her stomach still churning from the voyage, she had no idea what to expect.

The last month in Holloway Prison had been, in turns, stultifyingly boring and unbearably hellish. At the start, she'd shared a cell with a Jew, at least; some Jews had to share the small, barren cells with hostile Nazis sympathizers, which had seemed awful in the extreme, and they had come to both insults and blows, until the wardens had had the sense to separate them. She'd also been able to wear her own clothes, rather than the shapeless prison garments the other inmates wore, and so she was able to keep her sliver of emerald, which she had slipped into her brassiere, close to her skin.

It seemed the status of the German internees was somewhat in question; they were not quite prisoners, like the regular inmates, a rather rough group of women who eyed this new crop with surly suspicion, but they were certainly not free. They were able to move as they chose from their cells to the other areas of the prison, such as they were—a scrubby courtyard, a social hall—but they could not leave the prison and they were given nothing to *do*. They had no access to newspapers or a wireless, no ability to telephone or post letters, no visitors or contact with the outside world at all. Sometimes Rosa had felt as if she'd been enclosed in a tomb—a tomb with a thousand other women in it.

Rumors had flown, just as they had on that other, unlikely prison, the *St Louis*. The women would be interned at Holloway for the entire war; they would be moved on as soon as possible. They would be let go, as no one saw the point of interning thousands of innocent people, some of them British citizens; they would disappear, forgotten by the country that had taken them in, just as they might have been back in Germany.

Rosa had forced herself to stop paying attention to the pointless hysteria, keeping to herself as much as she could. She had been acutely conscious that she fell uncomfortably between the innocent Jews, which most of the internees were, and the few dastardly Nazi sympathizers, who incurred enmity among just about everyone. She'd had no desire to explain what had got her reclassed as Category B, that she'd entertained Adolf Eichmann, of all people, in her own home. She feared what might happen to her if she did.

Three days after she'd arrived at Holloway, she had been shocked to see her mother in a corner of the crowded social hall, standing by herself, looking pale, forlorn and frightened.

"*Mutti*." The name had fallen naturally from Rosa's lips. She'd crossed the room to take her mother by both shoulders. "What on earth are you doing here?"

"My letter came the next day." Her mother's lips had trembled as she'd attempted to smile. "They did the same to me as they did to you. Oh, Rosa, whatever shall we do?" She'd

sounded so pitiful, so unlike her usual self, that Rosa had felt a
sudden rush of not just sympathy, but love. Her poor mother.
Nothing could have prepared her for this.

Quickly, tightly, Rosa had hugged her. She had been
surprised at how glad she was to see her, a familiar face in this
seething sea of strangers. Her mother had put her arms around
her, hugging her back just as tightly in a way Rosa had not been
able to ever remember her doing. For a second, they were
united, a mother and daughter like any other, but in a prison, of
all places.

"Do you know where your father is?" her mother had asked
as she'd released her.

"I heard the men have been taken to a racecourse called
Kempton Park, somewhere outside London," Rosa had replied.
"It's been turned into a camp." She hoped her father was there,
and not somewhere further away, although in truth, as long as
they were in Holloway, she wasn't sure it mattered.

"Are we to stay here?" her mother had questioned in a
faltering voice. "Forever?"

Rosa had briefly closed her eyes against such a terrible
thought. "I certainly hope not."

Fortunately, she'd been able to arrange for her mother to
share her cell, as they'd waited to be moved on from Holloway...
but to where?

The days had crawled past, with so little to do; there had
been plenty of time to think, except Rosa hadn't wanted to
think. She couldn't bear to consider the future, and the past felt
far too painful. Oh, the sweet simplicity of the life she'd experienced so briefly in Belsize Park! Washing pots, taking coffee
with Peter, learning English... she'd chafed against the smallness
of it all sometimes, it was true, but now she'd take it all back
with such glad relief. With *joy*. And yet she'd feared she would
never get the chance. Every day, she'd kept hoping it would all
turn out to be a dreadful mistake, someone would tell her she

and her mother were free to go. *Other* women left—all Jews, clutching their children, weeping with relief—but Rosa's name had never been called, and neither had her mother's.

Two weeks after they'd arrived at Holloway, Rosa had finally been allowed to post a letter, only to realize there was no one she'd actually wanted to write, to tell them where she was, or why. She couldn't bear to admit to Sophie or Hannah or Rachel that she'd been interned, classed as a threat, as good as any Nazi... and for a reason. Neither had she wanted to write to Peter, who might have understood all too clearly why she and her parents had been interned. In the end, she didn't write to anyone, and the lack of friendship or support caused an emptiness to whistle right through her. She hated that she'd been brought to this place of loneliness and despair... all because of her father and the choices he'd made back in Germany, choices they were all paying for.

Then, at the beginning of June, news finally came. They were to be moved somewhere up north, where a camp was being built for both male and female internees.

"The Isle of Man," Rosa had told her mother. "I've never heard of the place."

Her mother had shaken her head wearily, too resigned and dispirited to make a reply. She'd looked so different from her usual, glamorous self; there were white streaks in her hair, and without her usual powder and lipstick, her face looked careworn and haggard. The peevish tone she'd often take with Rosa had softened into a resigned weariness that, in some ways, had worried Rosa more than her mother's petulance ever had. In Holloway, she'd spent her days lying on her bunk or listlessly flipping through one of the out-of-date magazines in the social hall.

"I don't suppose it matters where we go," she'd finally replied, on a sigh. "Do you think your father will be there?"

"I don't know, but you'd think they'd want to keep all the

internees together," Rosa had replied with more optimism than she'd felt. "Especially if the camp is on an island. We aren't likely to escape, are we, right into the sea?"

She'd had no idea just how far away the Isle of Man was until they'd taken a train up to Liverpool, first through flat green fields and then through gray-looking cities, the sky filled with smog; all the rail signs had been removed or covered up, so Rosa had never been able to tell where exactly they were. Outside some town or other, she'd found a newspaper discarded on a carriage seat, and she'd sank down in a daze as she'd read the headline.

We Will Never Surrender.

It was a summary of Churchill's speech, after three hundred thousand British soldiers had been evacuated from Dunkirk, just the other day. Germany had invaded France three weeks earlier, as well as the Low Countries; Belgium and the Netherlands had already surrendered, and France was about to. Rosa had had no idea about any of it until that moment. She'd feared, as everyone had, but she hadn't known. Now the knowledge weighed heavily inside her, lining her stomach with lead.

Hannah... Rachel... and Sophie's family, little Heinrich.

They were all already or about to be under Hitler's rule once again, suffering the same restrictions and persecutions as back in Germany... or maybe an even worse fate. Who could know what would happen, now that Hitler had expanded his evil empire? Rosa had thrust the paper away from her, her stomach churning, unable to bear reading any more of it. Her friends, she'd realized, were in a prison as surely as she was.

They'd taken another train from Liverpool to the city's port, where they'd been jeered by locals as they were herded along the dock to the waiting ferry that would take them to the Isle of Man.

"Nazi lovers! Go home to your Führer, why don't you, if you like him so much?" someone had shouted.

"You're not wanted here!" a red-faced housewife had spat. "You never were! Not you *or* your brats!"

A heavily pregnant internee, a toddler clasped in her arms, had angled her face away from the hateful woman, while Rosa had struggled to hold her own head high. She'd felt a maelstrom of emotions whirling within her: indignation, that she was being lumped together with genuine Nazis, and guilt, that maybe she belonged in that wretched category, after all. All of it, along with the awful taunts and shouts that dogged them all the way to the ferry, felt like too much to bear. She had held onto her mother's arm, who walked with her head down, her shoulders slumped, like an old woman. She did not look a single person in the eye.

And now, after an interminable, three-hour ferry journey, this little outpost of humanity bobbed before them in the Irish Sea, its green hills sweeping down to the seafront. Home—but for how long?

"It's not so bad, is it?" her mother murmured as they surveyed the promenade running along the beach of what they'd been told was the island's main town, Douglas.

It was a lovely, sunny day, the air surprisingly balmy; in any other instance, Rosa might have enjoyed being out on the water that sparkled so brightly underneath a benevolent summer sun. Ahead of them, the gracious Victorian buildings that lined the town's seafront were half-hidden behind hastily erected fences of barbed wire. The fences were everywhere she looked—along the seafront, up on the barren hilltops, even in the sea itself, foaming waves crashing over their bottom. Jagged and ferocious looking, they enclosed everything—and everyone—in. Rosa imagined that the island's non-German residents were not appreciative of their home being turned into what amounted to an enormous prison.

Rosa did not have much time to think about it, however, as she, along with all the other women, was ushered off the ferry and herded toward a train that would take them to Port Erin, on the other side of the island, where the women would be interned. Rosa had learned during their journey that the men would be housed here in Douglas, and she hoped to find her father at some point, although considering there would be several thousand men on the island, she did not know when that would be, or if she would even be allowed to.

When they arrived in Port Erin, everything was in disarray, the sky starting to darken over the sea, with shreds of clouds smudged with violet as the sun sank toward the water. Rosa glimpsed several impressive Victorian hotels perched high above the seafront; they had yet to be encased by barbed wire, but perhaps it was only a matter of time.

As the women were shepherded toward a church hall near the station, it was soon abundantly clear that they had been brought here without adequate staff or provision. The women walked uncertainly, milling about as twilight fell; Rosa could see no one in charge and she couldn't help but think that there was nothing to keep her from slipping away into the darkness, save that she had no idea where to go, and she was on a fairly small island. Where would she go?

She glanced around the crowded hall as women shifted and slumped where they stood, exhausted from their journey. Rosa and her mother had kept themselves mostly apart in the month they'd been in Holloway Prison, but now, as they waited, Rosa found herself sharing both bracing and commiserating smiles with some of the women she recognized. They were a motley bunch—some well-heeled, with hats and stoles and expensive-looking handbags, others still in the maid's uniforms they must have first been arrested in. Some women were fearfully young, little more than teenagers, or pregnant, or holding babies in their arms. Others were elderly and looked exhausted, sagging where they stood.

Rosa had discovered, in the last month, that very few of the women to be incarcerated actually were the Nazi supporters the British government feared. Many were Jews, and those who weren't, were hostile or at worst indifferent to Hitler and his regime. The few genuine Nazis, however, were vocal enough to make everyone notice them—and shudder, even as they did their best to ignore the mere handful of Hitlerites.

Still, Rosa felt a surprising and needed sense of solidarity with them all as they stood in the hall, waiting to be told what would happen to them. Right now, they were all just hungry, tired, frightened, and longing for home.

An impressive-looking woman in her sixties, dressed entirely in tweed, bustled to the front of the hall. She was clearly in charge, and looked it, seemingly unfazed by the dozens of women crammed inside, and more milling around outside.

"Ladies!" she boomed, her voice carrying easily across the hall. "Welcome to the Isle of Man. I am Dame Joanna Cruickshank, and I am in charge of the Rushen Camp for Women Internees. You are very welcome here."

Rosa had to swallow something close to a laugh at that. *Were they?*

"You will be given directions to your billet now," Joanna Cruickshank continued. "And we will continue to work to maintain a semblance of order as we get this camp up and running to everyone's satisfaction. You can all help with that! We want you to be as comfortable as possible during your stay." The smile she beamed at them seemed genuine, and for the first time Rosa felt a flicker of—no, not hope, not as much as that, but something that lifted her spirits just a little from the weary funk they'd been in for nearly a month.

Joanna Cruickshank did not look at the women in front of her as if they were prisoners as well as potential traitors. She smiled at them as if they were human beings, as if they *mattered*. It was enough to make tears sting Rosa's eyes.

A few minutes later, she and her mother were handed a slip of paper with an address and were told to make their way to a boarding house down the street facing the seafront, separate from the grand hotels on the cliffside. Women were walking in every direction, trying to find their billets, with no one to accompany or guard them. As Rosa walked down the street with her mother, she felt an exhilarating sense of freedom, even more than when she'd first arrived in London and had first felt the fear that had dogged her back in Germany and on the *St Louis* slip away. Perhaps their internment wouldn't be as awful as she'd feared.

The boarding house, when they finally found it, was small and homely, a terraced house facing the seafront, a "No Vacancy" sign in the window. They were welcomed in by the landlady, Mrs. Kneale, with what seemed like genuine warmth; she paid no mind to their German accents and remarked approvingly on Rosa's nearly fluent English. She helped them with their few bags—her mother had, at least, been able to bring more clothes to Holloway—and then made them toast and tea in the kitchen while they sat at a scrubbed oak table, wilting with exhaustion.

"You must have had a terrible journey," she clucked as she plied them with currant-studded buns. "Such a long way, and so much upheaval! I don't mind saying as plain as day that I don't agree with what they're doing. You can't put that many people behind bars, just on the *chance*, I say. And I expect you came to this country to get away from Hitler in the first place!" She puffed up, reminding Rosa of a hen ruffling its feathers, and making her smile a little.

"Yes, we did," she confirmed quietly, putting an arm around her mother, who looked as if she might fall asleep right there at the table. "We're Jewish, you see."

Mrs. Kneale shook her head, her lips pursed. "Jewish, and imprisoned like you're Hitler himself! It's a crime, that is," she

stated staunchly. "There's no other way of putting it. A crime."
And she poured them more tea.

Her kindness, after such an unsettling month of fear and
uncertainty, was almost Rosa's undoing. The tears that had
stung her eyes during Dame Joanna's welcome threatened to
roll right down her cheeks. She managed to blink them back as
she smiled at her new landlady.

"Perhaps we won't be here too long," Rosa said. "It can't be
that pleasant for you or your fellow residents, to have so many
people thrust upon you."

The woman's face softened. "We'll be fine," she stated
firmly. "Don't you worry about us. And drink up your tea. You
look like you need it."

Twenty minutes later, Rosa and her mother were up in their
neat and cozy room, two twin beds facing the windows, with a
chest of drawers each besides. As they unpacked their few
things, Rosa could hear furniture being dragged to and fro
upstairs; a group of young nurses had come in as they'd finished
their tea and, it seemed, were determined to sort their domestic
arrangements to their satisfaction before bed.

Finished unpacking, she stood by the window, watching the
moonlight gild the placid sea in silver. The moon had risen high
in the sky and reminded her of a silver coin tucked in a pocket,
with only a slim crescent visible. After the noise and dirt, the
crowds and mess of Holloway, Port Erin felt like a haven of
peace. It was certainly a beautiful, if isolated, place, the sea
stretching in every direction, the whole world seeming as still as
a hushed breath. There were, Rosa knew, far, far worse places
to be.

And yet, as thankful as she was that they seemed to have
washed up on a pleasant shore, Rosa was still dogged by uncertainty, and worse, a terrible sadness. How long would they be

here, and what would they *do* with themselves? And what about her father—would she ever see him again? How had he fared, this last month?

Her feelings for him were as complicated as they'd ever been; she loved him like the small child she often still felt she was, but she was still so very angry that it was his choices and actions that had led them to this terrible predicament. Even so, she knew she could not wish him ill.

She thought of Peter, too, wondering what he was doing. Had his life changed? Had he discovered what had happened to her—and if he had, what would he think about it? She was afraid to find out the answer. And yet she missed him, missed his wry smile and the familiar glint in his eyes, his dry sense of humor, and most of all, his inherent kindness.

Rosa also thought about her dear friends from the *St Louis*. In the frantic rush of moving from train to ferry to island, she had pushed the terrible knowledge of Hitler's invasion of France and the Low Countries to the back of her mind, but now it rushed to the fore, sickening in its awful implications. *Hannah... Rachel.* Little Lotte, and poor, dear Franz. What would happen to them all? As much as she might chafe against being treated like the enemy, Rosa knew her circumstances had to be far better than those of her two friends suffering on mainland Europe. What were they feeling now, with the Wehrmacht on the march, the Luftwaffe darkening the skies above them?

She imagined both Hannah and Rachel huddled somewhere, planes strafing the sky above, tanks rolling down the city streets, as they clutched their pieces of emerald and prayed for the day when all four of them would all be together again, safe and reunited.

Rosa slipped her hand into her pocket and let her fingers curl around her own shard of jewel, grateful for the comfort it always gave her. That day would happen, she told herself, even if she could not see a way to that moment from this. Even if, right now, it seemed utterly impossible.

Outside, the crescent moon glided beneath a bank of clouds, and the silvery sea turned into an expanse of black. Still Rosa stood there, gazing out at the darkness, as if she could see all the way to the horizon.

CHAPTER 19

When Rosa and her mother woke the next morning, their little room was awash with sunshine and she could hear seagulls cawing on the promenade out front. For a second, she simply lay there, enjoying the comfort of her narrow bed, the warmth of the sunlight on her closed eyelids, and the unexpected peace of the moment.

She glanced over at her mother, who was just stirring.

"The seagulls and sunlight... it reminds me of when we went to Binz," she murmured sleepily. "When you were small. On Rügen... an island much like this one, I imagine. You must have only been three or four. All you wanted to do was build sandcastles." Her mother smiled in memory, while Rosa blinked at her in uncertain surprise.

She suddenly pictured herself on the beach, knees and elbows sandy, face furrowed in concentration as she built her fleeting masterpieces. She couldn't remember it at all. Had it been a happy time? Sometimes she forgot that there had been happy times, before her father's affairs and courting of Nazis, before her mother, always so obsessed with her husband, had become so unhappy.

"We could be in worse places, certainly," Rosa replied as she pushed herself up onto her elbows. In the chink between the curtains, she could see the sparkle of the sea. It did feel like a resort here, and she supposed it was, or had been, judging by the hotels.

After Rosa and her mother had dressed, they went downstairs, to find Mrs. Kneale making them a hearty breakfast of eggs and toast with real strawberry jam, washed down with copious cups of tea. The nurses who had arrived after them joined them for the meal in the little dining room, chattering excitedly over the table; they seemed to view their internment as an extended holiday, with one remarking, with as much seriousness as flippancy, "Why shouldn't we like it here? We're fed, we're housed, and we don't have to spend ten or twelve hours rushed off our feet, being shouted at by doctors!"

That was true enough, Rosa supposed, but as beautiful as it was, they were still on a tiny island in the middle of the Irish Sea, encased by barbed wire. The holiday feeling would surely be fleeting. And yet... as she mopped up the last of her eggs with a piece of toast, it did, indeed, feel like an odd sort of holiday.

After breakfast, Rosa helped Mrs. Kneale tidy up, and the landlady told her what sights she might like to explore on the island.

"Are we free to do so?" Rosa asked in surprise after she'd been regaled with descriptions of the Great Laxey waterwheel and Milner's Tower. Despite the nurses' excitement, she had expected far more restrictions.

Mrs. Kneale looked as surprised by the question as Rosa was by her own assumptions. "I don't rightly know," she admitted, "but I can't see why not. Where are you going to go, after all? We're over seventy miles from the mainland, you know, in any direction, and it isn't as if they've got enough staff to police you. They can't lock you up, not when you're staying in a boarding house like mine!" She looked fierce then, as if she'd fight for Rosa's right to see the Laxey waterwheel, and that made Rosa smile.

"Yes, that's true," she conceded. Even so, the idea of being free to go where and whenever she liked had not actually occurred to her. She'd expected Camp Rushen to be like Holloway, only a little bit bigger, but as she wiped the last of the breakfast dishes, she had a sense that that might not be the case at all.

Over the next few days, the intoxicating extent of their freedoms became clearer. They were allowed to go anywhere they liked in Port Erin, but would need a police escort—female police constables had been brought in from London for such a purpose—to go anywhere outside the town. Still, Port Erin was freedom enough, especially as the weather remained warm and sunny, and there were shops to browse and the beach to stroll down, and the sea to swim in.

With a few of the young nurses from her boarding house, Rosa had gone down to the seafront, wading into the water up to her calves, her skirt caught about her knees. One of the women, from Norway, had stripped off her shabby dress—the only clothing she'd been able to bring—and dove neatly into the water, entirely naked. Rosa had never considered herself a prude, and, in truth, she'd felt more envy than embarrassment at the sight of the woman's pale body gliding easily through the water. Oh, to be so free! To care so little what others thought of you. To feel so unencumbered by the past, by guilt, by memories...

She'd stayed where she was, in only up to her knees.

As the days and weeks passed, the women internees, under the guidance and encouragement of Dame Joanna, organized themselves into industry. Schedules for housework and laundry for each boarding house or hotel were drawn up, and classes were offered, in spinning, weaving, and dressmaking; these were soon expanded to more academic subjects, including English, philosophy, and mathematics. A library was formed, with many local residents donating books, and run by a Jewish internee and former librarian.

After just a week, every internee was offered the opportunity to sign a repatriation agreement; those who were pro-Nazi did so, and were housed separately, at the Golf Links Hotel, which made, Rosa thought, everything operate more smoothly, without the fear of running into a genuine Nazi, for both the Jewish internees and wary island residents alike.

All in all, there was a strange sort of freedom about their lives in Port Erin—time she hadn't had working ten-hour shifts back in London was now hers for reading, learning, or simply enjoying the summery blue skies that continued all through June and July. She took classes in philosophy and mathematics and read just about every volume she could get her hands on. Sometimes she imagined the conversations she might have with Peter, debating ideas and discussing poetry. She could picture the way his eyes would light up, the small, crooked smile that would curve his lips, and it caused a great ache inside her, like a physical pain. She still hadn't written to him.

When the weather was fine, she had long walks along the promenade, and with a kindly police escort, even made it to the Great Laxey waterwheel, which was just as impressive as Mrs. Kneale had said.

In the evenings, which stayed light until past ten o'clock, she simply enjoyed the view of the placid sea or read a book, doing her best to live in the silence; the one thing there was not available was a wireless. Mrs. Kneale didn't own one, and none of the internees had access to current events except through the newspapers, which came to the island several days or even weeks out of date.

It was through those newspapers that Rosa learned that France had fallen to Germany and had been divided into two zones—the central and north regions of the country, including Paris, were under Nazi rule, while the south, from the Swiss border to Tours and the Bay of Biscay, was under a sovereign rule, at least in name. While there had been no news about restriction on Jews there or in the Low Countries, Rosa feared it was only a matter of time.

In the out-of-date newspapers, she also read about "the Battle of Britain"—how the English Channel and towns on the south coast were being bombed by the Luftwaffe, night after night after night, with devastating losses.

It felt as if it were happening so far away, when all Rosa could see was tranquil, sunlit sea in any direction. They were, she reflected, far safer out here in the middle of the Irish Sea than in London, which hadn't been bombed yet but surely would be, soon.

That possibility compelled her to finally write to Peter, needing to know if he was still safe, although she hardly knew what to say to him. Had he discovered where she'd gone—and why? And if he hadn't, could she admit that she'd been interned for the part she had played in her father's parties? As she sat at Collinson's Café on Port Erin's high street, drinking a cup of tea and composing her letter, Rosa found she didn't have the courage to do so. She wrote a brief note instead, keeping it light and airy, as if this was no more than an amusing detour in the landscape of her life. She wrote in the same tone to Sophie— describing the classes she was taking, and the books she was reading, and even blaming her father—and her father alone—for why she was on the Isle of Man in the first place.

It felt shameful as well as cringingly cowardly, to write such things without admitting the full truth, but Rosa knew she couldn't risk losing the best friend she'd ever had. What would Sophie, when her own father had been in Dachau, think about Rosa having drunk champagne with Adolf Eichmann? Or flirted and more—so much more—with SS Obersturmführer Ernst Weber?

And what would Peter think, with his poor, twisted hand that had been ruined by a brownshirt jackboot? Rosa couldn't bear to think about his reaction. He'd been disapproving enough, when he'd learned who her father was. She could not bear for him to know who *she* was... or at least who she had once been.

Despite all the pleasant and interesting activities available, the holiday mood, just as Rosa had feared, began to wear thin, flaking off like the cheap gloss to an ultimately unappealing proposition. The lack of meaningful work, of current news, of opportunities to visit husbands or have their children join them, all took their inevitable toll. The barbed wire fences that ringed them in every direction started to feel menacing—almost, Rosa thought, as if they were drawing closer.

As the weeks passed and summer waned, women became restless and bored, and arguments blew up like storms over the sea, quick and violent. Mothers who had been separated from their children fell into lethargy and despair. And women who still could not see their husbands, despite learning they were just across the island in Douglas, became frustrated and fractious.

The one person who *didn't*, to Rosa's surprise, was her mother. After a year of anxious waiting in London, and an interminable month in Holloway, the Isle of Man seemed to be the making of Elsa Herzelfeld. Always a dab seamstress, she took a dressmaking class and then began to work as a dressmaker, enjoying the challenge of turning the occasional well-worn donations into a beautiful frock or blouse. Her skills were in high demand, and a new color filled her mother's cheeks that had nothing to do with the rouge she usually wore, a gleam in her eyes that had nothing to do, Rosa realized, with her husband.

"Do you miss him?" Rosa asked one evening in August, when they were getting ready for bed. The nights were starting to draw in, the sun having already sunk between the smooth surface of the sea.

"Your father?" Her mother's voice was sharp, but also surprised. "Of course I miss him, Rosa. What a question."

"I know," Rosa replied quickly, "but..." She found she could not put into words quite what she meant, not, at least, without offending her mother. *You're happier without him. You seem stronger, brighter, with more purpose.*

No, she couldn't say any of that, even if she saw it, day by day, and was glad for it.

Her mother let out a long sigh, her shoulders sagging as she gazed out at the moonlit sea. "I do miss him," she said again, more quietly. "But... I'm happy here, in a way I never expected to be." She gave an uncertain little laugh. "What a strange thing, to be happy in a place like this! I suppose it's pitiable, but I don't mind. Your father..." She paused, seeming to weigh her words, and Rosa found herself holding her breath, wondering what her mother might admit. "Your father is like the sun, to me," she said at last. "I find I can't live without its light and warmth, but... I'm cast into shadow, next to it. I always have been. And I haven't minded, because... well, because I love him." She gave another little laugh, this one sounding sad. "But here... here I think I've found my own light. And I don't want to give that up." Her mother pressed her lips together, looking as if she'd said too much. "But I do miss him," she said yet again, more forcefully. "And I want to see him again."

It almost sounded, Rosa thought, as if her mother was trying to convince herself.

At the end of August, news finally came that the wives and husbands who had been separated would be allowed to meet, under careful conditions.

Life had improved in other ways, as well; wirelesses were now allowed to be listened to in public rooms of hotels and boarding houses, although only the BBC stations, and the newspapers were more current. More classes were offered in the social hall and even at a marine biology station on the island, and women were able to work, as well—in shops and cafés, or setting up their own businesses, such as her mother's dressmaking.

Some women kept a piggery, others hens, and yet others made plans to plant a vegetable garden in the spring. Rosa couldn't help but hope she wouldn't *be* there in the spring, although, as far as anyone could tell, there seemed no plans yet to free the several thousand internees that had quickly doubled the population of the island.

And now, the news that husbands and wives would be able to see each other, for a mere two hours at Derby Castle, a dance hall in Douglas.

"Oh, Rosa, what should I wear?" her mother exclaimed, her hands pressed to her cheeks, as giddy as a girl. "I don't have anything, and I've become so plain. Look at my hair..."

"*Mutti*, you're a dressmaker!" Rosa told her with a laugh. "You can make yourself something gorgeous and new. Use one of your old dresses, if you like, or one of mine." Her mother had thankfully brought Rosa's clothes with her when she'd first joined her at Holloway. "You've got to be dressed to the nines," she insisted, smiling.

To Rosa's surprise, her mother's eyes filled with tears, and she grabbed both her hands. "I don't deserve your kindness," she gasped out. "I know I don't."

Rosa stared at her, taken aback. "*Mutti*..."

"I haven't been a good mother to you," her mother continued in a rush, seeming to need to get the words out. "I don't think I knew how. And your father... sometimes it felt like he took all the air in the room, all the space in my head. He shouldn't have, I know that now. I shouldn't have let him, but... I did. I loved him so much, you see. I still do. And I was ashamed, how he treated me sometimes—the other women... that you knew about them. I blamed you, or tried to, and it was wrong. I know that. I've always known that." Her mother bit her lip, her face crumpling. "What must you think of me, Rosa?" she asked in a soft whimper. "What sort of mother have I been?"

Gently, overcome with both love and pity, Rosa squeezed her mother's hands. "It doesn't matter now, *Mutti*," she said. "It really doesn't. And I wasn't always the best daughter." It was the first time she'd thought as much, but she realized it was true. Her exasperation and disdain for her mother, for her relentless obsession with her husband, her jealousies and addictions, had bled through her words and actions, like a stain on a cloth.

"You adored your father," her mother said simply. "How could you not?"

Yes, she'd adored him, Rosa thought, which made her still feel so bitter now. She was glad it was her mother seeing him, and not her; she wasn't ready to face him, not yet. She didn't know what she would say—or feel. The months at Rushen had been pleasant, in their own way, but she still resented her father for having to be here at all.

Her mother created the most beautiful dress, snipping away at the green satin she'd worn to board the *St Louis* to turn it into an elegant tea dress, nipped in at the waist and swirling about her calves. She eschewed a stole or jewels, wearing a simple necklace of pearls instead. She had no makeup, and she pinned her hair back simply. Rosa decided she preferred her mother this way, elegant yet without fuss, although she did not say so. She simply kissed her cheek and told her she looked beautiful.

After her mother had left with two hundred other married women, to head to Douglas, Rosa decided to go for a walk. Although the air now possessed a chill, the sun still hadn't quite set, and long, lavender rays of light slanted across the promenade as she walked along, following the line of the barbed wire fence that stood between her and the sea.

They'd erected so many more fences since she'd arrived, Rosa noted. On the waterfront, along the streets, in front of the boarding houses. The Isle of Man had become an island of barbed wire. Everywhere she looked, she could see the jagged bits of wire, closing the world out, closing her *in*. As pleasant as these weeks and months had been, she was still acutely conscious that she was, to all intents and purposes, in prison, as impregnable a fortress as Holloway had been.

And yet... in a sudden rush of self-perception, Rosa realized she'd *always* felt she was in a prison. With the smallness of her life in London, on the *St Louis*, back in Berlin. She'd always felt trapped in some way and yearning for more. Maybe the problem wasn't her circumstances, she acknowledged, but herself. She could never escape the prison of her memories.

Her steps slowed as she wrapped her arms around herself and stared out at the darkening sea. For the first time in a long while, she let herself think of Ernst—not at the beginning of their doomed relationship, when he'd been charming and handsome and seemingly in love with her, but the last, when they'd been about to lose the villa on the Wannsee, when her father had no more work, and Jews weren't allowed anywhere.

Rosa, be sensible. You knew all along this could never go anywhere. Of course it couldn't! I like you, but... That little light laugh, touched with a scorn she'd forced herself to ignore. *You're a Jew.*

He'd stated it as if it were obvious, which it had been—painfully, glaringly obvious from the beginning—and yet she'd still fooled herself. She'd fooled herself, and worse, she'd compromised herself, utterly, and when he'd come back from Kristallnacht with bloody knuckles and a wild look in his eyes, she'd pretended not to see. Not to know.

How could she have betrayed her own people like that, her own self? How could she have been so callously indifferent to the absolutes of the situation, the stark right and wrong? She thought of her father's mocking words—*you think like a child. First, he was angelically good, then he was demonically bad.*

But Ernst had *never* been good, Rosa acknowledged wretchedly. He'd joined the SS at just twenty, thanks to his father's connections. He was friends with Heydrich and he'd dined with Hitler, and he'd boasted about both—if not directly to her. He'd spoken of getting rid of all the Jews the way you would rats, although he'd tried not to say such things in her presence. It turned her stomach now, just to think of it. To think of *her*, listening to him speak like that and still loving him, or believing she did.

It didn't mean anything, Rosa. It was just words.

Except it hadn't been.

Rosa didn't know how long she stood out on the promenade as the sky darkened and the sea turned black. The wind grew chilly, blowing her hair into tangles about her face, and still, she didn't move. Memories from the past whirled around her, swept through her. Hugging Ernst. Hating her father. Even the beach at Binz, building sandcastles as a child, feeling so happy and innocent and free. Did she even remember that, or was she making it up? Did it matter?

And then, more poignantly, on the *St Louis* with her friends —having their Spanish lessons, toasting each other with champagne. Making promises she no longer knew if she wanted to keep. How would she face them, at Henri's, if she had to explain that she'd spent the war in prison, tarred as a Nazi? How could she explain it to Peter, when he already judged her father for his connections?

How could she explain the *why* to any of them, that she'd fallen in love with a man with the *SS-Runen*, that hateful symbol of two lightning bolts, pin on his lapel? A man who had espoused everything Hitler ranted and raved about... even if he'd done so quietly, and insisted to her he didn't really mean it. To admit that she'd known all that, and yet she'd willfully chosen to ignore it...?

She couldn't, Rosa thought hollowly. She never could.

She'd been trying to escape her own sense of guilt for so long, choosing to be angry with her father instead, and yet... she was to blame, as well. She hated the thought, but she knew that if she wanted her father to accept responsibility for his choices, then she needed to for hers... no matter how much it hurt. The pain of it felt like a blade slicing her clean through.

Rosa closed her eyes.

"Rosa... *Rosa!*"

At first, she thought she was imagining the voice, high and shrill, that was snatched away by the wind. Was it Sophie, calling to her all the way from America, lambasting her for lying in her letters, or was it Hannah or Rachel, begging her to help them, *save* them, when she knew there was nothing—absolutely nothing—she could do?

She slipped her hand into her pocket, withdrew the emerald she still carried with her everywhere. For a single, wild second, she considered throwing it into the sea. She wasn't worthy of it, of their promises to each other...

"*Rosa!*"

Rosa let out a startled gasp as her mother hurtled toward her, grabbing her by the shoulders. The sliver of emerald slipped out of her grasp, clattering to the pavement, and rolling away. With another gasp, this one of alarm, Rosa lunged for it. No, she realized, she didn't want to give it up. She would keep her promises, no matter what it cost her.

"*Mutti*, what is it?" she asked as she slipped the emerald into her pocket. "What has happened? Why aren't you with Father?" Belatedly, Rosa registered the look of anguish and anxiety crumpling her mother's face, one hand clutched to her chest as her breaths came out in ragged gasps.

"He didn't come," her mother told her, and began to weep. "On the way to the castle, he was *attacked*. He's in the hospital, Rosa, and they say they don't know if he'll survive."

CHAPTER 20

Her father had been taken to the island's hospital for internees, in the Falcon Cliff Hotel in Douglas, and then transferred to the island's main hospital, Noble's, on Westmoreland Road, due to the extent of his injuries. Rosa learned all this in stages, as she'd appealed to Dame Joanna for information, as well as the opportunity for her and her mother to visit her father in hospital.

"I understand your distress, child," Dame Joanna had said in her firm yet kind way, "and we will arrange for your transport as soon as we can. But there are three thousand women at Rushen, and many of them want to travel to Douglas, just as you do, to see their husbands or fathers. We simply haven't enough constables to accompany everyone. You will have to wait, and in the meantime, we will give you what news we can."

How many of those women, Rosa had thought in frustration, had fathers or husbands who were hovering near death's door? And why should she need a constable anyway, simply to visit her own father, considering how impossible it was to leave this forsaken island? Her helplessness infuriated her, and perversely, it made her feel even angrier at her father, for his part in why they were here in the first place. And yet he was injured, badly so, and she feared for his life.

The details of the attack were sparse, and given with seeming reluctance. Those in charge of the camps prided themselves on the order they instilled, and Rosa suspected they did not want to admit when it failed. What she did know was that three men, fellow internees, had set upon her father while he'd been walking to Derby Castle, and beaten him into a bloody unconsciousness. The doctors did not know the extent of any internal damage, but three days on, at least, her father was alive and seeming, slowly, to recover, although, according to Dame Joanna, doctors had warned that he might have lasting effects from the attack.

Then, finally, five days after it had happened, Rosa and her mother were allowed to be taken to Douglas in the company of a constable to see her father in hospital. Her mother clung to Rosa's arm as they entered the ward, while the female constable remained outside by the door.

Her mother had been beside herself ever since she'd had word of the attack, lamenting how she hadn't been there, as if, somehow, she could have stopped the men setting upon her husband, when, surely, she would have only been hurt herself, as well.

"Oh, Fritz! *Fritz.*" Her mother began to weep freely as she flew to her husband's side.

Rosa hung back by the foot of the bed as she gazed down at her father, shaken by how injured he truly was. His right arm was in a sling, and his chest and stomach were heavily bandaged. He had another bandage wrapped around his head, and one eye was swollen completely shut, his face covered in cuts and bruises. Despite all these injuries, his left arm was chained to the bed, the handcuff heavy on his wrist. How on earth, Rosa wondered, did they think he might be able to escape?

"How could they have hurt you so?" her mother exclaimed, pressing gentle kisses to his damaged face. "How could they have done such a thing? I hope they've caught the monsters, I hope they've *flogged* them—"

"They weren't monsters."

It took Rosa a few seconds to realize what her father had said, in such a low, weary voice.

He closed his eyes, a heavy sigh escaping him as her mother eased back, wiping her face.

"Fritz, what do you mean?" her mother protested, her voice wobbling with uncertainty.

"Who were they?" Rosa asked quietly. "Do you know?"

His father kept his eyes closed. "My fellow internees, as well as fellow Jews."

Fellow Jews. A cold and creeping suspicion took hold of Rosa. Had her father been attacked because his past had become known?

"I knew one of them, at least," her father continued in the same weary voice. "Aaron Horowitz. He would have killed me if he could. The others held him back, but only because they didn't want to hang for murder, I should think."

Her mother let out a little whimper. "Oh, *Fritz...*"

Her father opened his eyes, managing a lopsided smile as he patted his wife's hand. "It's all right, Elsa. I'm all right—or I will be."

"But why would they hurt you so?" Rosa's mother exclaimed. "It's diabolical..."

"It's justice," her father replied.

"Justice—"

He stared at her bleakly. "They found out about how I treated Nazis, back in Berlin."

So, it was true. Rosa took a steadying breath as she pressed one hand to her middle. How many other people knew? Would the women in Rushen find out? What would it mean for them?

Her mother drew herself up, all indignation. "What else were you meant to do—"

"Elsa, you know that wasn't just it," her father cut her off, his tone turning almost gentle. "I entertained them. I courted them, even. I accepted what power and privilege they threw my way, never caring what it looked like. What it might have cost other people." His gaze moved to Rosa, who still stood at the end of his bed. She sensed something different and defeated in her father, as if an essential part of him were missing, and she did not know what to make of it. Was he finally showing some regret for his choices, or was it simply because he'd been attacked for them? "*You* know," he told her, his gaze locked on hers. "Don't you? You're probably going to tell me that this serves me right."

Rosa's mother's mouth dropped open in outrage. "*What—*"

"No, Father," Rosa said quietly, realizing that she meant it. "I'd never say that."

His gaze, challenging yet also resigned, never left hers. "But you'd *think* it?" he pressed, and Rosa hesitated.

Would she? Could she be that callous, that cruel, especially when, just a few days ago, she'd been forced to acknowledge her own sorry part in the whole wretched affair? Was she really any better than her father? He might have made the first move, inviting those men into their home, but she'd followed his lead, even if she hadn't wanted to.

"No," she said at last. "I wouldn't."

"Well." Her father let out a huff of breath as his eyes fluttered closed again. "*I* would."

"Fritz..." Her mother's distressed protest trailed away as she gazed at her husband in consternation. "You only did what you had to," she said after a moment, her tone quiet and intense. "To protect us. We both know that, Rosa, don't we?" She turned to give Rosa a quelling look.

"Yes," Rosa said after a moment. "But it's had consequences, hasn't it?" She thought of her interrogators, back when she'd first been detained.

And yet many Jews, in fact just about all other Jews, did not use such means as a way to survive.

Her father had made a choice, one that many reviled and disdained. Rosa certainly had, even as she'd been complicit, which, she supposed, made her even worse than her father. In addition to a traitor to her own people, she was a hypocrite. She certainly wasn't about to blame her father now, not without also blaming herself.

"Yes," her father agreed as he opened his eyes once. "Consequences. More, perhaps, than you could even realize. This changes everything."

Rosa stared at him uneasily. "What is that supposed to mean?" she asked.

Her father just shook his head.

He grew tired soon after that, and so Rosa and her mother came away, her mother trying not to weep in her distress, the dour-faced constable trotting behind them. The happy, productive woman who had thrived at Rushen, Rosa thought sadly, had reverted to the wife she'd once been—emotional, desperate, obsessed with her husband. Rosa hoped it would only be temporary, and her mother would find her strength and spirit again.

"Oh Rosa, I can't bear to see him like that!" her mother cried once they were back at the boarding house. "It's as if the most vital part of him has drained away. He was always such a handsome, charismatic man. No one could take their eyes off him, and especially not the women. Well..." She sighed. "You know that already."

"He's injured and suffering," Rosa reminded her gently. "He'll get that vitality back in time, I'm sure." Although hopefully not with the other women. Again, she wondered what her father had meant, that this changed everything.

"He has no need to feel guilty," her mother stated abruptly, with a challenging look. "You shouldn't make him feel guilty, Rosa."

"I..." She *had* made him feel guilty, Rosa knew. She couldn't deny it. "He shouldn't have made a deal with the devil, *Mutti*," she said after a moment. "It's affected us all, terribly. You know that."

"Making a deal with the devil doesn't make you the devil himself," her mother returned hotly. "And what do you think would have happened, if he hadn't? Where do you think we'd be now?"

"Back in London, at the very least," Rosa replied evenly. "Able to hold our heads up high."

"Or your father in a camp, us all in camp, or even *dead*!" her mother shot back. "Do you think your father didn't know what was at stake? It's easy to have principles when nothing is actually at risk."

Rosa opened her mouth to fire back a similar retort, and then closed it. How could she possibly argue against her father, when she knew she was no better? Her shoulders sagged as she shook her head. "You're right, *Mutti*," she whispered. "It is easier. And I'm no better than Father."

"Oh, Rosa." Her mother's face softened, suffusing with sympathy. "Are you talking of Ernst? You were a child. A child in love. How could your head not have been turned, when you were approached by a man so handsome and charming?"

"But he wasn't," Rosa whispered. "Not truly."

"Does that even matter?" her mother returned, with a small, wry smile. "He was to you."

It occurred to Rosa then that for all she'd disdained her mother for her desperate obsession with her husband, she herself had not been much better, falling for a man like Ernst, ignoring so many things about him because she'd felt so happy, so desired. Was there no end to her self-deceit, she wondered, as well as her hypocrisy? The realization filled her with shame and exasperation. She'd been trying to distance herself from her parents for years, only to learn just how like both of them she was.

"Yes," she agreed after a moment, "He was, to me. But... he was a Nazi."

Her mother raised her eyebrows. "And? They don't have horned tails and forked tongues, you know." Her lips twitched. "Well, not all of them, anyway."

Rosa shook her head, denial a matter of instinct. Thinking such a thing was akin to the Nazis telling children Jews had horns on their head, hidden under their hair. And yet... "It was wrong," she stated. "To have those parties. To enjoy them. To... to fall in *love* with Ernst."

"Did you enjoy them?" her mother asked practically. "The attention, yes, but the events themselves? Those men in our house, stomping around in their boots, being free with our things? You always seemed to me as if you dreaded them." She paused. "*I* dreaded them, but I was more cowardly than you. I claimed headaches instead of facing up to your father."

"That's why you didn't always act as hostess?" Rosa exclaimed in surprise, and her mother shrugged.

"And I didn't like being made of a fool of, watching your father flirt with whatever floozies those men brought in." A sigh escaped her, long and low and weary. "But I loved him, and love him still." She straightened, giving her daughter a direct look. "In any case, what's the point of raking all this up now, Rosa? It's in the past. Your father did what he did, and at the time he felt it was right. We made our own choices, for better or for worse. But we must think to the future now, and whatever it might hold for us here. There is nothing gained in constantly looking back with regret."

With a jolt, Rosa realized how right her mother was. When she'd boarded the *St Louis*, she'd thought she'd been facing the future. She'd told Sophie as much; she'd told everyone. She'd even convinced herself. Yet, all this time, she'd been looking back, with guilt and shame. It had trapped her more than any fences of barbed wire ever could.

"You're right, *Mutti*," she said, and leaned over to kiss her mother's cheek. "We must look to the future."

The next day, Rosa volunteered to help teach in the kindergarten that was being organized, now that some of the internees' children were joining them, at long last, at Rushen, after having been separated for so long.

They set up a small school in Collinson's Café, which had been used for social activities and crafting. Rosa was tasked with teaching the younger ones English, and she found, somewhat to her surprise, just how much she enjoyed taking them through their letters, words, and simple phrases.

It reminded her of the whimsical conversational classes at the Jewish Day Center, with Peter. *Would you like one lump or two?* She could picture him smiling as he mimed pouring the teapot, and it caused an ache deep within her. She missed him more than she wanted to, because whenever she thought of him, it made her realize how futile any hope of a future for them was. She didn't even know if he thought of her romantically, but if he ever learned about Ernst, she feared he would reject her completely.

In any case, she hadn't had any reply to the light letter she'd sent him, although she'd heard from Sophie, as well as Hannah and Rachel. Sophie was still working at the Jewish Center in Washington, and living at a boarding house. She'd also written about how she'd gone on a date with a young American navy man, Sam, confessing she was quite besotted with him. Rosa thrilled to think of her friend experiencing a bit of romance in her life. She recalled back on the *St Louis* how Sophie had bashfully admitted she'd never been kissed. Well, perhaps she had been now.

Rosa had also had letters from Hannah and Rachel, written before the fall of France, and taking ages to get to Rushen.

Rachel had written that she and Franz were in Haarlem, managing—just—to keep body and soul together. *There is a woman here who is so kind and helpful. She has given us food, and more besides. I am so thankful for people who think of us.* It almost seemed, Rosa reflected, as if there was more Rachel wanted to say but couldn't. She supposed they all had their secrets, especially in these dark and troubling times.

I don't want to be afraid, Hannah had written, *but I might as well tell you that I am. I want to do something, fight this evil, but I don't know how. Where even to begin? It's all around me, and yet it feels impossible. I envy you, Rosa, for at least you are living in a country that is fighting! You can do your part, whatever that turns out to be.*

Yes, she was in a country that was at war, Rosa thought, but she was still behind barbed wire. How could she do her part? And yet, she realized that, like Hannah, she wanted to. That, too, Rosa thought, was all part of looking toward the future.

In late September, when the leaves were starting to change color and the wind off the Irish Sea had turned bitter, her letter to Peter came back unopened, with *Addressee Unknown, Return to Sender* stamped across the envelope in stark, black ink. Rosa gazed down at the crumpled letter in dismay. So, Peter had not even received her letter! He had no idea where she was, and more alarmingly, she had no idea where *he* was. Was there any way to find him? The prospect of never seeing him again at all filled her with a deep sorrow, akin to grief. She'd feared for their future friendship, but she'd still thought she'd see him someday.

What had happened to him? she wondered. Had he been sent off somewhere to volunteer? Or worse, had he been interned, as she had?

In October, she made the journey to Douglas to inquire whether there was a Peter Gelb at any of the male camps on the island. There wasn't.

Back in Port Erin, Rosa couldn't keep a deep disappointment from settling over her like a fog. She would never be able to find him, she thought, even when she was released from Rushen... whenever that was. A tribunal had been set up to examine cases for release, and an announcement of who had been chosen was made every night at five o'clock. A steady trickle of internees was being released in this way, but none of the Herzelfelds had ever been on such a list, and Rosa sometimes doubted whether they ever would be. Her father, at least, had made a full recovery from his injuries, although his arm pained him on occasion. He'd been moved to isolation after the attack, to avoid any further aggression.

Rosa's mother had been able to see him twice, at the monthly socials now held for married couples at Collinson's Café, the only time husbands and wives were reunited, although there was talk about creating a camp for married internees to be together. Some of the local residents were against it, fearing it would create greater security risks.

"I think it's ridiculous!" Mrs. Kneale claimed in her staunch way. "Keeping married couples apart for no good reason! It's not right."

Meanwhile, news of the war continued to filter in, through newspapers and the nightly updates on the BBC. Although it had been declared that the Luftwaffe had officially lost the Battle of Britain, at the start of September, German planes began to bomb London, with almost nightly raids for the next two months, battering the city.

Rosa became aware of a growing hostility of the Manx residents toward their German visitors; shopkeepers who had always been cordial and even friendly now acted with a decided coolness toward the internees who bought their goods. Residents cast darkly suspicious looks at groups of internees walking past, and there were more complaints about the fact that the whole island had become a detention center, a simmering resentment for all the barbed wire. A concert of internee musicians had been canceled, deemed inappropriate "considering."

"Considering what?" Mrs. Kneale fumed. "Most of the musicians, I heard, were Jewish, and some were famous, back in Germany. I'd have liked to have heard them, at any rate."

"So would have I," Rosa replied. "Perhaps another time." She was becoming more philosophical about these little setbacks and disappointments, trying to find pleasures where she could.

Sometimes, at night, she heard the drone of bombers heading to Glasgow or Belfast, and once she'd been woken by the muffled thuds of bombs being dropped, and the sky glowing red from the ensuing fires.

"Liverpool," Mrs. Kneale told her the next morning, over a meager breakfast of porridge made with water; rationing had started to bite. "They bombed the docks. It might not go well for us, if there was a great deal of damage. The steamers with supplies come from there, you know."

Over the next few days, it was announced that, due to the damage, no steamers would be heading to the Isle of Man with supplies, and no internees would be leaving, either. This continued all through the fall, with limited arrivals or departures, lending a subdued note to residents and internees alike, as supplies became scarce and internees who were due to be released couldn't leave.

Rosa tried to keep busy with the kindergarten, as well as her own classes. She helped Mrs. Kneale in the kitchen and took long walks along the seafront, trying to ignore the jagged barbed wire and look out to the horizon instead, where anything was possible, one day...

Sometimes, she lay on her bed and held her sliver of emerald up to the light as she wondered where her friends were, and more importantly, how they fared. She'd had another letter from Sophie, early in the new year; her sweetheart Sam had been posted to Hawaii, and she was desperately worried for her family in Belgium as she'd had no news but it looked like they had brought in restrictions for all the Jews.

Just like Germany, Sophie had written. *How can it be? I feel so guilty, for being here, safe and well, when they are not. Sometimes it is all I can think about...*

Yes, Rosa knew all about guilt, and how crippling it could be. She wrote Sophie back, encouraging her to look toward the future, just as she was trying to do. *The Luftwaffe have taken a beating, and from what I hear and read, London is still holding strong. Hitler will be defeated, Sophie, and one day we'll all be living somewhere safe. We'll be at Henri's, toasting our freedom and our futures! I'm sure of it.*

At least, she wanted to be sure of it. She held onto it like a promise, when she knew, in her heart, it was only a hope.

The months passed drearily enough, although still offering some small yet precious pleasures—a party for the children in the kindergarten, with games and cake, made from preciously hoarded butter; a new dress sewn by her mother, cut down from one of her evening gowns in bright pink taffeta. It was the nicest dress Rosa had had in a long time, and when she wore it, she felt beautiful in a way she hadn't since being in Berlin. She allowed herself to feel beautiful, which she hadn't done after Ernst; her mother clapped her hands and laughing, proclaimed she was very glad indeed she no longer had a "drab pigeon" for a daughter.

Rosa had no further news from her friends, save a letter from Sophie saying she was no longer working at the Jewish Community Center, but she couldn't say where she was. From Hannah and Rachel, there was nothing, and the nightly news on the wireless Mrs. Kneale had finally acquired made Rosa fear for them, just as she knew Sophie did.

Then, in April, when spring was just starting to warm the air and the buds on the cherry blossoms were beginning to unfurl into riotous, pink bloom, Rosa was summoned by Dame Joanna.

One of the great lady's aides came to find her at the kindergarten, where she'd been bent over a primer, listening to a little boy haltingly sound out his first words.

"Miss Herzelfeld?"

Rosa had glanced up in surprise, one hand on the boy's shoulder as she murmured her encouragement. "Yes...?"

"Dame Joanna wants to see you immediately."

As Rosa straightened, the blood rushed from her head and, for a second, she felt so dizzy she swayed where she stood. The aide's face was severe and unsmiling. What could the head of the whole camp possibly want with her? Rosa wondered. Had something terrible happened? She did not think it could be good news; releases were announced publicly, in the evening, not by a private summons to the head of the camp. What had gone wrong? Her mind raced as she thought of her mother, whom she'd seen only that morning, and her father, a few weeks ago at the café social. Was one of them hurt?

"Thank you," she murmured, and putting down the primer, she followed the aide to Dame Joanna's office, in a repurposed boarding house along the high street, every step she took filling her with yet more dread.

"Ah, Miss Herzelfeld." Dame Joanna's smile was kind but brisk. "I have had word that you are to leave us."

Rosa stared at her blankly, the words not making any sense. "Leave you...?"

"Yes, as soon as possible, as it happens. You can take the first ferry tomorrow morning, and then the train to Liverpool and onto London. Someone will meet you at Cockfosters Station."

Now Rosa's head was truly whirling. To go all that way on her own... and what for? "But... why?" she asked, caught between fear and a cautious excitement. "Where am I going, exactly?"

Dame Joanna's smile softened as she cocked her head. "I don't know right know, but it seems, my dear," she said, "that you might be wanted for war work."

CHAPTER 21

APRIL 1941—COCKFOSTERS, LONDON

Rosa stepped off the train at Cockfosters and glanced around at the near-empty platform. Only a few people had got off with her, and they were walking briskly away while she stood there, holding her single, shabby suitcase, having no idea what to do or where to go. She was supposed to be met, according to Dame Joanna, but she had no idea by whom and in any case, no one was here.

The day had passed in something of a surreal haze. After Rosa had returned from speaking with Dame Joanna yesterday afternoon, she'd found her mother and explained her unexpected turn of events. Her mother, somewhat to her surprise, had been excited for her.

"Oh Rosa," she'd exclaimed, "what an opportunity! And you'll finally be able to leave Rushen, which I know you've always wanted."

"Yes, but... why?" Rosa had not been able to shake a deepening sense of unease, that she'd had such a mysterious summons. "Why would they request *me* in particular? How do they even know my name?"

Her mother had shrugged. "I imagine they have files on all of us," she'd replied. "This is good news, Rosa, surely?"

"But I don't want to leave you," Rosa had admitted, half surprised she was saying it. She'd become close to her mother while they'd been in the camp, closer than she'd ever been before. She didn't want to lose that, or the camaraderie and industry she'd found here—teaching at the kindergarten, taking classes.

"Oh, my dear." Her mother had put her arms around her, and Rosa had hugged her back, breathing in the familiar scent of her perfume, Chanel No. 5, eked out a precious drop at a time. "We'll be together again soon, I'm sure of it. More and more of us are being released—one of the ladies at the hairdresser's told me three thousand internees have been able to go home since September."

"That many?" The thought had been encouraging. Surely, her mother and father would both be released soon, then.

Although Rosa hadn't been able to get word to her father about her news before she'd left, she'd written a letter for her mother to give to him at the next social. It had been short and simple, stating that she no longer blamed him for his choices, and she wished him well. It had felt oddly final, to write such a letter, and no matter what her mother had said, Rosa had wondered when—and even if—she would see her parents again. The future felt more unknown than ever.

She'd left the Isle of Man on the morning ferry, just past dawn, the sea still covered in shreds of mist. There were a handful of residents going to the mainland for one reason or another, as well as another handful of released internees, eager to start their life of freedom. The two groups kept resolutely separate. Rosa had stood at the ferry's railing, watching the island and its jagged lining of barbed wire get smaller and smaller, until it was no more than a smudge on the horizon, and then it was nothing at all.

The other internees were talking excitedly about returning to their homes and jobs, yet with some apprehension about what still remained, ten months on from their detention. Rosa had not really been able to join in the conversation; she wasn't returning to anything, and Dame Joanna had warned her not to speak of what she was doing—not that she even knew or could guess.

From the docks, she'd taken a train into Liverpool, and then another to London. Both were delayed and filled with soldiers, as well as women in various uniforms; now over eighteen months on from the start of the war, it had seemed as if everyone was serving in some way. After the relative isolation and quiet of the Isle of Man, Rosa had found it all chaotic and loud—the shouting and chatting and laughter, the squeeze and crush of too many people piled into a train, passing around a flask of tea, all very good-natured. She'd ended up pressed next to an elderly lady who was determined to keep on with her knitting, her suitcase on her lap, the ends of the knitting needles poking her in the arm as the excited jabber of a group of Wrens flew around her, for most of the wearying journey.

As the train had trundled slowly into London, she'd seen, with some shock, the extent of the city's bomb damage—whole streets obliterated, houses half-crumbling, roads impassable with rubble. She glimpsed a house with its entire front ripped off, so it looked like a dollhouse, every room visible. On another street, a church had been reduced to nothing but its steeple, cracked in half and lying on the ground. Amidst it all, people went about their business, stepping over rubble, skirting craters in the pavement. Their stoical resilience, glimpsed from the window of a train, humbled her, and it had brought the awful reality of war home to her in a way like nothing else possibly could.

And now she was here, on this empty platform, wondering what on earth she should do.

"Miss Rosa Herzelfeld?" A young woman in the olive-green uniform of the Auxiliary Territorial Service, or ATS, walked smartly up to her.

"Yes..."

"I'm Lance Corporal Elaine Lister. If you could come with me...?"

"Yes, thank you," Rosa murmured, and followed the woman to a waiting car. She was surprised to see the woman slide into the driver's seat, as she hadn't known many women to drive. Rosa put her case in the boot and slid into the back of the car, wondering what on earth would happen next.

"Where are we going, if I may ask?" she inquired after the lance corporal had started the car.

She threw Rosa a smiling glance. "Cockfosters Camp. I don't suppose you've been told anything at all about it?"

"Not a word," Rosa admitted, and Elaine nodded in under-standing.

"That's how it is with everyone. You're told to take a train, you show up on a platform, and you're more or less whisked away. It almost feels like a fairy tale."

"As long as I don't get eaten by a witch in the woods," Rosa joked, and Elaine laughed.

"No fear of that, although Mrs. Gibbins, who runs the kitchen, has a fierce tongue when she's of a mind to! Don't worry, though. It will all be explained to you—well, not *all*, but enough. Everything we do is hush-hush, it's true, and we're not meant to talk among ourselves about our work. That is defi-nitely rule number one, and it's important you keep it."

"All right," Rosa replied, startled and more than a little alarmed by how stern the lance corporal suddenly sounded. It sounded, she thought, like Dame Joanne might have been right, and she *was* wanted for war work. But what kind of war work, that was so hush-hush?

"There was a story going around," Elaine continued, "that

during one interview, Colonel Kendrick passed an Enfield pistol across the desk and told the poor chap that he knew what to do with it if he spilled any secrets! Mum's the word, well and truly."

"Oh my..." Rosa murmured faintly. She hoped that really was just a story.

"But the colonel's a good man," Elaine reassured her. "Although it's true he can be quite lively, and he can have a devilish sense of humor when he wants to. But as long as you keep your tongue in your head and are sensible about it, it should all be just fine." She glanced back at Rosa again, her eyebrows raised. "Are you German?"

This was said in such a friendly, interested way that Rosa was a little taken aback. Mrs. Kneale's kindness aside, she realized she'd become used to the suspicion and wary hostility of many of the Manx residents, with their small island infiltrated by so many Germans.

"Yes," she admitted. "I'm Jewish."

"There are loads of Jewish émigrés working at the camp," Elaine told her. "The colonel recruits them specially. Ah, here we are."

She turned the car through a pair of impressive gates flanked by brick pillars. Rosa glimpsed an elegant country house that had now clearly been repurposed for the war. Prefabricated huts and buildings made of concrete blocks dotted the grounds, and the whole estate was surrounded by a brick wall which had been topped with three rows of barbed wire.

More barbed wire, Rosa thought, and almost laughed. What was going on here, that required these stringent security measures, along with such secrecy?

Their identification was checked as they went through the guard posted at the gate, and handed back without a word. As they drove in, Rosa glimpsed what looked like watchtowers at the corner of the estate; she had no idea what to make of any of

Was this another prison? Maybe she wasn't wanted for war work; perhaps she was simply being detained somewhere else. But Elaine Lister hadn't acted as if she was...

The car drew up to the front of the great house, which was also made of brick, flanked by two impressive wings, window-panes glinting in the late-afternoon sunshine, and slowly Rosa climbed out and went to fetch her bag from the boot.

"Colonel Kendrick will see you in the Blue Room," the lance corporal said, and Rosa nodded, although she had no idea where that was.

"Thank you. Where..." she began, only to have Elaine nod toward the impressive set of paneled front doors.

"Inside. Someone will direct you, don't worry." She gave her a conspiratorial smile. "Trust me, it's all going to be absolutely fine. Welcome to Cockfosters Camp!" And with a smart salute, she drove away.

Slowly, her heart hammering, her suitcase knocking against her knees, Rosa mounted the few, shallow steps to the front doors. Inside the grand foyer, a young man in a military uniform took her name and then directed her to a chair in front of a pair of ornate double doors; several led out from the hall in various directions.

From somewhere in the huge house, Rosa heard the clack of typewriters, the click of heels, the murmur of voices. Although the foyer was empty save for her and the guard, the whole place seemed to be a quiet yet bustling hive of industry. It made Rosa wonder, again, what it was all for... and why on earth she was here.

After about ten minutes, when a few people, both men and women in uniform, had crossed the foyer, giving Rosa no more than cursory, if friendly, glances, the guard sprang to attention. "Colonel Kendrick will see you now," he told Rosa, and she rose from her chair on decidedly unsteady legs.

She tapped once on the door and then turned the handle,

stepping into a large, elegant room with deep blue walls and long, sashed windows overlooking parkland.

Colonel Kendrick stood up from behind a desk in the center of the room; he was in his late fifties, with a sagging, jowly face and bright eyes, his dark hair parted with razor-sharp precision. "Miss Herzelfeld," he said, stretching out one hand, which Rosa took gingerly; she felt as if she were at a party, and yet... not. "I trust you had a good journey? It is a long way, admittedly, from the Isle of Man." He let go of her hand as he sat down, indicating with a nod of his head for her to sit in the chair in front of the desk.

"It is," Rosa agreed after a second's pause. She knew it shouldn't unnerve her that he knew she'd come from Rushen, but it did all the same. How much did he know about her?

She sat down, placing her suitcase on the floor next to her.

"I am sure you are curious as to why you are here," Colonel Kendrick told her with a small, sympathetic smile. Rosa managed a nod. "And what it is we do here. There are many people who are certainly curious about *that*." He leaned back, steepling his fingers together. "Unfortunately, there is very little I can tell you. We operate on a strictly need-to-know basis, Miss Herzelfeld, and the less you know, the better."

Rosa, having expected this thanks to Elaine Lister, simply nodded again.

"Before I go any further," he continued after a moment, "I must ask you to sign this document." He pushed a piece of paper across the desk toward her. "This is the Official Secrets Act," he explained. "When you sign it, you are swearing not to disclose any—and I mean *any*—of the information you might learn here." He paused, steepling his fingers together once more. "If you were to do so, then I'm afraid the Manx internment camp would be far preferable to what would await you."

So, this was her version of the Enfield pistol, Rosa thought wryly. She suspected the colonel was trying to scare her, but she also believed he was deadly serious.

"I see," she murmured and then reached for the pen, dipping it in ink before she carefully signed her name in the relevant place. As she laid the pen down, she forced herself to ask in a voice that quavered only a little. "Now may you tell me what I am doing here? And how you got my name?"

"Your name?" Kendrick sounded surprised. "From your father. I thought you might know that piece of the puzzle, at the least."

"My *father*?" It was just about the last thing she'd expected. Her father had had dealings with whatever went on here, with the British government? She shook her head slowly. "No, I didn't know that," she admitted. "He's being held at a different camp. I don't see him very often. But... how do you know him?"

Kendrick rocked back in his chair. "Your father gave us some very interesting and relevant information," he told her. "Information he'd gathered before the war, back in Berlin, about some of the officers he came into contact with. It's always helpful, you see, to know a man's preferences and predilections. His weaknesses and wants, as well as his hopes and ambitions. Your father gave us quite a lot of information in regard to all that, as well as a few choice titbits he overheard, by the by."

Rosa struggled not to gape in shock at this news. Clearly Kendrick knew about her father's pre-war associations; just as, clearly, he did not take the same view of them as the interrogators once had. Her head spun.

"He also mentioned *you*," Kendrick continued with a smile. "And how you might be of service to us."

"How?" Rosa asked helplessly. She still felt completely lost, as well as a little afraid.

Kendrick was silent for a moment, his gaze fixed somewhere on the ceiling, before he leveled it at Rosa. "Did you happen to notice the watchtowers outside, Miss Herzelfeld?"

"Yes," she admitted unsteadily.

"It reminded you of the Manx camp, perhaps."

"Yes." Her voice wavered and she forced herself to lift her chin, meet his thoughtful yet shrewd gaze directly. "It did."

"That's because this is another internment camp, of sorts, but one for German prisoners of war. Soldiers, pilots, officers, the lot. Those we have captured come here for a week or two usually, a respite of sorts, before they are moved on to a proper camp. They are interrogated here and any information they give us is then analyzed."

He paused again, as if waiting for her to speak, yet Rosa had no idea what to say.

Prisoners of war? She was still reeling from the knowledge that her father had something to do with her being here. Was this what he'd meant when he'd said everything would change? Had he given the information then, back on the Isle of Man, and mentioned her, as well? But why hadn't he explained any of it to her?

"Your role here," Kendrick continued, "would be to translate the transcripts of the interrogations."

This seemed to require some response, so Rosa murmured, "I see."

"When we first started this business," Kendrick's tone turned almost jocular, "it was all Brits who were fluent in German. They served well, but having it as a second language can only take you so far. We soon realized we needed proper German speakers, those who knew dialects, slang, specialized language." He raised his eyebrows as if expecting an answer, and Rosa did her best to nod her understanding. "We've got people here who know all the parts of an airplane, and others who know all the Wehrmacht lingo." He gave her an appraising look. "You were recommended because of your knowledge of the Berlin dialect, as well as some of the regional slang. You've rubbed elbows, I believe, with a number of Nazi officers, some of them high-ranking?"

Rosa could not keep a flush from rising to her face. So, he knew. "Before the war, yes..." she admitted quietly.

Kendrick nodded, unsurprised, matter-of-fact. "That could prove to be immensely helpful in your translations," he stated briskly. "We've become stumped, you see, on some of the words these blighters use." He smiled then, looking quite cheerful, yet Rosa remained deeply shaken by it all. She thought of Peter, telling her at the beginning of the war that her German might prove useful. She had never expected her former associations to be useful, as well, quite the opposite, but that seemed to be what the colonel was saying...

"I will do whatever I can to help," she finally remarked.

"Good." Kendrick nodded again, like an ending to their conversation. "You can see the quartermaster for your digs. Naturally, there is to be no discussion whatsoever about what you are doing with others who work here. Remember, it's all on a need-to-know basis. *Strictly.*"

"Yes," Rosa agreed as she stood up; it seemed the interview was over. "I won't say a word."

She was almost at the door when Colonel Kendrick spoke again. "You know, I worked as a British Passport Officer in Vienna, years ago."

Rosa turned around slowly, having no idea why he was telling her such a thing now, yet clearly, he'd waited until just this moment to mention the fact. "Oh, yes?" she replied politely.

"Yes, I struck a bargain with Adolf Eichmann, a few years ago now. He wanted the Jews out of Germany, just as I did. We agreed, between the two of us, to give a thousand Jews visas for British Palestine. The British authorities never knew a thing about the deal."

Rosa simply blinked at him.

"Sometimes," he finished softly, "you have to do a deal with the devil. There's no shame in it. In fact, I think it requires its own kind of valor." He nodded toward the door. "You may go, Miss Herzelfeld."

Rosa walked out of the room in a daze. She felt as if she needed to sit somewhere quiet for a long time, and simply let all she'd learned settle inside her. Right now, everything felt jumbled up; she had a strange yet strong urge to burst into tears.

Then, quite suddenly, she felt a pair of hands grip her shoulders rather hard, making her gasp.

"*Rosa,*" a man said, and Rosa lifted her head to blink him into focus. He was standing right in front of her, his hands still on her shoulders, a look of wonder and joy on his face.

Rosa's mouth dropped open as her mind reeled yet again.

"*Peter...*" she whispered.

CHAPTER 22

"I can't believe you're here!"

Peter squeezed her shoulders before dropping his hands as he shook his head wonderingly. "How did you... Have you just arrived?"

"Yes, just this moment almost," Rosa replied.

It seemed truly incredible that Peter was standing there in front of her, looking exactly as he always did—mussed hair, glinting eyes, a wry smile. He'd tucked his right hand behind his back, just the way she remembered. He looked wonderful, she thought with a rush of both awe and affection, as her heart turned over. *Wonderful.* She let out a little laugh of disbelief and joy.

"I just finishing speaking with Colonel Kendrick," she explained, and then, not knowing if she should have admitted even that much, she shut her mouth abruptly.

"I went to look for you, back when you first disappeared," Peter told her. "I was so worried! The Rosenbaums told me you'd been taken away to be interned, but they didn't know where." His mouth twisted. "It was because of your father and his wretched activities, I suppose."

A bitter edge corroded his voice, and Rosa swallowed. Now was hardly the time to admit her whole part in the business, and yet Peter's words, as well as his tone, reminded her that not everyone was as pragmatic or understanding as Colonel Kendrick.

"I was interned," she acknowledged carefully. "On the Isle of Man, in the north."

"I can't believe it." Peter briefly gripped her shoulders again before dropping his hands as he gave her an abashed smile. "I'm sorry. I'm overwrought. It's just... I thought I might never see you again. The Rosenbaums couldn't tell me anything. They've kept your things, by the way. They were very concerned for all of you."

"That's very kind of them." Rosa paused before admitting, "I thought I might never see you again, either. It... it distressed me terribly, Peter."

He smiled a little at that, and she felt her heart skip another beat. She really had missed him, more than she'd been willing to admit even to herself... and he'd clearly missed her! The thought was, in its own way, intoxicating.

"Are you busy now?" he asked. "Could you spare the time for a cup of tea in the canteen?"

Rosa nodded. She still felt jumbled up inside, but she was so very glad to see Peter. "That would be wonderful," she told him. "I'm meant to find out where I'm staying, but I suppose that can wait."

"Good, because there's so much we need to catch up on."

Peter led her through a warren of corridors back to a big, comfortable kitchen with a scarred and well-used butcher's block and massive cooking range at one end and a long trestle table at the other. Several Welsh dressers lined the walls, filled with blue and white crockery. Peter guided her to the table and then went to fetch cups of tea. The cook, the aforementioned Mrs. Gibbins, Rosa supposed, was elbow deep in flour. She gave her a quick, distracted smile of welcome as Rosa sank into a chair.

She felt as if her whole world had tilted, upended, *scattered*... and she was still coming to grips with how to feel about it all. And now *Peter*... Peter here. It was truly incredible to her that they would have found each other again, and in such a place as this.

"Here we are," Peter announced, returning with cups of tea. "Milky and sweet as you like it."

"Where did you get the sugar?" she exclaimed, only for Peter to tap the side of his nose knowingly.

"We're vital to the war effort now, don't you know. Rationing isn't quite as severe here as it might have been where you were—where was it, again?"

"The Isle of Man." Rosa took a sip of the hot tea, savoring its sweetness.

"I'm so sorry," Peter said quietly as he sat down opposite her, cradling his good hand around his own cup. "You didn't deserve that."

Again, Rosa felt the need to come clean, and again she recognized that now was not the time. "It wasn't so bad really," she told him. "I was able to take classes in all sorts of subjects, and there was a wonderful library. We had quite a bit of freedom. I helped with the kindergarten, and my mother set up her own dressmaking business." She felt a surprising pang of nostalgia for the life they'd both made at Rushen, such as it had been. She'd been beginning to find her place there, and now she was somewhere entirely new and strange. At least here, she told herself, she'd be able to help with the war effort.

"Still," Peter persisted, "to come to this country and be treated so... It's unconscionable, really."

Rosa shrugged, more pragmatic now than she'd been back at the camp. "It's a war."

He reached over to clasp her hand with his good one. "I

admire your attitude." He paused, his hand still on hers. "I... really missed you, Rosa."

She smiled at him, laying her other hand on top of his. "I missed you, too."

"I mean..." He swallowed, glancing down at their hands. "I *really* missed you."

Rosa's heart stuttered in her chest. Was he implying what she thought he was? It felt like too much, on top of everything else she'd learned that day. She wasn't ready to process it all, to figure out how she wanted to respond, and yet she also knew she was pleased.

"I'm glad we've found each other again," she said, and Peter nodded, removing his hand from between hers.

"I am, as well."

They lapsed into a short silence as they sipped their tea, and then Rosa asked, "Have you been here long? I don't know much about this place, only what Colonel Kendrick told me, but it does seem very secretive."

"It is, rather. I've been here for three months. They recruited quite a few Jewish émigrés, for our German. Do you know what you'll be doing?"

"Translation." She hoped she was allowed to admit that much.

Peter gave a quick nod. "And that's probably all you should say about it, I imagine. They don't like us talking amongst ourselves... some of the typists and things think we're a supply depot, although..." He lowered his voice. "It's rather hard to hide the prisoners. You see them about, taking the air. They're given quite a lot of freedom here."

"Are they?" Rosa didn't know how she felt about that. What would she say or feel, if she were to come face to face with a Nazi soldier? Hopefully that would never happen, especially if she was closeted in an office somewhere, poring over transcripts.

"Anyway, I don't suppose we should talk about it," Peter

conceded with a wry grimace, before his eyes lit up. "There's a dance at the local pub on Friday—will you come to that? I've got two left feet, as they say, but I'd still be glad for a spin with you. A lot of the staff here go along, and it can be quite a laugh."

"I'd love to," she said.

Rosa smiled, filled with a shy pleasure at the thought. A dance, and with *Peter*. They were together again at last.

A short while later, having finished her tea and said goodbye to Peter, Rosa headed upstairs, following the directions given to her, to the room she would be sharing with another translator. The ground and first floors of the great house had been turned into a rabbit warren of offices; as Rosa mounted the stairs, she heard once more the murmur of voices, the click of heels, the rustle of paper and the clack of typewriters. Everyone seemed very busy.

Two more floors and she found herself in the attics, right under the eaves; the room halfway down the narrow corridor was clearly hers, with one side completely empty, regulation sheets and blanket folded on top of a bare mattress. Rosa put down her suitcase and let out a long, low breath. She still could hardly believe she was here, and really, she didn't truly know where *here* was... or what it would mean for her.

She moved to the room's one dormer window, stooping a little so she didn't hit her head on the ceiling, as she peered out at the house's grounds. Rolling parkland was covered with prefabricated huts and an L-shaped concrete-block building that she suspected must house the prisoners.

Prisoners of war, here! It was odd, she reflected, to go from one internment camp to another, and yet have a very different role in each. Now she was essentially on the *outside* of the barbed wire... her freedom had been gained so quickly she couldn't quite believe in it yet. She was almost afraid to trust it, to test it. And what of the prisoners themselves? Rosa didn't know if she would even see them, but the prospect gave her a shudder of apprehension. The last thing she wanted was to come face to face with a dyed-in-the-wool Nazi... again.

As for all the other things she'd learned—about her father, as well as Peter being here... Rosa pressed one hand to her cheek. It really felt like too much to take in.

She turned from the window and began to unpack her belongings, sliding her few garments into the drawers of the bureau at the end of her bed. The skirts and blouses she'd made do with for the last ten months at Rushen seemed worn indeed, but she supposed everyone would begin to look a little shabby, what with clothing about to be rationed. At least her mother had managed to freshen up a few of the pieces—new buttons on a blouse, stitching on a skirt.

Rosa had just finished putting it all away when a woman in the drab olive of the ATS uniform came into the room, stopping abruptly when she caught sight of Rosa.

"I say," she exclaimed, "are you my new roommate? Jolly nice to meet you." She was tall and strong-boned, with a friendly, freckled face, her auburn hair pulled back into a neat bun under her cap. She stuck out a hand which Rosa shook. "I'm Sally Heyward."

"Rosa Herzelfeld."

"Oh, are you German? How brilliant." Sally sounded warmly enthusiastic, just as Elaine Lister had. "We truly do need the real deal here, you know. We're getting awfully stumped on some of the slang. You're a translator, as well, aren't you?"

"Yes," Rosa admitted, still feeling cautious, despite Sally's friendliness.

"Well, you know we're not meant to talk about anything," her new roommate confided with an amiable roll of her eyes, "but I guess you've gathered the gist of it?"

"We're... we're translating transcripts of the interrogations of prisoners of war, aren't we?"

"That's it, yes. Although not just their interrogations. It's what they say in their cells that's really important."

Rosa frowned. "In their cells?"

Sally looked startled, and then guarded, and then she let out a laugh as she shrugged. "Did no one tell you about that? Well, it will be obvious soon enough, I should think, when you read a transcript and see the kind of things they're saying. The trick here is that they *think* they're being interrogated and that's all that's happening, but it's really not." Her brown eyes gleamed with humor as she leaned forward, lowering her voice as she explained it all. "We've got the whole place bugged with microphones! Their cells, the social rooms, even some areas outside. That's what we're translating, really, along with the interrogations, but those aren't nearly as useful. A lot of our interrogators play dumb to lull the prisoners into thinking they don't know anything—and then they spill it to each other in their cells!" She let out a hoot of laughter. "Genius, really, isn't it?" She stopped suddenly, an uneasy look crossing her face. "Golly, I hope I was all right in telling you all that. Maybe you're just translating the proper interrogations and aren't meant to know about the other stuff..."

"I won't tell a soul," Rosa promised her quickly. "And really, I imagine everyone knows more about what's going on here than they're letting on."

Sally looked a little relieved. "Yes, I'm sure they do. They must do, if they've any sense! But pretend to forget I said all that, all right? My mum was always telling me off for having a big mouth. But this isn't the place for it, that's for certain!" She let out another laugh, this one sounding a bit hollow. Rosa could tell she was genuinely worried she'd said more than she should have, and in truth she probably had.

"No, it isn't," she agreed, smiling. She liked Sally's easy

friendliness and was grateful for her ready acceptance of Rosa's nationality.

As for keeping quiet about such secrets... well, Rosa reflected with a sober ruefulness, she certainly knew how to do that.

CHAPTER 23

Rosa soon found herself falling into a routine that was both interesting and challenging. Each day, she showed up in the large, pleasant reception room on the first floor that served as an office for about a dozen translators, many of them, as Rosa had been told, Jewish émigrés like herself. Although they were busy with work and tight-lipped about what they did, they were friendly and approachable outside the office; those without officer rank ate together in the kitchen, at the big table where Rosa had had a cup of tea with Peter. In the evenings, there were card games or singalongs around the piano, or occasional forays out to the pub or village hall. It was more socializing than Rosa had had since she'd arrived in Great Britain, and she found she enjoyed it. She was finally starting to feel as if she belonged somewhere... somewhere she wanted to be.

Each day's work followed the same format—she sat herself down at her desk and worked her way through the pile of transcripts that inevitably appeared in the wooden filing box. It hadn't taken her long to discover that Sally had been right—the transcripts of the interrogations were far less informative and interesting than those of the prisoners talking to each other in their cells, when their words were unguarded. Rosa found the prisoners were either carelessly boastful or sorrowfully despondent, and both emotions, rather poignantly, came through in the transcripts.

Rosa translated conversations about movements of battleships and mine-laying techniques; engine sizes and U-boat losses. Everything she translated was sent onto another facility for analysis, only known as "Station X," and while Rosa knew she wasn't meant to make assumptions or judgments about what she translated, she found it was becoming abundantly clear that many of the German prisoners, especially those of lower rank, felt they were losing the war.

In one transcript, she translated that of the seventy U-boats in operation, thirty-five had already been sunk. *And no trained crews to replace the ones that were lost*, she translated. *We'll lose this war one boat at a time.*

The mood at Cockfosters Camp was, Rosa found, cheerfully energetic and infectious. There could be no doubting that they were doing important work; the information they gathered and sent on was, she suspected, critical to intelligence operations. It put a spring in her step, a note of enthusiasm in her voice, to realize she was actually, amazingly, doing something important, when just weeks ago she'd been languishing back at Rushen, trapped behind barbed wire, wondering if she'd ever make a difference in the world.

She'd written to her parents, as well as Sophie, with an address to write to her—no more than a postbox in London where mail was forwarded on to the relevant place and person. While she could divulge no details about what she was actually doing, she assured her family and friend that she was happy and productive, and that the work was interesting.

Three days after she'd arrived, she'd gone to the dance at the local village hall with Peter and a few dozen others from the camp—they all tended to be young and enthusiastic, and the dance floor was crowded for the entire evening. Rosa had danced with Peter, and then with several other young men whose faces blurred and whose names she'd forgotten if she'd ever known them in the first place; there were far more men than women at Cockfosters and so Rosa, like the ATS girls, was in high demand.

As she had come off the dance floor, breathless and laughing, Peter had pressed a glass of lemonade into her hand.

"You looked like you needed a drink," he'd remarked wryly, "and this is the only way I think I'll be able to spend time with you!"

"I'm sorry," Rosa had replied, regretful but also energized. She hadn't had so much fun—hadn't *let* herself have so much fun—in years. "I can't remember the last time I danced so much!"

"Maybe back in Berlin?"

Rosa had glanced at him sharply, but she could tell from the relaxed look on his face that there was no hidden edge to the question. She really needed to tell Peter about her life back in Berlin, she'd acknowledged as she'd taken a sip of lemonade. But how to do it? She didn't want to jeopardize their friendship, and in any case, it was all in the past. She wasn't the same girl who had fallen for Ernst Weber, SS Obersturmführer.

Sometimes, as she read the transcripts of the prisoners, men who had served in the Luftwaffe or the *Kriegsmarine*, she wondered what Ernst was doing in the war. Was he still in Berlin, working in administration, or had he joined the Waffen-SS, the military arm of the *Schutzstaffel*? He'd always been so keen to prove himself, his valor, and as a young, fit man he would, Rosa suspected, be expected to fight.

When, at the end of June, it was announced that Germany

had invaded the Soviet Union, with all of the Waffen-SS forma-
tions involved in the operation, she wondered if Ernst was
among them, pushing forward in a never-ending line of tanks
toward Moscow.

The news had been a cause for celebration at Cockfosters,
and indeed throughout most of the country. With Hitler's forces
amassed along an eighteen-hundred-mile border with the Soviet
Union, there was little leftover to fight the other Allies. The
relentless bombing of London and other cities began to subside,
and it felt, especially when taking the mood of the prisoners into
account, as if the tide might slowly but surely be turning.

"The end is a long way off yet," Peter warned her as they
walked through the house's parkland, away from the prisoner
block.

It was a lovely summer's day in late July, the trees in full
leaf, the sun shining high above in a hazy blue sky. They'd taken
to going on such walks during their breaks from work, or into
the village for a drink in the evening. They were still just
friends, but Sally had remarked, with a waggle of her eyebrows,
that she'd like a *friend* like that. Rosa had simply smiled, hoping
she was right.

"But Hitler's completely abandoned the Western Front,"
Rosa argued now, good-naturedly. She felt optimistic, almost
fizzy with hope; while the news from Russia was bad—with the
Wehrmacht now a mere two hundred miles from Moscow—it
did seem as if Germany's Western front was collapsing under
the lack of manpower. And meanwhile, her parents, along with
thousands of others, had been released from internment camp;
they were back in Belsize Park, sharing their old flat with the
Rosenbaums, who had kept everything safe for them, just as
Peter had assured her.

Her mother had written, and Rosa had been able to feel her
excitement leaping off the page.

Zlata and I are going into business together. Dressmaking, of course! Zlata as seamstress and I doing the designs. We are mainly serving the émigré community, repurposing what they've brought with them. I like to think, in our own small way, we are contributing to the war effort. As is your father, would you believe! He is taking English classes and volunteers with the Home Guard, to treat those who have been injured in bombing raids who can't get to hospital—the air raids have been terrible, but at least they are tapering off now. It is good to see your father occupied. It is what he has needed. Something changed in him while in camp, and I think it has been for the better.

Rosa had marveled at the change in her parents, and been thankful that they were free, and more importantly, were making something of themselves in this new life, just as she was. She still wasn't quite sure how her father had arranged for her to come to Cockfosters Camp, but she was grateful for his hand in it. She hoped one day she'd be able to tell him so. It all gave her a heady sense of the future, formless as it remained, and all it might hold... Something she was acutely conscious of, walking in the summer sunshine with Peter.

"But just because Hitler's stopped bombing us here," he continued seriously, his hands shoved into the pockets of his trousers, his hair flopping down on his forehead, "doesn't mean we've beaten them, or even come close to beating them. We've got to take back all of Europe, for a start, and that surely means an invasion."

It was an inevitability that was on everyone's minds, and yet still felt so far away. "When do you think that will happen?" Rosa asked.

Peter shook his head. "Not for some time, I should think. We can't have another Dunkirk. This time it's got to stick."

"When the Americans get involved..." Rosa began hopefully. She'd heard from Sophie, and it seemed, judging from the vagueness of her letters, that she was involved in some kind of hush-hush work, as well. And if that was the case, Rosa reasoned, then surely the American government was preparing for war? It just had to be a matter of time.

"When," Peter asked ruefully, "or *if?*"

"They can't give up all of Europe!" Rosa argued. "No one wants war, I understand that, but some things must be fought. Surely the Americans realize that. They might be all the way across the Atlantic, but a Europe controlled by Hitler couldn't be good for them."

"You sound so fierce," Peter replied with a smile. They'd slowed to a stop underneath the spreading branches of a cherry tree, and now he turned to her, a serious look coming over his face that made Rosa's heart skip a hopeful beat. "And you're right. Some things must be fought... and some things must be said."

Rosa caught her breath, her heart starting to beat double time. Did he mean what she thought he did? What she *hoped* he did?

Peter reached for her hands, clasping them in his own. She could feel the crooked, bent length of the two injured fingers on his right hand and it made her ache with both pride and sorrow. He was such a brave, good man. A man she knew she was falling in love with, bit by cautious bit.

After Ernst, she'd been so wary to give her heart away again, and she'd felt she didn't deserve such happiness, but those old fears had blown away like cobwebs in a clean, healing wind. She wanted to be happy now... and she knew she wanted to be happy with Peter Gelb.

"What sorts of things?" she asked, her voice coming out in a breathless whisper.

Gently, he squeezed her hands. "I think you know, but I'll tell you anyway. I'll gladly tell you, because I've been wanting to say it for weeks now, if not months." Once more, his hands tightened briefly on hers. "When the Rosenbaums told me you'd been interned... and I didn't know if I'd ever be able to find you again..." He swallowed hard. "It made me realize what I'd almost thrown away, Rosa. I know I let your father come between us, and that was stupid and wrong. Why should you be beholden for another's choices? I didn't expect to feel that way, honestly I didn't. I'm not even sure why I did." He paused, his throat working, his forehead furrowed in thought. "I suppose because I knew so many people who suffered terribly under those beasts. Men who died in Dachau, or wished they had. Neighbors who were arrested in the middle of the night, taken away, never to be seen again. The thought that your father had avoided all that by cozying up to the people I've hated, that we all should hate..." He trailed off, shaking his head.

Rosa's heart, once beating so hard with hope and happiness, now felt as if it had completely stilled in her chest. Her hands were cold, clasped in Peter's. She'd put off telling him the truth about her past for so long, had convinced herself it had become irrelevant, but Peter's words put paid to that naïve notion.

"Peter," she said quietly, slipping her hands from his, "if you are going to judge my father for his choices, then you must also judge me for mine..."

Peter's forehead creased, his mouth pulled down into a frown. "Rosa, what are you saying?"

She expelled a shaky breath, wiping her now-damp palms along her skirt. "I'm saying I was complicit in some of my father's choices," she stated, surprised at the sudden rush of relief she felt, to finally be fully honest. "I didn't mean to be, and I certainly didn't *want* to be. When he first started treating Nazi officers... well, I don't remember exactly when, but I must have been fifteen or so. He became known as someone with something of a magic touch—for venereal diseases, as you've said before." She grimaced slightly. "A rather sordid element, I know, but the men appreciated his treatment, and they found him... amusing, I suppose. Charming. They'd been coming to our house for discreet treatment, and it sort of started from that. They'd stay for a drink, and then they were joined by others. This was before the race laws, you understand. Before Jews were truly vilified."

Peter's lips tightened but he didn't say anything, just gave a terse nod to indicate she should continue.

"I didn't have anything to do with it, not at first, and I didn't want to. The men seemed so... loud to me, so *big*. And my mother acted as hostess to begin with." She stopped, conscious of Peter's frown deepening, as well as apprehensive about telling any more of the story.

"But then?" he prompted after a moment, and she could not tell anything from his tone.

"But then my mother started claiming she had a headache, and could not act as hostess, so my father asked me." She glanced away, steeling herself to say more. "I think the first time I must have been sixteen or seventeen. Young, but old enough to know better, perhaps, especially as things had become more dangerous to Jews. There was a sense, every evening, that you weren't quite sure what might happen. Whether one of the officers would suddenly stop laughing and point his pistol at you instead." She shivered, remembering that feeling of tension and fear, like everything in her had been pulled tight. By the end of every night, she'd been trembling with exhaustion, desperate not to do it again.

Until she'd met Ernst...

She swallowed, staring down at the ground. "I admit, there were times when I enjoyed dressing up, feeling grownup and elegant. Sometimes I enjoyed the attention the officers gave me —looking back, I think they thought it all one big joke. '*Look at*

*us, drinking a Jew's schnapps and flirting with his daughter!
Playing his piano and there's not a damned thing he can do about
any of it!'"* Her voice had become hard without her realizing. "It
suited my father, though, because while they came and while he
treated them, we were sheltered from the sorts of things you saw
—camps, arrests, even just being bothered in the street. It was
like we had a special shield around us."

She glanced up at him again; his face was expressionless,
which worried her, and she was so very tempted to not say the
rest. But, no. Now was the time for truth, for honesty. No
matter what happened. No matter how much it hurt.

"I admit, I was glad about that, as well, even though it alien-
ated us from our Jewish friends. We existed in a bubble—it was
lonely, but it was safe. Mostly, anyway." Although, in the end,
that sense of safety had been an illusion, just like Ernst's
affection.

"How difficult it must have been for you," Peter remarked,
his tone terribly flat, and Rosa couldn't help but recoil.

"I'm not excusing *any* of it, Peter," she protested, her voice
catching. "I'm simply telling you the truth. Yes, my father
treated Nazis for venereal diseases. In that, he had no choice. If
he had not treated them, he would likely have been arrested. As
for entertaining them... did he have a choice then? Yes, perhaps.
And did I? Again, *perhaps*. I could have refused my father, I
suppose, and stayed hidden upstairs. The officers enjoying his
hospitality would have never known I existed. Sometimes I do
wish that I had done that." She drew a shaky breath, recalling
the many times she'd thought such a thing, wished for it desperately, while knowing such regret was useless. "But I was young,
impressionable," she continued. "I wanted to please my father,
and yes, I confess, have the attention of those officers. Some of
them, anyway." One in particular.

Peter's mouth twisted. "How could you resist the charm of a
Nazi officer?"

"I know it sounds terrible," she replied in a low voice, "but surely you've encountered some of the prisoners here?" She knew she was on shaky ground; they weren't meant to talk about what they did at the camp, but with his knowledge of German, Peter had to be involved with the prisoners in some way. Judging by the way he gave a curt nod, she was right. "Some of them are vicious and brutal," she continued, "but others... they're just *men*." She'd heard their voices coming through the transcripts—the fear for their wives, the affection for their children, their wry sense of humor, or their enjoyment of the simple pleasure of a sunset or a stein of beer. They weren't *all* monsters, even if they had certainly been a part of incredibly monstrous things.

"They're not just *men*, Rosa," Peter replied harshly, his whole face twisting into a ferocious scowl. "Or at least not men like me, like those I admire or accept or simply understand. They are *evil*. They chose to do the most evil, heinous things imaginable, to innocent lives. Yes, they are fellow human beings, with the natural desires and weaknesses of any such creature—but they do not deserve either my pity or my respect."

Rosa swallowed hard. She knew he was right, and yet... "Peter..." she began helplessly.

"How could you think otherwise?" he demanded, and she stared at him miserably, having no answer. How on earth could she now tell him about Ernst?

"Hey, Herzelfeld!"

Startled, Rosa whirled away from Peter's glare, squinting to see a fellow translator standing a few dozen yards away. How much had she heard?

"Yes?" Rosa called, her voice wavering.

"You're wanted in the Blue Room ASAP. Something important, it seems."

Rosa's heart, already sore and wounded, did a freefall of

fear. *What now?* she thought in dread. She glanced at Peter, who simply shrugged.

"You need to go. We'll talk later."

"Peter—"

"Herzelfeld, you're needed *now*."

Rosa hurried back to the house, her heart like a stone inside her.

CHAPTER 24

"Ah, Miss Herzelfeld. Please sit down."

Rosa lowered herself onto the chair in front of Colonel Kendrick's desk, just as she'd done nearly three months ago. Now she wasn't facing the kindly but shrewd colonel, however, but his second-in-command, Lieutenant Richard Pennell. Colonel Kendrick had been absent from the Cockfosters Camp almost since Rosa had first seen him; all that was known was that he was on an important mission up north. Rumors had swirled around the camp, that Intelligence had managed to snag a high-ranking SS officer Kendrick was now interrogating, but no one knew who it was.

"Lieutenant Pennell," Rosa murmured, clasping her hands together tightly in her lap. Her heart ached with grief for Peter and the conversation she knew they still needed to have, but she forced herself to push it down as she focused on the man in front of her. What could he possibly want?

"You have done good work here, since you've been with us, Miss Herzelfeld," Lieutenant Pennell remarked. "Very good work."

Rosa would have been relieved by such a comment, save for

the rather calculating look in the lieutenant's eyes, the narrowed purse of his lips. "Thank you, sir," she said quietly.

"I have a different sort of task for you now," he continued, "but one that could help us greatly in our efforts. In this line of work, we sometimes have to do the unexpected, don't we? Think outside of the box, as it were." He smiled, as if inviting her to share a joke, but Rosa had no idea what it was, and in any case, she wasn't in the right frame of mind to find anything funny.

"Sir?"

He took a file from on the desk in front of him and tossed it to her. Rosa found herself having to lunge forward to catch it, drawing it closed before the papers within fluttered out.

"Have a look at that," he said, and then turned away to face the window, as if he hadn't a care in the world.

With great trepidation, Rosa opened the file—and then gave a revealing gasp out loud at the photo of the handsome man on the first page, his blond hair brushed back from his forehead just as she remembered, his bright gaze staring straight at the camera, unwavering, piercing.

Hauptmann Ernst Weber.

"I can see he's familiar to you," Pennell remarked, turning around as Rosa gaped down at the photograph of the man she'd once thought she'd loved, her heart twisting inside her as a thousand memories flashed through her mind in a poignant kaleidoscope. Ernst smiling tenderly down at her. Ernst laughing, plucking a glass of champagne from her fingers as she grinned up at him, silly with love. Ernst threading his fingers through hers. *Rosa, if I could change the world...*

"Yes," she said after a moment, her voice a little hoarse. She knew she could not deny it. She closed the file, and Pennell raised his eyebrows.

"You don't want to read any further?"

"No," Rosa replied quietly.

"Weber was captured a few months ago," Pennell told her, "but he's only come to us in the last few days. Perhaps you didn't see in his file, but he commanded a squadron of fighters that have been bombing Britain for the last year." He paused, as if waiting for a reply.

Rosa slowly shook her head. Ernst was here, in England? At Cockfosters Camp? Maybe just meters away from her right now... the thought made her head spin. "I..." She licked her lips. "I didn't know."

"I didn't expect that you would."

"I didn't even know he was a pilot," Rosa told him. "He wasn't... when I knew him."

"He started his training in September 1939," Pennell told her. "Just after war was declared. The Waffen-SS, as you might know, are only involved in land operations. Weber must have asked to be transferred to the Luftwaffe... or perhaps it was a punishment of some sorts?" He glanced at her in query, his eyebrows lifting, his eyes flashing with insight. "You know the average lifespan of a pilot in the Luftwaffe is just five weeks? About the same as the RAF, but I imagine it starts to feel like a death wish. You might have noticed, from the transcripts you've translated, that some of the pilots are starting to seem, shall we say, a bit despondent? Thirty percent losses across the board, with not enough air crew to replace them. It must all begin to feel rather futile, don't you think?"

He withdrew a cigarette from his jacket pocket and lit it while Rosa watched him, having no idea what sort of response he expected from her. What could he possibly want with her, in regard to Ernst? And yet... Ernst was here. After the conversation she'd just had with Peter, it seemed incredible. Impossible. And most, most unwanted...

"I would imagine it does, yes," she agreed after a moment. She hesitated, and then decided to be direct. "Is there a particular reason you have called me here, Lieutenant Pennell?" she asked. "Is there a way you believe I can help?" Even if she had absolutely no idea how, and in truth she didn't want to know. Didn't want to have to even *think* about Ernst Weber.

Pennell smiled briefly before he took a drag of his cigarette. "As a matter of fact, yes, but it's not what you might think. Weber is in an interesting frame of mind—quite disillusioned, I'd say, with both the Luftwaffe and Hitler himself. I gather he was something of an acolyte, back in the day? Quite young, when he joined the SS."

"His family..." Rosa swallowed. Ernst had told her he had joined at his father's urging, a shrewd political decision after Hitler came to power. He'd insisted he wasn't like some of the other officers, who were rabid in their convictions. And yet what had she really been able to believe?

Still, it had been the so-called gentlemen, the Nazis who managed to seem like reasonable men, who had come to her father's house. Sometimes Rosa wondered which type of man was actually more dangerous; at least with the officers who were vociferous in proclaiming their convictions, you could not let yourself be deceived.

"If he had strong convictions," she said after a pause, "he tried to hide them from me." *I don't like it any more than you do, Rosa...* She swallowed. "How... how did you come to know of my... association... with him?"

"It came through the transcripts, Miss Herzelfeld. Weber mentioned it himself, to his cellmate, another disillusioned soul. Talked about a sweet Jewish girl he knew, back in the day, and how her father treated officers for the clap. It wasn't hard to put two and two together." He smiled, coolly. "We are intelligence officers, after all."

"I... see," Rosa said after a moment, her voice faint.

The knowledge that Ernst was *here*, and he'd been talking about her, and other staff had heard and understood, felt utterly overwhelming—and defeating. What must they think of her?

She knew that secret listeners eavesdropped on all the conversations between prisoners; they were the ones who recorded the transcripts that Rosa then translated. She suspected Peter was one, although he hadn't spoken of his work, just as she hadn't of hers. Could he have heard Ernst himself?

The prospect was appalling. But surely not... he'd seemed so surprised when she'd told him about her association with SS officers. She hadn't had the opportunity, or really, the courage to mention Ernst to him then... How on earth, Rosa wondered with a sinking feeling, would he react, knowing the SS officer she'd fallen in love with was right *here*, at Cockfosters Camp? It felt like some sort of monstrous joke, and her life was the punchline.

"Miss Herzelfeld," Pennell said, sitting up straight and stubbing his cigarette out, "I will be direct, as you seem a young woman who appreciates candor. Weber undoubtedly has information that could be essential to the war effort, in particular regard to some wireless transmitter codes. He's mentioned them in passing, but kept himself from giving the actual codes away. All he needs is a little nudge in the right direction, and we think he'll offer those codes up himself. We need *you* to give him the nudge."

Rosa's mouth dropped open. "What..." she began faintly, shaking her head as if to clear it. "How?"

"Not in the way you'd think. You're not a trained intelligence officer, obviously, nor an interrogator, so naturally we don't expect you to do either. We don't want you to do either, in fact. The last thing you should be doing is talking shop with a man like Weber!" He paused to give her a stern look, his dark eyebrows drawing together. "But you did know him," he continued, "once upon a time, and he's still clearly fond of you. We want to act on that knowledge."

Rosa shook her head again, dread pooling in her stomach. "I... I still don't understand how I can help."

Pennell leaned forward. "Weber is despondent. He's started to question the whole purpose of the war. He's called Hitler a madman. This is strong stuff for someone who once was in the SS, you understand. If he truly believes the war could be lost, if he can see a future where Germany is defeated... then there is a good chance he will aid us in making that happen."

"You want to... *turn*... him?" Rosa asked slowly.

"Turn him?" Pennell spoke as if this were a novel idea. "Perhaps," he allowed. "Or perhaps just act on his sense of disillusionment. Either way, that's where you come in, Miss Herzelfeld. We will arrange for you to meet him at a nightclub in London—"

"*What*—" Rosa could not keep the astonishment from her voice. She felt as if Lieutenant Pennell had just completely switched directions—a *nightclub*? He was surely talking nonsense!

"Yes, a nightclub," he continued calmly. "We are giving Weber and a few others a tour of London—the kind of tour that avoids bombed streets and shows our lovely buildings of Parliament operating as usual. We'll add a few plucky commoners for him to meet—staged, naturally—to show just how amazingly well good old Blighty is resisting the Jerries and will do so for the foreseeable future. While he's contemplating this, we'll take him to a nightclub for drinks, dancing, music— and he'll see you, looking utterly beautiful, from across the room."

Rosa found herself flushing. Part of her—a tiny, treacherous part—yearned for such a scenario. Another, larger part backed away in horror. "I don't see how..."

"You won't talk about the war, or anything to do with what goes on here," Pennell continued severely. "Not a peep. You're just a beautiful young woman in London, enjoying all our lovely, lively city has to offer. We'll give you all the relevant details of the background we've made for you, keeping as close to the truth as we can. And over the course of a few drinks, you'll show Hauptmann Weber all he's been missing."

"What is *that* supposed to mean?" Rosa asked in a taut whisper. Despite that flicker of longing, she realized she was truly horrified by the whole prospect. To see Ernst again, to pretend to beguile him... it made her stomach churn with both fear and dread. She couldn't possibly do it.

"There will be no improprieties," Pennell assured her smoothly. "You share a drink, a recollection of old times, an acknowledgment of how wonderful your new country is, how strong they've been and will continue to be. It will be, I believe, enough to push Weber over the edge, and he'll give us the information we need."

"This is... psychological warfare," Rosa surmised slowly.

Pennell raised his eyebrows, a small smile playing about his mouth. "Of course it is, Miss Herzelfeld. What do you think it is we've been doing here, after all?"

Rosa walked from the Blue Room in a complete daze, so much so that she didn't see Peter until he was right in front of her, looking tense and unhappy.

"Rosa... what was that all about?"

She shook her head slowly. "You know I can't tell you."

He nodded, accepting, but not seeming particularly appeased. "I feel like there is more to say between us."

Rosa nodded, her insides heavy. Considering what she'd just learned—that Ernst was actually *here*—she knew she needed to tell Peter about him. She just didn't want to. "Shall we go back outside?" she asked, and Peter fell into step with her.

They walked in silence back outside, where the sky was just as blue, the sun just as warm, and yet Rosa felt cold inside, so very cold.

"I'm sorry I seemed so angry before," Peter started in a low voice. "I don't mean to judge you... I apologize if I seemed as if I was. I know you were young, and you're not responsible for your father's actions. I can even acknowledge that your father had cause to act as he did, and little choice, as you said, even if I disagree with the way he chose to live his life. I know you didn't—"

"Peter, stop." Rosa knew she couldn't listen to any more, not without telling him the truth. "There's more you don't know."

Peter's face, drawn into determined lines, became wary. "More?"

"If you are to choose not to judge me, you need to know the whole of it," she said heavily. "At one of those parties... I..." Rosa faltered. It felt impossible to confess. She pictured Ernst as she'd first seen him—that wry smile, not all that different from Peter's. The blond hair, swept back. "I met someone," she admitted quietly, and Peter drew his breath in sharply. "He was young and handsome and very charming. Looking back, I think he was amusing himself with me, just as those men were amusing themselves with the whole idea of being friends with a Jew. It never meant anything to him, and why should it?" She lifted her chin, pressing her lips together to keep them from trembling. "The truth was," she stated bluntly, "that he thought Jews were little better than rats—I heard him say as much, when he didn't know I was listening."

How well she remembered that awful moment, when she'd been coming down the stairs, dressed in a new gown of white satin, her heart lifting at the sight of Ernst looking so handsome. His voice carrying, with the lilt of laughter... When he'd caught sight of her, he'd looked annoyed rather than guilty, although Rosa hadn't registered that at the time. She'd been too hurt.

Peter could not hide the horror on his face as he drew back from her. "He was SS?"

"Yes," Rosa replied simply.

Peter did not answer; he looked as if he were struggling to control his emotions.

"It was risky for him, of course," Rosa continued quietly, "and he broke it off when it—I—became too much of a liability, for his career. Not that our... attachment... was ever public. It was always a secret between us."

"Of course it was," he replied scoffingly, and Rosa acknowledged this with a nod.

"I'm ashamed of it," she confessed after a moment. "And I regret it deeply, more than you could possibly know. But..." She looked at him pleadingly, longing for him to understand. "I've also forgiven myself, Peter. Or at least, I'm trying to. I was young—I see that now. I had my head turned, and I ignored so many things... but Ernst, he wasn't... he didn't seem..." Rosa saw Peter's nostrils flare, his mouth tightening in distaste, and she decided to stop that line of reasoning. "I've come to see that punishing myself for a stupid, schoolgirl mistake—what is the point in that? I don't want to be mired in the past, Peter." Her voice took on an urgent, pleading tone. She longed for him to understand, but she feared he didn't. Wouldn't. "I want to live for the future," she explained softly. "That's something I began to realize at Rushen. How often I was looking back instead of forward. How I let what had happened paralyze me, keep me from doing anything good or useful with my life, because I felt so guilty. There was no point in it. No hope."

She paused, scanning his face for some small sign that he understood, that, like her, he could forgive. She didn't see it, and her heart sank with disappointment, and something even deeper. She knew she couldn't tell him that Ernst was here; it was secret. Would he find out somehow, and if he did, how would he react?

"Perhaps," she said quietly, "this changes your opinion of me."

Peter shook his head slowly, the look on his face despairing.

"Rosa..." he began, and then stopped. She waited. "I love you," he said helplessly. "I still love you, even knowing what you just told me, and hating that. And yet..." He swallowed. "I must admit, it is something I find very difficult to excuse."

"Not excuse, perhaps," she returned softly. "But *understand*, at least a little? Or... forgive?"

"I..." He shook his head, and her heart wilted within her.

She knew she couldn't regret being honest, and yet at what cost? It felt far higher a price than she'd ever wanted to pay, and she still had to face Ernst himself.

"The SS," he burst out, almost angrily. "Whatever you say, whatever you've let yourself believe... they were *monsters*, Rosa. Monsters! Brutal thugs who enjoyed torture, violence... The man who stamped on my fingers had a look of utter *glee* on his face when he did it. And at Dachau... there were women prisoners there, you know. Not many, but they were... brutalized. *Raped.* There was an SS training school attached to the camp, the men used to come and take their pick, as if they were choosing a chicken for their dinner. We were *animals* to them, Rosa, just dumb animals..." He trailed off, shaking his head again, looking near tears.

Rosa found she, too, was near tears. When he said all of that, she hated herself all over again. How could she have convinced herself she'd loved Ernst? And yet she had. "I know I can't excuse it," she whispered. "But, Peter, I didn't know any of that sort of brutality at the time. How could I? And Ernst... to me, he was just a handsome man who paid me attention. I let my head and heart be turned, I admit it. I'm sorry, Peter. I'm truly sorry." She looked down at the ground, blinking back the tears that filmed her eyes. What more could she say?

He let out a shuddering breath and raked his hands through his hair. "I do understand that," he told her after a moment, sounding more composed. "I do. And I accept you were young, as you said. I just... find it hard."

"I know." She glanced up at him, hope warring with fear. *Hard, or impossible?* "I should have told you before," she said. "I know I should have. I always meant to, yet the moment never seemed to come. I suppose I didn't want it to. But I knew I couldn't let things go any farther between us without you knowing. I suppose it changes things now." She tried to swallow past the lump in her throat. That Peter would reject her, just because of Ernst! It felt dreadfully unfair, and yet Rosa knew she'd been expecting it all along. She found she couldn't begrudge him for it.

"It shouldn't change things between us," Peter replied after a moment. "I know it shouldn't." He lapsed into silence, and Rosa wondered what he wasn't saying. *Yet it still did?* "Oh, Rosa," he said on something of a groan, and then he took her into his arms.

Rosa went willingly, wrapping her arms around his neck as his lips found hers, soft and sweet and yet he kissed her in a way that felt desperate, an ending rather than a beginning.

He broke off, looking anguished. "I'm sorry..."

Rosa didn't know what he was sorry for—the kiss, or the relationship they could now no longer have, or something else entirely—because he thrust her away from him, shaking his head as he walked away, leaving her alone in the park.

CHAPTER 25

Two days later, Rosa found herself staring at her wide-eyed reflection in the mirror of the ladies' room at the 400 Club in Leicester Square. Her lips were blood-red with lipstick, her cheeks pale, save for two hectic spots of color. Her hair had been styled into an elegant chignon, and she was wearing an evening dress in midnight-blue satin that was demure enough in the front, but draped shockingly low at the back, its whispering folds of fabric brushing her tailbone.

Over the last two days, she'd been drilled in her own fabricated history—working as a typist for a law firm in London, living with two other typists in Kensington, her parents still in Belsize Park. They'd scrubbed her German Jewishness from her, Rosa had reflected, and tried to turn her into a goodtime British girl; she had no idea if the ruse would work.

Despite the preparation she'd been given, she could not imagine what she would say to Ernst when she saw him. She was afraid of her own reaction, that she'd give herself away before she'd even begun... and also, more treacherously, that she'd feel something she didn't want to feel.

"He's here." The severe-looking woman who had been

assigned as her handler appeared in the doorway of the ladies' room. "It's time to go."

Wordlessly, Rosa nodded. She'd memorized and rehearsed her part in this charade well enough, but now that it was real, she felt faint and sick. She couldn't do it, she just *couldn't...*

She wondered if Peter somehow knew about this little drama, and decided that he couldn't possibly. Taken off her usual duties and busy with this new operation, she sadly hadn't had the chance to see him since he'd told her he loved her but acted as if he no longer did. Rosa had been too much in shock by the prospect of seeing Ernst again to feel truly heartbroken, but she knew the emotion was there, underneath the nerves, waiting to surge up and overwhelm her when this episode was over.

"Quickly!" the woman said, and Rosa, her heart beating hard, turned from the mirror.

Outside the ladies' room, she straightened, throwing her shoulders back, lifting her chin, as crowds circulated around her, chatting and laughing, drinking and dancing. For a second, she felt almost as if she were back on the *St Louis*, staring out at the sea all the way to the horizon, summoning the strength to envisage her new life, dizzy with both possibility and fear of the unknown.

She'd come full circle now, she thought, facing Ernst, and maybe there was something good and right about that. She could do this, Rosa realized with a ripple of relief, a frisson of something almost like joy. She could do this because this was what needed to be done to win the war, and end Hitler's evil forever, and in doing so she would find her own absolution.

"He's there," the woman hissed behind her. "*Go.*"

As elegantly as a cruise liner slipping into the sea, Rosa strolled across the floor of the club. An eighteen-piece orchestra was playing a slow, slumberous number, the perfect soundtrack for her assured, hip-rolling amble. She saw Ernst before he saw her, and for a second, no more, she checked her stride, before she made herself keep walking.

There were two other prisoners with him, looking around in wary wonder and dressed in plain suits, accompanied by several British officers, but they all faded away as Rosa gazed at Ernst, her heart feeling as if it had hollowed out, everything in her emptying.

He looked just the same, she thought with an ache, and yet entirely different. He still had his blond hair swept away from his forehead, his pale blue eyes as piercing as ever, but he looked... *diminished*, somehow. Defeated, even, with the slight slump of his broad shoulders. The expression on his face was wondering, a little lost. What had he thought of his tour of London, avoiding all the bombed-out buildings and rubble? Had he been impressed? Shaken? And what did he think now, of all the well-heeled people in one of London's premier clubs, dancing and drinking the night away as if they hadn't a care in the world?

She took a deep breath, threw her shoulders back a little more, and kept walking.

She'd almost reached the bar when she heard his sharp intake of breath, the incredulous note in his voice. "*Rosa...?*"

Rosa turned, eyebrows raised as she did a theatrical double-take, one hand pressed to her chest. "Ernst... dear heaven, *Ernst.*" She took a step toward him, and then checked herself, giving an embarrassed little laugh. "My goodness... but... what on *earth* are you doing here?"

"What on earth are *you* doing here?" he asked. He spoke in heavily accented English, his eyes wide as his gaze roved over her, taking in her hair, her lipstick, her gown.

"I live here," Rosa replied with a playful smile. "You remember, don't you, how my family emigrated? You were there, I believe, when we were ejected from our house on the

Wannsee." She made sure to speak without any edge, but Ernst's face crumpled a little.

"Rosa, I—"

"It's all in the past, Ernst." She dared to lay a hand, ever so briefly, on his arm, and was grateful she felt nothing at his touch. "Forgotten. Although..." She lowered her voice, keeping her tone conspiratorial. "I *am* wondering how on earth an officer in the SS can waltz into the 400 Club right here in London!" A tinkling laugh as she eased back to eye him appraisingly.

"It is... complicated," Ernst told her. "I am here as a... prisoner. But please, may I buy you a drink? And can we go somewhere private, talk more... openly?" He leaned forward to whisper, "I dare not speak German in here."

Pennell had suggested that he might ask something like this, and there was a booth reserved for them in the corner of the club, just for this purpose. Still, it made Rosa's heart stutter in her chest, to think of the two of them cozied up, having a private and intimate conversation. She realized she had no desire for it, at *all*.

"All right," she said after a moment, doing her best to sound puzzled and a bit wary. "But, really... how is it you can be here, Ernst? If you are a prisoner, shouldn't you be... in prison?" She gave a little, uncertain laugh as she widened her eyes.

Ernst laughed back, the sound somewhat hollow. "I am in prison. But they are kind here, and they have allowed a few of us out. We are guarded, of course. But today they have shown me the sights of London."

Rosa raised her eyebrows. "I had no idea they gave prisoners tours of London."

Ernst grimaced. "Neither did I. They have been very... decent to me. Far more than I had expected... or deserved."

For a second, no more, Rosa was assailed by a pang of guilt. She was complicit in deceiving a man who believed his captors to be acting in good faith. But this was war, she reminded herself. All was fair in love and war... and this, in its own way, was both.

"Well, if you're allowed, then, yes, I suppose we could," she told him with a shrug, and Ernst beamed at her.

"I will ask them."

Rosa stood there, trying to look unconcerned as the little charade was played out—Ernst asking the officer, who made a show of considering the request before reluctantly agreeing. Then Ernst returned, beaming, telling her it was allowed, and asking what he could get her to drink.

"Champagne, if they have it," Rosa replied, which had been her rehearsed line. She knew already there was a bottle of Pol Roger behind the bar specifically for this purpose... yet further proof that Great Britain was unaffected by the war, with champagne on tap for those who knew who to ask.

"Very well, I shall see," Ernst told her.

Rosa nodded toward the booth in the corner. "Shall I sit down?"

"Yes, yes, I'll bring it to you."

Making sure to sashay just in case he was watching, Rosa headed over to the booth, sliding deep into the velvet banquette as a shuddery breath escaped her. Then she steeled her spine along with her nerve, and in a show of unconcern, took out the silver compact she'd been provided with and reapplied her Yardley's cherry-red lipstick. She was just putting the lipstick and compact away when Ernst arrived, followed by a waiter brandishing the bottle of Pol Roger and two coupes.

"Excellent," Rosa said, sounding pleased but not surprised, as if drinking champagne were a regular occurrence in her life, and Ernst sat down across from her as the waiter poured them both champagne.

"Shall we toast?" he asked after the waiter had left, and then dropping his voice to little more than a murmur, he said,

"*Solange man nüchtern ist, gefällt das Schlechte. Wie man getrunken hat, weiss man das Rechte.*"

It was an old toast by Goethe—*when one is sober, the bad can appeal. When one has taken a drink, one knows what's real.*

Rosa hesitated, unsure how to respond. Was he trying to tell her something?

Then, putting down his glass without drinking, Ernst leaned forward, almost as if he wanted to take her hand in his, but he kept himself from it.

"Rosa, I am so glad to see you," he said, speaking in German, his voice a low, husky murmur. "I must apologize to you."

Shock rippled through her at his words, along with an undeniable little frisson of pleasure. Hadn't she once dreamed of him saying something like this to her? And yet she didn't want to be pleased. She wanted not to care at all.

"Oh?" She smiled and lifted her eyebrows, cocked her head. "What for, Ernst?" She spoke in English, but then deliberately switched to German, lowering her voice as he had his, their heads bent close together. "For something in particular, you mean?"

"Yes, you know it as well as I do. *More.*" He paused, his throat working. "I... I treated you... abominably."

Rosa leaned back to take a sip of her champagne, trying to order her racing thoughts, her jumbled feelings. She hadn't expected him to talk so honestly, so *emotionally*. She hadn't thought he'd felt anything for her back then, and she was both gratified and alarmed that it seemed as if he did. Their relationship *had* been real, on some level—but did that make it any less wrong?

"You mean," she said after a moment, "because I was Jewish." Her voice came out rather flat, and she realized she was veering off the script given to her by Lieutenant Pennell. She was meant to keep it all light and laughing, show Ernst what a

wonderful life she was having in even more wonderful Great
Britain, so he felt the war was already lost and gave away the
information they needed. Yet right then, she couldn't manage it,
because she realized she wanted to know too much what he
really thought... about her.

Ernst let out a restless sigh, his long fingers toying with the
stem of his champagne coupe. "Yes, I suppose. I never had
anything against the Jews themselves, you know. They were just
people to me, really. But there was a party line—"

"Yes," she said softly. "I know."

"If I was to succeed—"

"Yes."

He leaned forward, looking hopeful. "You understand?"

Rosa took a careful breath. "Tell me something," she said
softly. "What happened on Kristallnacht?"

Ernst stared at her for a moment, his brow furrowed with
perplexity, and then his expression fell and he slowly shook his
head. "Rosa..."

"I'd like to know." He'd ended things between them immediately after, but Rosa had already felt the fragility of their relationship, if she could have even called it that. Their meetings
had been sporadic, hidden, no more than moments snatched,
and those with seeming reluctance, as Ernst had cared more and
more about his career.

He let out a long, low breath. "I expect you already do. It
was a wild night. Emotions were running high..."

"No, they weren't," Rosa returned sharply. He made it
sound as if it had been a raucous party! "Jews were hiding in
their homes, Ernst, their shops boarded up as they feared for
their very lives—"

"I was under order, Rosa. Surely you understand that?"

"To do *what*?"

He shrugged, seeming a bit restive. "To rough people up.
Break a few windows. You know what happened that night."

Rosa glanced down at her barely touched glass of champagne. "You came to our villa that night," she said slowly. "I was waiting for you."

"I remember."

They'd already heard the news of what was happening through all of Berlin, and indeed all of Germany. They'd seen the smoke from the fires polluting the sky; the Fasanenstrasse synagogue had been burned to the ground. Thousands of Jews had lost their businesses, hundreds arrested, like Sophie's father. She thought of his frightened face and something in her hardened.

"What did you do that night?" she asked Ernst. "I know it doesn't really matter anymore, but I've always wanted to know." Even now, she could remember how he'd come to her at the villa, taken her in his arms. There had been a wild glitter in his eyes, his knuckles scraped and bloody. She'd pretended not to see, not to know.

He frowned, a petulant downturn to his mouth that alarmed Rosa, because this was not how he was meant to respond. This was not how she was meant to act. If Pennell could hear her now, he'd probably be furious. Still, she wanted his response.

"Ernst," she said quietly.

"I can't remember exactly," he replied, shrugging. "We went down the Kurfürstendamm, breaking windows. One old Jew started to make a fuss, and I hit him, I think. He fell, cracked his head." He gazed at her now with hard, defiant eyes. "I think I might have killed him. What of it?"

Rosa just shook her head. She felt sick inside, with shame and grief. She'd believed herself in *love* with this man once, and why? Because he'd smiled at her and told her pretty things?

"Why bring all that up now, Rosa?" Ernst demanded.

"I just wanted to know," she said quietly. "That's all."

"Do you know what happened to me after you left?" he

asked in a low voice, leaning over the table. "I was kicked out of the SS. Oh, they said it was a transfer, but I knew the truth. Instead of rising in the ranks, I had to start all over in the Luftwaffe. And you know why? Because of you. Associating with a Jew. One of the other officers at your father's house must have told them my name. Any chance to push someone else down, get ahead." He shook his head, his mouth twisting bitterly.

Rosa had no idea what to say. Was she sorry for him? No, she found she couldn't be. And yet... some small part of her still had the urge to relent. To forgive, or at least to understand. Was Ernst simply a product of his time, his upbringing, as anyone was? His father had hated Jews, Rosa recalled. Ernst had shared that as a point in his favor; he wasn't like his old man, he'd told her. He didn't care about the Jews either way, but if he was going to make his mark, then she had to understand...

Briefly, Rosa closed her eyes. What a fool she'd been. What a misguided, lovesick fool.

"Are you happy here, Rosa?" Ernst asked. "You seem to be doing well for yourself."

"Yes, I am." And with that, Rosa told him all her lies, surprised at how easily they tripped from her tongue—she was a typist, she lived in a flat with a few other girls, she went out every weekend, dancing the night away.

"I thought London would look worse," Ernst admitted, frowning. "Back home, we were told that the city was almost entirely destroyed, but I didn't see any bomb damage anywhere."

Rosa shrugged. "Oh, here and there, I suppose," she replied airily. "A little bit. But your bombers keep missing the city. And we've shot down so many of your planes."

His face darkened with anger, but when he spoke, he sounded grieved. "We've?" he repeated. "You really do feel you are part of this country now?"

"Why shouldn't I?" Rosa returned with an uptilt of her

chin. "Why should I have any loyalty to Germany, Ernst? Great Britain has been wonderful to me—welcoming, with so much opportunity, prosperity. My life here is far better than it ever was back in Germany."

He shook his head slowly. "I had no idea... it would be like this," he said slowly. "I believed everything they told me, back in Berlin."

"And now you are beginning to question it?" Rosa asked, finding she was genuinely curious.

"Yes." His voice was bleak. "Hitler... he has too much power. He wants the whole world, and I fear he will destroy Germany in trying to obtain it. The Soviet Union... there have already been grave losses there, far graver I think than even this country knows. And he simply won't stop. I know he won't."

Rosa filed away that titbit to tell Pennell later as she kept her expression softly concerned. "I'm sorry, Ernst," she said. "For you. But I cannot be sorry that Germany is losing the war. They will lose it," she added, keeping her voice strong but sympathetic. "You must see that."

Ernst didn't reply for a moment, his head bent, a lock of blond hair falling across his forehead.

"Yes," he said at last, his voice heavy. "I see that."

CHAPTER 26

AUGUST 1941—COCKFOSTERS CAMP

Rosa hadn't known what to expect in the aftermath of her evening with Ernst, but in the end, it felt as if nothing much had changed, and her work at the camp went on as before. She'd debriefed with Lieutenant Pennell, recounting almost all of the conversation, leaving out only what she'd asked Ernst about Kristallnacht; she decided that it hadn't been relevant, and, in truth, she wasn't willing to share those details.

"Interesting, about the losses in Russia," he'd mused. "It sounds as if all the Jerries are losing their mettle! Good work, Miss Herzelfeld. You may return to your post."

And that, it seemed, was that.

Rosa hadn't been expecting heaps of praise from her superior for what she'd done, but she still felt strangely deflated by the whole bizarre episode. She'd said goodbye to Ernst with a pang in her heart, but also relief she'd never have to see him again. He'd caught her fingers as if to kiss their tips, but Rosa had pulled her hand away before he could and walked away quickly. The emotional overload of having Peter say he loved her only to back away, and then learning about Ernst, never mind actually *seeing* him... it had all been incredibly overwhelming. She'd had an urge to pull the cover over her head and sleep for a week, but that simply wasn't possible. Transcripts had to be translated, and her shifts went on without a pause or a beat.

Rosa did her best to get back into the routine of work, but she often felt too shaky and jumbled up inside to concentrate. Every time she picked up a transcript, she wondered if it would be one of Ernst. Had he given up the codes? Had the whole surreal ruse actually *worked*?

As far as she could tell, she never translated one of his transcripts, and she wondered if that was on purpose. Perhaps they didn't want her getting too involved, too invested. She'd reviewed her conversation with him in the booth at that club endlessly, trying to untangle its confused threads, her own complicated feelings. She found she couldn't decide if Ernst was the monster Peter seemed to think he, along with all Nazis, was, or just a man who had been born and bred into a hateful way of looking at the world, essentially a victim of his own circumstances... and yet what were circumstances, but a reason to understand, rather than an excuse or justification? And what was anyone, she reflected, but the sum of their choices? And yet each new day provided an opportunity to make a different choice, a *better* one...

It was a thought which gave her both peace and hope.

A week after her tumultuous evening at the 400 Club, Rosa finally learned the fate of Ernst... and from Peter, of all people. He came and found her, after work, when she was having a cup of tea with Sally and a few of the other translators in the kitchen.

"Rosa." His voice was quiet, his tone somber. Rosa had not seen or spoken to him since their conversation in the garden, and she'd felt the loss keenly. She'd wondered if he'd been keeping his distance on purpose, and feared that he had. She hadn't possessed the courage to seek him out. Now, looking at his serious face, she felt a wave of dread. Whatever he wanted to say to her, it didn't seem as if it would be something she wanted to hear.

"Peter." She glanced at the other girls at the table, who were all looking avidly curious, their glances darting between her and Peter.

"Is there somewhere we could speak in private?" he asked, and then managed a small, wry smile for her companions. "I apologize, ladies."

"Oh, don't mind us," Sally assured him with a wink. "We'll gladly make ourselves scarce, won't we, girls? Especially if there's love in the air!" She giggled, and her friends followed suit. Color surged into Rosa's face.

"That's not necessary," Rosa said, standing up quickly. Whatever Peter did have to say to her, she didn't think it was a conversation she wanted to have in the kitchen. "Why don't we go for a walk?" she suggested. "It's a nice evening."

He gave a brief nod. "All right."

Neither of them spoke as they headed out of the kitchen, the other girls tracking them with their curious gazes, before bursting into giggles as they turned the corner.

"Sorry about that," Rosa said once they were outside, in the dusky evening. "Sally has a bit of an obsession with the cinema. She thinks life is like a romantic film."

"Maybe it should be," Peter replied, smiling a little.

His remark gave Rosa hope, but she still felt wary, bracing herself for whatever came next.

They began to walk down one of the meandering paths through the estate's parkland, the evening air as soft as silk, the sky striated with clouds of lavender and orange. After a few moments, Rosa summoned the courage to speak. "What is it you wanted to say to me, Peter?" she asked quietly.

"I know about Weber." He stopped mid-stroll and turned to face her. "About him being here, I mean. He was here, that is, but he's left now, gone to another camp. But I know about him seeing you."

Shock rippled through her, but she kept her voice even as she asked, "How do you know all that?"

Peter shrugged, his glance moving around the parkland, dusk deepening into shadow. "As part of my position. I know I shouldn't talk about it, but I... I heard him speak myself."

"You're one of the listeners," Rosa murmured, and Peter nodded.

"And that's all you should know about that, I suppose, but I have to tell you, Rosa... I've been in agony since we last spoke. I know I was unfair to you, I *know* it." He reached for her hands. "I just couldn't help myself, somehow. I felt so angry, but not at *you*, not really..."

"I understand, Peter." Gently, she squeezed his hands, grateful for what he was telling her. "When I... when I saw Ernst face to face, when I spoke to him..." She shook her head slowly, recalling that moment in painful clarity. "I felt sick inside, that I could have ever convinced myself I was in love with him. Maybe I'd simply been starved of affection, or maybe I was naïve, but... I should have known better. I *should* have." It was a thought which had been tormenting her since that night, but now she knew she needed to let it go.

"But, Rosa, don't you see?" Peter protested. "I'm saying the opposite. *Why* should you have known better? He was a kind and handsome man who charmed you. When I heard him speak, when I listened to what he was saying—not just about you, but about everything, the war, his life, being here—I realized he was that, only that... a *man*. Not a monster." He drew a shaky breath. "Perhaps it makes it easier, to believe such men are monsters, not worthy of any pity or regard. Perhaps it is harder to accept that men can act in monstrous ways and still be human—fallible, afraid, loving, weak. I don't know." He straightened, his expression turning resolute, her hands still clasped in his. "But the Nazis tried to demonize us Jews, turn us into something inhuman—beneath regard, unworthy of respect. Like rats, that's how they treated us. I won't do the same to another man—*any* other man—no matter how odious his beliefs. And I understand why you were able to believe yourself in love with him, I do."

"It was a long time ago," Rosa whispered. She tightened her grip on his hands, as if she could anchor him to her. "When I saw Ernst last week, Peter, he meant nothing to me. *Less*—"

Peter's smile was soft, his expression tender. "I know."

Her heart felt as if it were turning over in her chest. "Then..." she began, hardly daring to hope. *To believe.*

"You know I love you," he reminded her wryly. "I told you so, and I'll tell you again. I love you, Rosa Herzelfeld, maybe from the moment you first pretended to pour me tea, or maybe it simply grew from there, into something deep and strong and true. But it's real, and I want you to know it." He paused, squeezing her hands gently. "I suppose the question now is, do you love me too?"

Rosa gulped and nodded, her heart so very full, tears of both relief and elation starting in her eyes. "Yes, Peter," she whispered. "*Yes.* I do. So much."

"Good," he whispered back, and then he drew her to him. Rosa came with relief and joy in her heart, and as Peter kissed her, this time there was nothing in it but sweetness.

In retrospect, the next few months passed in a blur of wonder and happiness. Yes, it was wartime, and the news was often grim, and Rosa was still worried for her friends in Europe, but... Peter was in love—*in love!*—with her, and she loved him and was doing important work, and the tide was surely turning, just as they'd hoped it would. There seemed every reason to be happy, to *choose* to be happy. Even the news from home seemed

happy—her mother's dres
her father had sat his m
colors. The Rosenbaum
somewhat miraculously,

Like Sarah and Abr
her father had, somew
the liberal synagogue
by refugees in 1939
better and more com
hope, and seemed stro...
her father's indiscretions behind them.

She even heard from Hannah—a letter had been s...
through to Vichy France, and then posted on. It had taken
months to arrive, and had been covered in the red ink of British
Intelligence officers and signed only with her initials, H. L., but
at least Rosa knew that Hannah and Lotte were safe... or they
had been, all those months ago when she'd written it. Rosa
could only hope it remained the case.

I am doing good work now, Hannah had written, which
Rosa suspected was code for something secretive and probably
dangerous. *It feels more important than anything I've ever done.*

Rosa understood that sentiment well; indeed, she shared it.
She was glad Hannah had found a way to fight this war, even as
she feared for her safety.

She'd also heard from Rachel, who had managed to send a
letter through the channels in Portugal.

*We struggle on—food is very scarce, and they have ordered all
Jews to register with a central board, which doesn't seem like a
good sign, but who knows, maybe they just want to make sure
we're cared for! It is very difficult to get reliable news, but there
are good people here, and I know they will protect us.*

Rosa's heart had faltered at those stark words; it sounded as

e in terrible danger, even if Rachel was
ke light of it. In any case, the truth of the
lands could be heard on the BBC during the
n February, Jews there were segregated from
e population, and over fifteen thousand sent to
r camps. A month later, they were forced to wear a
tar on their clothing. It felt like the beginning of some-
truly ominous. Rosa prayed that Rachel and Franz had
been arrested, and the good people her friend had
mentioned had indeed been able to protect them from whatever
came next.

Rosa heard from Sophie too, in March, that her sweetheart
Sam had died in the attack on Pearl Harbor. Her friend's
matter-of-fact tone hid, Rosa suspected, an ocean of grief, and
she ached for her, and the love she'd lost. After she'd folded up
the letter, Rosa took out the sliver of emerald she still carried
with her everywhere. *What is happening to all of us?* she
wondered, her heart feeling as if it were twisting inside her,
with anxiety and fear. All four of them had already suffered so
much. Would they all survive—and not just survive, but emerge
stronger, braver? Rosa longed to imagine them all at Henri's,
laughing, weeping, embracing. Together again, the emerald
whole once more.

And yet the war was far from over. The happiness that she'd
found with Peter felt then as precious and fragile as a glass
bauble, achingly beautiful and yet so easily shattered.

In May, as the cherry blossoms came out on the trees in
beautiful, blowsy pink puffballs, Rosa received another unexpected summons to the Blue Room. It had been ten months
since that night at the 400 Club, and that whole evening with
Ernst thankfully felt like a distant, shadowy memory, one she
was more than happy to consign to history.

She'd had nearly a year of simply doing her work and falling more deeply in love with Peter, enjoying their snatched moments together—walks in the estate, drinks at the local pub, and twice, on their days off, a trip into London. He'd met her parents, and had shaken her father's hand, charmed her mother. She'd told him about Sophie and Hannah and Rachel, shown him the emerald and tried to explain what it meant. All of it, taken together, had felt so very precious and sweet, and she realized she didn't want any of it to change as she headed once more to the Blue Room.

"You're wanted at the War Office," Colonel Kendrick told her briskly, before Rosa had even sat down in the chair in front of his desk. "Seems they've found another use for you. I don't know anything about it, so you might as well not bother asking me any questions." He smiled to soften the words, but there was a flicker of something in his eyes that flooded Rosa with a sudden unease.

"Will it... will it be dangerous?" she asked.

"I've no idea, Miss Herzelfeld," Kendrick replied briskly. "But I will tell you that just about everything we do these days is dangerous. There is a war on, after all."

She left for London the next morning. It felt as surreal to leave Cockfosters Camp after a year as it had been to leave Rushen after ten months. Her life, Rosa reflected, was parceled out in days and months—first Belsize Park, and then Rushen, and then Cockfosters. Each experience felt strangely out of time, out of reality, existing in its own separate universe.

When she'd told Peter she'd been summoned to the War Office, he'd looked concerned. "The War Office? What do you think it's about?" he'd asked, frowning. "Will you be transferred somewhere, do you think?"

Rosa had shrugged, nerves warring with a cautious excitement. "Maybe? I don't know why I would, though, when I'm doing important work here." She'd hugged him, wrapping her arms tightly around his middle as she'd pressed her cheek against his chest, savoring the feel of him. "I don't want to be transferred," she'd whispered. "I want to stay here with you."

"I want you to, as well," Peter had replied, holding her close. "But you can't ignore the summons." He'd hugged her to him a little more tightly. "Perhaps it will be interesting work."

"This is interesting work," Rosa had protested. She'd known he was trying to make the best of it, but she'd still felt scared.

The address Kendrick had given her was not the impressive War Office building in the Horse Guards in Whitehall, but rather a branch on Baker Street she'd never heard of; there was no plaque or sign of any sort to say she was in the right place, and yet when she knocked, hesitantly, at Number 64, the door opened immediately and a plain-clothed and sober-looking man whisked her upstairs to a cupboard of an office, where she sat in trepidation for the better part of an hour, wondering what on earth was going on, before a man walked smartly into the room.

"Miss Herzelfeld." She glanced at him uncertainly; he looked to be only in his thirties, with a full head of wavy hair and a neat moustache. He smiled at her and then stuck out his hand. "Major Thurston."

Gingerly, Rosa took it. "How do you do, Major?" she murmured.

"Very well, thank you." He took a seat behind the one rickety table in the room and dropped a file on top of it, so it landed with a smack.

Rosa blinked. He flipped it open and scanned the contents; from the other side of the table, she could see her own photograph on the first page. It was a file, she realized, on *her*.

"You came to Great Britain in 1939... on the *St Louis*?" he began, glancing up at her in inquiry, and she nodded. "Worked in a Lyons teashop, interned for ten months at Camp Rushen, and then seconded to Cockfosters." He flipped the file closed. "Fluent in German, naturally, and some French?"

"Yes—"

Quickly, without missing a beat or a blink, he switched to speaking French. "*Parlez-vous bien le français, Mademoiselle Herzelfeld?*"

Startled yet enjoying the challenge, she answered just as quickly. "*Je crois que je parle assez bien la langue*, Major." She paused and then added boldly, "*Et vous?*"

He gave a short, approving laugh. "*Tres bien, mais bien sûr.*"

If Rosa hoped she had passed some sort of test with this little repartee, she soon discovered her mistake. The major launched into a long explanation of the work he was doing, all in French, which Rosa struggled to follow completely. He spoke of the need for secrecy, and manpower on the continent, and ways of fighting a war that to some might seem underhanded, but was necessary in these difficult and dangerous times.

"*Qu'en pensez-vous, mademoiselle?*" he finished. "*Est-ce que c'est quelque chose que vous aimeriez faire?*"

Was it something she'd like to do? He sounded as if he were asking her to attend a tea party.

"Are you," Rosa returned in careful French, her words halting not because of the language but because of the import of them, "asking if I would like to be a... a *spy?*"

"*Un espion?*" He shrugged, smiling. "Call it what you will. I will say, the training is rigorous. Many do not pass. It will take six months at a minimum, most likely more like nine. And after that..." He spread his hands. "We shall see."

A *spy*, in occupied France? Her? Rosa's heart quailed at the thought. It wasn't just dangerous, it was *insanity*. If she were caught, as a spy *and* a Jew... well, her life would be worthless, but worse than that, she was quite sure her demise would neither be quick nor painless. She thought of Peter's two twisted fingers, and suspected she would be begging for such a small injury in comparison to what the Nazis might do to her.

And yet... Her fingers, almost as of their own accord, slipped into her pocket and slid round that precious piece of jewel. Sophie, doing something secretive in America, having lost the man she loved. Hannah, in France, maybe even doing something as dangerous as Rosa was now contemplating. And Rachel and poor Franz, in hiding, perhaps, in the Netherlands, fearing for their very lives...

How could she be unwilling to risk her own life when her friends were all risking theirs? How could she not want to, and *gladly*?

"Why *me*?" she asked abruptly, and he raised his eyebrows.

"You were recommended."

She tried not to goggle at him. "I was?"

"You've shown a remarkable sangfroid in certain situations," he replied, and Rosa knew, with a sudden, leaden certainty, that he was talking about that night at the 400 Club, the role she'd been able to play. Would she be asked to do something similar... in *France*?

"Well, mademoiselle?" the major asked, smiling faintly, almost as if he already knew her answer... just as Rosa knew. There was only one answer she could give, one she wanted to give.

"*Oui*," Rosa replied firmly. "*J'accepte, avec plaisir*."

She was told to report to King's Cross the next morning, to take a train all the way to Arisaig, in the north of Scotland. The journey would take two days, and she would spend the night at a boarding house in Carlisle, in the far north of England. In the meantime, she was allowed to spend the night with her family in Belsize Park, as well as collect her things from Cockfosters Camp.

Returning to the great house where she'd spent such a happy time with Peter felt like an agony. Rosa knew full well she could not tell him where she was going, or why, and yet she was achingly conscious that this would be a far more final farewell than he could ever possibly imagine. What if she never saw him again? What if she was captured and killed in enemy territory? The thought alone was enough to weaken her knees and ice her insides... and she couldn't let him know anything about it.

All in all, there wasn't much to collect. After a year, she found she had little more than she'd arrived with—a spare utility jumper and skirt, a change of underclothes and two blouses, woolen stockings and a winter coat.

Peter was on shift, and with a pang Rosa wondered if she would be able to say goodbye to him at all. Was she simply to creep away like a ghost, invisible, forgotten?

She said goodbye to Sally at least, who was in the kitchen with a few others.

"Going?" Sally looked dismayed. "But we've had such fun together, and we need you here. What on earth are they having you do now?"

Rosa smiled as she playfully wagged a finger at her friend, amazed she could act as if it were all a lark. "Now you know you can't ask me that, Sally."

"No, you're right." Sally frowned. "It's not something dangerous, though, is it?"

"No more dangerous than what's going on here, I'm sure," Rosa replied lightly. "We're all in danger, aren't we, from the air raids?" Cockfosters Camp had been bombed several times already, although, thankfully, with little damage. She parroted Colonel Kendrick's well-used line, "There's a war on, after all."

"Well I know it." Sally stood up to give her a hug. "Write when you can."

"I will."

Rosa had just turned to leave, tears starting in her eyes that she knew she needed to hide, when Peter came into the room.

"Rosa!" he exclaimed. "Someone said you were back!" With an apologetic smile for the others, he drew her away from their prying eyes, lowering his voice to ask, "What did you find out?"

"I am being transferred," Rosa told him. She tried to smile, but her lips felt funny. "Tomorrow, as it happens. To some other establishment like this, I'm not exactly sure." She shrugged, tried for a laugh, but it sounded hollow. "They never tell you much, do they?"

He slipped his arm through hers, guiding her from the kitchen into an empty lounge. The stale smell of cigarette smoke hung in the air, and day-old newspapers littered the coffee table; it felt an appropriate place for an ending.

Peter gazed at her seriously. "You would tell me, wouldn't you, if it was something dangerous?" he asked quietly.

Rosa kept his gaze, although only just. "Peter, you know I can't tell you anything."

His expression turned bleak, his shoulders starting to slump. "It is, then. It must be..."

"Don't," she whispered. "There's no point, and you know we can't..."

His expression turned anguished, his face crumpling. "Rosa—"

"I love you," she told him, and put her arms around him, longing to hold him close. "So much."

He held her tightly, his lips pressed to her hair. "This feels like too much of a goodbye," he told her, an ache in his voice.

"It isn't." She'd probably be given some leave when she finished her training, Rosa told herself. And, in any case, she might not even pass it! Major Thurston had made sure she understood just how challenging it was. "I'll see you again, Peter, I promise," she told him. "And I'll write."

He pressed his lips to hers and Rosa closed her eyes, trying to imprint the memory of his kiss, his touch, on her very soul. As long as she had this to hold onto, along with her emerald and all it meant to her, she would have the strength to face whatever came next, she told herself. She would have to.

That evening, Rosa mounted the steps of her old building, smiling faintly at the familiar smell of sauerkraut and drains. Some things, it seemed, never changed.

When her mother opened the door, she gasped in surprise before throwing her arms around her. "*Rosa*! Why didn't you say you were coming?"

"There was no time," Rosa replied, as she hugged her mother back. "I'm off again—tomorrow, as it happens."

"But you'll stay the night?" Her mother sounded so hopeful and anxious that Rosa almost smiled. How their relationship had changed, and she was so very glad for it.

"Yes," she assured her. "I can spend the night."

"Come see Zlata's baby," her mother entreated as she drew her into the apartment. "He's only two months old but such a healthy, bouncing baby boy! He's already smiling."

Laughing, Rosa let herself be led into the sitting room, where Zlata was sitting in her mother's old armchair, a chubby, grinning baby perched on her lap. The apartment looked more comfortable now, Rosa noticed, with a few bits and pieces to soften the austere furnishings, including a dressmaker's dummy perched in one corner and covered in swathes of olive-green viscose.

"Utility clothing," her mother explained, following Rosa's gaze. "No one dares go out in silks and satins these days! Now come and look at this darling boy."

"Isn't he gorgeous!" Rosa exclaimed, and her former house-mate held the baby out to her.

"Would you like to hold him?"

"Yes, please!" Rosa took the baby gingerly, as she did not have much experience of infants, but as she breathed in his milky scent and saw his beaming, gummy smile, she felt an ache inside her as sharp as a dagger.

Would she ever have the chance to have children, Peter's children? Or was she being melodramatic, feeling as if she'd signed her whole life away, when she might fail a simple test and be sent back to Cockfosters Camp next month in near disgrace? She had no idea what the future held, but then she never had, all this time, and perhaps she never would; *no one* would. She would simply have to take whatever happened as it came.

"He is the most beautiful baby in the world," she pronounced solemnly as she handed him back, and Zlata nodded in perfect agreement.

"His name is Josef, after Moritz's father."

"A very good name."

The front door opened, and Rosa turned to see her father coming into the room, larger than life as ever, a scarf thrown about his shoulders, his hair rumpled. He checked himself when he saw her, before a wide smile appeared on his face.

"*Rosa!*" He held his arms open, and as naturally and easily as when she'd been a small child, Rosa went into them.

"*Vati,*" she whispered, and again she felt the sting of tears. Everything and everyone felt so precious at that moment, so unbearably fleeting. She longed to hold onto it all, to cling to it, and yet already she felt it slipping away from her, every last precious person and thing, as the future continued to loom, unknowable, in front of her.

"How have you come home?" her father asked as he eased back to study her, a faint frown creasing his brows. "You're all right?"

"Yes," Rosa replied, as firmly as she could. "I'm off again

tomorrow, a new assignment, something dull, no doubt, but I'm afraid I can't say anything more about it."

His expression softened, and he pressed his hand to her cheek. "I am so proud of you, my darling."

"And I'm proud of you," Rosa told him. "A doctor once again!"

"Yes, well, it was about time, wasn't it? But you are the one doing *proper* war work." Smiling, he tapped the side of his nose; Rosa suspected he knew more or less what she did, thanks to his own offering of intelligence.

"And you've done your bit, as well," she reminded him. "I wouldn't be at Cockfosters if not for you."

"It was a very small part I played," he replied, "and, truth be told, it was about time that I did." He paused, his face sagging so he looked every one of his fifty-four years. "I've made a great many mistakes, Rosa," he stated quietly. "You know I have."

She suspected he was not just talking about his regrettable relationships with Nazis back in Berlin, but also with the various women in the past, the ways he'd hurt both her and her mother. "We all have, *Vati*," she replied. "What is important is the choices you make in the future. And I mean it," she added quietly.

He hugged her again, and then her mother clapped her hands. "We must celebrate," she proclaimed. "I will use all our ration of butter and sugar to make a cake. Zlata, do we have enough eggs?"

"I think so," Zlata replied, hurrying to the kitchen.

Her mother was baking a cake? She'd never stepped foot in the kitchen back in Berlin. Some things never changed, Rosa reflected, and other things did... wonderfully so.

In retrospect, the whole evening felt as if it were rose-tinted, surrounded by a sunset glow of poignancy—the *baumkuchen* cake, one of Rosa's favorites, and little Josef gurgling happily as he was passed from knee to knee, her parents clearly so content together, in a way they never truly had been before. Moritz got out his violin, and they all danced to a rousing folk tune, with Josef shrieking his delight.

Rosa couldn't bear for the evening to end, but she knew it had to, and so it did after just a few short hours. She took her leave of her parents early the next morning, hugging and kissing them in turn, along with the Rosenbaums and dear little Josef, and then she headed out to make the eight o'clock train from King's Cross, wondering, with a pang, when she'd see anyone she loved ever again.

The station was full of soldiers and women in uniform bustling to and fro. Amidst the sound of the trains' whistles and the cry of the seagulls circling above, tearful farewells and joyful greetings played out on the platforms, a thousand poignant dramas enacted by the hour.

Rosa found the train for Carlisle and took her seat in one of the compartments. A soldier sprang up with alacrity to help her stow her suitcase above.

"Thank you," she murmured as she sank into the seat by the window.

"My pleasure." He sat down opposite her with a smile. "Are you going all the way to Carlisle?"

Rosa nodded, even as she thought, *And then onto Glasgow... Arisaig... and maybe France?* She turned to look out the window to hide the sudden tears that threatened. She'd left everything and everyone she knew and loved behind, *again*. Back on the *St Louis*, when she'd faced the same sort of uncertain future, she'd felt hopeful, determined. She wanted to feel that way again. She would choose to, despite the dangers and the loss.

Rosa slipped her hand into her pocket, her fingers closing around the emerald, savoring its smoothness. She thought again of Peter, working at Cockfosters Camp, determined to rid the world of Hitler's evil. And Sophie, over in America, doing whatever secretive work she was, maybe even risking her life in some way, and then Rachel, in the Netherlands, fearing and fighting for her life. And Hannah, in France... *I am doing good work... It feels more important than anything I've ever done.*

Yes, Rosa thought, and now she would be, as well. To fight for justice and freedom, to face the future unbowed and unafraid... it was a choice she would make and was already making. Just as she'd once thought of Ernst, of anyone, she, like him, was the sum of her choices—not one misjudgement years ago, but this—here, now. A smile touched her lips as her fingers curled even more tightly around the emerald.

With an exhale of steam into the pale blue sky, the train moved off, heading north, toward her future.

A LETTER FROM KATE

Dear reader,

I want to say a huge thank you for choosing to read *The Girl with a Secret*. If you enjoyed it, and would like to keep up to date with all my latest releases, just sign up at the following link. Your email address will never be shared and you can unsubscribe at any time.

www.bookouture.com/kate-hewitt

As with the previous book in this series, *The Girl on the Boat*, this novel was inspired by a friend's ancestors who had traveled on the *St Louis*. The plight of the doomed ship caught my imagination, and when I learned that the refugees had been dispersed between different countries, I immediately imagined four young friends, each assigned to a different place, and the adventures and trials they would all have. Many of the characters in the story, including Rosa's father, are based on real people, and the events on the ship are all taken from firsthand accounts. Of the 937 passengers on the doomed *St Louis*, 267 tragically ended up dying in concentration camps.

I hope you loved *The Girl with a Secret* and if you did, I would be very grateful if you could write a review. I'd love to hear what you think, and it makes such a difference helping new readers to discover one of my books for the first time.

I love hearing from my readers—you can get in touch on my

Facebook group for readers (facebook.com/groups/ KatesReads), through X, Goodreads (goodreads.com/author/ show/1269244.Kate_Hewitt) or my website.

Thanks again for reading!

Kate

www.kate-hewitt.com

✕ x.com/author_kate

ACKNOWLEDGEMENTS

I am always so grateful to the many people who work with me on my story and help to bring it to light. I am grateful to the whole amazing team at Bookouture who have helped with this process, from editing, copyediting, and proofreading, to designing and marketing. In particular, I'd like to thank my editor, Jess Whitlum-Cooper, as well as Sarah Hardy, Laura Deacon, and Kim Nash in publicity, Melanie Price in marketing, Richard King in foreign rights, and Sinead O'Connor in audio. Most of all, I'd like to thank my readers, who buy and read my books. Without you, there would be no stories to share. I hope you enjoyed this one as much as I did. Thank you!

PUBLISHING TEAM

Turning a manuscript into a book requires the efforts of many people. The publishing team at Bookouture would like to acknowledge everyone who contributed to this publication.

Audio
Alba Proko
Sinead O'Connor
Melissa Tran

Commercial
Lauren Morrissette
Jil Thielen
Imogen Allport

Cover design
Debbie Clement

Data and analysis
Mark Alder
Mohamed Bussuri

Editorial
Jess Whitlum-Cooper
Imogen Allport

Copyeditor
Jade Craddock

Proofreader
Tom Feltham

Marketing
Alex Crow
Melanie Price
Occy Carr
Cíara Rosney

Operations and distribution
Marina Valles
Stephanie Straub

Production
Hannah Snetsinger
Mandy Kullar
Jen Shannon

Publicity
Kim Nash
Noelle Holten
Jess Readett
Sarah Hardy

Rights and contracts
Peta Nightingale
Richard King
Saidah Graham

9 781837 902934